PRAISE FOR ANNIE SOLOMON'S LIKE A KNIFE

"Fast-paced...exciting romantic suspense that...the audience will relish."
—*Midwest Book Review*

"Fast-paced with multidimensional characters that are expertly written....*Like a Knife* takes off running and never stops."
—TheRomanceReadersConnection.com

"A chilling story...Ms. Solomon knows how to keep the reader glued to the pages."
—*Rendezvous*

"A riveting tale that will keep you on the edge of your seat."
—RomRevToday.com

"A powerful character study...[Ms. Solomon] blends the elements of romance and suspense...with the skill of a veteran."
—The WordonRomance.com

ALSO BY ANNIE SOLOMON

Like A Knife

DEAD RINGER

ANNIE SOLOMON

WARNER BOOKS

An AOL Time Warner Company

WARNER BOOKS EDITION

Cover art and design by Tom Tafuri
Hand lettering by David Gatti
Book design by Giorgetta Bell McRee

Warner Books, Inc.
1271 Avenue of the Americas
New York, NY 10020

Visit our Web site at www.twbookmark.com

 An AOL Time Warner Company

Printed in the United States of America

First Paperback Printing: October 2003

10 9 8 7 6 5 4 3 2 1

ACKNOWLEDGMENTS

Thanks to all who helped make this book possible, especially Linda, Jo, Beth, GayNelle, and Trish, my friends and fabulous critiquers. To Professor Frank Wcislo for help with Russian.

A special thanks to my agent, Pam Ahearn, and my editor, Beth de Guzman, for taking a chance on me and my stories.

And as always, to the people who keep me sane while I slowly drive them crazy: Larry and Becca.

DEAD RINGER

CHAPTER
~ 1 ~

"*Baby, oh baby, oh baby.*"

Like a hot breeze, a hoot of laughter drifted across the night-lit airfield as Finn Carver descended from the charter plane.

The laughing man crossed his arms and leaned against the car parked on the edge of the Memphis tarmac, the runway lights illuminating him. "My, my, my, don't you look good."

But Finn was in no mood for teasing. "Cut the crap, Jack." He pitched his briefcase and overnight bag to Jack Saunders and tried to ignore the way the younger man was making a big production out of admiring Finn's tuxedo.

"Yessir." Jack gave a long, low wolf whistle. "The storm troopers have definitely arrived."

Finn eyed Jack's baggy Hawaiian shirt, worn loose over a pair of rumpled khakis. "I wouldn't talk. You could take a few fashion lessons yourself."

Jack grinned and shrugged off the criticism the way he

always did. "Yeah, but then I'd lose the thing that makes me so . . . so me."

Behind them, the pilot hurried into the hangar, leaving Finn and Jack alone on the empty tarmac. It was past midnight, and the heavy delta air seeped beneath the collar of Finn's white dress shirt. But humidity wasn't the only thing making him sweat.

He scowled, crushing that thought. Nothing on earth would put him on the run, least of all a woman. He wrenched off the sleek black jacket and tossed it in the back of the car before folding himself into the passenger seat.

"Come on, Jack," Finn called out. "It's not like the bad guys are going to wait while you get your rocks off ragging me."

Jack stowed Finn's bag and briefcase in the trunk, then slid behind the wheel. "I gather you want to skip the how are you's?"

"Just brief me."

Jack shook his head. "Someday you're going to learn to slow down and say hello."

"Jack—"

"Just trying to save your life here, buddy. You saved mine."

"I didn't—"

"You gotta learn to loosen up. You don't want to keel over from a heart attack before you're forty, do you?"

"Jack . . ." He could give the younger man a heart attack himself and his voice clearly said so.

Jack only grinned at the threatening tone.

Jesus, the guy was worse than a puppy. Nothing you did put him off.

But Jack held up his hands in surrender. "Okay, I get it. Work, work, work. So here's the deal." Suddenly he was all-business. "I drop you off at the house where the party's at, then take your stuff to the motel. Here's the address." He fished a business card from his shirt pocket and handed it to Finn. "I stashed a cop at the house to keep an eye on things. I'll drive back to the house, leave this car there, and catch a ride back with the cop." He reached into the glove compartment. "Here," he said. "Credit cards, driver's license, social security card. Welcome back, Agent Carver."

Finn shuffled through the identification, saw his own name printed on everything, and replaced the cards he'd been carrying in his wallet for the past six days. He let out a tense breath and leaned back against the headrest. It was good to be clean for once. Twelve hours ago he'd been unshaven, scouring dockside bars and low-life coffee shops for even the slightest hint of where the package he'd been hunting might land. All he'd unearthed were the same rumors they'd been hearing for weeks. Something big, powerful, and nuclear was going on the market but no one knew where or when.

Then Roper had contacted him, said they'd found the girl.

Finn had grabbed a fast haircut, a tux, and boarded the charter almost before he'd had time to breathe. And now here he was, about to resurrect a ghost.

"You're sure this is her?" Finn asked.

"People told me you had a problem with trust," Jack said in a mock mournful voice, "but I didn't want to believe it." He reached for a manila envelope imprisoned by the visor in front of him, flipped it into Finn's lap, and started the engine.

As the car pulled away from the hangar, Finn slipped out the surveillance pictures and swore softly.

"What'd I tell you," Jack said. "It's her."

"Now this is hard to believe."

"The eyes don't lie."

Finn nodded thoughtfully. No, they didn't, but pictures did. He'd have to see for himself. "Where is she?"

"At Beaman's digs. Partying. Hence the party clothes." Jack nodded toward Finn and the tuxedo he wore.

"I thought Beaman just died."

"A week ago." Jack gave a cynical snort. "But everyone handles grief in their own special way."

Finn slipped into silence, thinking about the woman in the pictures. He didn't know much about her, but what he knew was keeping his palms slick, even in the air-conditioned car. His record was piss-poor when it came to working with women, especially this kind. Third-rate "actress," second-rate country singer, first-rate gold digger.

Well, everyone had their talents.

And clearly men were hers. Old men. With lots of money. Lucky for him that was exactly the skill he needed right now.

Yeah, real lucky.

"Beaman was what," Finn said, scanning the report enclosed in the envelope with the pictures, "soul mate number four?"

"And counting," Jack replied. "She chews 'em up and spits 'em out. Can't help but admire her, though. At least she's well paid."

"Those extra bucks are going to come in handy since old Uncle Sam doesn't pay top dollar."

"That's assuming she'll do it."

"Oh, she'll do it. With Beaman out of the picture, her free ride's gone—"

"She's vulnerable," Jack said, egging him on. "Probably lonely, afraid—"

"Exactly. Just ripe for the picking."

Jack shook his head. "Jesus, you're a cold bastard."

Not cold enough if his sweaty hands were proof. "It's a cold world, Jack, and we're the ones keeping it from getting colder. I do what it takes to get the job done."

Twenty minutes later Jack headed up a long winding drive that led to a large estate overlooking the Mississippi River. A columned portico set the front of the house off from the stately brick wings on either side. Greenery climbed the brick; thickly flowering shrubs adorned the entryway. The house was old and dignified, or it had been. Right now lights blazed out the windows like cut-rate diamonds, and raunchy, bass-heavy music pounded so loudly through the front door Finn could hear it outside.

His pulse notched up, pushed by a big fat slice of déjà vu. Scanning the grounds, he checked the perimeter and picked out Jack's cop, who was dressed as a uniformed valet.

At a nod, he came to the driver's side. Jack rolled down the window and murmured softly, "Everything okay?"

The cop knelt to window level. "Party's still going strong. The other valet tells me it'll rage for hours yet." He eyed Finn curiously. "Heard a rumor they were sending in some hotshot undercover guy. If it's you, you're in for a real treat, pal. But I got some advice." He leaned in close and grinned. "Make sure you hold on to your zipper."

Angelina Mercer stood in a corner of Arthur Beaman's large, luxurious living room and watched the party swirl around her. Because of the June heat and the crush of people, the air-conditioning was set at arctic, and she was cold.

Truth was she'd been cold for a week. Ever since she found Arthur Beaman crumpled on the floor, dead from a massive stroke. Tears pricked her eyes but she blinked them away. God, she missed the old man.

She looked around at the drunken bodies crowded into Beamer's house. The party was exactly as he'd specified: loud, crowded, and full of booze. He would have loved the send-off.

Too bad it wasn't doing much for her. She looked down at the vodka in her hand. She should be drunk; she needed to be drunk.

Trouble was, she didn't feel like drinking tonight.

Darling girl, she heard Beamer's crusty voice say in her head. *Life is too short for the mopes.*

Suddenly she felt the old man frowning down on her from wherever the hell he was now. And more than anything, she wanted to wipe away that frown and put the mischievous smile back on his eighty-year-old face.

The hell with the mopes.

The hell with death and loss and moving on. This party was for Beamer, and she'd be damned if she'd disappoint him. She raised her glass heavenward.

Here's to you, old man. She tossed back half her drink and plunged into the crowd.

Finn stepped inside Beaman's house and grimaced at the full force of the sound. Tuxedos and gowns swarmed over the plush interior. He pushed his way past the laughing group gathered under the hallway's vaulted ceiling. Screaming to be heard over the noise, the party-goers paid no attention to him. Balloons and streamers lay in disarray over a gleaming black and white marble floor. He stepped over them, pushed some away.

Someone handed him a drink, but he set it down. He needed a clear head tonight.

The crowd thickened as he moved inward, black satin over white brocade. Well-fed men stood in clusters around marble sculptures. Wraith-thin women draped over expensive furniture. A few turned his way with an interested eye, but he ignored them.

A burst of laughter came at him from the sidelines, sharp as a gunshot. Somewhere someone was coking up, dropping Ecstasy or whatever designer drug was the trend of the hour. There was sex here, too. In the coatroom, the closet, in furtive corners, people mating like rats in a dark alley. And somewhere there was betrayal. Not his own this time, but it was here, he could smell it. The knowledge rose up like a sickness, the haze of booze and smoke sliding over his shoulders like a coat he hadn't worn in a long while.

A banner that read "Bye-bye Beamer" spanned the living-room entrance. Inside, the room looked as though it had been packed into a dice cup, shaken up, and rolled out, furniture landing every which way. Green and gold striped sofas with green velvet pillows stood uncomfortably out of place against the edges. Gilt-edged mirrors still hung on the walls, but the marble-topped tables that should have been beneath them sat askew. A baby grand had been stuffed into a corner to make more room for the horde, which roiled, shifted, and all of a sudden split in two.

And then he saw her.

The hair was looser, the clothes outrageous, the face younger. But the resemblance was unmistakable.

A shaft of something almost like fear pierced him quick and sharp. Deep down he'd been hoping the pictures had been deceptive, that Roper and Jack and everyone else had gotten it wrong.

But they hadn't.

She held a drink in one hand, her lithe body undulating in an impromptu belly dance while a ring of men clapped and cheered her on. Thick blond hair fell in voluptuous waves around her face and shoulders. A clingy white skirt, shimmery with silver thread, hugged the curve of her hips and exposed the top of her navel. Although it reached her ankles and the knife-sharp heels she wore, the skirt was also slashed open to the top of her shapely thigh. Encased in a skimpy, sequined halter, her full breasts shone white and shiny as her skirt. Between the two, bare skin gleamed tan and supple, and exquisitely tempting.

Your mouth's watering, Carver.

No, it isn't.

He leaned into the living room's arched entrance and watched Angelina Mercer work the room. Her long, tanned leg swung sinuously in and out of the opening in her skirt. Her smooth arms wove above her head, her hips gyrated, her eyes glittered with the challenge, *Come get me if you dare.* He'd bet that every male in the room felt something move in his shorts.

Including him.

A final guitar chord screamed, and she upended her drink, downing every drop. "Here's to Beamer!"

Her crowd of admirers cheered. "To Beamer!"

Ample breasts rising and falling in breathlessness, she headed out of the male circle, skin glistening with exertion.

"More!" the crowd took up the cry, stamping their feet in time with the chant. "More, more, more!"

"You know what they say about too much of a good thing," she shouted over the blare of the next song. With a laugh, she threw herself at one of the men and gave him a loud smooch on the mouth. "Get drunk, everyone!"

And she whooshed out of the circle toward Finn.

He lounged against the arch, making no overt move to catch her attention. She'd notice him soon enough. Then the man she'd just kissed pulled her roughly back into his arms, and the problem of meeting her took care of itself.

She laughed and tried to squirm away, but the drunk had her fast. "Come on, baby, let's have a little more of that."

"Let go of me." Rising panic edged her voice and Finn pushed himself off the entry. He strolled toward the struggling couple and casually placed an arm around the drunk, looking for all the world like his best friend. Except Finn tightened his grip, squeezing so hard that the drunk gasped in pain and dropped his hold on Angelina.

Finn smiled. "You may want more, but the lady's had enough." Before the guy could react, Finn spun him around until the drunk staggered dizzily and faced the center of the room. "Back to the party, pal." He gave the man a gentle shove, and he disappeared into the crowd.

Then Finn turned to the woman, who raised an amused eyebrow at him. "Well, well, Sir Galahad. Nicely done."

A cool one. Good. For what he wanted she'd need to be cool.

"Thank you." She extended her hand in a graceful arc, as though he should kiss it. Something on her left shoulder caught his attention—an odd-shaped beauty mark or tattoo—but before he could examine it, she levered herself closer and he found himself staring into a pair of ice-green eyes.

That's right, Angelina. Come to Papa. "Not Galahad," he said.

"Robin Hood?" She poked him playfully in the chest with one long, slim, manicured finger. "Whoever you are, I don't know you." Her breasts brushed his arm, her perfume coiled around him, and the blood went straight to his groin.

Silently, he cursed his own weakness and winked at her. "Sure you do."

"Friend of Beamer's?"

"I knew him, yeah."

She appraised him, a shrewd expression on her face. "No. I don't think you did."

He smiled. "Friend of a friend."

She grinned back; she had his number now. "*You* are a party crasher."

He didn't deny it. "What's a party without a few uninvited . . . friends?"

She dropped an arm lazily over his shoulder and looked up at him. Her hip grazed his. He forced himself to stand still and ignore the sweat starting at the back of his neck where her arm lay like a cool steel trap.

She smiled, her lips promising worlds. "Do you have a name . . . friend?"

A moment ago, he would have sworn her eyes looked bright, but up close the green was tinged with sadness. Weary eyes. Old eyes.

Where had he seen eyes like that before? He said, "Finn."

"Fin?" She threw him the 'that's weird' look he always got when he introduced himself.

"Yeah, Finn. Like in shark."

She laughed, throwing her head back. "Well, *Fin*," she gave his name mock emphasis, "sharks like to swim around in the cool and the wet, and you're all dry." She held up her empty glass, swirling the ice. "Me, too."

She told him what she was drinking and he went to find her a refill.

When he returned, she was gone.

Figures.

But chasing her was part of the game.

He found her outside on the deck where thick summer air drenched him in the overripe smell of damp soil and honeysuckle. A wooden railing surrounded the space on three sides and she was standing on it, leaning against the home's outer wall. Hands behind her back, face to the stars, she'd closed her eyes as if absorbing the moonlight.

Thirty feet below, the Mississippi River lay shrouded in woods and darkness, and the only thing separating her from the abyss was six inches of railing.

"Why don't you come down and join me?" All he needed was to have her break her cheap, beautiful neck.

"Where's my drink?"

He handed the glass to her, and she swallowed a third of the contents, laughing as some spilled down the side of her mouth. A ripple of distaste ran through him, but he kept it off his face while she wiped her chin with the back of her wrist and gazed down at him with excited eyes. "Why don't *you* join *me*, Mr. Sharkman?"

"Because someone needs to catch you when you fall."

"I won't fall." To prove it, she stepped away from the wall and began to pace the railing like a tightrope walker.

Jesus Christ.

Honed to stilettos, her four-inch heels barely found

purchase. "See? Graceful as a cat." She giggled and almost lost her balance.

"Watch out!" He jumped toward her, but she righted herself, laughing.

"Nervous? Didn't know sharks had nerves."

Beneath his jacket, sweat glued his shirt to his back. Eyes fixed on her, he paced the length of the railing, following her highwire dance.

When she reached the middle, she raised her arms wide and cried out to the night. "Hallooo, Beamer!" She cocked her head, but no answer came. "Do you think he's out there, doing the rumba in heaven? God, but that old man loved to dance."

"Did he?" He watched closely. Was she wobbling?

"Poor Beamer." Her voice caught. *Tears?* He would have thought her incapable of it.

To prove his point, she laughed again, shouting into the chasm below. "Did you hear that, Beamer, you old coot? Poor you!" She giggled and wavered again. "Whoops . . ." Her arms pinwheeled.

Fear spiked; he'd had enough. Fastening one hand on the back of her halter, he pulled her toward him. Her drink went flying and she landed with a thump in his arms.

"Hey . . . what'd you do that for?"

"You want to kill yourself, do it on someone else's watch." She twined her arms around his neck and smiled lazily up at him. "You're the only one who would have missed me."

"What about all your 'friends' in there?" He nodded back toward the party still raging inside.

"All party crashers. Like you, Sharkman." She snuggled up against him.

He tensed, trying not to like the feel of her bare midriff beneath his fingers. Or the curve of her hip or the view down the front of her tiny halter. She wiggled, settling in.

"Mmm, I like sharks." Her eyes closed, then opened again. "Big, black-haired sharks"—her head drifted onto his shoulder—"with ocean eyes, and sharp, cruel mouths."

He looked down; she was asleep. And suddenly he knew why the party smelled familiar and where he'd seen that sick-and-tired look he'd observed in her eyes.

His wife.

Angelina put a hand to her eyes, shielding them from the morning light.

Who the hell opened the curtains before she was awake? Slowly, she sat up. Groaned.

God, was that her tongue or a ball of wool?

Staggering off the bed, she stumbled on the floor and looked down.

Her Versaces were still strapped to her feet.

In fact, everything she'd worn the night before still clung to her body.

Holding on to the headboard, she undid the tiny straps and slid out of the torturous heels. What in God's name had ever possessed her to buy the things, let alone wear them?

Beamer liked them.

Yeah, good ole Beamer. Sweet, tender, lovable Beamer. He'd loved buying her clothes.

Tears threatened, but she sniffed them away.

Why couldn't you have stayed a little longer, Beam?

Someday she was going to find a young man, one who'd stick around more than a few years.

Fat chance.

What young man would let her have her own bedroom and make no demands except that she look good and bring a little fun into his life?

Before she could stop it, a picture of Beamer's crumpled body rose in her head, and with it the panic that had rushed up her throat. She remembered the frantic phone call, trembling fingers pushing 911 and screaming for an ambulance. Before it came a squad car arrived, complete with a uniform who asked a lot of questions and acted as if he didn't believe her answers.

Not that she expected any different. Not from a cop. They'd looked at her the same way all those years ago when they refused to believe the truth staring them in the face.

She shuddered, then pushed the memories away.

Through the bathroom door she heard the shower turn on. Who was that?

She thought back to the night before. Who had she ended up with?

A picture of sharp blue eyes and a grim mouth rose in her head.

Sharkman?

But she still had her clothes on, so they couldn't have . . . Or maybe they could.

She didn't remember.

She didn't want to remember.

No more, party girl. You promised Beamer.

Sorry, Beam. But like I told you, promises are made to be broken.

Sighing, she padded out of the bedroom. The sight that greeted her was enough to depress a saint, let alone a wicked witch like her. Empty bottles, half-filled glasses swimming with cigarette butts, dead balloons. Beamer's banner tilted into the living-room archway, hanging by a string.

God, she was tired of her life. The weight of it thudded behind her eyes like a wake-up call. She fingered the edge of the banner and it sailed down to the floor.

Who are you going to be now, party girl?

She thought briefly of the fruitless search for the one person she truly belonged to. Not the pale, timid woman who had raised her, but the one who had birthed her. Not the one who had cowered in the face of a small town's blindness, but the one who would have stood up for the truth. Who would have thumbed her nose at them all. Just like her daughter.

But the records were sealed, and not even Beamer's millions had been able to unlock their secrets, though the old goat had tried.

Pushing aside a pleated shirt and tuxedo jacket, she plopped on the couch with a sigh. She had to figure out her next move. Beamer was gone, which meant the house was gone. Time to make some changes.

You'll never change.

I used to be smart once.

Yeah, and look where it got you.

She shut off the voices arguing inside her head. Too early in the morning for self-reproach.

Besides, she had to pee.

Stepping over dirty plates and strands of streamers, she made her way back to the bedroom and pushed open the bathroom door.

Spacious and airy, the marble bathroom was big enough to sleep in. Beamer had renovated it as a surprise for her, turning the tub into a rose-colored Roman bath with golden cherubs that shot water out of their mouths. She'd scolded him for his lavishness, but he'd just pinched her cheek, called her his darling girl, and told her life was to enjoy.

The shower stopped while she finished her business in the alcove that held the toilet. She came outside, but the door to the shower room remained closed.

Who was in there?

Sharkman?

Not his name, but for the life of her she couldn't remember . . . Something fishy. Flounder?

A pair of men's trousers lay over the gold and pink angel wings that held hand towels. Down the side of the slacks, a long tuxedo stripe suggested they matched the jacket on the couch. She searched the back pocket and came up with what looked like a wallet.

Opening it, she saw it contained only two things: an official seal and a picture ID. Finn Carver, Special Agent, Terrorism Control Force.

A cop. Sharkman was a goddamn cop.

When Finn came out of the shower with a towel wrapped around him, she was holding his ID, her hair an uncombed and tumultuous gold, her eyes bruised from too little sleep, her face a thundercloud.

"You get out of here."

Calmly, he took the ID from her and put it back in his pants. "How about I put my clothes on first?"

He dried his chest with a second towel and to his surprise, her face colored. "You gonna watch?"

Her eyes narrowed. "Like a hawk until you get the hell out of my house."

He found his briefs and pulled them on under the

towel, eyes never leaving hers. *You're nothing. Nothing I can't handle.*

She raised her chin as if to say, *Wanna bet?*

Oh, yeah. He'd take that bet. Thanks to his dear departed wife, he was an expert in handling women like Angelina. And he had a bullet wound to prove it.

"You had no right coming here last night. Certainly no right pretending to be—"

"I didn't pretend anything." He slid into his pants. "You knew I wasn't invited."

Her eyes narrowed. "You didn't say you were a cop."

"You were so busy trying to fall off the edge of the world, I didn't have time."

"You had all night."

"Not unless you believe in communicating through dreams." Pants in place, he left the bathroom in search of his shirt. It lay where he'd left it last night, over the back of the couch.

She followed, standing in the archway where he'd watched her the night before, making an exhibition of herself to a crowd of ogling men.

"Then we didn't . . .?"

"What's the matter—don't you remember?"

She blushed again.

Of course not. He shrugged into the shirt. "Wouldn't have been very sporting of me, since you were so . . . under the weather."

"Not to mention I would have sued your ass off."

"Not to mention."

She bit the inside of one full, luscious lip.

That's right, think about it. I'm pretty enough. I'm male. And if you take care of me, I'll take care of you. And I won't even make you sleep with me.

"What do you want?" She barked the question, her voice rife with suspicion.

"I want you to come work for me."

Her eyes widened, then narrowed again. "What makes you think I'd do that?"

"Because I have something you want."

She laughed. "Get real. What in this glorious hellhole of a world could you possibly have that I'd want?"

He found the snapshot in his jacket pocket and held it up, a corner grasped between two fingers. "Your mother."

Angelina gasped, the breath sucked out of her. "Wh-what? What did you say?" She reached for the photograph, but he snatched it back.

"You heard me."

His face was impassive, the eyes hard. His expression gave nothing away. Just like a cop. The most calculating, self-righteous, cold-hearted bastards in the world. She'd had her share of them when she was eighteen and if she never breathed the same air as a cop again she'd count herself lucky.

"I don't believe you."

He shrugged and started to put the snapshot away.

"Wait!" She stretched out her hand, heart pounding. Damn him. "What's her name?" She eyed the picture hard enough to burn a hole through it, but all she saw was the white back.

"Carol."

Carol. The sound rolled around in her head, a loose stone echoing, a cannonball ready to explode inside her. "Carol what? Who is she? Where is she?"

"I'll tell you everything when you agree to work for us."

"I don't like you, Sharkman. I don't trust you. Why the hell should I do anything you ask?"

"Because your country needs you."

The mawkish phrase made her laugh again. "You're kidding, right? For what?"

But his face was dead serious. "A little lost and found."

"You lost something and you want me to find it?"

"Smart girl."

"And if I do you'll tell me who my mother is."

"That's right."

"That's blackmail."

"No. It's a simple, straightforward business proposition. Given all this . . ." He waved an arm indicating Beamer's luxurious home. "I assume you're familiar with them."

She saw the contempt in his blue eyes and was stung by it. "What do you know about me and Beamer? Nothing. So get the hell out of my house."

But he didn't move. "It's not your house. It belongs to Beaman's heirs now." He gave her a pointed look, a reminder that she would soon be homeless, rootless again.

But she didn't need any reminders. Not from him. "You have a damn sick way of asking people for favors."

"I'm not asking, Angel, I'm selling." He wiggled the photograph between his two fingers. "Just like Beaman."

She growled at the implication, but didn't bother setting him straight. Instead, she stared him right in the face, trying to get past the hard blue wall of his eyes. "Who burst your balloon, Sharkman? Girlfriend? Wife? Whoever she was, she must have been something to make you so god-awful judgmental."

Some emotion flickered across his face, something he shut down as quickly as it had come.

"Well, well, well." She arched a brow. "Struck a nerve." He glowered at her. "You want to trade potshots or make a deal?"

"A deal? Smells more like a scam to me. Arthur spent a fortune trying to track down my mother. And now some two-bit *federale* walks in and just hands her to me? I don't think so."

He shrugged. "Fine." And put the snapshot away.

"Don't!" The cry was more anguished than she'd intended, but her deep desire to see the picture warred with her desperation not to give him control. She licked her lips. "Why me? I'm not exactly Jane Bond. You must have a million people who do this kind of thing every day."

His face grew colder, if that was possible. "You're the right type."

"For what?"

"For the job." He picked up his tuxedo jacket and slung it over his shoulder. "You want to close the deal, give me a call." He flipped a card at her and walked out of the house.

Angelina didn't bother picking up the card. She turned her back on the sound of the door slam and tried to slow her breathing.

Her mother. He said he knew who her mother was. Where she was.

She straightened her spine. That gave him power over her. And no man would ever have power over her again.

Facing the mess in the living room, she swooped down and picked up the fallen banner, crushing it into a ball and marching into the kitchen where she threw it in the garbage. She was *not* going to have anything to do with cops, local, state, federal, or planetary. No matter what they claimed to know.

She pulled a plastic garbage bag from a box in the pantry, jerking it free from the roll. Back in the living room, she plucked the empty beer cans and plastic glasses from the floor and dumped them inside the sack.

Your country needs you.

Right. What could she do anyway? She wasn't a cop. She wasn't anything. Just a fly-by-night party girl who was suddenly sick to death of parties.

Wouldn't it be nice to be different? To be the good girl for once?

She shut off the argument by dumping the overflowing ashtrays into the sack. The residue of ashes and cigarettes was so disgusting, she threw the ashtrays in there, too. One by one they crashed against the cans, each one a loud reproach. She spotted the card Finn had flung at her lying on the carpet and quickly turned her back on it. *Don't do it, party girl.*

Hell. Double, triple hell.

She threw the garbage bag down and stalked into Beamer's room. She fingered the expensive cuff links in the jewelry box on top of his dresser. Opening a drawer, she ran a hand over dozens of silk pocket scarves, each one brighter than the next. In her mind's eye she tucked one into the pocket of Beamer's white suit, a beloved morning ritual.

Profound sadness washed over her and she sank onto his bed. Beamer was gone. Her dear friend. Her protector. She felt naked again. Exposed. With no one on her side.

She surveyed his room, gaze skimming over all the

places he used to be. When she came to the mirror over the dresser, her eyes caught on the sight of herself, hair a wild snarl, eyes puffy, white halter creased from a night of sleeping in it. Beamer would have been appalled, but she merely stared, facing her flaws head-on.

Automatically, her hand went to the tiny, heart-shaped birthmark on her shoulder. She covered the spot, fingering the faintly raised edges of the mole. Her adoptive mother, Adele, used to say the shape marked the spot where an angel had kissed her. Had her real mother seen it? Had she taken one look and thought it a sign of some deeper defect?

Heat rose up Angelina's neck to fill her face, and all at once she knew without a shadow of a doubt that whatever trap Agent Finn Carver was laying, she had already taken the bait.

Finn slipped into the car Jack had left for him the night before, rummaged in the glove compartment for the keys, and fit one into the ignition. Gripping the steering wheel, he stared out at the dense trees and perfect lawn of Arthur Beaman's estate.

As though it seeped out of his pores, Angelina's lush fragrance curled around him. He'd planned to wait her out right there, but if he didn't ditch last night's clothes, the smell would drive him crazy.

Scrubbing a hand down his face, he tried to shut out all traces of her. The last thing he needed was another floozy getting under his skin. Once a lifetime was enough.

He pushed the thought away, and to make sure it stayed gone, he punched in the secure number to Roper at their temporary headquarters in Memphis. While he waited for the connection to clear, he started the engine and drove off.

"She agree?" his boss asked first thing.

He pictured Roper's bulldog face. "Not yet. But the bait's out there."

"We don't have time for haggling. Get her cooperation. Take her out to dinner, buy her something. Try being nice instead of your usual charming self."

Finn's jaw tightened. He didn't trust her as far as he could throw her. "She's a civilian. She isn't trained. I can do this job—"

"Alone." Irony edged Roper's voice. "I know. Finn Carver, one-man army. Look, we've already lost a week since the rumors started. Right now, she's our best option, so get used to it."

Finn's gut churned at the set-down. Roper may have been right, but Finn couldn't help hoping to avoid prolonged exposure to Angelina Mercer. Then again if his luck held out, she'd stay true to type and he wouldn't have to worry about her.

He promised Roper to report in person later that day, then drove to the motel, got the key from the desk clerk, and let himself into the room.

It was antiseptically neat, with the sharp smell of disinfectant just below the surface. Single bed, plain dresser, table with briefcase and overnight bag carefully placed. Like a thousand other motel rooms in a thousand other places.

His thoughts flashed on a house in St. Louis. A small brick Cape Cod, painted white. It had been a long time since he'd seen his boyhood home. Since his mother's death, he'd had no reason to go back. He should have sold the place, but something held him back. Nostalgia, maybe. Sentiment. Some vestigial desire for a real life.

Fuck that. He had a real life.

No, he had a job.

And as soon as this assignment was over he'd sell the damn house. He'd tried real life. Tried the whole love and marriage thing, and it had nearly killed him.

He'd take a job any day.

He plunged into the shower, the hot water cutting off the argument, and lingered in the steam.

He was taking off his rumpled clothes when his cell phone rang Finn picked it up. "Carver."

"Is that you, Sharkman?" Angelina's voice came through the receiver, low and close.

"Fins and all. So . . . what can I do for you?"

"I thought it was more a question of what I can do for you."

His pulse quickened. "What we can do for each other."

A pause. He heard her take a deep breath. "I'm listening."

His heart jolted in satisfaction and alarm. They were on.

CHAPTER
～2～

"So what exactly do you want me to do?"

"How about letting me in?"

Angelina stepped back from her front door so Finn could enter. The rumpled tuxedo had been replaced by a charcoal suit, crisp white shirt, and burgundy tie. A briefcase added the finishing touch.

"Special Agent Carver. How nice to finally meet you."

He shot her a deadpan look and moved wordlessly past her, scanning the place as if checking for booby traps. "What are you hunting for?"

"You cleaned up."

"I do know how to use a vacuum cleaner."

Finn's eyebrows rose as if he didn't believe her. Stepping around an antique table that held a pair of Italian marble urns she and Beamer had found in Paris, Finn crossed into the living room, placed his briefcase on the coffee table in front of the Scalamandré sofa, and parked himself on one of its green and gold, satin-striped arms. His eyes took her measure, and clearly she came out lacking.

She flushed, and that reaction sent a spark of irritation through her. She could handle this. She could handle any man. "Are, you going to tell me what you want me to do, or are we going to play twenty questions?"

His jaw tightened, his eyes became two black stones. "Game playing may be your idea of sport, but it isn't mine. What we're looking for is simple. Four kilograms of weapons-grade plutonium."

She stared at him. Whatever she'd expected him to say, it certainly wasn't that. "You're kidding."

"I don't kid about enough plutonium to fuel a dirty bomb that could spread radioactive waste in all directions."

"You want me to find a nuclear bomb?" Her voice rose in incredulity.

"Not a bomb. Not yet. Just one of the main ingredients. Four kilograms of plutonium. The amount that could sit in the palm of your hand."

Despite the seriousness of the situation, she couldn't help laughing. "And how do you expect me to find something like that? I may know a thing or two about bombshells, but I don't know anything about bombs."

His lips compressed as he visibly reined in his patience. "We'll show you what to look for."

"Great," she said, rolling her eyes. "How about where?"

"We think the plutonium was smuggled into this country for purposes of resale. We've been hearing rumors among domestic terror groups that mention a man named Victor Borian, a wealthy businessman with connections in Russia and Central Asia where the plutonium was stolen."

She shook her head, still baffled. "Why me? Don't you have men in astronaut suits who do this kind of thing?"

Ignoring her gibe, he clicked open his briefcase. "You have something no one else does." He held out the snapshot he'd taunted her with that morning. "Your mother." She stilled. "She was married to Borian."

She heard the words but couldn't take them in. Was this some kind of trick? She examined his face for signs he was joking, but he only gazed at her, stiff and sober as Sunday. "Go ahead, take it." He pushed the photo at her.

But now that she could finally see what her mother looked like, she wanted to put off the moment. She wasn't ready. Not yet. Heart pounding, she took the picture from him and placed it facedown on the coffee table. "You said 'was' married? Is she divorced? Remarried?"

Finn hesitated, a shimmer of guilt wafting through him. He'd used her mother as bait, and it had worked. Now he had to tell her the truth, and given her reaction when he'd first mentioned the possibility of meeting her mother, what he was about to tell her now would be rough. "I'm sorry, Angelina, but she's dead. She died three years ago. Cancer."

The light in her beautiful face faded as the words sank in. "I see." She turned away again, but not before he saw bitterness and disappointment in her eyes. "So this was all a scam. You want me to help you and in return you give me a dead woman."

For half a minute he was tempted to put a comforting arm around her, but that was only his soft streak speaking. The farther away he stayed, the better. "Look, I can't bring her back to life, but I can get you as close as you'll ever get to her. Into the house she lived in, near the people she lived with. Her sister works for Borian."

"Her sister."

"That's right."

She nodded slowly, as though thinking it through. *Come on, 'Lina, work it out. An aunt is better than nothing.*

To help her, he took out the sheaf of reports and documents Roper had gathered. "We did a deep background check on Borian and his wife, and discovered she'd had a child when she was fifteen."

She gazed at him, green eyes wide and vulnerable. He looked away, not wanting to lose himself to their pull.

"Fifteen," she murmured. "So young."

Blindly, Angelina took the papers he held out to her. She had never been fifteen and pregnant, but she knew how it felt to face the world's scorn alone.

"She had the baby out of state in a home for unwed mothers," Finn said, "far away from friends and family. Here are the papers backing this up. Your birth certificate, the adoption records. Not that you'll need them. One look at the photo should convince you."

"What about my father?"

He shrugged. "There's no name on the birth certificate and the only person who could tell us for sure is dead. I'm sorry."

She heard the sympathy in his voice and shut it out. She didn't need pity. Not from someone like him.

"There is the sister," he continued casually. "Marian. She might know."

She looked at him, not for a second buying into his offhand tone or his implication: do this for me and find Daddy, too.

Instead, she touched the papers she'd tried for years to obtain. "How did you get these?"

As if it had been the easiest thing in the world, Finn said, "The court agreed to release your records to us in the interest of public safety."

She nodded, numb. Even the judicial system was in on the deal. "And this?" At last she pushed the photo out from under the other papers.

"Our research team dug it up. Take a look. The resemblance is uncanny."

Heart in her throat, she turned the picture over. Staring up at her was an attractive blonde in her late thirties, maybe ten years older than Angelina was now, but still youthful.

Her mother. The one person in all the world who was truly hers.

Tears gathered in the back of her throat and she swallowed convulsively, suddenly panicked. She would not break down. Not in front of him.

"Are you all right?"

His voice was gentle, too gentle. It nearly undid all her efforts not to cry, and for half a second she almost leaned against him, wishing for someone who loved her, someone to share this moment with, someone who would understand and help her absorb it.

But there was no one, only him, and when she trusted herself to look, she caught him appraising her, measuring her reaction, calculating . . . something. Her hackles went right back up again.

"What else is going on here, Sharkman? You want me to get into Borian's house. What does this"—she shook the photograph at him—"have to do with it?"

"Everything," he said curtly. "Borian adored his wife and never got over her loss. You're going to give her back to him."

Puzzled, she frowned. "Me? What do you mean?"

"Your job is to look as much like Carol Borian as possible. That's the hook we'll use to get you inside the house."

Her jaw dropped, but before she could get any words out, he slid off the sofa and walked past her as if he lived there. His familiarity with Beaman's home sent another flash of irritation through her. She followed him into the bedroom.

"This is my bedroom. I didn't give you permission—"

"We have a deal, and I just held up my end. So let's skip the niceties. We don't have time."

He opened her closet and began riffling through her clothes. She shoved past him and closed the doors. "What are you doing?"

He lifted her off the floor and set her down a few feet away. The hands circling her waist were warm and strong, and she didn't like the way her heart thumped at their touch.

"Checking your clothes for something more . . ." He examined her from head to toe and back again. "Appropriate." Reopening the closet, he began wading through the clothes.

Who the hell did he think he was?

She stepped toward him, and like that, he turned, blocking her way.

"I'm going to do this whether you like it or not."

His gaze was steely and she returned it. "Just so we're clear—I don't like it."

He turned back to the closet and she leaned against the bed, staring moodily at the picture of her mother. Face it, the woman was a stranger. She looked refined and elegant, blond hair pulled back into a soft chignon, a string of pearls around the neck of her tailored dress. Nothing like the rebellious spitfire Angelina had imagined all these years. Nothing like Angelina.

A nip of disappointment bit and she caught her reflection in the mirror. She'd toned down the bright red lipstick, but her lips were still a beacon of color. "You really think I look like her?"

Finn spoke over his shoulder, his fingers moving through the clothes. "Enough to make her husband's hair stand on end, we hope. Especially if you lose the makeup and the Veronica Lake hair." He scraped back a section of clothes to examine a glittery black dress with a plunging neckline.

"What's he like?"

"Old-fashioned. European." He pushed the black dress into the "reject" section and held up a red strapless pant suit. "Does everything you own have sequins?"

"No."

"Good."

"Some of it has feathers."

He shot her a don't-mess-with-me look and she sent him one back. She didn't bother telling him that most of the flashy stuff had been presents from Beamer. That little red number had been one of his favorites.

Her heart squeezed. *Oh, Beam. Why did you have to go?*

Finn rehung the outfit in the closet and closed the doors. "Nothing here. You'll have to lose the trashy wardrobe."

Trashy? As if apologizing for it, she glanced down at her clothes, then caught herself. No cop was going to tell her what to do or how to dress. Especially one who'd lied to her. Well, not lied. Not exactly. But she hadn't missed the fact that he'd neglected to say her mother was dead— at least not until he'd reeled her in.

She rose and crossed to where he was leaning against the closet doors, watching her the way a cat does, intense and ready to spring. *Do I make you nervous, Sharkman?* She glided up to him, feeling his almost-imperceptible tension mount as she approached. "You don't like my clothes?"

He sidestepped, neatly avoiding her. "It's not me you have to worry about. Victor Borian's blood is three-quarters starch. You want to hold up your end of our bargain, you'll play the part."

Oh, she'd play a part, all right. The part that paid back liars like him. Why else had she agreed to this?

Because you're tired of being you, party girl. Here's your chance to be someone else.

She *had* felt different after she'd agreed to work with Carver and hung up the phone. She'd showered and changed into the most conservative outfit she owned, a white silk suit that covered her from neck to mid calf. At the time, she thought it appropriate for her transformation into Finn Carver's little angel, but now she saw nothing she did would make a dent in his icy contempt. *Well, who the hell cares?* To prove it, she undid the top button of the high, Chinese-style neck, fingers working slowly, provocatively. Without taking her eyes off Finn, she moved on to the next button.

"What are you doing?" His voice was hoarse and he cleared it.

Payback time. "It's hot in here. Don't you think it's hot?"

He grabbed her wrist, stopping her at the third button. "I told you I don't play games."

"I'm not playing games." *Now who's the liar?* "I'm just hot."

His eyes narrowed. "Let's get out of here, then. We have work to do." And before she could protest, he grabbed her purse, tossed it to her, and led her out the door.

The spring afternoon washed over her, warm and fecund. She *had* been playing games, pushing to get back at him for manipulating her, but now she really was hot. His hand on her wrist gave her an electric thrill she wasn't too happy about. *You do nothing to me, Sharkman. I'm in control.* She tugged herself away and instead of getting into Finn's government-issue Ford, she opened the door to the '58 T-bird convertible Beamer had bought her last year. A classic in mint condition, he'd paid a small fortune for it.

"Can't cool down inside that tin box of yours." Not waiting for Finn, she slid behind the wheel, found her car keys, and turned over the ignition. Flooring the gas pedal, she squealed away, laughing at the slow burn in Special Agent Carver's face.

The wind blew her hair into a wild tangle, and she reveled in the feel of it whipping her face. Finn's car roared behind, taking the curves of the hilltop road with difficulty. She glanced in the rearview mirror and could almost see the fury heat those cold blue eyes. He leaned against his horn, demanding her to stop, but she pressed down on the gas pedal, laughed and watched his reaction in the mirror. The horn blared, and something about its warning peal made her focus on the road ahead.

Oh, my God.

She'd drifted into the wrong lane. An oncoming car headed straight toward her. Wrenching the wheel, she braked and skidded off the road as the approaching car buzzed by on an angry horn blast. Her right headlight connected with a tree, snapping her forward and back.

Shock rendered her motionless, hands locked around the steering wheel. The only thing that moved was her heart, and it galloped inside her like a runaway stallion. A screech of brakes, footsteps pounding over gravel, and the car door swung open.

"Are you completely crazy? You could have killed yourself." *Breathe, party girl. Just breathe.* "Angelina." Finn barked her name. "Are you all right?" His voice closed in and then he was gently prying her fingers away from the wheel. "Angel." Softer. Something touched the top of her head. His hand. It slid down to cup her chin. He turned her to face him. He was kneeling beside the car. "Are you all right?"

His eyes were so blue for a moment she thought she was looking at pieces of sky. *Don't be nice to me, Sharkman. I'm a sucker for nice.* "I'm not that easy to hurt."

His gaze lingered on her, as though he were seeing past all the masks she wore. She looked away, focused on the trees lining the road, and he rose. "That's good," he said, and frowned at the crumpled front end of the convertible. "But you're damned lucky you didn't break your neck."

"Disappointed?"

He turned to her, the ice back in his eyes. "Let's go. I'll call a tow truck from my car."

She got out slowly, her legs still shaky, and leaned against the car hoping he wouldn't notice. But he put an arm around her shoulder to prop her up. She shrugged it off.

"I'm fine."

One step and a leg buckled. In an instant, he caught her. Clasping her against him, he held her up so she could make the short journey to his car. His body was hard and strong beneath the dark gray suit, and she liked the feel of it. Too much. Way too much.

"I don't need your help." She twisted away, but he held on.

"Right." The edges of his mouth betrayed a hint of a smile. "How'd you get to be such a tough guy?"

"Vitamins."

He opened the passenger door on the Ford and helped her into the car, then got in himself. "We can stop at the hospital if you want."

God, she felt a fool. "What for? You want to get your head examined, that's one thing, but there's nothing wrong with me. It was a little fender bender. No big deal."

Once again, he observed her closely, then dismissed his concern with a little shrug and started the car. "Okay."

She leaned against the back of the seat and closed her eyes. Why did she do these things?

As if he'd read her mind, he said, "You like being reckless."

Reckless, careless, thoughtless—any word with 'less' in it described her perfectly. "It's called fun."

"You want to kill yourself, wait until after we get Borian." His voice was as cold as his eyes. "No more impulsive little dramas. You keep a calm, cool head. And you do what you're told, when you're told."

Not on your life, Sharkman. Not since I was eighteen. "You say jump, and I say how high?"

His mouth twisted into a tight smile. "First you say yes, sir. Then you ask how high."

Finn let her stew on that while he headed south. *Crazy, stupid* . . . He wanted to shake her. No, he wanted to comfort her. Make sure she was okay.

He clamped his jaw against the tender impulse. It had taken a bullet to get him to stop caring for self-destructive women, but he'd learned his lesson.

For a minute his wife's face floated in front of him. He remembered the way her lipstick never quite stayed within the lines of her mouth because her hands shook from booze or drugs. He remembered her wild hair and the blowsy smile she bestowed on him and whatever other man happened to be near. And with Suzy there were always men. She'd been the life of the party. Or had the party been her life?

He cut a glance at Angelina, who was glowering out the passenger window as a way to avoid connecting with him, and remembered his dead wife's eyes. Those sick, haunted eyes that couldn't quite hide her fear and self-loathing. It was her eyes that had gotten to him. They'd convinced him she could be saved, that his love could save her. But nothing could.

Disgust washed over him, familiar, even after years of living—and nearly dying—with his greatest mistake. Disgust with himself. His weakness. His damn inclination to feel too sorry for people. His fingers tightened around the steering wheel. Never again.

Twenty minutes later, he parked in front of Bradfords, one of the most exclusive clothing stores in town.

Angelina broke the angry silence she'd maintained during the ride. "We're going shopping?"

"That's right." He got out of the car and opened her door. "Angelina Mercer, you're in for a whole new look, courtesy of Uncle Sam."

He steered her toward the store, watching closely to make sure she wasn't limping. All he needed was to have her injured before they even got started. But her body parts were all back in prime working order. Unfortunately.

Inside, the store's cool quiet was ripe with the smell of old money. Perfectly laid-out clothes in muted tones spilled over polished wood tables or draped from carefully placed cabinets that seemed as though they belonged in a museum.

Angelina stood in the middle of the boutique looking like a refugee from Fredericks of Hollywood, her body-hugging suit clinging to every curve. She scanned the room, frowning.

"What's the matter?"

"Do you think this stuff could get any dowdier?" She held up a silky blouse. "What a cute little Peter Pan collar." She picked out a pale blue dress with some kind of floral pattern. "And this nice tidy belt and all those teensy-weensy flowers."

"I told you, Borian is conservative."

"Borian is boring."

A saleswoman approached them. "Can I help you find something?"

"Yes, you can," Angelina said, her green eyes innocent as a baby's. "Where do you keep the crotchless panties?"

Jesus Christ.

"I beg your pardon?" the saleswoman said.

"The cr—"

"We're just browsing." Finn took her arm and steered her away. "Behave yourself."

"Or?"

He gritted his teeth. "What size do you wear?" He'd

held her last night, and her body had yielded under his hands, soft and fleshy, nothing like the stripped down, bony women he'd held in the past. But if she was anything like them, she'd pare herself to the smallest possible number. "Two? Four?"

She laughed. "I'm a woman, Sharkman, not a little girl. I wear an eight. Sometimes a ten. Even a twelve. Depends on how skimpy they cut things. In case you haven't noticed, I've got a few curves. And they take up room."

Oh, he'd noticed all right.

She smiled like she knew it.

"Here." He gathered up the first things he saw and thrust the pile in her arms. "Try them on." Still grinning, she sashayed into the fitting room.

Finn made himself look away from the sweet sway of her very shapely bottom. He focused on a display of linen suits instead, noting their simple lines and understated cut. A nearby mannequin wore the same outfit, and it looked polished and well bred. Exactly the kind of look Victor Borian would expect. The skirt was a modest, knee-skimming length, the jacket a square coverall that lent the outfit a quiet, moneyed air. A strand of pearls at the throat completed the civilized look. Once Angelina was stuffed into that Finn knew his hands would stop sweating.

But when she came out a minute later, he saw he'd been wrong. She wore the same skirt, the same jacket, but somehow on her it looked entirely different. He would barely have known the mannequin had breasts, but the jacket hugged Angelina's waist and the rich curves of her chest. She did a slow turn and he saw the skirt fit snugly around her well-rounded bottom. She'd played with her hair, pulling it off her shoulders and into some kind of knot at the back of her neck, imitating Carol Borian's hairstyle in the photo he'd shown her. But unlike Mrs. Borian's hair, a strand of Angelina's refused to stay in place, drifting across one cheek like a sultry invitation.

An invitation he had no intention of accepting.

As if she knew what he was thinking, a faint, mocking smile curved her lips. "Conservative enough for you?"

His jaw tightened. "No. Try on the dress."

Her eyes narrowed. "What's wrong with this?"

He wasn't about to explain. "Try on the dress."

But the same thing happened. The mannequin wearing the dress looked like she'd be at home at a Junior League meeting. Angelina looked anything but. The silky material clung to her breasts, outlining the lush curves. The tidy belt she'd made fun of accented the way her waist squeezed in and her hips flared out. The skirt floated over her thighs and knees like gossamer, moving in a seductive dance as she walked.

They spent two hours at Bradfords, and despite his vow not to let her get to him, in the end Finn was sweating in more places than his hands. Everything that looked prim on the hanger looked sexy on her. The final getup—a simple skirt and sweater that should have looked elegant but somehow looked provocative—was the last straw.

"This is ridiculous, Sharkman. I've tried on every damn outfit in the place." She glared at him, hands on shapely hips. "This *was* your idea, remember?"

"Well, it was a bad idea. Get dressed."

She flounced away, but not before he saw a glimmer of hurt in her eyes. *Now what?*

Angelina slammed into the dressing room and examined herself in the mirror. No horns growing out from the top of her head. What the hell was wrong with that man? She smoothed down the front of the lavender sweater she wore over a straight skirt in shades of lilac and mauve. A short-sleeved cashmere crew, the sweater was soft as a baby's breath. It blended perfectly with the gentle heathered colors of the skirt. She sighed, gazing at her own image. In spite of herself, she liked what she saw. She looked young and sweet, the way she used to look years ago. Before she found out what a rat hole the world was. Looking at herself in the mirror, she felt a pang of nostalgia for the girl she used to be. That naive girl from Ruby, Texas, who believed in American justice. And herself.

Remember her, party girl?

Andy Blake and Sheriff Maxwell Dodd had taken care of that other Angelina. And her mother, the one who she'd called mother all her life, had helped.

She pushed back the hair escaping from the makeshift chignon, dismissing the memories. Everyone knew she could never be that girl again. Even Sharkman. Especially Sharkman.

Now why did that bother her so much?

Glancing at the mirror once more, she tried to see what he saw when he looked at her. Her breasts were high and firm, her waist small, her hips ample. Men usually liked her. More than liked her. Then again, was Sharkman really a man, or some kind of cold ocean creature?

She took one last look at the skirt and sweater, then began to tug it off. Before she pulled the sweater over her head, she changed her mind. *The hell with it.* Leaving the outfit on, she scooped up her suit and all the other clothes she'd tried on. So Sharkman didn't like them? The hell with him, too.

He was on her case the minute she walked out of the dressing room, the pile of clothes in her arms. "What are you doing? I told you to get dressed."

"I am dressed."

"I thought I made it clear these clothes won't work."

She shrugged. "I don't need your permission to buy clothes." Transferring the pile into the arms of a waiting salesgirl, she fished in her purse. "Who needs you when I have Citibank?" She handed the girl a credit card.

She could see by the way his mouth pinched that Finn wasn't happy, but she didn't care. She turned her back on him and tried not to blink when the salesgirl read her the total.

Oh, Beam, I could really use you now.

She thought about Beamer as she signed the credit slip. He'd have gotten a good laugh out of this shopping spree. No glitter, no boas, no plunging necklines. Nothing but simple elegance.

Like Carol.

The thought sent a ripple of longing through her. Would her real mother have liked the clothes in Bradfords? Pictures lie. Maybe the snapshot Finn had showed her hid the real Carol Borian. Maybe she had sequins and feathers in her closet, too.

As soon as Angelina's transaction was over, Finn hurried her away. He bundled her into the white Ford and her packages into the trunk.

"Where are we going?"

"You'll find out when we get there."

Typical closemouthed cop answer.

"There" proved to be a nondescript office building. Without explanation, he led her into the elevator and up to the third floor, where he pushed open the door to suite 301.

No one occupied the receptionist's desk, but that didn't seem to bother Finn. He led her past it and through an interior door to a vacant office.

Inside, an old Naugahyde couch sat across from an empty desk pushed against a dull beige wall. Lying on the couch was a pudgy man short enough to fit with his feet just barely dangling over the edge. His eyes were closed and he seemed asleep, but the minute they walked in, he said, "You're late."

"We got held up."

The man sat up; he was the ugliest man Angelina had ever seen, with a bulbous nose and a bulldog face. But when he stood and beamed at her approvingly, the smile was so warm she forgot his unattractiveness.

"Beautiful, Miss Mercer. Stunning, actually."

She laughed. She couldn't help herself, he was so transparent. "Thank you." And in a stage whisper, "You have better taste than he does." She indicated Finn, who stood stiffly to one side. "And now, don't you think you better tell me who you are? How do you know my name?"

Finn stepped in. "This is my boss, Ron Roper. Roper, Angelina Mercer."

"A pleasure." He extended his hand, enclosing Angelina's in his own.

"We're still working on the clothes," Finn said.

"The clothes? They're perfect. She's perfect. Victor Borian won't know what hit him." She tossed Finn an I-told-you-so look, but before he could respond, Roper led her to the couch and sat beside her. "I wanted to thank you personally before you began, Miss Mercer. Right now, you're our best chance of stopping this dangerous material from falling into the wrong hands. We don't have the luxury of infiltrating Borian's organization on our own. That could take weeks, if not months, of carefully building his trust. Time we don't have. We need someone to get close to Borian as quickly as possible."

Something in his voice set off alarm bells. She frowned. "Close? How close?"

Neither man responded right away, and she looked between the two of them. Finn's gaze was cool and mocking. "As close as you have to."

She flushed as his meaning dawned. "You want me to sleep with him." *Figures.*

"It's not like you haven't done it before."

The blood drained from her face and Finn could have kicked himself. Why the hell did he turn into such a bastard every time he was around her?

She sucked in a sharp breath. "He's my stepfather."

Finn exchanged a glance with Roper. This was an issue they'd discussed, one of the many objections Finn had made. He still didn't like it and he'd be damned if he'd defend it. He quirked his brow, giving the floor to Roper.

Not that his boss had any trouble going solo. Roper smiled sweetly at Angelina, a smile that hid the steel behind it. "Borian is your mother's husband, true," Roper said, "but you never knew your mother. You were fourteen when she married Victor Borian. There's no blood relationship, no relationship at all." Roper took her hand in a soothing way that made Finn squirm. God, the man was good at the fatherly act. "How far it goes is entirely up to you, my dear. All our information tells us Borian was devoted to his wife. Her death devastated him. Your resemblance to her could be the only lure that will trap him. Will you help us?"

Rising, Angelina walked to the window and stared blindly at the parking lot below. A bitter wave washed over her. Looked like her reputation had preceded her.

So what? It was her one chance to learn about her real mother.

Yeah, but Mommy was dead.

And a zillion-odd people would be dead, too, if Borian sold his radioactive loot to a bunch of crazies.

Do it.

The words echoed inside her chest like a heartbeat.

Do it.

Not for her mother, or a nation of strangers. For herself. For a chance to do good. Or to find out if she still could.

Angelina Mercer, the tramp of the new millennium, a do-gooder? She almost laughed.

Instead, she turned around to face them, crossed her arms self-protectively, and didn't bother to hide the sarcasm.

"Sure, why not? Anything for Uncle Sam."

CHAPTER
~3~

"**W**elcome to the team." Roper flashed Angelina another hearty smile and pumped her hand.

She looked around the nearly-empty office and back at Roper, waiting for more. "That's it?"

Finn rolled his eyes. "We stopped tattooing our agents last year, but your secret decoder ring is in the mail."

Patronizing jerk. She opened her mouth to respond in kind, but before she could, Roper interposed. "There's some paperwork to go through, but we can worry about that later." He turned to Finn. "Did you set up the briefing?"

Finn nodded.

"Good. Then this is good-bye for a while, Ms. Mercer. Finn will be your AC—Agent-in-Charge."

Damn, she didn't like the sound of that. "In charge of what?"

"You," Finn said with a gleam in his eyes she liked even less.

"He's the team leader," said Roper. "Your contact. He makes the rules and you report to him."

"You can call me sir," Finn said as he led her out of the office, down the elevator, and into his car. Once there, he turned on the ignition and set off without another word.

Angelina glared out the window, already regretting her decision.

Five minutes into the ride, Finn spoke. "Look, I know we got off to a rocky start, but how we feel about each other comes second to completing our job."

She crossed her arms and continued looking out the window. "And how *do* we feel about each other, Agent Carver?" She examined her own feelings and didn't like the way part of her wanted to nestle closer to the hard length of his thigh next to hers.

He shrugged. "I'm not going to lie to you. I have my doubts about this whole idea."

"You mean you have doubts about me." She swung around to face him and saw that grim muscle working his jaw again.

"I mean—" He sucked in a breath and let it out. "I mean you don't have any training and we don't have time to give you any."

She barked a curt laugh. "From what I heard back there, I've got all the training I need."

"Look, dammit, you don't trust me, I don't trust you. Fine. But we have to work together. I never expected you to agree to do this, and now you have. So maybe I was wrong about you. And maybe you're wrong about me."

"And maybe we're both dead right."

Brakes squealing, he careened into a seedy motel. "I hope to hell not, because dead is the operative word here." He parked in front of a room around back and pulled up the emergency brake with such force it sounded like he would wrench the thing off.

He shoved open the car door, got out, and slammed it shut. Through the windshield she watched him take a room key out of his pocket and insert it in the knob of a numbered door. He stood in the open doorway staring at her, his face dark and cold as a winter night, and she realized that he expected her to follow him.

She couldn't. The dank wall with its row of bent and battered doors closed in on her. She hadn't been to a cheap motel in years. Without warning, nausea surged through her. She couldn't have moved if her life depended on it.

Finn stood in the doorway waiting for Her Majesty. As the seconds stretched, he muttered a curse and stalked back, yanking open the car door. Then he saw her face. She was staring at something beyond him, her eyes wide and scared. He turned and saw what her gaze had fixed on: the room door gaping open like a black hole.

And then it hit him. What had happened to her years ago. Cursing himself for a fool, he bent down and put his hand on the tense fingers in her lap. They were ice-cold. For the first time since he'd met her, she looked small and fragile, not the indestructible wiseass she pretended to be. The enormity of what she'd agreed to do came back to him, and with it, a twinge of admiration. She had guts, he'd give her that. And now, when she needed it least, her courage deserted her. He cleared his throat, reaching for gentleness and half succeeding.

"It's just a briefing, Angel. Nothing more. There's another agent waiting inside with slides and pictures."

She licked her lips. "Don't you have an office?"

"I don't want anyone connecting you with a government agency. I picked this place because it was out of the way. That's all."

He gave her a small, encouraging smile, and her shoulders straightened imperceptibly. He could almost see her force the fear away, covering it up with her usual mask of hard cynicism.

He didn't know whether to admire her or feel sorry for her. He knew a thing or two about covering up, so he held out a hand to help her out, but she swung her feet around and got out by herself. "I don't need an escort."

Fine. Go it alone. The less she leaned on him the better. He slammed the door on his tender impulse and stepped aside to let her pass.

Angelina shook off the pity she'd seen in Finn's face. Who was he to feel sorry for her? Besides, he couldn't know how she felt about places like this—or why.

For half a second she hesitated on the threshold, then took a breath and plunged into the motel room. Inside, it was everything she expected, a lumpy bed, a wobbly chair, a scratched table. But unlike the rest of the room, which looked like a remnant from the sixties, the table held twenty-first-century tools: an open laptop computer with an attachment the size of a small video camera.

As promised, another man was waiting for them, a young, beefy blond with a buzz-cut and nice-guy brown eyes. "Hey, Carver, where you been?"

"Escorting our secret weapon around town." Finn nodded in her direction. "Jack, meet Angelina Mercer. Angelina, Agent Jack Saunders."

Agent Saunders? Not exactly the Terrorism Control Force uniform here. Unlike Sharkman, who was sewed up neat and tight in his federal grays, this one wore a vintage shirt that looked like it had barely survived Pearl Harbor. Complete with palm trees, pelicans, and pineapples, it hung loose over a pair of slept-in khakis. She liked him immediately.

Jack extended his hand and shook hers. "Glad you decided to help us out."

"Looks like you're the only one." At the confusion on his face, she shook her head. "Never mind." She glanced around the second-rate room and the third-rate setup, trying to distance herself from the memories. "You're kidding. This is the best the mighty TCF can do?"

The other man grinned. "Government work is so glamorous."

But Finn remained cool and aloof. "Like I said, you're safer in a neutral setting."

"Well, you got beige down pat."

Saunders laughed, but Finn only hit the lights. "Let's go."

Agent Saunders tapped a few keys on the laptop, and the attachment whirred on, illuminating the opposite wall. Into the beam of light a photograph appeared showing four women around a luncheon table. Her mother was in the middle wearing a severe navy suit. Slowly, Angelina sank on the edge of the bed and peered at the picture, drinking in the image.

Her mother. Come to life in a photograph. Angelina could hardly breathe.

"Become familiar with her smile, the way she holds her head. The closer you can come to duplicating her expressions, the easier your job will be."

What were you like, Mother? Carol looked happier here than in the snapshot Finn had showed her earlier, more relaxed. What lay behind that angelic smile?

Another keystroke, and another photo appeared. This time, Carol was arm in arm with another woman.

"That's the sister."

Aunt Marian. What stories could she tell? Had the sisters been friends? Had they giggled and shared confidences, or fought all the time? All at once, Angelina had a family. Her breath caught, her body went cold, then hot. The realization was almost too much to take in.

Marian had small dark eyes pinched close together. Carol was clearly the beauty. She smiled into the camera, dewy and fresh-faced, like a commercial for Ivory soap. Even in her innocent days, Angelina had never used Ivory.

Click. Another picture. "There he is," Jack said, and she caught her first glimpse of Victor Borian.

Thinning light hair pushed back from a strong forehead revealed deep-set, magnetic eyes. He had a full mouth and high, Slavic cheekbones that showed no sign of sagging even though he looked to be fifty. A brown suit with a vest completed the picture of a grim Russian intellectual, one familiar with using the ends to justify the means.

She shivered. He didn't look like a man to bargain with.

A new snapshot slid into place, a picture of Carol and her husband. She smiled at the camera, he gazed at her, and the expression on his face said he clearly adored her.

That was the trap they would use to catch him. Love. The ultimate Achilles' heel.

You know what that's like, party girl.

She pushed the thought away and focused on what Jack and Finn were saying. That Victor Borian spoke several languages and did odd jobs for a variety of governments including the United States . . . under-the-table tasks they couldn't complete themselves. That he used those connections to gain inside knowledge that financed his empire, an empire that included ties to the Russian mafia and the heroin trade. That he lived in remote places with armed guards, including a Montana ranch.

"Rumor has it that he had a falling out with Anton Ivanov, one of the most powerful Russian mob lords, which is why Borian's living here instead of overseas, where he has several homes," Finn said. "Since his wife's death, he's been a fixture at the ranch. Underground chatter and a variety of intelligence sources lead us to believe the plutonium is there."

The information set her reeling. Carol's pictures showed a woman with understated, old-world grace. A member of the local charity board. Yet all along she'd been married to a gangster. "Did she know what Borian was up to?" Angelina asked.

Jack nodded at Angelina and grinned at Finn. "I thought you said she couldn't put two and two together. That's a good question, Ms. Mercer."

"Angelina." She flashed him her most dazzling smile. "And thank you."

"You're entirely welcome." He smiled back, an expression that lasted a few moments too long . . . at least for the other man in the room.

"Jack," Finn barked. "The briefing."

Sheepishly, Jack tore himself away from staring at Angelina and scrambled for the next picture. "Sorry."

Angelina smiled sweetly at Finn: *men are so predictable, aren't they? Even big, strong special government agents.*

Finn scowled back and turned to look at the next photograph. "To answer your question, no, we have no indication that Carol Borian knew anything about her husband's activities. But she must have suspected."

"Must have made for strange pillow talk."

"Love does a lot of strange things. Combine it with a strong personality, like Borian's, and it can easily corrupt a weaker mind."

She peered over at him. The light from the laptop projector lit his face, making his eyes appear colorless, like a wolf's. "Love corrupts. Is that your motto?"

Jack cleared his throat in an obvious effort not to laugh. "Man, she's got your number, Carver."

Finn ignored that. "All we know is that she stayed with him. That's tacit support if nothing else."

"Maybe he lied to her and she believed him."

"And maybe she didn't want to know," Finn said bluntly. "Love is often blind."

She shivered. Love had blinded her only once, and she'd paid for it. Had Carol?

Before she could pursue the question, Jack hit the keyboard and another photo appeared. "That's Borian's ranch." He identified an elaborate stone, glass, and timber ranch house. "The property covers close to ten thousand acres in the foothills of Devil's Teeth." The next picture showed three mountain ridges, dark and forbidding. "As you can see here"—a new series of slides clicked into place—"the estate is virtually impenetrable, bordered by cliffs and mountains. There's a guarded gate in front."

A slow chill crept up her back. All that space and no escape.

Jack ended the slide show and the room filled with silence. Finn turned the lights on and tossed a folder in her lap.

"There's a detailed map of the ranch. Memorize it. Also prints of some of the pictures you saw. Study them."

She gave him a sloppy salute. "Yes, sir," she said dryly.

They left the motel while Jack was still shutting down the computer. Finn drove her back to the house and unloaded her parcels from the trunk.

"Pack your bags." He dumped the packages from Bradfords in the driveway. "We leave tomorrow."

"What?" She stared at him, floored by the pace of events. "I barely said 'I do.' Don't I even get to catch my breath?"

He gave her a grim smile. "We're running out of time. Breathing's not an option."

She ground her jaw down, knowing he was waiting for her to complain. "Where are we going?"

"Montana."

Montana. Borian country. She saw the expectation in Finn's face, but she wouldn't give him the satisfaction of quitting.

Instead, she smiled at him through half-lowered lids. "Terrific. I have a little cowgirl outfit I've been dying to try out." She picked up the bags and unlocked the door, stepped into the house and kicked the door shut with her heel. Behind her she heard the sound of his car speeding down the drive. She was glad to be rid of him, glad to get rid of the suffocating, can't breathe feeling being close to him created.

As Finn drove away, his gut churned. Despite her constant lip, Angelina had surprised him, and he didn't like surprises. She'd been upset by the seedy motel room, but had quietly suppressed those feelings. She'd watched the slides attentively, asked good questions, and made no complaints. He couldn't have asked more of a trained operative.

He let himself into his motel room, part of him wishing Angelina would have lived up to his expectations. He was already dangerously attracted to her. He didn't want to like her, too. That was a lethal combination. Although he'd loved his wife with a feeling bordering on obsession, he'd never liked her very much. She'd been weak and manipulative, and somewhere deep inside he'd known that. The knowledge had kept him from going crazy himself, especially after she'd betrayed him.

For a moment he was back in the warehouse, staring into the leering eyes of Pedro Morales. *We know who you are, Mr. Federal Agent. Thanks to your wife, we know everything about you.*

Inside his head the gun went off, the sound exploding in his mind the way the bullet had exploded in his body.

He shook off the memory, but couldn't shake the cold sweat as easily. Tossing his briefcase on the bed, he loosened his tie, undid his top shirt button, and turned up the AC, hoping the deep freeze would kill off the part of his brain where the memories lived. He was tired and hungry and his hip ached where the bullet had plowed into it. He just wanted to get some food into him before hitting the sack. Tomorrow would be another long day.

He found a steak place not too far from the motel and ate a fast dinner. When he returned to the room, the message light on his phone blinked red in the darkness. He looked longingly at the bed, but punched in the number to retrieve the message. It was from the front desk: Uncle Jack had left a package.

The minute Finn had gone, Angelina took a deep breath and opened the file he'd handed her. Standing in the entryway, she scanned the meager contents—a few snapshots and a sheet of paper with a brief biography of Carol Simmons Borian from Percy, Alabama.

On impulse, Angelina hurried into Beamer's study and took down the huge U.S. atlas and flipped the pages to Alabama. She couldn't even find Percy on the map.

Small towns. That was one thing she had in common with her mother. Had she hated hers the way Angelina had hated Ruby? Or was Carol one of those cutesy women who loved sweaters with pictures of cats on them and knowing what her neighbors were up to every second? Angelina picked up one of the photos of Carol Borian from the file and peered deeply into the dead woman's eyes. *Tell me your secrets, Mother. How did you go from Miss Percy, Alabama, to the wife of a mobster?*

Hell, maybe any way out was a good way out.

Angelina went into her bedroom and, holding the picture in one hand, pulled her hair back into a style similar to Carol's. She examined the effect in the mirror, comparing it to the photograph. Without the waves of hair framing her face she looked different.

She rubbed her lipstick off with the back of her wrist, and her whole face paled to a distant memory of herself—decent, law-abiding, smart, in control. And even more like Mrs. Borian. What would Special Agent Carver say if she looked like this?

Bet he wouldn't ask her to sleep around for old Uncle Sam.

Fat chance. Sharkman had already made up his mind about her.

Not that she cared. Let him think what he wanted. He would anyway.

Yeah, but what if he didn't? What if he thought her pretty damn terrific? Though she barely admitted it to herself, some small, wretched part of her yearned to be good and merit his esteem.

Good girls get used, party girl. And they get hurt.

She let her hair go with a sigh, and the thick waves tumbled to her shoulders again. Returning to the living room, she picked up her packages and toted them into her bedroom.

She took out two suitcases from the closet and heaved them onto the bed. Then she unpacked her new things, holding each item up with a critical eye before refolding it into a suitcase. The subtle colors and expensive cuts made everything in her closet look cheap and flashy. But the bright colors of her own belongings made the new ones look dull and boring. She sighed, the two sets of clothes like two incompatible identities.

Which one was she?

She finished packing, adding her own clothes to the suitcases, including a pair of jeans. A ranch meant horses, and this was one Texas girl who knew how to ride.

By the time she finished, her closet was empty and her back ached. She rubbed her shoulder, then stripped off the skirt and sweater she'd put on at the store, packing them as well. She closed the two cases, tugged them off the bed, and carried them to the doorway.

A red silk peignoir was her reward. She sighed with pleasure as the smooth silk slid over her body. Slipping into the matching robe and a pair of silk mules, she closed the door on the bags with her new identity inside, and padded into the living room to pour herself a brandy. She was just taking the first sip when a knock sounded.

She checked the peephole on the front door. Her heart sank. Reluctantly, she opened the door to Finn. "I thought we were done for the day."

"Until we find what we're looking for we're on twenty-four/seven." His gaze raked down her body, sending unforeseen heat through her. "Who were you expecting, Clark Gable?"

Instinctively, she wanted to pull the edges of the flimsy robe together to cover herself. But if she gave in to the impulse she would give him power over her, and when it came to men, she was in control. So she leaned into the door frame, one hand on her hip pushing the robe to the side giving him a nice clear view down the revealing dip in the front of her gown. She smiled as his gaze fixed on her breasts. *Don't play with fire, Sharkman. You might get burned.*

"I was expecting to be left alone, Agent Carver. Now why don't you fulfill my expectations and leave?"

He tore his gaze away from her chest and shot her a look as cool and lethal as a wave of black water. Then he stepped past her and held up a videotape. "This just came in. I wanted you to see it as soon as possible."

"What is it?"

"It's the only thing we have showing Carol Borian in the flesh."

She froze, the words reverberating through her entire body. Her mother. Moving, talking. Her chest tightened, her heart thudded in sudden anxiety. What if she didn't like what she saw?

What if she did?

Hiding her roiling emotions behind a blank expression, she led Finn to the media room, a state-of-the-art haven filled with big-screen TV, two VCRs, a stereo system, and a computer.

Finn glanced around the room and whistled. "Your boyfriend really knew how to spend his money."

A flash of anger spiked through the nerve-wracking anticipation. She was tired of the innuendo and disdain in his voice every time he mentioned Beamer. "Stop calling him that."

"What—your boyfriend? He was, wasn't he?"

For a minute, she thought of telling him everything, then decided not to. Her arrangement with Arthur Beaman was none of Finn's business. "He was a wonderful man and he had a name. Why can't you use it?"

"Fine. Didn't mean to upset your sensitive feelings." He put the tape into the VCR, turned on the TV, then joined her on the leather sofa facing it. She tried to swallow, but her mouth had dried up. On the screen, Carol Borian glided into view.

She was carrying a platter of cookies, blushing into the camera and trying to avoid the lens, but the camera operator followed her.

"I don't like having my picture taken." She put down the plate and covered her face with her hands. Her voice was soft and feminine, tinged with the rolling sounds of the South.

"Go on, shoo." She laughed into the camera, then scurried out of the frame. The picture went dark.

Angelina stared at the blank screen, overcome by the image of her mother made suddenly real and alive. She grabbed the remote, rewound the tape, and played it again. And a third time. That was her mother's voice. Her mother's laugh. My God. Angelina's hands shook and she buried them in her lap so Finn wouldn't see.

The tape scrolled to black and she sat there unable to say a word. Finn, too, was silent, as if he understood the enormity of the moment and respected it.

"She seems so . . . so ordinary," Angelina said at last.

Finn nodded. "Maybe she was."

"Hard to believe."

"Believe it."

His arrogant certainty hit a nerve. "Why, because you say so? I'd sooner believe a gangster than take the word of a cop."

"Not all of us are like Sheriff Dodd of Ruby, Texas."

She gasped and her head snapped up, the sound of that long-ago nightmare name coming out of his mouth like a specter suddenly floating in the room. Mouth dry, she could barely make her tongue form words. "What the hell do you know about him?"

"I know about him and his nephew, Andy Blake, all-star quarterback for the Ruby Warriors. And I know about the beautiful young honor student Andy Blake took to Homecoming and later raped at the hooker hotel on the edge of town."

The words slammed into her like a shock wave, their impact creating a curtain of silence around her. No one knew about that. No one except Arthur Beaman.

She looked down at her lap, unable to meet Finn's gaze. "That's . . . that's not what happened. Not according to the sheriff. Not according to anyone in Ruby." Not even Adele, her so-called mother.

"Date rape is hard to prove." His voice was soft and gentle. "Especially if the guy is the town's biggest asset and the girl is a nobody."

A fierce pain wrenched her heart. God, she didn't want to feel that way ever again. She raised her head, glaring at him. "I don't like you spying on me, Sharkman."

He shrugged. "We don't run blind. We did a background check on you. Standard procedure. Besides, you do such a good job of telling the world what a loose piece of change you are, you make people think Sheriff Dodd and Andy Blake were right."

She narrowed her eyes. How dare he? "What do you know about it? About me? Zero."

For a minute she saw something move in his face. Pity? Tenderness? No, not Finn Carver.

"You're right," he said. "I don't know a thing." His penetrating blue gaze lingered on her a moment longer, then he rose and nodded to the TV screen. "Add that to your homework." Just then he took out his cell phone, which must have been set to vibrate as she didn't hear it.

"Carver." He said the one terse word, then listened. A stubborn look came over his face. "No, wait until we get there. Smitty can take them—no, I don't see why . . . Hell no, we can't wait that long!" He cursed under his breath. "All right, okay. Hold on." He covered the mouthpiece with his hand and looked over at Angelina. The harsh lines in his face told her he wasn't happy about whatever he was going to say. "Do you have a tape measure?"

She blinked. "A what?"

He visibly reined in his temper, lips crimped together in a thin, cruel line. "A tape measure. I need to . . . to measure you. Bust, waist, hips, back."

She quirked her eyebrows in amusement. This was good. "You're going to put your hands on me, Sharkman? Is this some kind of new TCF con?"

"If I wanted to put my hands on you, believe me, I wouldn't need an excuse to do it. Not with the way you've been shoving yourself at me."

Stung, she raised her chin. "You're a real class act."

"Takes one to know one." He sucked in a deep breath, then spoke into the phone. "Let me call you back." He disconnected, then turned to her. "We're having clothes made to match the pictures of your mother." His words were overly calm and distinct as though he were barely able to say them without shouting. "Seems it takes a while to get them tailored. If I can get the measurements now they can start tonight and might have something ready in the next couple of days. So, do you or don't you have a tape measure?"

"Maybe. Somewhere . . ." She left to look for one, returning a few moments later with a crumpled yellow strip. Finn removed a small notepad from his inside suit pocket and a pen. "I need chest, waist—"

She thrust the tape into his hands, dying to see him squirm. "Go to it."

"You can do it yourself."

She smiled lazily at him. "More accurate if someone else does it for you. You want those clothes to fit, don't you?"

I dare you, Sharkman.

"Jesus Christ." He yanked her around to face him squarely, then placed the tape around her shoulders, sliding it down so it fit just above her breasts.

"Right through the center, please." She lowered his hands so the tape went over her breasts. His knuckles grazed her nipples, and she met his eyes as the nipples rose to meet his hands. And now the joke was on her, because something blazed hot and wild between them, a feeling that raked through her like Texas brushfire. Her heart hammered, setting off a pulse between her legs, liquid and quivery as fear. She clamped down on it, pushing it away so she could control it, but the heat shimmered inside her, even after she told it to go away.

She grabbed the tape out of Finn's hands. "Thirty-eight, right?"

"I . . ."

She refitted the tape around herself, glanced down at the number. "Thirty-eight. I don't need the damn tape. Thirty-eight, twenty-four, thirty-six."

He nodded, mute. Then he gathered himself and a moment later wrote the numbers down in the little book. She thought his hand was shaking but she couldn't be sure.

He cleared his throat. "Two more." She jumped when he touched her shoulders, turned her around, then stood stiff as a spiked heel while he measured the width of her shoulders and the length of her back from neck to waist. By the time he was finished, her own hands were trembling.

"That it?" she said through clenched teeth.

"That's it."

"Good. Get out."

For once, he didn't have a snappy comeback. He left without another word.

Angelina sank into the couch and closed her eyes. No man had ever affected her that way before. And no man ever would. Especially Sharkman.

Forget about him, party girl. Your date is with Uncle Sam.

Her brandy was still on an end table where she'd left it to let Finn in. Now she swallowed the rest in one gulp. She breathed deep and poured herself another. Carrying it with her, she retreated to the bathroom and slid onto the padded bench at the vanity.

Opening a drawer set into the marble, she fished out a bottle of nail polish remover, some cotton balls, an emery board, and a sturdy nail clipper. She swallowed more brandy, then extended her hands in front of her. They trembled just the tiniest bit and she hastily buried them in her lap. He was gone, she could breathe now. Nice and slow and even. She tried again and this time her hands held steady, the deep red of the polish glistening back at her from each long, perfectly manicured nail. She sighed. Twenty bucks a pop.

This better be worth it, Sharkman.

She picked up the clippers and with one crisp bite cut off the first of all two hundred bucks.

CHAPTER
~4~

The trip to Montana was interminable. No one flew from here to there, not in a direct line anyway, and after three takeoffs, the first at the crack of dawn, Angelina was sick of the smell of jet fuel. On the last leg of the journey, she watched the clouds drift by her airplane window, wishing she could hop aboard one and float away. The plane was nearly empty, the usual murmur of bodies and activity replaced by the hum of jets and an anesthetized quiet. In the silence, a wave of nervousness set her heart pounding. She'd never make it. Somehow, some way, she'd screw up. She always did.

"Let's go over it again," Finn said.

Turning away from the view outside, she stared at the empty seat in front of her, rather than Finn, dark and intense beside her. *Give me a break, Sharkman. Ten seconds without thinking about nuclear holocaust. Ten seconds without thinking about him.*

"We've been over it a hundred times," she said.

"Make it a hundred and one."

She struggled for calm; she was not going to let him

get to her. "You know, you have a real problem with trust." She reached for the vodka on her tray. Finn stopped her with a hand on her wrist. A hand that burned through her skin.

"And you have a problem with booze."

She wrenched her hand away, letting the anger come. Anger was a lot easier to deal with than the ragged, edgy buzz of awareness of him sitting next to her. "One drink is hardly a problem."

He glanced down at the bottle. "Until one drink leads to two, three, and four."

For a moment she felt as though he'd physically slapped her. *Bastard.* Hadn't she done everything he'd asked? She was stuffed into a dainty little suit with fricking pearls at her throat. She wore sensible, no-heel pumps and her hair was pulled back into her mother's boring little bun. She'd cut her nails, thrown out most of her makeup, packed her bags, and agreed to put her life on the line without so much as a whimper. Why couldn't he pat her on the head and tell her what a champ she was?

Because he's a cop, stupid. And they're not human.

Deliberately, she poured the vodka into her glass and brandished the empty bottle at the passing stewardess. "Another please." She smiled at Finn, raising her glass in a toast. She had no intention of touching the second drink and was carefully sipping the first, but if she was going to be condemned as a bad girl, she might as well let him think she was the baddest girl around. "To the grand and glorious U.S. of A."

Finn's eyes narrowed. "Keep this up and you'll blow whatever shot you get at Borian."

"Borian is my job, not yours. You don't have the right equipment, remember?" She smoothed down the front of her suit, watching the subtle change that came into his eyes whenever she reminded him she was a woman. The change that said, *I want you.* She smiled to herself, feeling her power over him. "But just so you don't have a stroke, I'll be happy to review the plan with you."

He grunted in reply, which she supposed in his vocabulary meant "continue."

In a voice pitched for Finn's ears alone, she said, "I am Angelina Montgomery, a young but well-connected widow, interested in land-use issues. On an invitation from my dear friend, the governor, I'm taking my hot little fanny to the wilds of Montana, where Mr. Victor Borian resides, to study Montana's efforts in promoting development while preserving the land." She glanced over at Finn's cold, dark face. "How'm I doing, coach?"

He didn't reply, and a small swell of satisfaction rolled over her. God, she loved goading him.

"Tomorrow is Friday. Every Friday, Victor Borian comes into town to do business. He eats at the same restaurant, where I will happily float by like the ghost I'm supposed to be. This Friday night, he attends the Governor's Ball. I will be conveniently seated at his table. I meet him, and by the power vested in me as a dead ringer for his dearly departed wife, I lasso him, reel him in, and as we used to say in Ruby, Texas, hog-tie him 'til the rope burns. Oh, and don't forget, let him poke me if he wants."

"That's enough." Finn grabbed her arm and pulled her close. "You may not take this seriously, but I guarantee Borian will. He's interested in two things: money and power. And don't think for a minute he won't crush you in order to protect them."

For half a minute, she saw genuine concern in his eyes. The sight startled her.

"Afraid of losing me, Sharkman?"

His eyes iced over. "I'm not going to let your adolescent self-destructiveness put this operation in danger."

"Oh."

Don't be stupid, party girl. J. Edgar Hoover Jr. here doesn't give a damn about you.

Finn released her and slumped against his seat. He was sweating again. Christ, he was always sweating when he was around her. The last thirty-six hours had been sheer torture. In spite of everything he knew about her, his fingers still itched to touch her, feel the soft expanse of curve and skin. Every time he thought about Victor Borian getting near her, he wanted to punch something.

And she knew it, damn her.

Now he not only had to worry about stifling his response to her, he had to worry about stifling her recklessness. He was responsible for the case, which meant he was responsible for her. Somehow he had to keep her safe, even when everything indicated she didn't want to be safe.

If she didn't give a damn, why the hell should he?

Because she'll endanger the mission.

Yeah, right.

He heard Roper's voice inside his head. *Try being nice to her instead of your usual charming self.*

Being nice meant caring. And he'd already served his time in that army.

They flew into Helena a little after seven. As the plane approached the city, Angelina could see it laid out in a broad valley between mountains and deep rolling hills. Trapped between two weighty forces, just as she was.

They secured their luggage and caught a cab to the hotel. Ensconced in the backseat, she tried not to think about tomorrow, when she would see Victor Borian and set their scheme in motion. An electric tingle of excitement nested in her chest, as though she were on the verge of stepping off a cliff into either the greatest adventure of her life or certain death. Half of her wanted to take that step, and the other half was terrified. Exhausted by the struggle, and from fencing with Finn, she couldn't wait to arrive at the hotel, shed her government escort, and soak in a tub for hours.

In keeping with her status as a wealthy widow, the TCF had arranged for them to stay in the priciest suite at the Colonial Hotel. Not without a little fuss, of course, because it was expensive, but Borian always stayed in the best when traveling, and Finn thought Angelina should do the same.

When they got to the room, she couldn't help but be glad. The hotel was no Trump Tower—Helena had no high-rise accommodations—but the VIP suite at the Colonial was spaciously designed with a living area, dining area, wet bar, a large bedroom with private bath, and an adjoining bedroom. Plenty of room so they wouldn't knock into each other. Finn poked his head into both of the bedrooms, then nodded toward the one attached to the suite.

"You take the room in here," he said. "I'll take the adjoining bedroom, but keep the door between unlocked. I'm going downstairs to scout the place, maybe map out an escape route in case we need one."

Fine. The less she saw of Special Agent Carver the better. She went into the bathroom and turned on the hot water for the bath, desperate to get out of the stifling suit and into something more comfortable. Stripping out of her clothes, she sank into the tubful of water and let the warmth soak away her lingering resentment. She knew she was bad news, but would it kill Finn Carver to like her just a little?

She didn't know how long she spent in the tub, but Finn must have been doing a whale of a job because she hadn't heard him come back in all that time. When the water had saturated her muscles and melted into her bones, she climbed out and reached for the towel. Slowly, she dried off, realizing she didn't have clothes to change into; they'd left their luggage downstairs for the bellhop to bring up. Holding the towel against her, she opened the door and peeked out to see if the suitcases had arrived.

"Sharkman?"

No answer. He must still be in the lobby. Or wherever the hell TCF agents go to "scout" things.

She found the luggage in the living room, and was hunting through a suitcase for a pair of leggings, when the latch clicked and the door swung open. Whipping around, she clutched the towel tighter around herself as Finn came in.

He took one look at her and his whole body tensed.

"What are you doing?"

"What does it look like I'm doing? Getting dressed."

His gaze ran over her, searing every inch. For a minute she thought he was going to stand there and watch. Then slowly he turned his back, letting her finish in privacy.

"You do have a bedroom." He clipped the words. "With a door. That closes."

"Yeah, but you know me. Too much of an exhibitionist to go for anything as dull as a bedroom."

She wiggled into the black leggings, all too aware of who was standing a mere ten feet away. But it was the leftover warmth of the bath—and not his presence—that made her face hot as she slid into a glittery pink tube top. Glad to be in comfortable clothes at last, she slipped her feet into a pair of shiny black thongs with tiny heels and said, "Okay, you can look now."

But when he turned around again his eyes widened with instant heat that he immediately doused with a frown. Ignoring the scowl, she picked up her key card and headed for the door. He caught her arm and pulled her around to face him.

"Where do you think you're going?"

"Downstairs for dinner. I'm starved."

"You're not going anywhere looking like that."

"What's wrong with the way I look?"

"Nothing if you want to work a street corner."

She flushed and yanked her arm out of his grip. "Did anyone ever tell you you're a real asshole?"

"Did anyone ever tell you to get your mouth washed out with soap?"

That was it. She pushed past him toward the door, but he got there ahead of her and blocked her way.

"You're going to starve me now?"

"You're supposed to be Carol Borian's double. How did that"—he gestured up and down her body—"even get in your suitcase?"

"I put it there. We're in the hotel, for God's sake. Borian's out on his ranch a million miles away. What does it matter what I wear?"

"It matters. Someone could see you and report back to him. It's stupid to take chances."

"I'm tired of mincing around in panty hose and ugly shoes."

"Stay here. Order room service."

"I just got off a plane, dammit. I'm sick of being holed up."

"Then change your clothes."

Her mother's sensibly styled shoes were still on the floor where she'd kicked them off. She picked one up and threw it at him, but he ducked and it missed his head. And then, without knowing she was going to, she launched herself at him. Arms flailing, pared-down nails scratching, she screamed at him, cursing. He made a grab for her wrists and she kicked him in the shins. He yelled in pain, and before she knew what had happened, she was face-down on the floor, arms pinned behind her. With a quick flip, he turned her over, knees straddling her stomach.

"I ought to take you over my knee."

"Go ahead. Taking me is what you've wanted to do ever since you laid eyes on me."

He'd been breathing hard, his blue eyes fired with anger, but her words stopped him instantly. Without another sound, he released her. She lay on the floor, her chest rising and falling with breathlessness. He didn't extend a hand to help her up and he didn't say good-bye. He didn't say anything. He just wheeled around, opened the door, and left.

Finn stayed away as long as he could, long enough for his hands to stop shaking and for the scotch to blunt her words.

Because she'd been right. She'd been absolutely goddamn right.

He would have stayed away all night, but the bar closed at two, and the hotel staff wouldn't let him sleep in the lobby. So he stumbled into the elevator, not drunk enough to deny he was drunk, but too far gone to do much about it.

A mess of plates and silver covers lay on the floor outside the room, testimony to the fact that Angelina had taken his advice and stayed in. He noted that she hadn't eaten much, despite her protestations of hunger, and a shaft of guilt speared through him. Had the scene with him killed her appetite?

Whether it was the state he was in or the fault of technology, he had to pull his key card through the lock three times before the little green light unlocked the door. Turning the handle, he took a breath and tumbled inside.

Please, God, let her be asleep in her room.

He saw immediately that his prayer had been answered. Sort of. She was asleep, but not in her room. Slumped in an armchair, she faced the TV, which was muted but on. Its changeable light cast a blinking blue glow over the darkened room. Edging closer, he saw she'd changed out of the skintight stretch pants and breast-defying top. Instead, she wore a simple white nightgown that left her arms and shoulders bare. Trimmed in delicate lace with tiny buttons down the front, the fabric was so fine as to be almost transparent.

He swallowed. *Don't look.* But he couldn't help himself. Her feet were curled up under her and through the sheer nightgown he saw the outline of her breasts and the swell of her hips. With her eyes closed, she looked almost angelic. Virginal. Her golden hair lay tousled around her face, her full lips sweet and kissable.

He knelt down beside the chair, a little unsteady, and tried to rouse her. "Angelina. Wake up."

Let her sleep there.

She'll be stiff tomorrow.

What do you care?

He drowned the argument by touching her shoulder. He'd meant to shake her, but his fingers closed on the mark he'd noticed the first time he'd seen her—not a tattoo, but a beauty mark in the shape of . . . He peered closer. A heart. She had a heart on her shoulder. He smiled to himself. Even in his half-fogged state it seemed wildly ironic that a tough cookie like Angelina would wear her heart where everyone could see it. His fingers traced the outline of the mark and the soft, warm skin around it. *Maybe not so tough.* Somehow his hand moved from her shoulder up her neck to her jaw and then her face.

Christ, she was beautiful.

Knowing he shouldn't, he leaned in close and whispered her name, his lips grazing her ear. Slowly, she opened her eyes and turned her head toward him.

"Sharkman." She breathed the name as if she'd been expecting him to appear out of the darkness.

Her green eyes gazed at him unafraid and huge as the sea, and despite every resolve, he whispered, "I'm sorry."

She tilted her head, looking at him curiously. "What did you say?" Her fingers traced the line of his lips as though she couldn't believe the words had come out of them. Her touch made him dizzy, made his chest soft and hollow and weak. He knew he should pull away, but he didn't.

"About . . . what happened earlier. I'm . . . I'm sorry."

Her mouth tilted in the barest hint of a victorious smile. He'd lost a battle, but didn't care.

"Why do I rile you so much?" Her voice hummed low, intimate, asking a question to which there were a thousand answers, if only he could think of one.

"I'm doing my best, Finn. I'm trying hard." Her gaze wandered to his mouth, then back to his eyes. His heart skittered across his chest.

"I know."

She took his hand, held it over her cheek, and rubbed her face against his palm. "Tell me, Finn. Tell me I'm doing a good job."

He could barely get out the words. "You're doing a great job." And he meant it, too, though some distant part of him knew he'd regret saying it.

She gazed at his mouth and whispered, "Tell me I'm good." Her fingers moved over his lips again, sending an arrow of desire straight to his groin. "Tell me I'm a good person."

He opened his mouth to speak and she slipped her fingers inside. *Jesus Christ.* He sucked one long, slender digit and kissed the tip. He was drowning, suffocating with the lush smell of her, the hot taste of her. "You're very good." He sucked another and kissed that one, too. "You're a very good person."

And then her arms circled his neck and he was lifting her out of the chair and kissing her mouth. She opened to him readily, hungrily, as if she'd been waiting years for his lips and his tongue to possess her. She moaned and arched into him, gasping his name, and he was gone. Lost. The fight to resist her over. And he was going down in flames.

"Touch me, Finn. Touch me with your good hands. Make me feel good."

Was he breathing? He didn't know. Didn't care. Her hands made sweet circles on his back, gliding lower, pressing him into her. God, he wanted her. Like he'd never wanted anything or anyone before. She filled his hands, his arms, soft and rounded and plentiful. Her hips against his rigid flesh sent a shock wave of pleasure through him. On the tail end, a voice penetrated the sex and scotch clouding his brain.

What are you doing, pal?

He shut off the nagging, but the voice wouldn't let up. *Don't get sucked in. You're drunk. Don't do this.*

Her fingers reached around his waist to tug at his zipper. Her voice moaned in his ear. "Don't stop."

But he already had.

She looked up at him, the green eyes hazy, her beautiful breasts rising and falling in a rapid dance of desire. "What's wrong?"

What wasn't? *Those who don't learn from history . . .*

His own breath none too steady, he pushed himself away and retreated to the chair. "Look, we can't."

"Why not?"

Been there, done that. "We just . . . can't." Head in his hands, he leaned over his knees. "I'm your boss, for God's sake. There are rules about that."

"Believe me, I won't sue."

"We have a job to do, and we don't need complications. Besides, last I heard, you hated my guts."

"The feeling is mutual, isn't it?"

He glanced at her. The haziness had left her face. She stared at him coldly, the defiance back in her eyes. But beneath the hard shell he saw something else, something he didn't want to see, but couldn't avoid. A softness, a tender vulnerability, as though a little girl hid behind a grown-up. He thought of the eighteen-year-old honor student, of what the town of Ruby had done to her. He wasn't about to do the same.

"Right." He got up and ran a hand through his hair.

"Let's not get confused about where we stand with each other."

She rose, green eyes shooting fire. "No confusion here."

"Good." He looked around for a graceful exit and found none. "Well then, good night."

Angelina watched him walk into his bedroom and close the door. She wrapped her arms around herself, trying to stop the trembling. What had just happened? She had one powerful weapon against men and when she used it, no one ever turned her down.

Panic bubbled and she crawled into the chair before her legs gave out. Was she losing her touch? If she couldn't get to Finn, who had coveted her from the start, how would she ever get to Victor Borian?

She pictured Finn's face if she failed, and couldn't bear the disappointment she imagined in his eyes.

Her tongue slicked over dry lips and she tried to still the frenzied clatter of her heart. Failure was not an option. Neither was backing out. She'd stick with the assignment until Finn Carver told her she was the best thing that happened to the TCF, law enforcement in general, and him.

Especially him.

Her stomach flopped. What did she care what he thought?

But she did care. With every fiber of her weak, little-girl-lost soul. She wanted him to think well of her. Wanted him to like her, respect her. Wanted him to—

In horror, she slammed a hand to her mouth. She wanted him. Her body still trembled with wanting him. Not just for the power it gave her over him, the power that made her feel safe, that put her in a place where he could never hurt her. No, she wanted him the way a woman was supposed to want a man. The way she'd never let herself feel about anybody since she was eighteen.

Oh, God.

Pure terror sliced through her. She couldn't feel that desperate, fist-clenched wanting again. If she gave into that, she'd be dead. It would be like Andy Blake pushing into her all over again.

Never.

That naive, innocent girl was gone forever. And no one would make her feel powerless again.

Especially Finn Carver.

As for those few seconds with Finn when she'd felt herself falling, out of control . . . she shuddered. It couldn't happen again. It wouldn't. She wouldn't let it.

CHAPTER
~5~

Finn woke with a fierce headache and a raging attack of conscience. The minute he opened his eyes, he remembered what he'd almost done the night before and with whom. *Of all the stupid . . .*

Christ, he should know better. Hadn't Suzy taught him anything? But Angelina wasn't Suzy, and the fact that she was in the next room should prove it. His wife would never have come this far. Not without falling apart. And if anyone had fallen apart last night it was him.

Groaning, he staggered out of bed and ambled into the luxurious hotel bathroom. At least he remembered it as luxurious. The light would only make his headache worse, so he didn't turn it on. But he didn't need a light to tell him he looked a mess, because he felt like one. Overnight, a crop of cotton had grown in his mouth; a marching band played Sousa in his head.

What the hell had he been thinking?

He hadn't been thinking. At least, not with his big head.

With a grimace, he turned on the water and showered in the dark. The needles of hot water brought back some semblance of humanity, enough to let him turn on the light and shave. As he dragged the razor across his still-pasty face, he mulled over how to handle Angelina. *Try not handling her.* Apologize, be professional, move on.

The door to the suite opened and closed, and he heard the sound of her moving around. Rinsing the last of the shaving cream off, he went into the bedroom and slipped on his slacks. Might as well get this over with.

When he stepped into the living area he saw she was back in costume, her dress an understated cream knit, her heels low, a strand of pearls at her throat. She'd tied her golden hair back into a loose bun, but as always, some of it had come free in a soft, sexy frame around her face. Her makeup was subtle, her lipstick a mere slick of color. She looked elegant, moneyed, and very beautiful.

And more than anything he wanted to strip every tailored stitch off her, throw her on the bed, and have the wild goddess of the night before back in his arms.

Get a grip, Carver.

He clenched his hands to keep from reaching out for her. "Did you go somewhere?"

Back toward him, she busied herself with something on the coffee table in front of the couch. The dress clung to her rear as she bent over, outlining her curvy shape. He took a breath and clamped his gaze on a swath of drapery as she straightened holding a silver carafe. Coffee splashed into a cup.

"I didn't want to wake you, so I went for a walk."

He heard the unspoken message. *I didn't want to see you.* He cleared his throat. "Look . . . about last night."

"You were drunk. You're sorry."

"It won't—"

"—happen again. I know."

"Angelina . . ." He stepped toward her and she stiffened.

"Better get dressed. There was a message for you. We're supposed to be somewhere called CP in"—she checked the slim gold watch on her wrist—"twenty minutes. I assume you already have your secret decoder ring and know what CP means and how to get there."

He poured himself a cup of coffee, relieved at her businesslike tone. "Command post. And I hope you can put aside what happened last night, so we can resume our professional relationship."

She mocked him with a smile, the first one of the day. As her gorgeous lips tilted up, he realized how much he'd wanted to see them do that.

"Is that what we're calling it?" She pushed back the stray strands of hair—a gesture that also set off her perfect breasts—and gave him that sea-green, challenging look, the one that said, *I know what you want, soldier.*

Did she ever.

"I am sorry," he said. And he meant it, too. Sorry he'd been so tough on her, sorry he'd let his own weakness take over. Sorry he'd touched her, and most of all, sorry he wouldn't do it again.

Angelina stared at the elevator door, not daring to face Finn.

Sorry, he'd been sorry.

Well, really, what else did she expect from an uptight straight arrow like Special Agent Carver?

And what did she care anyway? The sorrier he was, the farther away he'd stay. And wasn't that exactly what she wanted?

Never mind that it had taken every ounce of strength

not to run her hands over his broad bare chest when they were in the room. It seemed like a year before he'd put on a shirt. And the smell of him. Man and soap, shaving cream. She'd wanted to press her face against his skin and inhale him.

He was back in uniform now, thank God. Dark suit, white shirt, maroon tie. If only he didn't look so damn good in it.

She kept her eyes straight ahead as they walked through the lobby and out to the car waiting outside. A bellman ran to open the door for her and she slid into the back while Finn got in beside the driver. She had only a moment to wonder how he'd gotten a car there so fast before the driver turned around and grinned at her.

"Ms. Mercer. Nice to see you again."

Agent Saunders. He'd traded his Hawaiian shirt for something western and denim, but it still looked like he'd slept in it. She threw him her best smile and watched the flustered look come over his face, exactly as it had in the motel room in Memphis. Exactly as she expected it to. "Nice to see you, too, Jack."

Finn waved an impatient hand. "Stop flirting, Jack. We have work to do."

Jack cleared his throat and turned back to the front. "Yes, sir."

"Where are we going?" Finn barked.

"I set up a command post in a nondescript office building. Nothing to make it stand out, like you said. The place is fully furnished; used to be an insurance office. We've got it for the month. Longer if we need it."

"Good. What about Roper? Has he shown up yet?"

Jack shook his head. "He's in Washington, but we expect him tomorrow or the day after."

During the brief drive, Angelina glimpsed hills to the south. They rolled and tumbled like the spine of a colossal prehistoric creature waiting to come to life. The car turned a corner and a snow capped Mt. Helena came into view. Incised into a crisp blue sky, it dominated the landscape, as inescapable as her meeting with Victor Borian.

A few minutes later Jack pulled up in front of a low building that was as unremarkable as he'd promised.

"Treadwell Insurance, third floor," he said to Finn. "The door is open."

Angelina followed Finn into the building while Jack parked the car. All through the elevator trip and the trek down the hallway to the door marked Treadwell Insurance, excitement prickled like nettles.

Finn led her past low couches covered in dull aqua and fake wood coffee tables scattered with out-of-date magazines. Like the office in Memphis, no one sat at the receptionist's desk, and he marched past it into the inner offices.

A very different sight greeted her there. Stripped of everything but the necessities, the room contained only a couple of desks, phones, what appeared to be a complicated computer system, and a dark bear of a man who descended on Finn the minute he walked through the door.

"Carver! About time you showed up."

Finn pumped the other man's hand, then turned to Angelina. "This is Agent Howard. Mike, meet Angelina Mercer."

"Our secret weapon." He shook her hand and whistled. "Yessir, I do think she looks the part."

He found her a seat in front of the computer, then Jack came back from parking the car and they got down to business.

"Everything set up?" Finn asked.

"The governor's been informed and you've been offi-cially attached to his staff," Mike said. "Borian has his usual reservation for lunch today. Noon at the Saddle House. That's a local steakhouse," he added for An-gelina's benefit.

Her heart lurched. She checked her watch. Three more hours until lunchtime. Three more hours until this whole charade became real. A shower of apprehension ran up her spine and she looked at the hands in her lap with their trim, virginal nails. The masquerade had already begun.

"Okay, good." Finn put a hand on her shoulder and gave her a reassuring squeeze.

The shock of his touch sent her heart thumping for a different reason. She sucked in a small breath. *What was that all about?* He couldn't possibly know how nervous she felt, and even if he did, she doubted he'd care. And yet the weight of his hand on her shoulder, even for a minute, was like the comfort of a thick, warm blanket.

"What about the clothes?"

Jack thumbed over his shoulder at an inner door. "In there. On hold for a fitting."

"Great. Angelina?" Finn held out a hand to help her rise, but she ignored it, not wanting to feel that heart-racing touch again.

Slowly, she stood on her own and to hide the fluttering in her stomach gave them all that killer smile. "More new clothes? A girl could get used to this." She sauntered to the office, but Jack raced ahead, and with an eager ex-pression, opened the door for her.

She glanced over at the other two men. Agent Howard was amused; Finn frowned. He crossed to the door and passed through, all innocence. "Why thank you, Jack, that was very nice of you."

Howard guffawed and Jack flushed.

"Yes, it was," Angelina said softly and followed Finn into the room.

A thin-faced woman with a tape measure around her bony shoulders glanced up from a newspaper folded at the crossword puzzle. She was sixty if she was a day, sucking on a cigarette, with dangling earrings peeking out from flyaway gray hair that reached her shoulders.

"Hey, Smitty, let's see what you've got for me."

She squished the cigarette into a tin ashtray. "Hello to you, too, Carver." The woman's voice grated like sandpaper, but she grinned at Finn, then turned her attention to Angelina. "Got a humdinger here, I see." She walked around Angelina, inspecting her from all angles. "Hard to believe in this age of less is more that those measurements I got were right, but looks like they were."

Angelina felt her face heat and raised her chin in spite of it. "I gather you two know each other?"

If Finn noticed her discomfort he didn't say. Instead, he put a friendly arm around the other woman's shoulders. "Smitty's got the gig with the TCF sewn up, no pun intended. Costumes, special clothes, hair—whatever you need, she can do it."

The older woman winked at Angelina. "But not on a moment's notice." She opened a closet and removed three outfits on hangers, each one in different stages of completion. "I got one done, Carver. Stayed up all night to do it, too, so you better appreciate it. The rest you can have tomorrow." She laid all three across an empty desk. Angelina recognized the completed outfit as the navy suit from the photo of Carol Borian.

Finn took out a couple of snapshots from his inside jacket pocket and compared them to the clothes on the desk. "These are great."

"The suit probably needs a nip and a tuck, but that won't take too long." She thrust the suit at Angelina. "Try this on, honey." And to Finn, she nodded over her shoulder. "Make yourself scarce, Carver."

When Finn left, Angelina changed into the suit. Smitty hummed through a mouth pursed around pins as she cinched the waist a little tighter on the jacket and pinned the raw hem on the skirt.

While Smitty worked, Angelina thought about Finn's hand on her shoulder. Was it kindness or just a random gesture? Did it mean he was finally starting to believe in her?

She gazed at the kneeling woman's steel-gray head. "How long have you known Sharkman?"

Smitty looked up, her brows quirked in surprise, and took the pins from her mouth. "Sharkman?"

"Agent Carver."

"Oh." She shrugged and returned to the hem of the skirt. "I've been dressing TCF undercover agents for the last fifteen years or so. Carver's one of my best customers." She gave Angelina a close look. "You getting ideas about him, honey? Don't break your heart."

"Why? Doesn't he like women?"

She laughed. "Oh, he likes 'em. Just not enough to stick around. He was married once if you can believe it."

Angelina couldn't. Sharkman didn't seem like he'd trust anyone enough to go steady, let alone marry. "What happened?"

"Oh . . . turned out pretty bad. She was no good. Into

drugs and wildness. He poured his soul into her and she sucked him dry. Almost cost him his career."

Angelina blinked, surprised. If she had to guess she would have imagined Sharkman falling for someone more like Carol Borian. Someone whose heels, not necklines, were low.

Suddenly a whole new side to Finn Carver opened up. He was a man after all, not a machine. And what do you know—he made mistakes.

Smitty tugged at the hem, smoothing it out. "Here now, I think that's got it. Go on out and see what the boys think."

But Angelina was suddenly nervous. "What do you think?"

Smitty levered herself up and grinned. "If I were a man, I'd be a train wreck. Here, see for yourself." She swung open the closet where a mirror had been tacked inside the door.

Angelina saw herself and someone else at the same time. The navy material made her appear even more pale and fragile than the dress she'd put on that morning. Chaste. Like herself if her life had taken a different direction. But also like her mother. The two women stared back at her, the images blending, and for an unsettling moment it seemed as though a fine hairline crack had fractured her world. *Who are you?*

"You all right, honey?"

She tore her gaze away from the mirror with a shaky laugh. "Of course. I'm fine."

"Let's put you to the test." She opened the office door and pushed Angelina out.

A bubble of excited talk greeted her. Agent Howard sat at the computer, deep in a heated discussion with Jack.

Finn was frowning over papers in a folder and throwing his two cents into the conversation over his shoulder.

Smitty cleared her throat, and one by one the men looked up and stopped what they were doing. The talk died, and they stared as Angelina walked toward Finn, his cool sapphire gaze warming to an admiring glow that for once he didn't bother to hide. Her heart did a little flip of hope.

"Jesus, will ya look at that?" someone whispered.

She waited for a word of praise from Finn. She saw it in his eyes, but she wanted to hear it out loud. Wanted to hear him admit that she could do this. That she could be as good as him. Instead, his gaze slipped from hers to somewhere over her shoulder.

"Great job, Smitty." He crossed the room and clapped the seamstress on the back. "Fantastic. It's exactly what we need. Can you have it finished in time for lunch?"

Angelina stiffened. She felt Jack's warm gaze on her.

"You look great, Ms. Mercer," Jack said.

"Yeah," Mike added quickly, glancing from her to Finn. "Borian's a goner for sure."

"Thank you," she said quietly.

"C'mere, honey," said Smitty. "Let's get that off you, so I can finish it."

Angelina swept past Finn, and as she stepped into the inner office, she heard the whispered scold, "Jesus, Finn, it wouldn't kill you to tell her she looks good."

And Finn's caustic response. "She knows she looks good."

The rest was lost as Smitty shut the door. The latch clicked, and Angelina's heart closed like a fist over a pin-prick of hurt.

She concentrated on the other two outfits, a black

cocktail dress from a newspaper photo, and a skirt and sweater set from one of the snapshots. *Don't get mad, go shopping.* Nothing like new clothes to soothe a woman's heart.

Then how come her teeth were on edge?

They weren't. The hell with you, Finn Carver.

At eleven-thirty, a knock sounded, and Finn's voice came through the door. "Time to go."

Smitty began packing up the other two outfits. "I'll have these delivered to your hotel room."

"Thanks."

"Good luck." The older woman winked and nodded toward the door. "With both jobs."

Finn drove Jack's car to the restaurant. He talked the whole way, going over the plan in a low, soothing voice that didn't give her a minute to think about what she was about to do. But even so, her heart raced and her hands felt clammy. *Don't screw up, party girl.*

When they got to the restaurant, he parked and escorted her inside. The murmur of voices and the clink of silverware blurred in her head. Would the plan work? Would she do something to give them away? One slip, and Angelina could blow everything.

The Saddle House was a beef eaters' paradise—home of the real man—with lots of heavy, dark wood and a polished oak bar that looked like it had come straight from a Hollywood set for cowboy sophistication. Finn took her elbow and guided her to a table, following the hostess who led the way. The touch of his hand sent a current through her, but she was glad for his support. Her stomach was doing cartwheels. This was it. Her work was beginning. And there'd be no second chances.

"Is he here?" she asked.

"Left corner. We're heading right toward him," Finn murmured.

Angelina looked quickly over to the left and her heart almost stopped. The face she'd only seen on a wall in a motel room jumped into view. She had no time to take more than a fast peek but the impression of taut menace was as evident now as it had been then.

She swallowed hard and glided closer to the corner table.

"Almost there," Finn whispered. Borian had yet to notice them and a rush of panic sped through her. What if he didn't see her? What if he did?

But just as they were about to pass Borian's table, Finn did something to her feet, and she stumbled.

"I'm sorry," she said softly. "I'm not usually this clumsy."

Casually, he steadied her. "No problem." And like that, they moved on.

But not before Victor Borian looked up.

"Good girl," he said in her ear as they followed the hostess.

She led them to a table set with heavy white linen and big-handled silverware. Finn pulled out a chair for Angelina, but she hesitated before sitting down.

"I'm not facing him," she murmured.

"If this is going to work, your profile should be enough to whet his appetite."

She sat and fingered the heavy linen napkin. "You don't think it will, do you?"

He shrugged. "It's a long shot. But it's the best shot we've got."

"I'll bet that sticks in your craw, Sharkman. Having to depend on me to make your case."

Bingo. His jaw tensed and he gave her one of his famous steely glares. But all he said was, "Pick up your menu. Smile. Pretend you're enjoying yourself. All you have to do is sit there and look pretty, which shouldn't be too hard."

Her heart skipped a beat. "Was that a compliment?"

The blue eyes beneath his coal-dark hair remained cool and noncommittal. "Take it any way you want. It's the truth."

Behind her menu she hid the warm flush his words created. "What's he doing?"

"Trying not to stare at you."

She did smile then, a full and, she hoped, dazzling example. Looking up from her menu, she found Finn's gaze on her. Slowly, the corners of his hard mouth tilted up in the faintest hint of a grin. "Come on, Angel. Let's order lunch."

CHAPTER
~6~

Back inside their hotel suite, Angelina gave a piercing rebel yell, then said, "Hey, Sharkman, I think we did it!" With a giddy laugh, she threw back her head and spun around the room like a crazy top.

Finn lounged against the door of his bedroom, unable to keep his eyes off her. "Careful there, Mata Hari. That was just the first step. There's still the Governor's Ball tonight." Not to mention the fact that today Borian had just looked. Tonight he would talk to her, touch her, a prospect that settled inside Finn like a dead weight.

He shifted position, taking the pressure off his right hip, which ached with tension. Keeping a firm rein on his attraction while watching over her all day, not to mention worrying about what would happen that night when she actually met Borian, had wound him tight. He massaged his hip to ease the muscles.

Unaware, Angelina sprinted into her bedroom and burst back with the clock radio. She plugged the machine into the wall, and suddenly a blast of rock music filled the suite. Then she turned to him, green eyes alight with excitement. "Come on, Sharkman." She waved him over. "Come dance with me. I feel like celebrating."

Without waiting for him, she began to undulate into the center of the living area, her lush body circling in deep, erotic curves. Her arms twined in the air, her hips rotated. She'd danced the same way that first time he'd seen her, but now she moved for a crowd of one. Him.

"You're not going to just stand there?" As further inducement, she raised the respectable hem of her dress, baring her thighs while she continued to twirl seductively.

Finn couldn't move. If he did, if he put his hands on her, he wouldn't be able to stop. But he couldn't turn away either. She'd caught him, a fly in a trap.

"Don't you ever stop being that uptight straight-shooter?" Her eyes challenged him. "Loosen up, Sharkman. Move that well-toned, gorgeous bod. Be a mensch."

Glued to the doorway, he cocked a brow. "A mensch?"

"That's right. It's something Manny Vise taught me."

"And who is Manny Vise?"

"Come on, Sharkman, you remember Manny Vise. You read my file, didn't you? Manny rescued me from the college sorority syndrome. He owned a string of car dealerships in Dallas, had more money than he knew what to do with, but his family was as uptight as you and wouldn't let him enjoy it."

"And that's where you came in?"

"You got it, Sharkman. I helped him get a kick out of life."

Finn crossed his arms, more to create a barrier between them than anything else. "Yeah, until he kicked the bucket."

"Well, he was eighty-five when I met him." She

grinned, held out her arms, and jiggled her fingers at him to come closer, a siren's call he fought not to heed. He hadn't forgotten what had almost happened the night before.

"Come on, Agent Carver. Let me show you how to be a mensch. A down-to-earth, live-and-let-live, ordinary, salt-of-the-earth guy like Manny Vise."

Just then the music slowed to a ballad, and she glided closer. Sweat pooled under his arms and spit dried in his mouth. God, she terrified him. And made him want her all at the same time.

She took his hands and put them around her. "Dance with me, Sharkman." Her voice was soft and low. "We did good today. I did good."

She was right; she'd done a great job. Borian had spent the entire meal craning his neck, and Finn had been pleased. More than pleased. But he couldn't tell her that. Not when her body moved against his in a languid rhythm. Not when she stared into his eyes with that bottomless green gaze, her mouth an open invitation.

Delilah tempting Samson.

But everyone knew how that story ended.

He jerked away, strode across the room, and pulled the radio's electrical cord out of the socket. The music cut out in midnote. A long silence followed.

"Well," she said at last. "Tell me how you really feel."

Not on your life, Angel.

He buried desire and the fear of desire beneath a manufactured brusqueness. "Grow up. We don't have time for this."

Angelina stood rooted to the spot where he'd left her, a stricken look on her face. "You know, I'm sick of this.

Sick of your all-work-and-no-play game. I'm sick of you, Sharkman."

Something was choking him, but he shrugged and collected his briefcase. "You don't have to like me, Angel. Just do your job."

"Right. The god-almighty job."

"It's why we're here."

"Oh, I'm clear on that."

He headed for the door. For escape. Once he got past the door he'd be able to breathe gain.

"Where are you going?"

"To make sure Jack and Mike are ready for tonight."

"What the hell for? You know they're ready, and so am I."

"Are you?" He pivoted as he opened the door. "Carol Borian's ghost doesn't swear."

She flushed, making her face even prettier. "Well, her daughter does. She has a foul mouth that you'd give anything to kiss, and without her your case would be nothing!"

He plunged into the hallway, slammed the door behind him, and leaned against it, sweating and gasping for breath.

Angelina stared at the door, the slam echoing in her head.

Damn him.

Damn yourself, party girl.

She should give up trying to win him over. It was a lost cause. And as long as he stayed the hell away from her she'd be fine.

Just fine.

She stomped into her room, ripped off her staid little dress, and kicked off her no-nonsense shoes. Then she swept into the bathroom and soaked her resentment away in hot water and deliciously scented bubbles.

Two hours later she answered the door wrapped in a plush white robe to find Jack carrying a garment bag.

"Cinderella's ball gown," he announced, holding it up.

"Where's Sharkman?"

He looked at her blankly.

"Agent Carver," she fumed. Why the hell didn't everyone know who she was talking about?

"He's still going over things with Mike," Jack said. But she could tell from the shuttered look in those nice brown eyes that he knew as well as she that Finn was staying away on purpose.

Fine by me, Sharkman.

"Look . . ." Jack laid the garment bag over the back of the couch, choosing his words carefully. "I know he can be a real shit." No one had to ask who "he" was. "But he can also be a real ace. You just have to learn that the job comes first with him. It's not personal. He's the best at what he does. He'll keep you safe and he'll get you home alive."

Yeah, but who will keep me safe from him?

The doubt she felt must have shown in her face because Jack plowed on. "You're doing a great job. Finn told us about the restaurant. He said Borian looked like he'd lost a gallon of blood the moment he clapped eyes on you."

Surprised, she raised her brows. "He said that? He said I was doing a good job?"

"He may not act it, but he's on your side."

She snorted, not ready to forgive and forget. "He's a big boy. He doesn't need you to stick up for him."

"Yeah, well . . . he saved my life once. I'm just returning the favor."

That stopped her short. "He saved your life?"

"Took a bullet for me."

"You're kidding." He shook his head. "How? What happened?"

"Oh, an undercover job went wrong. Bad guys were on to us and Finn pushed me out of the way."

My God. A real hero. Figures. How the hell was she supposed to live up to that?

"So cut him some slack," Jack said, voice light, eyes serious.

Reluctant to give in, she shook a finger at him. "Well, if I do, it's only because *you* asked." She nodded toward the garment bag. "What have you got for me?"

"A little black dress. At least, that's what Smitty called it. Oh, and the skirt and sweater thing is there, too." He shuffled his feet, thumbed over his shoulder. "I . . . I better get back."

"Or Simon Legree will whip you?" She walked him to the door. "Thanks, Jack. You're a real peach." She kissed him on the cheek and he gave her that sweet puppy-dog grin.

"You're not so bad yourself."

"Evidently that's a matter of opinion." She opened the door. "Tell Sharkman I'll be waiting."

Jack's grin widened and he lowered his voice as if imparting a deep, dark secret. "I think he knows that." He winked and left.

She shook her head in mock annoyance, but Jack's visit had lightened her mood. Grabbing the garment bag by the hanger, she went into her bedroom, unzipped it, and took out Smitty's reproduction of Carol Borian's little black dress.

It was simple and understated, not exactly boring but far from the spangly numbers Angelina was used to. She sighed and laid it out on the bed, wondering how she could spice it up and still stay true to the part she had to play.

Then a wicked, slow smile eased over her. She had just the thing.

Finn paced outside Angelina's closed bedroom door. What the hell was taking her so long? He pulled at the bow tie and tuxedo shirt strangling his neck and caught Mike's amused glance.

"What are you laughing at?"

Mike shrugged, all innocence. "I don't know. What are you growling at?"

"Borian will have gone home by the time she finishes primping." A sharp jab of his head indicated Angelina's closed door.

"Uh-huh." Mike's eyebrows rose in a picture of doubt. "I thought maybe you were nervous. You've had a wild hair up your butt all afternoon."

Had he been so transparent? "Don't be an ass."

"You should be kicking your heels up at this party thing. If what you said about Borian's reaction at lunch is even half true, the ball will cinch everything."

Hell. Mike was right. But as time for the Governor's Ball drew near, the knot in the back of his neck had grown tighter. He recalled Angelina's heady laughter that afternoon, the excited light in her green eyes. And in his mind that picture was replaced by the shocked, covetous look on Borian's face at lunch, as though he wanted to devour her.

Christ, he knew the feeling. He could almost feel sorry for Borian, if he wasn't such a slug.

And if exposing Angelina to him didn't put her in danger, he could almost sit back and watch the show.

Almost.

Finn checked his watch again. Damn the woman. She was a survivor. She didn't need him worrying about her. She'd be fine. Who was he kidding? She'd be great. This was right up her alley.

Right up her goddamn alley.

The door opened, and he swiveled his head to look as Angelina stepped out.

Jesus Christ.

Finn's mouth dried up instantly. Mike's jaw gaped open. Angelina smiled and pirouetted in front of them.

"What's the matter, boys? Never seen black before?"

"Oh, I've seen it," Mike said. "It just never looked this good."

Amen. She transformed the simple cocktail dress Smitty had finished that afternoon. Black as a nun's habit but not as concealing. Not that it revealed a whole lot, either. The clean, smooth lines clung sedately to her curves, and a scoop of a neck skimmed her shoulders, partially exposing them without revealing her heart-shaped birthmark. In keeping with her pose as the demure Mrs. Montgomery, the dress stopped just below her knees. But the modest length didn't hide the rest of her long, shapely legs, which ended in a pair of black heeled pumps that added three inches to her height. Around her neck a single strand of pearls lay luminous and creamy as the skin it caressed. She looked expensive and elegant. And sexy as hell.

Finn nearly melted where he stood.

Mike whistled, low and admiring. "You look fantastic."

"Thank you." She turned to Finn as if she expected a pat on the head. Damned if he'd tell her she looked good. She always looked good, and she knew it. The trouble was, so did everyone else. He pictured Borian dancing with her, his hands on her arms, her shoulders, places where Finn had touched her the other night. His chest tightened for the hundredth time that day.

"I'm ready." She picked up the velvet stole draped over the back of the couch.

"Not quite." Her brows arched inquiringly, those sea-green eyes daring him to argue with her. "We need to wire you up."

"I am wired." She ran a hand over her breasts and torso, causing him to repress a groan. "Unless the TCF is going into the lingerie business?"

Mike wagged a finger at her. "Behave." And held up a thin, snaggly black cable with a tiny microphone attached. "We need a record of everything Borian says to you."

She lifted the cable with an indolent finger. "And do I push that in his face and ask him to speak up?"

Finn restrained his temper. "We tape it to you."

"Really?"

"Underneath the dress."

An amused look flickered across her face as her eyes met his. *Touching me again?* He could almost hear her sassy voice saying the words aloud. *Not on your life,*

Angel. But despite himself, his fingers tingled with anticipation.

Slowly, she turned her back toward Mike, her eyes never leaving Finn's. Heat warmed his face under her challenging stare. "Would you mind?" Her voice held a note of promise and her luscious mouth tilted up in a slight, knowing smile. Mike unzipped the dress, and the sheath slid to the floor with a satiny hiss.

Oh, my God. If Finn believed in the power of saints, he'd call on one now.

She stood wrapped in a single piece of lingerie that clung like a second skin. Black lace, it started at her full breasts, barely contained inside the strapless bosom, then hugged her waist and hips and ended with beribboned holders that fastened onto the tops of a pair of sleek, black stockings. The only other items she wore were the black heels and the strand of pearls, and if Finn had been speechless before, he was dead dumb now. In front of him stood the living emblem of every man's fantasy.

In less than ten seconds he was steel hard.

Hands on hips, she cocked her head in an innocent expression. "Now, you want to put that . . . where?"

Finn bit down hard on the explosion about to erupt inside him. *You want to play games, Angel? I can play games.* With grim deliberation, he took two steps in her direction, reached for the cleft between her breasts, and tugged her forward by the top of the black lace.

She stumbled toward him awkwardly. "That's a hundred and fifty dollars' worth of French lace you're pawing, Sharkman." She smiled at him sweetly and for the life of him, he wanted to do nothing more than bury his mouth over her insincere lips.

"Give me the wire, Mike." In spite of the heat circulating inside him, his voice came out just the way he wanted it to: cold and harsh.

"Why don't you let me—"

"Give me the wire."

Mike handed him the device, and he began to slide the thin cable between her breasts. The nerve endings in his fingers jumped when they came in contact with her skin. *You can do this Carver. Without your hands shaking.* If it were possible to get any harder, touching the plush mounds of her cleavage made him hard to the point of discomfort. But he resisted shifting his stance to find a better position, and continued threading the wire between her breasts.

Her breathing changed when he touched her and she tensed to fight her reaction. Grimly, he smiled to himself. The soft, breathy sound told him she wasn't as indifferent to him as she pretended. Triumph zinged through him, and he knelt to finish the job. But when he was on his knees in front of her, his head level with her belly, he lost his composure all over again. Pausing for a moment, he longed to lay his head against her, to rub his hands over the lush curves encased in black lace.

Heart booming in his ears, he slowly raised his hands and placed them on her left thigh, above the top of the black stockings where her smooth, soft flesh was bare. He found the end of the wire and plugged a matchbook-size cassette recorder to it, then laid the recorder against her skin. God, she smelled good. He inhaled her scent, something lush and utterly feminine, and for a moment, he forgot what he was doing.

"You going to spend the night at my feet, Sharkman?" Her words floated down to him on a sultry whisper, and he raised his head to look at her. She was looking right back at him, as if she knew what she was doing to him.

Suffocating him. Taking him by the throat and throttling him with his own desire.

"Mike." He was damn proud of the coolness in his voice. "Finish her up."

Finn rose and stalked over to the sideboard, where the hotel had provided a selection of liquor. He opened a bottle, not even checking to see what it was, poured himself a fast drink, and downed it in one gulp. Turning, he watched Mike finish taping the recorder to her thigh. Finn's hand tightened around the glass, fighting the urge to shove the other man away when he touched her.

He poured himself another drink. It was going to be a long night.

CHAPTER
~7~

The Civic Center had once been a Shrine Temple, complete with white minaret and an arabesque arched entryway. Angelina took one look and had the stray thought that she'd fallen into a fractured fairy tale. Cinderella, as Jack had said earlier, but a cockeyed version where she goes to the ball to entrap the prince.

By the time Angelina and Finn arrived, the place was teeming with people. The Governor's Ball drew a large, wealthy crowd from all over the state, and guests stood in clusters clutching highball glasses or sat at their tables fingering gleaming white linen and talking politics. The women wore glittering gowns, the men tuxedos, some with bolo ties and sharp-toed boots polished to a high gleam.

Angelina's heart danced inside her chest as Finn guided her through the throng, moving toward the table they'd been assigned. Elevator music from the band up front filled the large room, but it was only so much background. She caught Mike's eye and then Jack's. Both were dressed as waiters and managed to look like they were putting finishing touches on the round dinner tables packed into the room when they were really keeping an eye on her and Finn. Jack nodded once, a signal of some kind, but she didn't stop to ask what. She didn't dare. Cut-'em-dead Carver was all business now, his voice curt, his body tense, his grip on her arm punishing.

Not that she blamed him. Not really. That little black number back at the hotel had pushed all his buttons, as she'd known it would. Served him right, too.

But a guilty voice way down deep kept up a nagging drumbeat. If she wanted him on her side, why did she antagonize him at every turn?

Finn's contacts had managed to get them placed at the same table as Borian. Would he be there? Suddenly, all thought of Finn vanished, and she forced herself to focus on one man only. Victor Borian.

But no one was seated yet at their assigned table, and Angelina couldn't help the small sigh of relief at the reprieve.

"Is he here?" she murmured softly as they took their seats.

"He's here," Finn said. "Jack spotted him."

She licked her lips, feeling queasy. Maybe she should go to the ladies' room and hide. Before she could, Finn squeezed her thigh under the table. At first she thought it a gesture of encouragement, even forgiveness for goading him back at the hotel, and a rush of warmth flooded over her. But she quickly bottled it when she realized he was only turning on the cassette recorder.

"Showtime," he said under his breath, and without another warning, a strangely smooth masculine voice spoke from behind her.

"Table five?"

Finn turned. "If that's where you're supposed to be, you're there." His voice was several degrees warmer than it had been a moment ago. He rose and extended his hand. "Stephen Ingram. Special aide to the governor."

"Victor Borian." The voice held the barest hint of a foreign accent.

"This is Angelina Montgomery," Finn said.

Straightening her shoulders, she took a breath and tried to steady her jittery heart. *Here we go, party girl.* She turned around and stood.

Borian protested. "Please, don't get—" then swallowed the rest of his sentence.

She extended her hand with a smile, making it small and tentative, and looked up into a face that her mother must have looked into thousands of times. The slicked-back hair, slashing cheekbones, and deep-set eyes, so familiar from photographs, came alive with an intensity she hadn't expected. Age lines marred the corners of his eyes; he was easily fifty, maybe older, but still youthful and attractive—even if at the moment he looked like something had sucked the blood out of him.

Her mother's husband. The man she'd loved.

"I . . ." He wavered, and for a minute she thought he might collapse.

"You are all right, Mr. Borian?" A large man with a deep, accented voice and a military-style haircut leaped in to steady Borian.

"I'm all right, Grisha."

"You are sure?" He hovered like a worried parent, an odd role for a man massive as a tree trunk.

"Yes, fine. As you were."

"Da, tovarish." The man called Grisha placed a metal briefcase on the floor near Borian, and as he did, An-

gelina's eyes met Finn's. No one had mentioned a Russian bodyguard.

Grisha retreated to the side, taking up a position where he could see the table clearly.

"Here, sit down." Finn pulled a chair out for Borian, and he sank into it. "Friend of yours?" Finn nodded over to where Grisha stood at attention, hands crossed in front of him, gaze squarely on their table.

"My employee," Borian said, his attention drifting over to Angelina. "My driver."

Finn smiled amiably. "What does he drive, a tank?"

Borian turned back toward Finn, a slow movement as though he were reluctant to tear his gaze away from Angelina. "We live in a dangerous world, Mr. Ingram."

"Yes, we do," Finn said quietly, the smile dying out of his face. She knew he was thinking of Borian and how much more dangerous the world was with him and his nuclear goodies in it.

Meanwhile, Borian had returned to staring at her. His small eyes, unclear in the photographs, were a strange amber color. They fixed on her like a copperhead's, steady and penetrating, and she looked away, uneasy.

But not before she caught the gleam of victory in Finn's face.

"How about a drink?" Finn looked around for a waiter. "Some whiskey should put you to rights."

Borian shook his head. "I never drink. Alcohol is the crutch of a weak mind."

Great. Another puritan.

Before she could suggest a soft drink, Borian raised the metal briefcase his "driver" had left, and clicked it open. Foam lined the interior, cut out to hold a dark blue bottle stoppered with a cork, and three small juice glasses. If he hadn't just said he didn't drink, she might have thought the bottle a special wine reserve.

"I have this bottled from the streams on Eden's Gate, my ranch." He lifted out the bottle and snapped the case shut. "Pure, mountain water. No chemicals, no additives. No one has touched it but my own people."

He poured some into one of the glasses, handed it to her, and she took a dainty sip. Just like he said. Water. With a slight metallic, mineral taste, but definitely water.

"Delicious." She lied with a smile and handed the glass to Finn, but Borian intercepted it with a sober glance.

"Once you drink, your essence is in the glass. I'm sure you wouldn't want to give that away."

Another glance exchanged with Finn. No one had mentioned Borian was nuts, either. At least, not in this way. "No, of course not."

Borian poured water into the remaining glasses, handed one to Finn, and drank from the other. He savored the taste, rolling it around his mouth before swallowing. He did this while his intense gaze burned her cheek.

"Did I see you this afternoon at the Saddle House?" Borian asked abruptly.

Her heart leaped. Had they gone too far? Was he suspicious?

She turned to Finn, all innocence. "Is that where you took me for lunch?"

Finn nodded. "Best steak sandwich in Helena," he said.

"If you eat steak," Victor Borian said, still studying her. "Did you enjoy it?"

"Well, I didn't have steak, but lunch was very good."

In fact she was so keyed up she could hardly remember what she'd eaten. *Where are we going with this, Victor?*

"You are visiting?"

Ah, interrogation. "Angelina is a guest of the governor's," Finn said.

"A guest. How nice. From where, Miss Montgomery, if I may ask?"

Heaven, Victor. Straight from heaven. "Oh, please, you must call me Angelina. And I'm from a small town in East Texas. Why?" She made her voice soft and feminine, with a trace of her childhood. Carol Borian had been a southern belle and Angelina tried to sound as much like her as possible. Besides, men liked the southern touch, and she was there to please.

He gave her a shaky laugh. "You . . . you look like someone I used to know."

Do I? She put a hand on his arm, gentle and comforting. "I hope it was a good someone."

Nodding, he licked his lips. "Yes, yes it was." He cleared his throat, looking as though he wanted to clear the room of mist. Or ghosts. "And how did you get from East Texas to Montana?"

She laughed prettily, silently reviewing their cover story. "By way of Memphis, where I live. I'm interested in how development affects land use, and I met Stephen at a conference there. He works for the governor and wangled an invitation for me." She gave Finn a wry smile. "I'm afraid he's stuck with me now, though."

"You know it's my pleasure," Finn said.

"I don't think escorting me around is top of your list for a Friday evening."

"Nonsense," Victor Borian said. "How could he not enjoy the company of such a beautiful woman?"

She blushed. At least she hoped she blushed.

"In fact, why don't I take her off your hands, Mr. Ingram?" He gave her a brief, courtly bow. "Would you like to dance?"

That didn't take long. She slipped her hand into Borian's, trying hard not to recoil at his touch. "I'd love to."

Finn watched them move toward the dance floor. Borian hovered over Angelina like a mad scientist huddling over his creation. A protective arm around her, he guided her through the crowd, deep-set eyes riveted to her face as though afraid she'd disappear the moment he stopped looking at her.

It was like that for the rest of the evening. She couldn't pry herself away for more than five minutes, and those she spent in the ladies' room with Borian waiting outside. To add to the confinement, the hulking mass of ever-watchful Grisha loomed close at all times. Finn couldn't get a single private word with her all night, and it made him tense with uneasiness.

Hours later, he slumped against the wall of the Civic Center ballroom while Borian and Angelina danced, one of the half-dozen couples still moving to the music.

How much longer would he have to expose Angelina to Borian without getting a damn thing in return?

But he was getting something, he reminded himself. A slow, careful seduction. That's what he recruited her for, and from what he could tell, she was delivering. She glided gracefully in Borian's arms, her head bent toward him in a gesture as submissive as Finn knew she was not.

He closed his eyes, remembering what it had been like to hold Suzy, to look in her lying eyes and tell himself he saw love. For a moment, the scar over that old wound gaped open as though the bullet that had shattered his hip had slammed into him all over again. The ghost pain in his leg throbbed and he moved to the table to sit down, imprisoning the memories with a brutal twist of will. Angelina wasn't Suzy; if she were, this whole job would have been over before it began.

But that didn't mean she was a paragon either. Too bad knowing he couldn't trust a thing she did didn't make him want her any less.

Or make him worry less about what could happen to her.

He stifled the urge toward protectiveness, telling himself he'd feel the same with any undercover operative on his team. But then he glanced back at the couple on the dance floor, and team spirit warped into something more primitive. Borian's arms encircled Angelina's smooth shoulders and his lips skimmed the soft, tender skin at her ear. She tilted her head up, smiling that dazzling smile at him, and a stab of jealousy cut into Finn.

From the dance floor, Angelina saw Finn push away from the wall and drift over to their table. He was scowling. What the hell was he scowling about? Things were going swimmingly. Borian had stuck like glue to her all night. What more did Finn want?

As though reading her mind, Victor said, "You know Mr. Ingram well?" His gaze followed Finn, as hers had done, and her heart froze. Did he know why she was there? Had she given herself away already?

"Stephen? Not really. We met at the conference and as I said, I twisted his arm to get an invitation from the governor. That's all."

"Ah. A political relationship." His voice held a trace of irony.

"You could put it that way."

"I think Mr. Ingram would put it quite differently. He doesn't seem happy with the way I've been monopolizing you all night."

That's where you're wrong, Victor. "I'm sure he's oblivious. I'm told he's quite the catch and baby-sitting me has probably put a crimp in his style." Afraid he would pursue the topic, she searched for a change of subject. She looked around the ballroom, felt his hand on her back, firm and proprietary as he waltzed her over the dance floor. "It's lovely here. Have you always lived in this part of the world?"

"Regrettably, no. It was a favorite of my wife's. I bought the ranch for her and we visited during the summer. When she fell ill, we moved here permanently. She died several years ago and I couldn't bring myself to leave."

His wife. My mother. Her skin tingled with anticipation. "I'm sorry."

"Yes, it is a great tragedy to lose someone you love."

"Tell me about her. What was she like?" She held her breath, heartbeat ratcheting upward. This was why she was here, why she'd agreed to this whole sorry idea—to discover some small scrap of insight into the woman she longed to know and never would.

"Lovely. Like you, in fact."

"Me?" She feigned astonishment.

"Yes, you remind me a great deal of her."

She tried to look flustered. "I'm . . . I'm flattered. How odd."

"Yes. I was thinking the same. Odd. Or . . . providential." His gaze fixed on her like a laser and she looked down, as much to retreat from his burning eyes as to appear shy and demure.

"Why did she like Montana so much?"

"Have you ever seen the moon creep over the mountains?" His voice dropped to a whisper, his breath a hot breeze over her ear. A finger of disquiet trickled down her spine. "It's like a glimpse of paradise. God knew what he was doing when he made the Rocky Mountains."

She swallowed. He was so close. Too close. *Don't lose it now, party girl.* "It must be quite a sight."

"It is."

"I'd . . . I'd love to see it."

"Would you?" Borian pulled away and brought the full weight of his amber gaze on her again.

She flushed. Had she moved too quickly? Her pulse quickened in fear and in something else. Something a lot like excitement. Like driving too fast. The speed exhilarating, but also terrifying. Would she crash? Or would she beat the odds one more time? She gazed up at Victor, adrenaline shooting through her veins like a high-voltage current.

"I'm here to study land use. Stephen"—she glanced across the room at Finn—"has been ordered to show me around. I hope your ranch is on his list."

The corners of Victor's mouth curled slightly. "Oh, I doubt it. But perhaps we can do something about that."

A surge of triumph pumped through her blood as the music ended. Victor guided her to the table, and it was all she could do not to shout out loud.

Finn watched them approach, a glass of ginger ale passing for the scotch he would dearly love to be drinking. He straightened as they came, watching Angelina's face for signs of how she was holding up. A small part of him wished she would crack under the pressure. If she folded like he hoped, he could end the masquerade before she went deeper into an alien identity, where she might lose herself. And deeper into Borian's territory, where she might screw up and get hurt.

But she was clear-eyed as she approached, and beneath the outward calm, he sensed an edge, a brittle excitement he hadn't seen before.

She was enjoying this.

The realization sent a wave of surprise through him. He knew how she felt because he'd felt it himself. The thrill of the hunt, like going into battle. Fear and excitement rolled into one. But recognizing the feeling only set his antenna humming. An inexperienced hunter alone in hostile terrain made mistakes. And mistakes were something he couldn't afford, not with nuclear disaster at stake.

"Angelina is tired," Borian said, clearly unaware of what Finn had sensed. "I'm going to take her back to the hotel."

"Please stay if you like," she said to Finn in a soft, docile voice so unlike the woman he knew.

"Are you sure?" Finn didn't like leaving her alone with Borian, liked it even less that he cared.

"I'll be fine."

"All right. I'll see you in the morning."

He waited for them to head for the ballroom doorway before following. Mike and Jack caught up with him, Mike wheeling a cart of dishes, Jack carrying a bundle of rumpled linen. For a few seconds all three of them were within speaking distance.

"He's taking her home." Finn spoke in an undertone, not breaking his stride. "I'll bring the tape to CP in an hour."

The two men nodded and split off in different directions, while Finn continued out the door. The three of them had already arranged for the car to be parked at a side entrance, just in case Borian left with Angelina. Finn headed that way, knowing he'd have a few minutes lead on Borian, who would have to wait for the valet to get his car.

He drove with grim determination, racing through yellow lights. At the hotel, he parked the car, plunged inside the building, and was in place outside the suite, when Borian stepped out of the elevator with Angelina. Flattened against a corner that allowed him to observe the suite without being seen, Finn watched as Borian guided her by the elbow, his casual but possessive grip setting Finn's teeth on edge. Angelina handed Borian the key card for the lock.

"Thank you for a very nice evening." She'd ended up with her back toward Finn, so he couldn't see her face, but her voice slid low and gentle, once again mild in a way that was completely unnatural to the Angelina he knew.

"You're more than welcome. It's the first time I've enjoyed myself in a long time." He put his hand under her chin and caressed her cheek. Finn's stomach turned over. "You're a very beautiful woman."

She lowered her head in what looked like modesty. Modesty! But the gesture also succeeded in disengaging Borian's hand from her face. "Thank you. You're very kind."

Borian used the card to open the door, then handed it back to her.

"I can see you're tired. I won't come in."

Nice of him.

"Good night." She kissed his cheek and slipped inside.

Head down, eyes closed, Borian touched the closed door, palm flat against the surface as though wanting to absorb what was behind it.

A wave of dismay washed over Finn. Angelina had done a good job. Too good.

When the elevator had swallowed up Borian, Finn let himself into his adjoining bedroom and through the connecting door to the suite. If he didn't know better he would have sworn Angelina had known he was in the hallway and timed his entrance, because when he walked through she had one shapely foot perched on the coffee table, her dress pulled up past her thigh. Golden head bent over the cassette recorder she was untaping, she presented a neatly curved and wickedly desirable picture.

Her head lifted when he came in. "Sharkman!" She threw him a teasing smile and raised the dress another half inch. "You did such a good job putting this on, maybe you'd like to take it off."

He slumped into an armchair and loosened the bow tie at his neck. "You're doing fine all by yourself."

She laughed and tossed the tiny tape recorder at him. He caught it one-handed and stuffed it into his jacket pocket.

With feline grace she glided across the plush carpet and sat on the arm of his chair. Too close for comfort, but he wouldn't give her the satisfaction of moving away.

"I don't think you'll find much of interest on it."

"Why not?"

She shrugged. "He talked about his wife and how much he misses her. He told me about his ranch. Nothing about stolen nuclear material or his business, and nothing you don't already know."

She stretched and he caught his breath at the sight, her generous body supple in its curves.

"You did a good job tonight." He tried to make his voice match the compliment, but he didn't quite succeed and she must have heard his begrudging tone.

"I'll bet that hurts." Her words were harsh, but she was smiling.

He found himself slowly grinning back. "Yeah, big time."

And suddenly, they were laughing. At themselves, at their situation, out of relief that the whole absurd mess had gone well and the first step was over.

She slid off the arm and into his lap, still laughing. "This is going to work. We're going to do it. You and me, Sharkman. I know it. I *feel* it."

Without knowing how, he was looking straight into her jade eyes. Slowly the laughter died out of them, replaced by something else. Something wary and hungry. The heat of her seeped into him, languorous, enticing, and his heart started to pound.

"It's good to see you laugh, Agent Carver." She cupped his face in her hands and his mouth went dry. He ached to touch her, to run his hands through the flaxen mass of her hair. Impulsively, he pulled the pins from the knot at the nape of her neck, and the shiny mass tumbled over his hands onto her shoulders, releasing a cloud of fragrant shampoo as sumptuous as she was. He lifted the tresses off her neck, loosening them so they fell in waves and framed her face the way it had the first time he'd seen her.

"Welcome back, Angelina."

Her eyes went soft, and his control went out the window. Without even knowing he was doing it, he leaned toward her and she melted against him.

One kiss, that's all he craved. But one kiss was never enough. He kissed her again, and again, sensation whipping through him as though she were a drug he couldn't get enough of. She groaned against his lips and wriggled in his lap, sending waves of desire through him. Lost in her again, he drowned in her softness.

Again. Memory of the other night shook him to awareness. "No!" He wrenched himself away, almost spilling her onto the floor as he surged out of the chair. "Jesus Christ, I can't spend two minutes alone with you." He was breathing so fast, he didn't think he would ever catch up.

"What are you doing?" She stumbled to regain her footing and her face went from surprise to confusion and finally to angry understanding. She glared at him. "You want me, I know damn well you do, so don't give me your self-righteous crap."

"I'm not giving you anything, and that's the problem, isn't it?" He ran a hand through his hair, knowing he was a damn fool. Anyone else would take what she offered, no questions asked. "Look, I know what this is. I know this is all a game to you. I understand. I know what happened to you and I know why you do it. But damn if I'm going to play."

Her spine stiffened with injured pride and her eyes grew stormy. "What are you talking about?"

But he wasn't going to bring up Ruby again, or explain what the psych profile said about her. That some rape victims acted promiscuous in an ongoing attempt to re-create the rape, control the sexual experience, and make the outcome safe. "Someday you're going to want me for real, Angel. Not because you're on some power trip, or because it helps you forget, or makes you feel safe, but because you want *me*, Finn Carver. Until then . . ." He wheeled and walked toward the penthouse door.

"Where are you going?" Her voice rang out hard and demanding, a far cry from the gentle tone she'd used with Borian. The harshness reassured him. His Angelina was back.

Without turning around he took the cassette tape out of his pocket and held it up. "To take this over to Mike and Jack for analysis."

"Well analyze this, Sharkman. Borian invited me out to his ranch."

Finn stopped cold, shaken by her abrupt announcement. Slowly, he turned to face her. "He what?"

Hands on her magnificent hips, green eyes filled with angry contempt, she raised her chin and strolled up to him.

"You don't want me? Borian does. For a nice, cozy visit as long as I damn well please."

A shaft of pure ice sliced through his chest, and he realized how much he'd been hoping she'd fail.

"Congratulate me, Agent Carver. I'm in."

CHAPTER
～8～

As far as Angelina was concerned the weekend began on a high note when Finn stomped off to the command post Saturday morning. Good riddance to bad rubbish, her mind screamed at the door that slammed behind him.

Fine. Great. Terrific. That only left her cooped up in the damn hotel with little to do but shop for last-minute items and wait for evening when Victor was supposed to take her to dinner.

She roamed the luxurious rooms trying not to remember how she'd thrown herself at Finn. What he did to her, the way she couldn't breathe around him, couldn't think, made her stomach cramp.

So why did she provoke him? Why not just stay away? That's what he wanted. That's what they both wanted.

With nothing better to do, she got ready for Victor hours earlier than she needed to. Sitting at the suite's watered silk vanity, she iced her lips with a sweet shell pink. A strange, unsettled feeling prickled over her skin. How was she supposed to concentrate on Victor when all she could think about was Finn?

Hands trembling, she put down the lipstick. It rolled off the table and onto the carpet, but she didn't care. She closed her eyes, trying not to remember the rush of heat his mouth had sent through her.

Truth was, she didn't want him to stay away. She wanted him to kiss her, touch her, hold her. Sex was the only power she had over him, the only way to keep safe. But so far, damn him, he refused to be controlled, refused to be handled, manipulated, put in a neat little box with the lid slammed shut.

She shuddered. Thank God, he stayed away. Thank God and all the angels.

The cold war with Finn lasted through Sunday, when once again, Victor fed her—lunch this time. She wore the last of the three outfits Smitty had copied from the snapshots of Carol Borian, a gently pleated gray skirt that fell gracefully over Angelina's knees. Coupled with a soft rose sweater set, the ensemble was the embodiment of nice-girl femininity. Victor's face paled when he saw her and then filled with a warmth that almost shamed her. He found excuses to hold her hand through most of the meal and was attentive to the point of suffocation, all of which made a nice change from Finn's wintry indifference, but also proved exhausting. Encouraging Borian without seeming to, repressing the sharp intake of disgust every time he touched her, smiling when she wanted to cringe . . . she was dancing on a high wire with no net below.

Both times she and Borian went out, she taped the cassette recorder to her thigh, so Finn could listen to every word they exchanged. That Victor was hooked was clear to anyone who listened. Her progress should have pleased Finn, but the more she saw Borian, the crankier

Finn became. If Roper hadn't arrived Sunday night, she was sure they would have started throwing punches.

But Roper eased between them like a silk sheet. As before, he was all gracious smiles and courtly manners, making her forget in an instant his squat little body and bulldog face.

They met Sunday night at the command post where she had her final briefing. Roper greeted her like she was a beloved niece and led her to a metal chair as though it were a throne. Pulling up another seat opposite her, he almost knocked his knees into hers as he leaned forward and patted her hand.

"I hear you're doing excellent work, my dear."

Her gaze flew to Finn, who loomed over her in a half ring with Agents Saunders and Howard. Had he praised her to his boss? Hope flared, but his dark, unapproachable form discouraged it. Fine. She could ignore him, too. Or try. Too bad his nearness sent an electric current through her. She felt like a mess of live wires, all spark and jump.

"Miss Mercer is doing a great job," he said, ice-blue eyes mocking. "One she seems born for."

She flushed at the barely concealed insult, and something died inside her. God, she wanted to wipe that cold, self-righteous look off his face. "That's right, Sharkman, I'm here because you don't have what it takes to get the job done."

Eyes narrowing, he visibly tensed, and Jack put a restraining hand on his arm. She smiled. *What's the matter, Agent Carver, hit a nerve?*

Roper glanced between the two of them. "Is there a problem here?"

Finn gritted his teeth. "No. No problem." Nothing except a great, big, fat something he didn't want to name. He itched to have her and hated the wanting all at the same time. Even now her scent—shampoo or perfume or simply Angelina herself—curled around him like a conjurer's trick, beckoning him closer. And while he fought his own weakness he had to stand by and watch her throw herself at Borian, who would crush her like a bug if he found out what she was up to, but not before taking whatever she gave out. Then again, what sane man wouldn't? *Except of course yours truly.* Did that make him insane? No wonder he felt as though a burr had lodged under his skin. "Everything's fine. Let's get this over with."

Roper's eyes were on him, the gaze deep and penetrating. Finn forced himself to relax, to ease the tension in his hands and shoulders, and after a long moment, Roper leaned back in his seat. "So, we're all set," he said.

"She goes in tomorrow." Finn concentrated on Roper, speaking as though Angelina weren't sitting right in front of him. The less he looked at her, the less he was reminded of how much he wanted to touch her.

And how vulnerable she'd be once she left his sight.

"You've got surveillance set up?" Roper said.

Jack nodded. "An abandoned homesteader shack across the highway. All Angelina has to do is plant the bugs."

"What bugs?" Angelina's upturned face was keen and wary.

"Slap-on electronic transmitters," Mike explained.

"Not the greatest," Jack said apologetically, "but we couldn't get a tech team in there to wire for sound because the house is always manned. We figured slap-ons were better than nothing."

She looked from one face to another, searching beyond the surface to what they all knew. "But?"

Jack and Mike exchanged glances.

"But we don't know they'll transmit from that distance," Finn said bluntly.

Mike shrugged. "We don't know they won't, either. Not until we try."

"And even if the bugs don't work," said Jack, "we still have the phone tap."

"Which isn't going to do her a hell of a lot of good if they've got a gun on her." The acidity in his voice matched the gaze he swept over the men. Didn't they see how crazy this whole thing was? What if something happened to her? He'd never be able to get to her in time. "She can't exactly excuse herself to make a phone call."

She paled at his words; he was scaring her. Good. He wanted her scared. He wanted her absolutely clear about what she was about to get into.

"What about contact with the team?" Roper asked.

"I'll have my cell phone, won't I?"

She looked hopeful and he hated to quash that, but Finn couldn't have her laboring under any illusions. "There's no signal out there, so a cell phone would be useless."

"So . . . what—are you telling me there's no way to contact you? Come on, you're the great and powerful TCF. You must have some high-tech doohickey I can use."

"Not if you're supposed to be little Miss Ladies Auxiliary."

He ignored the uneasy shift from Jack and the uncomfortable twitch from Mike, finally allowing himself to confront those huge green eyes. *Listen good, Angel. Absorb this, understand.*

He saw the message get through. She stilled, sharp, quiet. "You're telling me I'm on my own."

A small beat of silence followed, as though everyone was seeing this in a new way.

Roper broke the hush. "Not quite, my dear." He gave Finn a pointed look, and he sucked back a heated reply to obey the unspoken order.

Grabbing the map, he strode to one of the desks and spread it open. "There's an abandoned mine in the foothills of Devil's Teeth."

Angelina rose to follow, peering over Finn's shoulder at a spot on the map half an inch from the house and its outbuildings. Along with the view of the map, she inhaled shaving cream and man, closeness making her knees wobbly. She gripped the edge of the desk. "What about it?"

"You can slip out of the ranch and meet me there. It's not far."

"How are your hiking shoes, Ms. Mercer?" Jack winked at her.

"Fine if you like two-inch heels on them."

Finn scowled, but Roper beamed. "See?" As though that took care of everything. "Then we're ready. Good luck, Miss Mercer." He, took her hands in his and gave them a squeeze. "We're counting on you. I know you won't let us down." He turned to Mike and Jack. "Let's go over the surveillance setup."

Angelina had been dismissed. But before she could feel rejected, Finn was at her elbow. Her heart did an unexpected flip as he spoke low in her ear. "I want to talk to you."

Without giving her an option, he pulled her into the room where she and Smitty had worked on her costumes. When he'd closed the door behind them, he put his hands on her shoulders and turned her to face him. Her heart leaped again.

"Are you all right?" His voice was quiet and his face held none of the cold contempt she expected. "Are you sure you want to do this? It isn't too late to back out."

It was the first time he'd touched her in two days, and despite an effort not to let it matter, the feel of his hands sent heat spiraling through her. Warm and strong, the half embrace felt like a refuge and for a crazy second she wanted to slide forward into his arms and complete the circle of safety. Of course, she didn't. She raised her chin and looked him squarely in the eyes.

"I'm not backing out, Sharkman." She slid out of his hold, putting distance between them. "No matter how much you want me to."

A shadow crossed his face, but he didn't argue with her. Instead, he pulled something out of his coat pocket and showed it to her. A pearl-studded circle pin.

What the . . . ? Eyes narrowing, she tilted her head, curiosity aroused. "The way to a girl's heart *is* through jewelry. Are you trying to win my heart?"

His lips compressed. "I'm trying to keep you alive." He turned the pin over in his hand. "With the latch closed, the pin gives off an electronic signal that monitors your position. Get into trouble, unhook the latch. You can take it off to change, but relatch it immediately. If the signal stops for more than thirty seconds, I'll know something is wrong."

He pinned the pearl circle onto her sweater, just above her heart, which was suddenly skittering wildly. His ocean gaze flooded over her, drawing her into deep blue water that was warm and inviting, but way over her head. She couldn't move. Couldn't breathe.

Then a knuckle scraped the bottom of her chin, and he stepped back. "Be careful," he said softly.

Monday afternoon, Borian sent Grisha to pick her up in a black Chevy Suburban stenciled with the Eden's Gate logo, a mountain with the sun rising behind it. Behind the wheel, Grisha was like a mountain himself, huge, silent, and menacing.

To keep the fear at bay, she sat in the back and fingered the brooch Finn had given her, reviewing what she'd learned the night before after assuring him she would stay on the job. He'd drummed the route from the ranch to the abandoned mine into her head until she wanted to scream. Now, she could stick Jack's bugs to chairs, desks, or light fixtures without anyone seeing her do it, and could install the filter into the phone jack that would allow them to monitor all calls. Finally he'd told her to look for a small metal container that could hold four kilograms of machined plutonium. And not to open it, because inhaling the radioactive dust was far more dangerous than touching it.

By three in the morning they'd declared her ready, patted her on the back, and told her she'd be outstanding. All except Finn.

She pushed that tiny hurt aside and gazed out the window at the view of emerald scrub and golden hay backed by deep purple mountains in the distance.

As she watched, the jeweled images distorted and changed. Mushroom clouds filled her head, heat so intense it peeled skin off bone, light so bright one look could blind. Finn had told her the amount of plutonium she was looking for wasn't enough to arm a bomb the size of Hiroshima, but it could still do plenty of harm. She'd seen pictures of nuclear bomb survivors. Skeletal children, deformed adults. She swallowed, the price of failure a heavy burden.

Hours after leaving the city, the rolling hills became sharper and taller, hills no longer. On their left they passed a beat-up weathered shack with a dusty pickup and rusted van parked outside, along with a stack of hay bales. The site looked ordinary enough for a mountain ranch and though she didn't see anyone hanging around, it comforted her to know Jack and Mike were there.

Ten yards farther along, the car made a right turn onto a gravel road and stopped at a large metal gate with the rising sun logo embedded in it. Grisha punched a code into a numbered keypad and the gate swung open.

As the car drove through, a barb of excitement and fear sliced through her. Soon she'd see her mother's beloved home. Breathe the air she'd breathed. Meet the woman who was her sister.

And hope to God no one found out.

The road curved until the gate and the country highway behind it disappeared. Beyond the bend, a two-man, armed checkpoint waited. The men, dressed military style in camouflage fatigues, carried machine guns. The sight thrust her into hyper-alertness, the guns a siren screaming in her mind.

One of the guards grabbed a clipboard and poked his head into the driver's side window. She noticed the Eden's Gate logo on his uniform pocket.

"Who you got here?"

Grisha stared straight ahead, his face expressionless. "Guest of Mr. Borian. Angelina Montgomery."

The guard flipped through the paper on the board, and checked something off. He eyed Angelina, his gaze lingering on her chest, then a sly grin spread across his face.

"Mr. Borian have a good time in town?"

Grisha frowned and turned to the guard. She couldn't see the look the large man gave Clipboard, but it quelled the nasty gleam of amusement on his face. His mouth spasmed into a twitchy smile, then he tugged the brim of his cap and backed away.

Check-in done, Grisha put the car in gear and drove off, for once leaving her grateful for his hulking presence. She looked over at his huge mass. The knuckles on the steering wheel were larger than two of her fingers combined.

"Why is the gate locked and guarded by armed men?"

"Mr. Borian, he like it that way." He used the same stiff tone on her that he'd used on the guards. She bit her lip. Clearly Grisha was not going to be much help in the way of information.

The Suburban bounced over a gravel road that soon wound around a crystalline lake. The ranch and outbuildings lay along its banks, scattered among tall mountain firs. She caught glimpses of the structures between the thicket of lofty trees whose greenery only began dozens of feet up. Quickly, she identified stables, barn, and guest house, ticking them off from what she remembered of the map. Then the imposing sight of the expansive ranch house came into view, capturing all her attention.

Encircled by a bilevel wraparound porch, the multistory stone and log home imposed itself on the landscape as though carved out of the Rocky Mountains towering in the distance. Huge beams crisscrossed over the high, arched entry. Windows and glass caught the sun, sparking against her eyes. Rockers and wooden swings dotted the porch, making the facade warm and inviting.

She stared at the house with morbid curiosity. This was where her mother had lived. Laughed. Loved. And somewhere inside, her husband may have hidden a small package that could lead to thousands of deaths.

Grisha braked in front of the house, turned off the ignition, and got out of the car to help her out. As she rose, Victor bounded down the steps, hands outstretched. "You're here at last!" He wore an ascot and tweedy sports coat, a European aristocrat playing at casual. Yet there was nothing casual about the way he pulled her toward him, clasping her fingers to his heart. "I missed you." He shot her a rueful smile. "I've been like a boy all morning waiting for you."

She lowered her gaze, hoping he would take her gesture for shyness. "I . . . I missed you, too. It seemed to take forever to get here."

Lifting her chin with firm but gentle pressure, he gazed at her with such intensity, she thought he was going to kiss her right there in the middle of the yard. Her heart shuddered and she quickly changed the subject.

"Your home is beautiful."

"Only more so now that you're in it." He smiled and put a sheltering arm around her, guiding her up the steps and inside. Grisha followed with her bags, closing the door behind them. Her stomach iced over. She'd entered the lion's cage and the door had just clanged shut.

Still holding her in his stifling embrace, Borian gave her a squeeze. "Come, let me show you around."

Inside, the vaulted ceiling soared up to massive cross

beams, many of which still retained their natural shape and beauty. He'd said her mother had loved the ranch, and Angelina tried to imagine the woman in the photographs here. How many times had she stood where Angelina now stood? The thought overwhelmed her and she craved a moment to herself, a breather while she adjusted to being surrounded by Victor's mountain castle and his world.

And she needed time to plant the bugs she'd been given.

She looked around for her things, now firmly in Grisha's grasp and moving away from her. "Can I see to my bags first? Unpack a little?"

Without giving her request a second's thought, Borian turned her in the opposite direction. "Grisha will take care of your bags. And one of the maids will unpack."

She acquiesced; Carol Borian probably never argued with her husband anyway. But as Victor led her away, she sent a small prayer of thanks that no special equipment was hidden where a careful search might have found it. Mouth dry, she remembered the three bugs taped to the inside of her bra. Unless Victor ordered a body search, they'd stay hidden until she could place them, which clearly wasn't going to be soon.

Impatience fluttered in her chest like too much caffeine. *Take it easy, party girl. You just got here.*

She tamped down her edginess and concentrated on the layout, charting the interior as she went. Lofts and open staircases leavened the heavy beamed architecture, but moose heads and bear claws marred the airiness. Everywhere she looked, dead animals stared down at her. How had her mother stomached it? Angelina tried to ignore them, but their lifeless eyes burned into her back as she passed. A shudder ran through her. Would she be up there someday? Would Victor find her out, slice off her head, and mount it over a doorway?

She swallowed and forced herself to smile up at him. In a moment he guided her into a sunken, wood-paneled space lined with glass along one wall. The wide window opened to a vista of charcoal mountain and silvery scrub. Wildflowers bloomed, dotting the view with specks of bright yellow and white. Drawn to the sight, she caught her breath, unable to believe something evil could happen amid such beauty.

"I warned you it would take your breath away." Borian's voice whispered in her ear, sending goose bumps up her arm.

"You were right," she murmured, all at once understanding what had drawn her mother to this place. "The flowers are magnificent."

"Wild English daisies. They were my wife's favorite."

She stored that tidbit away. Her mother liked daisies. Somehow that fit; they were such simple, innocent flowers.

"They're very happy," she murmured. "Like sunshine."

"She said they stood for purity and loyal love." He gazed out the window, lost in thought.

Purity and loyal love—not exactly her specialty.

"Is the rest of the ranch this spectacular?"

Victor turned and smiled. "See for yourself." He gestured her into the corridor again, then led her through a maze of stone and log hallways to a series of equally astonishing spaces. Lounges, dens, a library. His office was another paean to the hunter's art, with animal heads hanging over the room. Distasteful as it was, she noted the room's location; it was one of her prime search targets. Bug one in here.

From the office, they went to the dining room. Vaulted to the ceiling and decorated in mountain colors of granite and deep green, its centerpiece was a huge oval table carved out of what looked like a single tree, with raw, beveled edges that showed a web of tree rings.

"This is wonderful," she told Victor, and found herself speaking the truth. "Do you use it every day?"

"Yes. You can see why." He gazed around the spacious room appreciatively. "I'm glad you like it."

Great. Bug two here.

"And now," Victor said, ushering her toward the doorway, "perhaps you would like to refresh yourself before dinner? Let me show you to your room."

She cut Victor a sideways glance. He seemed pleased with himself. The ranch had impressed her and he liked impressing her. It looked like the wide-eyed routine had worked, but how much longer could she keep it up?

She tightened her jaw. As long as she had to. Until she found what she'd come for.

And what about the other—her mother and God, her aunt? *Marian.* When would she meet Marian? A ripple of yearning caterpillared over Angelina's heart, coupled with an equally strong wave of apprehension. What if Marian took one look and recognized her as family? Worse, what if she didn't?

Meanwhile, Victor was leading her into the stone-lined hallway. "I took the liberty of inviting a few friends this evening. I hope you don't mind."

She looked suitably alarmed, not only as the self-effacing woman she was trying to be, but as herself. Hard enough to pretend in front of one person. Several would be even more difficult. And the more people underfoot, the harder to escape and begin the search she'd been sent to undertake.

At her expression, he smiled indulgently. "Nothing to worry about. Just a few neighbors. A small dinner party. Wear the black dress you wore to the Governor's Ball."

She sent him a look of dismay, as though disappointing him were the worst thing she could do. "Oh, but I didn't bring it. I'm sorry, Victor. I thought this was going to be casual."

For a quick moment, a frown crossed his face, and she couldn't help tensing. Then he smiled again and shook his head as if shaking off his irritation at her. "Never mind, darling. I'll find you something appropriate."

I'm sure you will, dear.

But she was oddly relieved at how easily he'd capitulated.

He led her up a spiraled staircase cut out of the same honey wood as the rest of the house, then accompanied her down a passage lined with a rustic railing overlooking the lower floor. Turning a corner, he opened a door and escorted her inside.

"The family rooms are in this wing," he said. "Mine is just down the hall."

Apprehension rose at the disturbing thought of his bedroom's proximity and she glanced around, wondering how much longer he'd stay. The room was inviting if you liked quaint, with a stone fireplace for added mountain charm. A bent willow rocker matched the bed, which was covered with a colorful quilt. Someone had left a vase of flowers on the dresser—daisies, lilies of the valley, and blue cornflowers. Over it all hung a faint scent, sharp and spicy—not pine exactly, but something fresh and woodsy.

"It's charming," she told him, hoping her approval would send him on his way. "And smells divine."

He smiled and kissed her hand. "I'm glad you like it. My wife used to read in here." A shadow crossed his face before quickly disappearing, but a lump of pleasure struck Angelina. *Mother's room.*

"Rest," Victor ordered sternly. "Rest and restore. A woman's essence is fragile and needs constant replenishment. Make sure you get plenty of Eden's Gate water." He pointed to the blue bottle and glass resting on the bedside table. "I'll see you tonight. Refreshments begin at seven." And he whirled out.

A woman's essence?

She'd met some crazy men in her time, but no one who cared about her essence, whatever the hell that was. Most were too busy with her more . . . physical attributes.

As Victor had predicted, her bags had been unpacked and stowed, her clothes folded neatly in drawers. She pulled one open to find white bras, pink panties, and robin's egg-blue nightgowns staring back at her like eggs in an Easter basket. She grimaced at the nun's collection and wished fleetingly for her red silk peignoir. But her most provocative things were stored back in Helena, somewhere in the offices of Treadwell Insurance. She picked up a white, lacy bra and wondered who had folded it and placed it neatly in the drawer. It made her hair stand up to think of a stranger touching her things.

Relieved to be alone, she eased into the rocker and glanced around. The mountain decor was homey, peaceful. A far cry from the spangles and bright lights of Angelina's other life. Once she could have imagined herself in a room like this. Now . . .

She leaned back and closed her eyes, trying to absorb her mother's presence. *Are you here, Mother?*

She rocked gently, waiting for a reply, but none came.

Would her mother have sanctioned Angelina's assignment? Would she have wanted her husband trapped, caught, and punished?

Not likely, party girl.

Abruptly she stood, not wanting to think about her mother's approval. Instead, she checked her watch, calculating how much longer she should stay put before venturing back downstairs to place her listening devices. It was five now. She had two hours before Victor's dinner party began. Time enough to do a little exploring and still make it back to change.

She peeked out the door. The log beams in the hall looked back, round and silent. Heart thudding, she stepped out, praying she'd be able to retrace her way back to Victor's office.

Without getting caught.

CHAPTER
~9~

Finn stepped into the abandoned mine and shrugged off his heavy backpack, rolling his shoulders in relief. The thing weighed a ton. It should, packed as it was with blankets, sleeping bag, hiking gear, communications equipment, spare battery packs, weapons, and ammo.

Leaning the pack against the mine entrance, he opened it and riffled around for the compact monitor that registered Angelina's position. The signal flashed reassuringly, but did little to relieve the uneasiness he'd felt all day. Three hours ago, a helicopter had dropped him on the side of Devil's Teeth and it was all he could do to concentrate on his footing during the climb down.

Of course Angelina was all right. Women like her always landed on their feet.

Swallowing apprehension, he wiped sweat off his forehead and peered into the mine's blind-dark blackness. The interior felt cool and welcoming after the heat of the climb down, but he could barely see a few feet ahead.

Tugging the flashlight off his utility belt, he clicked it on, and a bright halogen glow filled the space. He passed the light over earthwork and wooden supports, some of which looked none too sturdy. No footprints marred the ancient dirt floor. No sign of habitation or visitation. It looked like the place had been forgotten by time. And he hoped, Victor Borian.

As he trudged farther in, Finn discovered fallen beams blocking some of the deeper recesses, but he was able to penetrate far enough to map out a fork in the passageway. To the right, a busy warren of channels had been hewed into the rock. To the left, a narrow track led to a bolt-hole and secondary supply route, complete with an ancient ladder cut into the stone. He threw some light on the top end of the ladder and peered up at what looked like a warped trap door, dusty with cobwebs. He made a note of it in case of emergency, but retraced his steps; the path here was too narrow to set up camp. Instead, he chose an open area about fifteen yards from the entrance that looked as stable as any he'd seen.

His pack held a battery-powered fluorescent lantern, which he switched on, settling in under its clear, white light. He unpacked the satellite phone, stowed his weapons and ammunition where he could get at them quickly, and unrolled the sleeping bag. As he worked he saw Angelina's face in every crevice, her smile in every shadow. What was she doing? If Borian hurt her . . . Finn clamped down on the thought before it set off a small panic.

Ease up. She'll be fine. She's smart. She can do this.

That litany had played in his head all day, but barely disturbed the swirl of anxiety in the pit of his stomach. Growling in frustration, Finn checked his watch. Seven. Another five long hours until their rendezvous.

A picture of her rose in his head, her luscious lips tilted

in that tempting smile, her mossy eyes challenging, egging him on. He smiled. Man, she was a handful.

But gutsy. It took nerve to do what she was doing.

Not for the first time, he wished she'd taken the chance he'd given her and backed out. If anything happened to her, anything at all . . .

A squeeze of guilt tightened his chest. He'd almost lost a partner once. He didn't want to go through that again.

Those goddamn bugs better work. They were his only link to her. The transmitters and the pin. He gazed at the monitor again, the green blip steady in the darkness.

His stomach growled, reminding him that he hadn't eaten since early that morning. Digging into his pack, he found some of his food stores and tore open a power bar. The thing tasted like old rubber, but he had a feeling nothing was going to taste right until Angelina showed up.

Angelina darted down the night-lit hallway toward Victor Borian's reception. She caught a reflection of herself in a window and paused for a moment. Were her eyes too bright? She put a hand on her heart, hoping it would somehow force her breathing back to its normal pace.

The dress she wore had been delivered to her room by a maid with a note from Victor. *For tonight.*

"It was Mrs. Borian's," the maid had explained.

When Angelina had slipped into the dress, an eerie feeling crept through her. How many times had her mother worn this? Had she been happy when she put it on?

Now, Angelina stared at herself in the window, remembering how the midnight-blue satin made her face translucent, as it must have done to her mother's. The high neckline and bouffant skirt covered most of the skin Angelina would normally have exposed and transformed her into a pale, virtuous version of herself, as though the nice girl she might have been was just waiting for a chance to get out.

Liar. Fraud.

A boom of laughter sent panic careening through her. She turned her head in the direction of the party noise, dreading the evening, but knowing she'd better hurry before Victor sent his troops out looking for her.

One last time, she fingered Finn's circle of pearls, its luster creamy white against the rich, dark blue satin. He was nearby, huddled in the recesses of an abandoned mine, but close. All she had to do was take off the pin and he'd come for her. Suddenly the piece of jewelry felt like a lifeline, a direct connection to the cool, mocking gaze she never thought she'd miss, and all at once did.

Would he be pleased at her work today? She'd planted all the bugs, installed the watchdog filter on the phone in Victor's office. And she hadn't been caught. Not yet at least.

She closed her eyes and took a deep breath. *Exhale, party girl. Time to shine.*

Heading toward the sound of voices, she found the get-together spilling over the hallways and living area near the front of the house. She scanned the crowd, looking for Victor. A few neighbors? There must be fifty people mingling amid small, linen-covered tables and twinkling lights. Women wore cocktail dresses, bright with summer colors, turquoise, and hot pink. Men wore sports coats without ties. They were noisy in a subdued way, too polite to have a really good time.

A makeshift bar occupied one corner, but she couldn't

imagine the serving selection beyond the ubiquitous Eden's Gate water. Too bad, because she could really use a drink. Since that was out of the question, she stood on the threshold and scanned the room for her quarry. But Victor saw her first.

He hurried over, then slowed as he came near. A brief kind of crumbling happened to his face, and a small sting of shame pricked her. What was she doing to this man?

She hardened her heart. *Preventing him from helping thousands die.*

"You look . . ." He swallowed. "You look magnificent."

"Thank you." She smiled sweetly. "The dress is lovely. The maid said it belonged to your wife."

He nodded. "You look . . . remarkably like her in it. You even smell like her."

She tilted her head up at him, trying not to feel suffocated by his powerful gaze. "That's because I borrowed her perfume. I left mine in Helena and the girl who delivered the dress was kind enough to find me some. It's the same fragrance that scents my room." That had been a surprise. The sharp smell hinted of spice and earth and layers of mystery. Perfect for her, but not at all what she expected from her mother. "I hope you don't mind me using it."

"Mind? It's wonderful." He proffered his arm, and she hoped he wouldn't notice the slight tremble as she placed her hand on it. "Did you have a chance to rest?"

Not exactly. "Yes, thank you. I feel wonderful."

He drew her arm through his, and she snuggled close, letting him smell her perfume. Nothing like fragrance to renew old memories.

"Come, I'd like you to meet someone," he said.

He led her to a clump of people clustered around a woman whose back was to Angelina. Victor touched the woman's shoulder, she turned, and Angelina found herself face-to-face with a photograph.

Her mother's sister. Marian.

Angelina's heart thumped, her whole body stiffened in shock, in expectation, in hope, and in fear. God, what would Marian say? Would she claim Angelina as her sister's child? Surely she knew about the baby.

In the space of a heartbeat, Angelina saw the other woman throw her arms around her neck, weeping in welcome. Then the fantasy dissipated and Angelina was left standing next to Victor, dry-mouthed and aching.

No one seemed to notice. Not even Marian. Her first glance was toward Victor, and her eyes lit up at the sight of him. "Oh, Victor, I was just telling—" Her gaze slid naturally from Victor to Angelina. The smile died and the blood drained out of Marian's face. The glass she'd been holding tumbled through her fingers and smashed against the polished oak floor.

Heat crawled up Angelina's neck and into her face. In the background she heard murmuring, knew heads were turning, people staring. But in Marian's eyes she saw no eager welcome. Nothing but shock and dismay. Angelina's heart clenched and the moment seemed to stretch forever. Then a gasp of voices jumped into the silence.

"Marian, are you all right?"

Victor's voice penetrated the other woman's stupor. She put a hand to her head.

"I . . . yes. Oh, I'm so sorry."

The other people drifted away, and Victor signaled to a maid. The girl ran up with a towel to wipe the spill and pick up the broken glass.

"Angelina, this is my sister-in-law, Marian. Marian, this is the treasure I've told you about, Angelina Montgomery."

For a moment, the breath backed up in Angelina's lungs. Then Marian extended her hand, covering Angelina's with a strong grip.

"I'm . . . I'm delighted to meet you." She stumbled over the words, clearly trying to regain her composure. "Victor said he had a surprise for me tonight. He was . . . he was right."

"It's wonderful, isn't it?" Victor gazed at Angelina with a fond expression, seemingly oblivious to Marian's shock.

She sent Victor a tiny glare, a small pinprick of rebuke, then covered it up with a faint smile. "The resemblance is uncanny. You . . . you're even wearing her favorite dress."

Marian turned toward the wall behind them. A portrait of Carol Borian stared down at them. Angelina gasped. The woman in the canvas looked back at them with Angelina's own face. Both were wearing the blue dress. A wave of nausea quivered in her stomach, and she clutched at the satin skirt. Victor must have sent it on purpose.

"I . . . I had no idea. I'm so sorry if I've brought back unpleasant memories."

"Not unpleasant at all." Victor stared up at the portrait ardently. "It's almost like having her back again."

Marian looked down quickly, but not before Angelina saw the haunted look in the other woman's face. Losing a beloved sister was bad enough without reliving the pain. It had been unkind of Victor to spring this on her. Then again, what Angelina was doing had its own share of cruelty. She glanced up at the painting again and imagined her mother's eyes accusing her.

Angelina put a hand on Victor's arm. "I . . . I didn't mean to upset anyone. Perhaps it would be better if I left."

But a quick smile replaced the pain in Marian's face. "No, please, not on my account. The dress is lovely. And the pin makes it entirely your own."

At the mention of Finn's monitor, a flash of alarm surged; instinctively Angelina covered the pearl circle, reassured by its solid shape. "Thank you. It was my . . . my mother's." Her lie brought a gleam of approval to Victor's eye.

"How nice," Marian said, no indication that she knew who Angelina's mother was. "Well, I . . . I hope you'll enjoy your visit with us." The words were polite, the tone one used with a stranger. Deep disappointment wrenched Angelina, though she did everything she could to hide it.

"I'm sure I will," she said.

A stranger. She was nothing to Marian. She glanced up at the painting of her mother and imagined her scoffing down.

What did you expect—a brass band?

What had she expected? Carol's parents had kept the baby's existence from everyone; maybe even the baby's aunt. Good news for Finn, as the assignment could proceed as planned. Bad news for Angelina, though she hadn't realized how much she'd been hoping for something different until it hadn't happened.

A waiter with a tray of refreshments passed by, and Victor snagged two glasses, handing each of them one. Angelina sipped sparkling water laced with a hint of sweet raspberries and searched for something to say that wasn't about family or how easily they could let you down. Something that would help with the real reason she was here. But she felt her mother's gaze on her, screwing with her concentration, and all she could come up with were banalities. "The ranch is lovely. You must enjoy it." *Talk to me, Marian.*

But it was Victor who replied. "She better. We wouldn't know what to do without her. Marian has been here since my wife's death. She nursed her during that last horrible year, and then kindly consented to stay on as my hostess."

"You must have loved your sister very much," Angelina said.

Marian looked away as though the thought were too much to bear. "We all did."

"She was . . . she was very beautiful." What was she like, Marian?

"Not unlike you," Victor said, wrapping an arm around Angelina's shoulders.

Marian saw the gesture and her small eyes widened just the merest bit, and Angelina found herself embarrassed. Casually, she disengaged herself from Victor's embrace.

"Victor tells me she loved the ranch and the mountains."

"Very much," Marian said. "She liked the outdoors, hiking, riding."

"And you?"

She smiled ruefully. "Oh, I don't have time for fun."

"You don't make time," Victor scolded.

She sent him a mock grimace. "A thankless job, caring for a man." A twinkle in her crimped, mud-colored eyes said she was teasing.

"But one she does well, I can assure you." Victor waved his hand, indicating the room. "She's responsible for this whole event in fact. She contacted the guests and made all the arrangements. And did it in two days."

Marian sighed. "Unfortunately, I'm very efficient."

"Maybe you can give me lessons," Angelina said. "I'm hopeless when it comes to planning."

"That's because you're too pretty to worry about it." Victor ran a proprietary finger down her cheek, sending a flutter of unease through her that she deflected by turning to Marian.

"Oh, don't tell her that. She'll think I'm some kind of blond bimbo."

"No one would think that," Marian said kindly. "Some people have a gift for organization, and some people don't."

A burst of laughter drew Angelina's attention away momentarily. The crowd parted and she saw Grisha's hulking form. He stood on the sidelines, in the same ready stance he'd taken at the restaurant, hands crossed in front of him, eyes on Victor. Her awareness sharpened, but she quickly repressed her small intake of breath and the sudden thump of her heart. The bodyguard was an enormously tangible reminder that she wasn't there solely for a family reunion.

"Thanks for the reprieve, but I still might hold you to those lessons. And in the meantime, I'd love a tour of the ranch." *Where have you stashed your deadly trinkets, Victor?*

"I'm sure Victor will love to give you one," Marian said.

"Oh, but you must come, too. It would give us a

chance to get to know one another." And give Victor a chaperone.

Marian shook her head. "Oh, I couldn't possibly. Too much work—"

"I insist," Angelina said. "And so does Victor."

In truth the man seemed less than enthusiastic, but he did bow his head gallantly. "By all means. Please join us."

"Well . . ." Marian smiled tentatively. "I'd . . . I'd like that."

"So would I," Angelina said. "Tomorrow, then?"

"Tomorrow," Marian said. "And in the meantime, would you excuse me? I need to check on the food."

"Certainly."

The rest of the evening passed in a blur. Victor introduced her to so many people the faces melted together into one oversized smile. Most seemed ordinary enough for Victor's neck of the woods—wealthy landowners, mining executives, businessmen, politicians and their wives. All gave Victor a certain narrow-eyed deference, as though he were someone they didn't dare cross, but didn't dare like either. Many looked at her oddly, remarking on her likeness to Carol or her portrait until Angelina grew tired of hearing it.

But no matter where she went or with whom she spoke, her mother's eyes stared down at her from the painting on the wall, an indictment against the impostor in the crowd. By the time the party ended Angelina felt raw and bruised as though her skin had been peeled back to reveal what was hiding beneath.

When everyone had gone, Victor escorted Angelina to her room. He kissed her hand at the door and looked deep into her eyes.

"You pleased me very much tonight."

She didn't know what to say. The way he looked at her, the intensity of his gaze, the fervor, was the same he'd turned on his wife's portrait, and it made her skin crawl. "I . . . I'm so glad."

He cupped her face with his hand, trapping her. "Good night, *milaia*."

What had he said? She raised a brow in question, and he smiled. "It means 'my dear one' in Russian."

"My dear one." She forced herself to appear contented. "It's . . . it's very beautiful. Thank you, Victor. Good night."

He made no attempt to embrace her, merely stepped back and let her slip inside.

She slumped against the closed door, glad for the barrier.

In the moment it took for her to regain her composure, she glanced around the room. How long to wait before escaping to Finn? She started for the dresser and a change of clothes, then stopped.

Something about the room was different.

The hair on her neck stood on end. Had someone been there? She ran a rapid inventory. Clothes, makeup—nothing was missing. And yet, something was wrong.

She scanned the space again. Daisies stood shoulder to shoulder with lily of the valley, all perky in their vase, the blue of the cornflowers reflecting off the water bottle on the nightstand. Nothing out of place. Nothing . . . *looked* different.

But something smelled different. The strong, spicy scent of Carol Borian's perfume permeated the air like a thick presence. Had Angelina left the bottle open? She checked, found the stopper off. Quickly she closed it up, but the ghostly fragrance lingered.

Is that you, Mother?

Angelina stood in the middle of the room, heart hammering. An icy, unnatural feeling washed over her. Carol felt close, as though her spirit had floated down from the portrait. Watching. Waiting. Hoping for a chance to stop Angelina.

Don't be an idiot.

But she couldn't shake the eerie feeling. Slowly, she turned, searching every corner for something she couldn't name.

You can't protect him, Mother. If Victor has those radioactive goodies, he deserves to be unmasked and punished.

Silence. Nothing moved. No spirit appeared, malevolent or otherwise.

Careful to keep a watchful eye, Angelina sidled over to the window and raised the glass. Fresh air rushed over her, earthy and real, and she inhaled a deep, ragged breath. A few moments, and the spicy scent receded.

She swallowed, her mouth dry. She was going batty and could only imagine what Finn would say if he knew.

Good thing he'd never know.

She shook off the nerves and shucked Carol Borian's dress in a sudden frenzy to be free of her mother's clothes. Rummaging in a dresser drawer, she came up with a pair of black jeans, a black tank top, and a matching cardigan to throw over it. A little warm for June, but Finn had warned her to cover up as much as she could to avoid detection. It would be easy enough to remove the cardigan when she was clear of the ranch, although mountain nights were notoriously cool. She pinned the pearl monitor to the tank top and grabbed a black scarf, stuffing it in her pocket. Once she was clear of the house, she'd cover her head with it. Finn had been adamant about that.

"Your hair glows in the dark," he'd said in a tone that told her he lusted after the shine even as he begrudged her its gleam. "Cover it up."

She smiled, remembering. The man had a funny way with a compliment.

She checked her watch. Finn had insisted she get one with a luminous dial, and the greenish numbers shone up at her even under the room light. Twelve-fifteen. She would have liked to duck out the window, but the drop was a good twenty feet down, and a broken leg was not part of the plan. Turning off the light, she picked up the low-heeled pumps she'd worn earlier, eased back the interior label on the left shoe, and extracted a square of paper. Wadding it into her pocket, she slipped into the quiet hallway, skin tingling at the thought of seeing Finn again.

Two minutes later, she stood flattened inside the front door, heart in her throat as she waited out the nightly Jeep patrol. She checked her watch, melting into the shadows until the spotlight skimmed the front facade and faded into the dark. Seventeen minutes after the hour. She'd have fifteen minutes before the next patrol passed by. Cracking open the door, she peered out, saw the empty grounds ahead, then slipped out and scrambled down the porch steps.

Stomach in a knot, she took off at a brisk pace, praying she'd make it out of the immediate area in time. Above her, the huge sky stretched endlessly, stars thick as glitter against the black velvet night. The full moon sat among them, a queen surrounded by her consorts. Together with the dim night lights of the ranch, there was enough illumination to see the outline of Devil's Teeth to her right. Keeping the three-headed mountain dead ahead, she strode toward the stables. Once past those, she'd put on the scarf. The Jeeps patrolled all night, and she didn't want to be caught anywhere near the mine. One look at the equipment Finn was likely to bring and their cover would be blown for sure.

Ahead of her, the stables loomed beautiful and neat, carved out of the same stone and dark wood as the house. She made a mental note to search them tomorrow; the stables might make the perfect place to hide the plutonium. Besides, it had been years since she'd been on horseback. A ride would give her an excuse to get out of the stifling atmosphere at the ranch.

Tapping into vestiges of her old self?

Maybe.

What would Agent Carver say to that?

She threw back her shoulders. Who cares?

She did.

Before she could continue the argument, the stable doors swung open and Grisha stepped out.

Her heart nearly flew out of her chest. She drew in a sharp breath and back-pedaled furiously into the shadows around the side of the ranch house. Had he seen her?

Damn, damn, damn.

Her mouth went dry as he lumbered toward her, his massive shoulders rolling bearlike. If he caught her, would he search her? The paper she carried could be a dangerous indictment.

But Grisha didn't round the corner toward her hiding

place. Instead, he lumbered up the stairs and went into the house.

Legs shaking, she collapsed against the wall. God, there must be a better way to get her thrills. She peeked around the edge, saw the way was clear, and leaned back, taking a moment to check her sanity.

Definitely on the blink.

She stepped out, cautiously at first, tiptoeing away from the house like a cartoon. But the tiptoeing gave way to a fast walk that soon turned into a trot. Before she knew it, she was flying away from the ranch toward the mountain. And Finn.

CHAPTER
~10~

The minute he heard footsteps, Finn drew his weapon, flattened himself against the mine wall, and crept up to the entrance. Tracers of moonlight filtered through the scrub he'd placed to camouflage the opening. The brush rustled and a shape broke through the ragged branches. A hand.

In a heartbeat, he grabbed the wrist, pulled its owner through the thicket and into his arms, the gun pointed at her head.

Her. Angelina. He'd know that body anywhere. In the dark, deaf, and blind. He inhaled her scent, different now, with a sharp, spicy edge, but still her. Undeniably. A wave of relief washed over him.

"I hope that's you, Sharkman," she whispered.

"Yeah, it's me," he whispered back, sick at how glad he was that she'd finally arrived, and in one piece. "Don't move." He shoved the Glock into the waistband at his back, retrieved the flashlight from his back pocket, and turned it on.

His chest squeezed. She looked so good in the dim

glow. She'd covered up her hair the way he'd told her to, and now she reached for the bandana and slid it off. White-gold tumbled to her shoulders in a froth of light. Against her black clothes it gave her face a pale, angelic cast so unlike the woman she wanted him to think she was.

"You all right?"

She threw him one of her tough-guy looks. "Why wouldn't I be?"

Because undercover work is damn hard. Lying about yourself, your motives, your feelings, takes a toll. Because it's dangerous. But he only shrugged. "I don't know, Angel. Just thought I'd ask. Come on—I'll take you back to the camp I set up and you can brief me."

He flashed the beam ahead and gestured for her to proceed him. She moved gingerly, favoring her left foot. He frowned. "What's wrong with your foot?"

"Nothing."

She walked ahead, her stride definitely off. "Nothing my ass. Come here." He pushed her onto a small outcropping and knelt to check her foot.

"It's nothing," she repeated, holding back her leg. He heard something like embarrassment in her voice.

Without another word, he pulled off her black slip-ons and shone the flashlight over her feet. Blisters had torn the skin in two places, leaving raw, ugly sores.

"I told you it was nothing." She snatched her foot out of his hand and put her shoe back on.

He thought about the long walk from the ranch. "Where are your sneakers?"

"Did you ever look at a pair of sneakers, Sharkman? No heels, no pointy toes, no rhinestones."

"They're a damn sight better than those"—he pointed

to the thin-soled shoes she wore—"for walking long distances."

She slapped a hand to her head. "Now you tell me."

A flash of anger raced through him. What the hell was wrong with her? Why would she want to hurt herself? If she couldn't take care of minor things like her feet what would happen when she had to take care of the big things? Like her life?

The fear that had been stalking him all day and most of the night—fear for what might happen to her—stabbed him, sharp and hard. He rose in an instant, hands on her shoulders shaking her.

"Jesus Christ, Angelina. Are you *trying* to screw this up?" He'd meant to say be careful, don't put yourself in danger, but it hadn't come out that way. Hurt flit across her face before she smothered it in the shadows beyond their beam of light; he wanted to kick himself.

"Yeah, Sharkman, that's exactly what I'm trying to do." She wrenched herself away and headed farther into the mine, limping as she went.

I'm sorry. But he couldn't get the words out. Instead, he caught up with her, handed her the flashlight, then scooped her into his arms.

"Whoa," she said. "They're just blisters." She gave him one of her insolent grins. "But any excuse to put your hands on me, right?"

He compressed his lips, refusing to rise to the bait. "Just keep the path lit." He set off, but had only gone a few steps when the thought that was uppermost in his mind burst out. "Why the hell do you take chances with yourself?"

With a sigh, she snuggled closer, making him grit his teeth against the instant wash of pleasure her body created in his. "If I knew this was going to be an Olympic event I would have made sure I had the right equipment, okay? Like I said, they're just blisters, not leprosy. They won't kill me."

"How are you going to explain limping around to Borian tomorrow?"

She didn't respond right away. Uh-huh. Hadn't thought that one through, had you, Angel?

But her speechlessness didn't last long. It never did.

"I'll tell him it's from all the dressing up I've been doing. That I'm not used to high heels."

He snorted at that whopper. "What dressing up?"

"Victor threw a party for me tonight."

His interest quickened. "A party?"

Briefly she told him about the gathering, about the dress Victor had asked her to wear, and about meeting Marian.

Her voice changed at the last piece of information, a subtly different inflection that sent up warning signals. "How did that go?"

They'd reached the campsite, and he unloaded her onto a ledge he'd covered with his sleeping bag. He switched on the lantern, flooding the area with light, then put the Glock in the holster he'd hung from a rusty nail embedded in one of the mine supports.

"Piece of cake," she said. But her face wore that shuttered, don't-come-close look that said she wasn't telling him everything. A pulse began to hammer in his head.

"She recognize you? Make the connection with Carol?"

Angelina shook her head. "Nope." Her smile was wide and brittle. "So . . . I'm fine. No problem."

He studied her in the lantern light, and she avoided

looking at him. All at once, he understood. She was such a liar. A beautiful, expert, and right now very vulnerable liar. But she wasn't hiding something dangerous. At least, not to their assignment. "I'm sorry, Angel," he said softly, resisting the powerful urge to comfort with more than words.

She shrugged. "Don't be."

But he sensed the hurt she was hiding. "It's better this way. Having Marian tie you to your mother would only have complicated everything."

She nodded and busied herself with her injured foot, and he let her. No point in pursuing what couldn't be altered, especially if it made him weak when he needed to be strong, tender when he should be tough. So he took the hint and changed the subject.

"I think I have something for that." He rummaged around in the first-aid supplies he'd lugged down the mountain, found the salve and bandages, and tossed them to her. "That should help. Fix yourself up."

That was when she reached into her pocket and handed him the map.

"What's this?"

"A rough map of the ranch house interior. I thought it might come in handy."

He glanced at her sharply, then slowly unfolded the paper to reveal a hand-drawn diagram, crude but easy to interpret. "I'm no Da Vinci, but I think you can figure it out. Entry, living areas, den, library." She pointed to squares representing rooms. "Here's Victor's office. And here's where he's got me stashed." She pointed out a room on the western corner of the second floor. "Great view of the mountains. His room and Marian's are on the same floor."

Finn glanced at Angelina, reviewing the implications. He'd told her she would meet her aunt, but having her so close . . . "Can you handle that?"

"Do I have a choice?"

He didn't mince words. "No. But you'll have to do it all the time. Hiding your real relationship on an everyday basis won't be easy."

"Look, I'm not going to throw my arms around her and suddenly blurt out I'm her long-lost niece."

No, but you'd like to, Angel. And despite himself, he was sorry she couldn't. "Good. Because you can't. Not without compromising yourself and your assignment."

"I know."

And she did. He heard it in her voice and saw it on her face. Something he never expected. Something Suzy never had.

Commitment.

He blinked at the realization, and at whatever it was he felt in his chest. Pride. That's what it was. He was proud of her. Damn proud.

His breath caught. Christ, what a shocker that was.

But she'd already moved on. "The only part of the house I haven't seen yet is the north wing." She pointed to a section that was outlined but not squared off into rooms, and he turned his attention back to the map.

"How come?"

She shrugged. "Victor decided I'd had enough touring for one day. Didn't want to weaken my essence."

A smile tugged at the corners of his mouth. "Doesn't he know that's impossible?"

The same half smile answered him back, accompanied by a teasing glint in her green eyes. "I don't know, Sharkman. Did you tell him?"

She was flirting with him. Worse, he was flirting with her. "No, but next time I see him I'll be sure to."

For a moment their gazes held, heat and liking flaring up between them. God, she could be so smart about some things. How had he missed that?

He cleared his throat and broke the connection between them before he did something he would regret. "This is good, Angel."

A slow smile spread across her beautiful face and she jumped down from the ledge. "Thanks," she said simply, holding out the tube of salve and the extra bandages as though she were thanking him for the medical help and not something else. Something neither of them wanted to name.

"You're welcome," he said. "And keep them. You may need them when you get back."

He focused his gaze back on the map rather than stare at her. Scanning the drawing, he took in the layout, trying to decide where she might concentrate her search.

"Is there a safe in his office?"

"I didn't see one. But I didn't do any heavy lifting to look for one either. I plugged the doohickey in the phone jack and got out of there."

He pursed his mouth, considering. "See if you can get back inside and poke around."

She nodded. "You don't think he'd keep the plutonium in his office? Seems a little too obvious."

"Probably is, but let's start with the obvious and go from there."

"Okay. I guess I should check out his room, too. It's next to mine."

The minute she'd said the words, Angelina wished she

could take them back. His brows quirked up and the warmth she'd seen in his eyes up to now cooled.

"That's convenient," he said.

She tried not to bristle. "It's what you wanted, isn't it? Me, getting close to him. Can't get much closer."

"Oh, I'm sure you could manage." She heard irony in his voice, and in his face . . . something else. Something there and then not there.

"What's the matter, Sharkman. Jealous?"

His eyes narrowed.

"Because you don't have to be jealous." She ran a finger lightly up his arm, giving him her best seductive smile. "Anytime, anywhere." He jerked away as though she were a rattlesnake.

"Save it for Victor."

"Oh, I will."

There it was again. That flash of anger where she'd expected delight. After all, sleeping with Victor was part of their bargain.

And yet.

A buzzer went off. His phone. He grabbed the gun he'd stashed earlier and nodded toward the entrance. "Outside. I can't get a signal in here."

"I thought you said there were no cell phone towers in this part of the state."

"I've got a sat phone. Satellite," he said at her questioning look. "But I can't link up from inside here."

She followed him out, watching the strong line of his back encased in a faded blue workshirt rolled up at the wrists. It had been a shock to see him in something beside a suit. The jeans and hiking boots softened him somehow, made him seem a different person, less of a hard-ass. At least it had up until a few moments ago.

At the entrance, he held her back and went through the camouflage thicket first. Then separating the branches enough for her to step through, he signaled her to move forward.

"Looks clear," he said in a low voice. "Patrols come by once a night, but we should have plenty of time."

Once through the thicket, he turned off the flashlight and moved away from the mine, staring up at the sky. It was black and silver, covered in stars, the moonlight bright enough to see by.

He unhooked his phone from his waist and punched in some numbers. "Carver," he said. His glance went to her and then back to the rocky hills around them. "Yeah, she's here. Hold on." He turned to her. "Mike wants to know if you planted the bugs."

"In the dining room, the den, and the office. He should have picked up something by now."

He unfolded her map and located the rooms. "She says you're hot, Mike. You should have—"

His face hardened. "I told you . . . Jesus Christ, Mike, she's fucking alone in there . . . Don't give me that crap . . ." He blew out a breath. "Okay. *Okay.* Yeah." He punched out and turned to her. "There's no reading on two, one goes in and out. Useless, cheap . . ." His jaw tightened, and he walked away, running a hand through his hair as though trying to stem his frustration.

She bit her lip, reaching for confidence. "Look, Finn, I'll be fine."

"Why is that? Bullets bounce off of you?"

"No one's going to shoot me." She sounded more certain than she felt.

He blew out a breath and shook his head. "Not much

we can do about it anyway. Look, it's late. I should get you back."

"We're not on a date, Sharkman. You don't have to walk me home."

He shot her a grim smile. "But I want to, Angel."

She didn't know if it was a sign he didn't trust her or if he was just worried about the damn blisters. The salve had helped and the bandage gave her a bit of cushion. "My foot's fine."

"Yeah, I know. And you can leap tall buildings, too." He took her arm and helped her along, letting her lean on him. They walked in silence and she tried to concentrate on something beside the two most obvious distractions, her foot and him.

"Look . . . about Victor," he said.

She glanced up at his face. Big surprise. His eyes were sober, without an ounce of scorn. "Take your time. Don't push."

What did that mean? "I thought you were in a big hurry to find this stuff."

"I am. But I also want you to be careful. Don't . . ." He cleared his throat. "Don't rush into anything." He didn't say it, but she knew what he meant: don't throw yourself at Victor. She nearly lost her footing at that bolt from the blue, but all he did was tighten his hold on her.

"You still have the pin I gave you?"

She unbuttoned her cardigan and showed it to him, flushing like a stupid schoolgirl at his concern. "I'll be okay," she said softly.

"I know you will." He looked down at her with something close to affection. Even respect. And maybe, just maybe, a bit of regret for being such a jerk. "After all, you're the toughest guy I know."

He didn't say anything after that, but she trudged beside him in silent happiness, hugging that last look to herself.

He took her to the edge of the ranch site and she walked the final quarter mile alone, woozy from feeling so good.

Watch it, party girl. Don't go too deep with this. You'll drown.

But the night sky was gloriously huge, the stars twinkled with fabulous shine, and the moon stared down with a kind, jolly face that reminded her of Beamer. How could she be cautious on a night like this?

She was so absorbed, she didn't notice the figure in the shadow of the porch.

"Angelina, is that you?"

She jumped, her heart bolting into overdrive. "Oh, fu—for God's sake," she exclaimed, swallowing the curse her mother would never have uttered. "You startled me." That was an understatement. Mind whirling, she stood frozen while Victor Borian rose from one of the rockers and stepped out into the moonlight.

"Where have you been? I went to your room to say a last good night and you weren't there. The bed didn't even look slept in."

God, she hadn't thought to rumple the bed. She looked at the stern suspicion on Victor's taut face, and tried to think. Think.

And suddenly a cold calm descended over her, a gossamer veil cloaking her true identity. She caught a whiff of spice, like her mother's perfume, but shook it away. No time to worry about Carol's ghost. Time only to become one.

She laughed lightly, trying to appear carefree, her

mind speeding ahead for an explanation. "Oh, I had such a wonderful time at the party, I just . . ." She threw open her arms as though embracing the night. "I just didn't feel like sleeping. I decided to take a walk."

"It's the middle of the night." Victor's voice was filled with distrust, and something more. Concern. He'd been worried.

"Oh, Victor . . ." She covered her mouth with her hand, hoping he wouldn't notice it trembling in the dim light. "Did I worry you? I'm so sorry. I didn't think . . ." Her palms were beginning to sweat and the saliva in her mouth seemed to have disappeared. "You've told me so much about the sky out here . . . I, well, I wanted to see what it looked like at night."

Victor's face softened. "Foolish girl," he said, his voice a fond scold. "I didn't know what to think." Arm around her shoulders, he led her into the house. "Don't wander off alone again. Especially at night. There are cliffs and gullies out there. If you don't know your way around, you could get lost or hurt. I'll always be glad to take you anywhere you'd like to go. Even in the dead of night." He nuzzled her nose, and she giggled, hearing how inane she sounded and knowing he was lapping it up.

"Thank you, Victor. And you're right. I've been very thoughtless."

"Do you think you can sleep now?" He walked her through the maze of hallways and up the stairs to the second floor. "I'm sure Marian has something to help if you need it."

"Oh, no—I'll be fine. After all that fresh air, I think I'll fall asleep the minute my head touches the pillow."

They'd reached her room and she paused outside the door to say good night, but Victor came right inside.

"Forgive me, my dear, but I won't sleep tonight until I see you settled."

"Of course." She made herself sound gracious, but she wanted to choke on the words. Especially since his presence shrunk the space, making the bed loom huge and foreboding.

As if he'd heard her thoughts, he strode to the bed and turned down the blankets.

Not yet. Please, not yet.

"Thank you, I'll be fine now," she said.

But instead of leaving, he stepped closer and stroked her cheek. "Yes, I can see you will." He smiled tenderly. "Shall I tuck you in?"

Her heart sank. Had he hovered over Carol like this, too?

"Would you like that, *milaia*?" His voice was low, whispery, his eyes searing her face. She couldn't tear her gaze away.

"Yes, Victor."

"Ahh," he breathed, as if the answer gave him great pleasure. "Get into your nightclothes then."

As if in a trance, she slid away to gather her things, then went into the bathroom to change. Thank God, he hadn't asked to watch. Heart rattling, she slipped into the baby-blue flannel nightgown she'd bought in Helena, and for once was glad something covered her from neck to ankle.

Stepping back into the room, she saw him at the edge of the bed.

Oh, God.

He gazed at her hungrily. "You look very young, my dear. Sweet."

She felt like Red Riding Hood facing the wolf.

"Now hop into bed."

She slipped beneath the covers.

"That's right," he soothed, and turned off the light. "Close your eyes." She felt him move toward her and braced herself for the touch of his lips. But they only grazed her forehead.

"Sleep tight, precious one," he whispered.

And he was gone.

The minute the door had closed, her whole body began to shake. She reached for a glass of water, the bottle clanking against the glass as she poured with trembling hands.

Calm down. He's gone.

She drank the water and collapsed backward on the bed. That was close. Too close.

She closed her eyes, and popped them open again.

The pin.

When she took off her clothes, she'd hidden Finn's monitor in the folds. It was her only link to him, and she wanted it near.

She returned to the bathroom where she'd left her clothes and found the circle of pearls. Clutching it in her hand, she slipped back into bed and slid it under her pillow.

It took her a long time to fall asleep.

Angelina scrunched open her eyes, then shut them against the morning light. Groaning, she sat up, rubbing her temples. While she was sleeping a nasty pulse had developed in her head, and now it drummed a sharp steady beat.

Great. Just what she needed. A headache.

Then again, she'd been traipsing around in the dark pretending to be someone she wasn't, hiding the someone she was, and all the while trying not to get caught at it— that would give anyone a headache.

Before she could worry further about it, her gaze caught on the back of the door. Slowly, she cocked her head, but the image didn't change. Clothes on hangers suspended from a hook. Not her clothes. Not clothes that had been there last night. But clothes that were certainly there now.

Sliding out of bed, she padded over to them. Slim navy slacks, a soft white sleeveless sweater, and a scarlet cardigan trimmed in navy. A note pinned to the blouse said simply, "Wear this for me." Victor's name was scrawled at the bottom. She knew without being told what they were. They still exuded her faint, spicy scent.

Angelina ran her hands over the sleekly soft cashmere sweater, trying to ignore the eerie quiver at the pit of her stomach. While she slept, someone had been in her room. A maid? Victor? She looked around for signs of a search, but didn't see any. Not that there was anything to find if someone had searched, thank God. She'd gotten rid of the map and all the handy little electronic devices Jack had given her.

Except the pin. She dashed to the bed and felt underneath the pillow. It was still there. Still latched. Still looking for all the world like a pretty piece of jewelry.

Breathing relief, she glanced at the clothes on the door once more, then closed her eyes against the throb in her head. The last thing she wanted was to put on her mother's clothes again.

But she took a shower, used a restrained hand with her makeup, carefully wound her hair into the sleek chignon Carol Borian had favored, and slipped into her clothes.

For a finishing touch, she attached Finn's pearl brooch to her mother's crimson sweater. She remembered the way he'd looked at her last night. As though finally, he liked her a bit. Admired her even.

Her lips compressed, half grimace, half smile. Tonight she would see him again. The prospect sent an unwanted zing of electricity through her, part uneasiness, part anticipation. God, just thinking about that man stirred her up.

Repressing the feeling, she rose and checked herself in the mirror one last time. The heat of the shower had eased her headache, although it still lurked beneath the surface. She rummaged through her purse, found a bottle of aspirin, and downed two tablets with some Eden's Gate water.

Then she slipped out the door. Her goal for the day was the office safe and the north wing. But she wouldn't know how fast she could get to them until she scoped out the action downstairs.

Who was in the house? Where were they? She headed for the dining room, hoping for some indication of everyone's whereabouts. The smell of hot coffee turned her stomach, but no one was there, so she didn't have to pretend to an appetite.

She glanced around the hallway, then back to the empty dining room. Where was Victor? Marian? Silver chafing dishes marched in a row down a sideboard along with plates and silverware. It was late. Was breakfast over?

As if on cue, Grisha rounded a corner, saw her in the entryway, and stopped.

"You are looking for something?" He loomed over her, voice bass deep, accent thick, face twisted in a scowl as though he knew she had no right to be at the ranch.

Disregarding his frightening expression, she tried out a smile. He was a man after all. "Victor. Do you know where he is?"

But Grisha was impervious; the scowl remained. "In the morning Mr. Borian works."

"I see." She held on to her patience, but only just. "Very clever of him. Where exactly does he do this . . . work?"

"Office."

"Ah, the office. Good." She waited for him to leave, but he only stood there, a giant redwood rooting through the floor. "Thank you," she added.

"You know where is it?" He started to show her, but she held up a hand. The less she saw of Grisha the better.

"I can find my way. Thank you."

She turned around feeling the bodyguard's eyes bore into her back. The encounter had overridden whatever good the shower had done, and now her head pounded in earnest.

When she got to Victor's office, the door was closed. She knocked.

No answer.

Keeping a careful eye out, she opened the door a crack. "Victor? Are you there?"

Silence. She pushed the door open farther, peeked in.

The room was empty. She stepped in and closed the door behind her.

How long until he came back?

She didn't know, but she wasn't going to waste the opportunity.

Ignoring the mounted deer heads that seemed to track her every move, she did a quick scan of the roomy log interior with its wrought-iron lamps and large fireplace whose stone facing climbed to the roof. In the center, a chunky pine desk dominated the space. Early hunter-gatherer. God, whoever had done the decorating should be shot, stuffed, and strung up along with the deer.

It took less than thirty seconds to search the walls for a safe, but it felt like thirty years. Her hands shook as she ran them under picture frames, behind bookcases, under furniture. Her ears strained for the sound of approaching feet, and she kept looking over her shoulder at the door. In the end, though, she didn't find a safe. That left . . .

She glanced at the desk, then at the door. How much longer could she remain undetected?

With a deep breath, she approached the desk and rummaged quickly through the surface and all the drawers. She didn't find a safe, but she did find a few other interesting things. She stared at Victor's PalmPilot and at the strange leather journal she'd found hidden in the back of the bottom drawer.

Don't do it, party girl.

But she paid no attention to the warning. In a rush, she slid the electronic device into her pocket and stuffed the book at her back underneath her sweater.

You're an idiot.

I know.

Before she could talk herself out of it, she raced to the

door, opened it, and yelped, the breath whooshing out of her body.

Victor.

Looking as stunned to see her as she was to see him. But not for the same reason.

"My God," he whispered. "For a moment, I thought . . ."

The rest of his words hung between them as though they'd been said aloud.

He thought his wife had come back.

Heart racing so fast it could have taken off without her, she reached desperately for the icy calm of the night before. For that other Angelina, the one that was also Carol.

She touched his face. "Are you all right?"

He took her hands and holding her at arm's length, scrutinized his wife's clothes. "You look . . ." He swallowed and gave her a shaky smile. "You look spectacular. Thank you." He pulled her toward him in what would have been a tight embrace, but she inserted her arms against his chest to put distance between them. Then she leaned against the closed office door so he couldn't get his arms around her and feel the book at her back.

"I'm glad you're pleased." She fingered the ascot at his throat and looked deep into his eyes. "I want to please you, Victor." God, she could wash her mouth out with soap.

"You do. More than I can say." He stroked her cheek and gazed at her fondly, then seemed to realize where they were. "But whatever are you doing here?"

Liquid fear shot through her, but she forced a smile on her face and leaned over to kiss his cheek. "Looking for you, of course." She tucked her arm through his. "I thought we might have breakfast together."

"Did you?" He looked down at her indulgently. At least she hoped that expression was indulgent and not predatory. "I had breakfast hours ago, sleepyhead."

She turned her mouth into a little-girl pout. "Have a second cup of coffee then."

He laughed and tweaked her nose. "You are a little temptress, and I wish I could. But I've things to do this morning."

She tugged him away from the office. "Do them later. After coffee." She stroked his arm and turned on the full wattage of her smile. "Please."

How could he refuse? He didn't. "All right, my dear. Sweep me away."

"Oh, I intend to." She snuggled closer. "Don't forget you promised me a tour of the ranch today, and I always hold handsome men to their promises."

Head on his shoulder, she led him away from the office.

CHAPTER
~11~

It was nearly two in the morning before Angelina appeared at the mine. "You're late," Finn said. He'd been pacing since midnight, cursing and trying not to panic.

She slumped against the rock wall, eyes closed. "Last night Victor caught me coming back."

A buzz of alarm started inside him. "And the fallout?"

"Nothing. I handled it. But tonight I wanted to make sure he was asleep before I left."

Her posture looked ragged and her voice lacked its usual fight. He pointed the flashlight closer to her face to get a better look at her.

His heart tap-danced beneath his chest. Christ, he couldn't even look at her without hyperventilating. Forcing the breathlessness away, he examined her closely, glad to see she wore dark clothes as he'd instructed, her head covered by the same dark scarf she'd worn the night before. But she seemed even paler than usual and though her eyes were closed, the minute the light hit her face, she raised an arm to ward it off.

"Cut the lights, Sarge. I'll talk. I swear."

He shifted the light, but only a fraction. "Are you sure things with Borian are okay? What's wrong with you?"

"Nothing a little vodka and tonic wouldn't fix." She gave him a wan smile, eyes still closed.

"Feet okay?" He shone the light down to her shoes, which accomplished what she'd asked.

"Fine." She lifted a pant leg to show him. "This time I wore these amazing things called socks. So they're fine. I'm fine. Everyone is fine."

"Borian didn't give you any trouble about them?"

"Believe me, my feet were the last thing Victor noticed today."

The alarm started clanging. "Why? What happened?"

Straightening her shoulders, she pushed off the wall. "Look, I've had more fresh air in the past two days than I have had in the past two years. Not to mention the exercise. I'm tired. Are we going to do this here or back there?" She nodded in the direction of his camp. "Either way, I'd like to sit down."

He peered at her as closely as the light would allow. She did look tired. And sounded cranky. "Sure. But brief me on the way."

She started to follow him, but the flashlight only lit the path ahead and she stumbled a few times. Finally, he took her hand, pulling her close to him.

It felt good to have an excuse to touch her, and to feel the warm solidity of flesh and bone. Her fingers fit nicely in his, smaller and finer. Womanly.

Automatically, his mind raced to other parts of her, parts that were equally smooth, equally fine, and equally feminine. Had Borian discovered them for himself? A line of anger, like a lit fuse, raced through Finn and he misstepped.

She grabbed his arm with her other hand. "You okay?"

Not as long as she was around. "Uh-huh. The damn ground is filled with stones." He made himself remember why they were here, and it wasn't for a game of touchy-feely. "So what happened with Borian?"

"Oh, he had me wear his wife's clothes again, like I'm his own personal real-live Barbie. And then he took me on a tour of the ranch."

"That's it?"

"That's it? Jesus, Sharkman, do you know how big ten thousand acres is? We were gone all frigging day and I still didn't see everything. I even had to hunker down on the ground and eat lunch out of a wicker basket."

"Torture."

"You have no idea."

"Fill me in."

"Did you know the property includes a small gorge called Russell's Canyon? One wrong move and . . ." She used her hand to simulate a nose dive. "Oh, and Hangman's Rock is an outcropping that someone supposedly hung himself from when his sweetheart rejected him."

"How romantic," he said dryly. "Dying for love."

"My thoughts exactly." Her tone was just as sarcastic.

They reached the campsite, and he lifted her onto the sleeping ledge.

"And Marian? Did she show up today?"

"I wanted her to go with us, but Victor said she had business in town. I didn't see her all day."

That was something. The less she saw of her aunt, the better.

"So in the midst of all this . . . sightseeing, I don't suppose you happened to make any progress on the other little task you're there for?"

She sighed. "O ye of little faith. Before you get your panties in a wad . . ." She took something from her pocket and handed it to him.

A PalmPilot.

"It's Victor's. From his office. And . . ." She fished under her sweater and pulled out a small, leather-bound journal. "This. It's written in some kind of foreign language so I don't know what it is. But he'd hidden it away in the back of a drawer. It might be important."

He stared at the two items she held out to him, his mind careening in shock. The personal digital assistant could be a big windfall. If Borian kept his appointments and contacts there, that information alone might be enough to intercept a meet and stop him dead in his tracks. Then Angelina could go home and he'd never have to see her again, never have to smell her again, never have to touch her . . .

Christ. He shifted his attention away from the woman to the book she held.

He took the journal and leafed through it. The cover was warm from contact with her skin, and the heat rattled him before he ruthlessly buried it. Forcing himself back to the book, he turned page after page of what looked like old-fashioned, fountain-pen handwriting. Occasionally, pictographs and diagrams interrupted the narrative, whose language he didn't recognize, except to guess it was some kind of Slavic dialect.

He looked over at Angelina. "This is . . ." He searched for the right thing to say.

"Useful?" she supplied.

"Oh, yeah," he said softly. "Very useful." Her gaze met his and for once he didn't hide his respect. "Good job, Angel."

He thought he saw a flush of pleasure steal across her cheeks, but in the dim light, he couldn't be sure. It didn't matter anyway, because she deserved the praise. She deserved to be heaped with it. He grinned. "I take that back. It was a great job."

She leaned against the rock wall and closed her eyes again, a smile playing around the corners of her mouth. "Yeah, I thought so myself. So what do we have?"

"I don't know yet. Let's see." He bent down and turned on the electronic device. "There's probably a password. I don't suppose you managed to obtain that, did you?"

She cracked open one eye and then the other. "I'm good, but not that good."

He let a small grin escape, but the warmth in her eyes was too potent and he forced his gaze back to Borian's computer. Without the password, he couldn't get very far. "Looks like I'll have to call in a little expertise, which means going outside where I can catch a satellite signal. We'll do that later." He set the PalmPilot aside and searched through his backpack for the tiny digital camera. "Hand me the lantern next to you." He set the journal on the ground and positioned the lantern for the optimum amount of light. Then he began snapping pictures.

He was so focused on the task, Angelina could relax without fear of being caught. She leaned back and closed her eyes, rubbing her temples. She hadn't been able to shake her headache all day, and now it was killing her. But she wasn't going to tell him that and ruin the perfect moment when he'd said she'd done a great job.

Because she had. She was proud of herself.

And wasn't that a kick in the teeth?

Now if she could only find the damn plutonium.

As if he read her mind, Finn asked if she'd scouted out the north wing yet.

"I'll try to do that tomorrow. I didn't find a safe in the office, though, so we can probably eliminate that room. I still think hiding it in the house doesn't make sense. That leaves the stables, the outbuildings, staff quarters, about nine thousand nine hundred and ninety-nine acres."

"Easy as pie."

"Oh, absolutely."

At the teasing tone, Angelina opened her eyes. His dark head was bent over the journal. For a moment the only sounds were the click of the camera and the flip of a page. Click, flip. Click, flip.

The sight of him in hiking boots and jeans still shook her. The casual clothes made him seem all too real, the jeans worn and faded through dozens of washes representing dozens of days of living. It was almost as though behind the wall of suit and tie hid another Finn Carver. A man she didn't know, whom she hadn't suspected existed. The Finn Carver she knew lived in places with initials . . . HQ, CP. The other Finn . . .

"What's your favorite color, Sharkman?" She settled on the ledge, ignoring the undertow of pain in her head, and hugged her knees to her chest while he continued taking pictures.

Click, flip. "My what?"

"Your favorite color. Come on, everyone has a favorite color."

"I don't."

Big surprise. "Read any good books lately?"

He thought a moment. "*Law Enforcement Response to Weapons of Mass Destruction Incidents.*"

"Hmm. Sounds like a bestseller."

He turned another page and took its picture.

"How about movies? You like movies?"

"Sure."

"What's the last movie you saw?"

He put down the camera and scowled at her. "How the hell am I supposed to concentrate with you blabbing in my ear?"

"You don't remember, do you?"

"I remember fine."

So? The last movie you saw was . . .?"

He frowned. "What are you getting at?"

"The real you. There is a real you somewhere deep inside that stiff-necked shell, isn't there? A guy, not a cop. With a life, not just a job."

Or maybe there wasn't because he only rolled his eyes and went back to photographing the journal.

"Do you have a mother, Sharkman?" She hadn't planned to ask that, but once she did, she knew it was exactly what she wanted to know. Who was he? Where did he come from?

The click of the camera stopped momentarily, then started again. "Doesn't everyone?"

She thought of her own situation. "Some people have two."

"Well, poor unfortunate me, I only had one."

"How about a dad? Brothers, sisters?"

"A dad. No brothers or sisters."

Somehow that fit. Always the lone ranger. "Where'd you grow up?"

Again, the click, flip rhythm stopped. This time he looked over at her. "The sooner I finish, the sooner you can get back."

But she knew a dodge when she heard one. "What's up,

Sharkman? Don't like talking about yourself? You know so much about me, why can't I know a little about you?"

"What difference does it make?"

All the difference in the world. You got to know someone, you got to understand them. How they thought. How they felt. That gave you power over them, and power was dangerous.

Unless you could be trusted.

You can trust me, Sharkman. "No difference," she said softly. "I just . . . I'd just like to know."

His sharp eyes examined her a moment longer, then he turned his head and went back to snapping pictures. "St. Louis." Click, flip. "My dad was a cop. Killed in the line of duty when I was sixteen. My mother never had a job, never learned how to drive, was entirely dependent on him. Which was how he liked it, believe me. But when he died . . ." Click, flip. Click, flip.

"What happened when he died?"

"Oh, I guess you could say she fell apart."

"And you picked up the pieces?" The answer was loud as his silence.

Click, flip. Click, flip.

"You see her much?"

He sighed and closed the book, snapped a last shot and turned to her. "She died five years ago. End of story."

Not by a long shot. "Smitty told me you were married once."

He tossed the journal to her, his face expressionless. "Smitty has a big mouth."

"She said your wife did drugs. You pick up the pieces for her, too?"

He rose and crossed his arms, eyes a narrow strip of blue steel. "What's it like fucking an eighty-year-old?"

She drew in a sharp breath and jumped down from the ledge, meeting his gaze head-on. His face was hard as the rock wall, but hooded, too, as though he didn't want her peering past it. In an instant she understood what he was doing. Not insulting her. Okay, he was insulting her, but only as a way of telling her to back off. "I stay out of your life, you stay out of mine?"

"Something like that."

"Fine." She shrugged. Let him keep his damn privacy. He was right. What the hell did it matter to her?

"Ready to go back?"

Right. Go ahead. Change the subject.

She repositioned the journal under her sweater. "Sure."

"Good." He held up Victor's PalmPilot. "Let's head out and see what we can do with this sucker. You can leave from there and take it with you."

As he'd done the night before, he slipped his gun into his waistband, then picked up what looked like a laptop. Switching off the lantern and reverting to the flashlight again, he led her the way they'd come.

This time, though, he didn't take her hand, forcing her to latch on to the back of his shirt to keep herself steady in the gloom.

Below the material, his muscles worked hard and strong. She licked her lips. Her head felt like a jackhammer run wild, but she still wanted to stroke those muscles, feel his heat beneath her skin.

Talk about fools.

Outside, a light breeze cooled her flushed face before he could notice. Not that he'd notice anyway. He was too busy picking up a signal for his phone.

Ignoring her.

Finally, the call went through.

"Jack, it's me, and you won't believe what I've got here. Borian's PalmPilot . . . I don't know how she did it, I didn't ask." He looked over at her, his expression shrouded. "Yeah, magic fingers are right. Look, patch me into one of the techies. If they can get me through the password, I'll upload the whole shebang and you can sift through it . . . Yeah, every name cross-referenced, every phone number checked. Whatever's on there."

Still on the phone, he knelt and put the gun on the ground within easy reach. Then he opened the laptop. It took twenty minutes for whoever was on the other end to talk him through the upload process. He spent the entire time concentrating on that as though she weren't there.

You'd like that, Sharkman, wouldn't you? You'd like it if I just disappeared. Too bad you need me so much.

Yeah. Too bad.

When the keyboard tapping had ended and the on-screen data had stopped flashing, he handed the Palm-Pilot back to her.

"Make sure Borian doesn't know it was missing."

She pushed it back into her pocket. "No problem. He's not going to be doing a whole lot of work in the next few days anyway."

She'd meant that she'd keep Victor busy with exploring the ranch, that she'd demand to be entertained and refuse to let him near his office—just as she'd done all day. But that's not how the words came out, and not how Finn interpreted them.

He picked up the laptop, throwing her a cool glance. "I'll bet," he said dryly.

She opened her mouth to reply, to deny the implication in his tone and in his face. But she'd be damned if she'd defend herself against his obvious prejudice. Let him think whatever the hell he wanted. Besides, "entertaining" Victor was exactly what he'd asked her to do. He should be thrilled.

But he didn't sound thrilled. Or look it. Like the night before, he looked angry. He snapped the laptop closed as though he were snapping someone in two, then hefted it. "Wait for me behind that boulder," he ordered, nodding toward a massive rock near the mine entrance. "I'll stow this and walk you back."

"I'll be fine," she said stiffly.

"I didn't ask for a medical report. Just do what I say." He grabbed her arm and dragged her toward the rock. "Get down." And when she didn't move fast enough, "I said . . ." He put a hand on her head and pushed until she was crouched behind the rock. "The patrol shouldn't be by for another couple of hours, but it's stupid to take chances. Stay there. I'll be right back."

Finn escaped into the mine, letting darkness cover his churning emotions. Christ, he needed to keep a clear head, but all he could think about was how much he didn't want to send her back to the ranch. To Borian.

The thought of the sick son of a bitch putting his hands on her . . .

But that's what he was paying for. For Victor to put his hands on her and more.

A twist of disgust shifted deep in his gut, but he ground his teeth, flicked on the flashlight, and headed toward his makeshift camp, where he stashed the computer. Before heading back, he ran a hand through his hair. His fingers were shaking.

Calm down. Just calm the fuck down.

She was here to do a job. That was all. A job. An assignment. He'd done a million of them. Each one was different in its own way, but every one was the same in one way. Catching the bad guy.

That was the point. The only point. He couldn't stop Borian without her, and he damn well should understand that by now. She had to go back, and he had to send her. Had to.

Right.

But the least he could do was apologize for being such a jerk.

He proceeded outside, stopping to make sure the scrub in front of the mine still hid the opening from any but the closest examination. Satisfied the mine and all his equipment would be safe while he was gone, he crept over to the boulder where he'd concealed Angelina.

"Angel," he called in a low voice. "Let's go." He braced himself for the sight of her, for the face that challenged him even as it pulled him in. "Come on. Look, I'm sorry I was so . . . so rough back there. I just don't want you to get"—he strode behind the rock to extract her—"hurt."

But the hiding place was empty. The damn woman was gone.

In her place something white fluttered at his feet. He bent to pick it up. A blank sheet of paper from Victor's journal held in place by a stone. Scrawled on it with what looked like—he rubbed a finger over the letters, which instantly smudged—like lipstick was a message.

Hasta mañana, baby.

Tomorrow. Until tomorrow.

Shit.

CHAPTER
~12~

However long it had taken Angelina to trek to the mine, her trip back was shorter. Despite the headache and the leftover blisters, she was so angry at Finn, she practically raced back. Damn the man. What more did she have to do to prove herself?

Plenty more. She had to find where Victor was hiding the stolen plutonium, and to do it she might have to look under the bed.

Or in it.

And wasn't that the hell of it? Damned if she did, damned if she didn't.

Just plain damned.

Nothing new there.

Not true, an opposing voice cried. Not true. Not true. The words stamped out in time to her footfalls.

If only it were as easy to believe the good as the bad.

She slipped into the house undetected, and on soft, silent steps wove her way to Victor's office where she replaced the PalmPilot and the journal.

Relieved of that secret burden, she slid into the eerie

silence of the hallway and crept up the stairs and oh-so-quietly crawled past first Marian's and then Victor's room.

Once inside her own room, Angelina closed the door, leaned against it, and breathed again.

Safe.

Perspiration chilling on her skin, she stood propped against the door a moment longer, the aftershock of adrenaline quaking through her body.

She'd done it.

A tremor of pride grazed her, and she smiled.

Twice in one night, a record for her.

Yeah.

And deserving of a medal. Or at least a week's worth of sleep. She crossed to the bed and collapsed backward on it.

She was asleep in seconds.

Sunlight was pouring into the room when Angelina woke. She moaned and rolled over. Who the hell had turned on the searchlights?

Ohmygod. She'd fallen asleep. In her clothes. With Victor's things still on her.

With a high-speed surge upward, she felt around for the journal underneath her sweater and the PalmPilot in her pocket, then remembered she'd taken care of them the night before. That's when the hammer went off in her head. She groaned and clapped a hand to her temples.

For God's sake, this made two days in a row. Was it a migraine or just tension? She'd never had a migraine before, but who knew what the stress of her situation might cause?

Satisfied that Victor's things were back in place, she

clawed open her purse, which she'd left hanging over one of the bedposts, dug around for the bottle of aspirin, and shook out two. She washed them down with a swig from the bedside bottle of water, then looked at the aspirin bottle again.

What the hell. She swallowed two more. Finally, she sat on the edge of the bed, wondering what time it was and feeling too tired to lift her wrist and look.

Instead, she stared at the back of the door, her heart sinking. Another outfit waited for her.

If wearing them brought her closer to her mother, she wouldn't have minded. But the clothes only made Angelina feel used and manipulated. And somehow ashamed. As if she knew Carol wouldn't approve.

But Angelina didn't have much choice. She stumbled off the bed, took a shower that didn't do much to ease the throb in her head, then put on the soft black skirt and pink sweater that Victor had left for her.

By the time she made it downstairs it was almost noon. She hadn't intended to sleep that long, but she hadn't intended to spend all day yesterday outside with a pile driver in her head either. Too much fresh air could put anyone to sleep. Not to mention be a real pain in the ass.

Or in her case, the head.

A maid told her Victor was in the stables. Angelina peeked out the window and saw the stable door open. Someone was cleaning out the stalls; hay, a water hose, and buckets were strewn around outside.

She bit her lip. She'd promised Finn she would scout the north wing. Would she have time now?

Life is risk, party girl.

Don't I know it.

It was also a bore without a little excitement.

Before she could change her mind, she turned around and made her way north.

After twisting and turning down meandering hallways, she found herself in a long, glass-lined corridor with a fine view of the trees, foothills, and the wide blue sky.

And a clear view of herself for anyone outside.

Luckily, no one appeared on this side of the house, and she continued undisturbed. The hallway led to a smaller passage with two rooms off it. One was a media screening room with rows of theater seats, the other a game room with pool table and dart boards. She searched both rooms, but found no safes or secret hideaways, and no lead-lined box of plutonium.

Back out in the corridor, she noticed it dead-ended a few feet away and was about to retrace her steps when a crook in the wall caught her attention. She continued on and discovered a narrow corner to the left. Tucked into the corner was a door.

She hesitated, looked around, saw she was alone, and peered in.

Darkness greeted her. A basement? An underground vault? Whatever it was, it looked isolated enough to be a good hiding place.

Her pulse picked up speed. She had no reason to be poking around here. Pausing outside the entrance, she looked right, then left. Victor was outside. No maids, no Grisha. No one watching. She ducked through.

She'd expected a staircase of some kind, but a switch on the wall turned on a dim light that revealed a small, stone-lined corridor slanting downward. Stepping warily, she followed it. Empty of doors or other rooms, the walk narrowed as it went, trailing into little more than a slim passageway. Halfway down, a sound caught her attention, and she stopped dead still. Was someone following her? She looked over her shoulder. No one.

She swallowed and continued down the tapering passage. When it ended, she found herself facing a metal door, a door with a bulky keypad embedded in its surface instead of a knob.

She pushed against the door; as expected, it was locked. Did the keypad open it? Frowning, she stared at the numbers. So far, she'd seen nothing overtly suspicious in the house. Now suddenly she'd found a door that looked like it belonged on a military installation. What was Borian hiding that required a locked door, and a complicated one at that?

A chill ran up her back. If she'd stolen contraband nuclear material, she'd hide it behind a steel door, too, wouldn't she?

Heart beating fast enough to fly, she shoved against the door again. It didn't budge.

"What are you doing there?"

The sharp voice sent her heart leaping into her throat. She whirled to see Marian scurrying down the passageway.

"Marian!" She laughed nervously, which wasn't hard to fake. "My goodness, you scared me."

Marian eyed her, waiting for an explanation.

"But I'm glad to see you. I . . . I was looking for the dining room and somehow ended up here." A lame excuse, but the best one she could come up with, given the fact that her heart was thudding so loud she couldn't hear herself think. "I have a terrible sense of direction."

Marian studied her closely. "You passed the dining room to get here."

Panic surged, but she tamped it down. "Did I?" She

shook her head as though helpless. "What a ninny. I could get lost in my own room."

Marian stepped back, gesturing for Angelina to precede her. "I'll be glad to show you the way back."

"Thank you." She exhaled a low sigh of relief and started up the narrow hall, butterflies playing tag in her stomach.

"What's down here anyway?"

"Victor's private space. It's off-limits to everyone." Marian's voice was tight, almost curt.

"Really? That's mysterious. I'll have to ask him why."

"I wouldn't advise it." Marian's mouth pressed into a thin line. Clearly, she didn't want to talk about the locked room.

Why? Did she know what was in there?

She looked at Marian, wishing they could be friends. But of course, friends tell each other everything and there was so much she couldn't tell her aunt.

And vice versa?

God, she wished she knew. She didn't want Marian to be part of Victor's dirty dealings. Then when this was all over, they could have a real family reunion. She and Marian could get to know each other without lies and deception between them.

"Did you have a nice day in town yesterday?" She put as much interest into her voice and face as possible. It wasn't difficult, as she really wanted to know.

Marian shot her a surprised look, as though attention to her life was the last thing she expected.

"Victor told me you had business in town yesterday. I was sorry you couldn't come with us on the ranch tour."

Marian looked at the floor and then back up again, a

tight smile on her face. "Maybe another time," she said, but they both knew Victor hadn't wanted her there, and another time probably would never come.

They emerged out of the passageway and Marian led her down the hallway to the dining room. In the stronger light, she noticed Angelina's clothes for the first time, and her face paled.

"What's the matter?" Angelina asked, though she knew damn well what the matter was.

"Those clothes. They . . . they were—"

Angelina looked down at herself, then back up to the shocked face of the other woman. "Oh, God. Were these your sister's, too?"

"Yes. It's . . ." She swallowed. "It's amazing how much you look like her."

"Oh, I'm so sorry." She made herself sound appalled without working too hard. She didn't like lying to Marian, and she especially didn't like hurting her. "I only put them on because Victor asked me to. I'll change if it makes you uncomfortable."

"V-Victor asked you to wear that?"

A wave of annoyance at Victor flashed through Angelina. It was cruel of him to parade constant reminders of his sister-in-law's loss in front of her. And using Angelina to do it made her even angrier. "I'd be happy to change, if it upsets you . . ."

Marian stiffened. "No, of course not . . ." She continued down the hallway. "Victor insisted on saving everything and Carol's clothes are in perfect condition. No reason why they shouldn't be used." Another taut smile flashed across Marian's face, but she was clearly upset.

They entered the dining room and Marian pulled out a chair. "Here, sit down. Let me pour you some coffee."

Angelina felt genuinely terrible. "Please. You don't have to wait on me."

"It would be my pleasure. I always waited on Carol. It will be like having her back again." She looked so apologetic and eager to please that Angelina couldn't think of a way to refuse without arousing suspicion.

"All right. But please, pour yourself a cup and sit down. You make me feel like a guest and I'd rather feel . . ."

"At home?" Marian threw her a sideways glance, then looked quickly away.

Angelina understood. She could see why having her there on a permanent basis would upset Marian. She still hadn't adjusted to the resemblance to Carol; just looking at Angelina seemed to disturb her almost as much as it enchanted Victor. Not that Angelina could blame Marian. What a shock to see someone you love come back from the dead, but in the guise of a whole different person.

"It's such a beautiful home. I can see why Carol loved it. Why you all love it."

Marian placed the coffee in front of Angelina, but the smell almost turned her stomach. She pushed the cup away a bit, the pulse in her head pounding out the questions she was dying to ask. Should she risk them?

"Would you . . . tell me about her?" The words were there before she'd decided to speak.

"About Carol?" Marian started, and Angelina wondered if talking about her sister would upset her again. But Angelina was so desperate to know, she plunged on anyway, no better than Victor.

"What was she like?"

Marian poured a cup for herself before answering.

"Carol was the kind of woman everyone loved to love," she said at last.

A twinge of disappointment hit Angelina. *Everything you're not, party girl.* "Gracious, kind, warm?"

"Oh, yes. You have it exactly." She hadn't added cream or sugar, but she stirred her cup anyway, as though needing something to do.

"Were you close?"

She took a sip. "Not really. Not until the last few years. She was five years older, so we didn't share school or many activities. And when I was ten my parents sent her to boarding school. I didn't see her much after that."

Angelina's breath quickened. If Carol was five years older, she would have been fifteen. Boarding school. That's what they told everyone.

Another thought occurred to her. If Marian believed her sister had gone to boarding school, she wouldn't know who the father of her child was. *Who my father was.*

Another dead end.

Can't think about that. "Victor seems to have loved your sister very much."

Marian laid down her cup and it clattered on the saucer. "Oh, he doted on her."

Sorry, Marian. Please understand. Just a few more minutes, a few more questions. "How did they meet?"

"I introduced them."

An emotion Angelina couldn't identify flickered into Marian's face. With the pinched look of her eyes, she was hard to read, but something had affected her. Angelina was feeling worse by the minute.

"I was working for Victor by then, and we were in Paris. She flew over on a vacation and we all met for dinner." She smiled ruefully. "She never left."

"They have no children." Angelina looked down at the coffee to hide her face when the subject of children came up. The dark black liquid stared back at her, blank and inscrutable.

"No. Carol was unable to conceive. They tried for a while and then, well, she got sick."

Well, she'd conceived once, that was for sure. Did Angelina's birth leave her mother with some permanent damage? She'd never know.

"You don't like your coffee?" Marian was changing the subject, and Angelina let her. She'd put Marian through enough that morning.

"I . . . I have a bit of an upset stomach. I think I'll pass on coffee this morning."

Marian peered at her with mild concern. "Oh, I'm so sorry. What can I get you? Some broth, perhaps?"

"No, really. I'm fine. I think I'll just skip breakfast."

"All right. We'll have lunch soon. Maybe you'll feel better by then." She started to clear away the cups, then stopped, holding them in her hand. "Please, if you wouldn't mind . . ." She hesitated, then sighed. "Don't mention it to Victor. He's a bit obsessive about illness."

"I've noticed." If he brought up her essence one more time she'd scream.

"Carol's death nearly killed him," Marian said. "He can get quite panicky when anyone is ill. If you need anything, come to me."

"Of course."

"Thank you." She smiled, and the expression nearly transformed her plain face, making her seem younger, warmer. All at once the gap between their ages narrowed, and the possibility of friendship bloomed.

Angelina ducked her head to hide the hope flaring in her eyes. "My pleasure."

One day soon, Marian, I'll tell you everything.

One day soon.

"What have you got?" As he spoke into the phone, Finn kept a wary eye on the open ground around him. He didn't like being outside the mine during the day, but Jack wouldn't have buzzed him if it weren't important.

"We have preliminary analysis of the journal and PalmPilot," Jack said. "I'm downloading visuals and data."

While the information was sent, Finn gave the rocky canyon another fast sweep. No one in sight.

"Okay," he said, looking back at the computer he'd wedged between two boulders. "I see it."

"Take a look at the first page."

Finn punched in the keys to access the information. A head revolved on the screen, then settled into the image of a face boxed by a square and bordered by information. Name, vitals, occupation. Finn squinted at the face. Something about it was familiar.

"Who is it?" he asked.

"Borian's first appointment of the week. Tomorrow. Take a look at the address."

Finn skimmed the information. Name: Dennis Copley. May birth date. Occupation: Owner, Copley Farms. Henley, Tennessee. "What does Borian want with Farmer Greenjeans?"

"He's not a farmer, he raises horses. Horses Borian likes to buy. At least he did until his wife died. We're wondering if our friendly temptress has inspired him to another buying spree."

"Could be. Could also be a cover. Is Copley connected to any groups on our radar screen?"

"Haven't found a connection yet."

"Keep digging."

"Already on it. We're also looking into the rest of the names here. So far, nothing's turned up a red flag, but—"

"This guy Copley looks familiar," Finn said, frowning at the face on his screen. "Where's Henley?"

Jack sighed. "I knew you were going to ask that. Hey, Mike—" Jack's voice muted as he yelled to his compatriot—"didn't I tell you he'd ask about Henley?" Back into the phone, he said, "Hold on, Mike's checking."

Finn peered at the screen, hoping the face would jog a memory. In the phone he heard the faint sounds of Jack and Mike conferring in the background. He imagined the two of them holed up in the surveillance van, cans of Cheez Whiz and bags of Fritos strewn around the electronic equipment.

"Looks like it's north of Memphis, some place called Crockett County," Jack said at last.

A warning bell went up. Memphis. Finn stared at the picture again. Why did the guy look so familiar?

He thought back over the last week, his mind flying over images. The dockside bar he'd been in when Roper contacted him about Angelina. The charter to Memphis, meeting Jack at the airport, Beaman's house, the party, meeting Angelina . . .

The party. Jesus Christ.

The drunk at the party who wanted one more smooch from Angelina.

"He was at the party," Finn said.

"What?"

"The party. Beaman's wake. He was there. Drunk as a

skunk by the time I arrived, but he must have known Beaman, which means he—"

"—knows Angelina," Jack said at the same time. "Shit."

The tension in Finn's neck ratcheted up tenfold. "Look, it's okay. I'll see her tonight and we'll work something out. Maybe she'll go into town for a shopping spree tomorrow. Or better yet, maybe Stephen Ingram needs to make an appearance and take her to another ranch for a few days."

Jack let out a breath. "Okay. Sounds good. Let me know if you need any arrangements on the ranch front."

"What about the book? What's it written in?"

"Belorussian. How and when Borian obtained it we don't know, but it looks like the genuine article."

"No codes?"

"No, it's pretty straightforward. A scientific journal."

"Nuclear? Could Borian be using it as a blueprint for bomb making?"

"It's not nuclear, Finn. It's, well . . . it's about cryonics."

Finn blinked. "Cryonics? You mean . . . ?"

"Yup. Freeze-drying the dead so you can bring them back to life later."

"Christ." Finn paused, astonished. "That's twisted." Then he started to smile. "That is fuckingly, amazingly, shit-facedly twisted."

Jack laughed. "Yes it is, brother. And I guess Borian won't be needing his little book anymore."

Finn's grin broadened from ear to ear. "Thanks to us. You know, I think Victor Borian owes the TCF a huge debt of gratitude. We brought the dead back for him."

CHAPTER
~13~

Lunch was a disaster, dinner worse. Angelina picked at the food, moving it around her plate so it looked like she was eating, but Victor wasn't fooled.

"Is something wrong?" he asked with a worried look.

Angelina exchanged a glance across the table with Marian. Had her aunt mentioned she'd caught Angelina sneaking around Victor's secret room? Neither Marian nor Victor had referred to it, leading Angelina to believe her aunt had said nothing. As though the two women had entered into a pact of silence, Angelina returned the favor and kept her promise to say nothing about feeling ill. "I'm fine. Just not very hungry today."

"Nonsense," Victor said. "You hardly ate anything at lunch. Your essence needs fuel. Eat up. Food will do you good."

She forced a forkful of potatoes into her mouth and tried not to gag. "Of course, Victor. I'll try."

He patted her hand. "Good girl."

"Perhaps Angelina should rest tonight," Marian said.

"I think you exhausted her yesterday." She threw Angelina a sympathetic look.

"Oh, no. I have something exciting planned for tonight," Victor said with a smooth smile. "That's why you must eat up, my dear. Build up your strength."

"Not more hiking?" The last thing she needed was more fresh air.

"After your midnight stroll the other night, I thought you might like to see Eden's Gate the way it should be seen. From the back of a horse." He leaned over, dropping his voice to a low, intimate rumble, and clasped her hand in his own as though they were alone. "I'm taking you riding tonight."

Angelina's stomach tightened. Oh, God, not tonight. Not with her head killing her and her stomach a mess. Tonight, she had to see Finn.

"I don't think I'm up for a ride tonight."

"Really, Victor, she's awfully pale," Marian interrupted, "and besides, I have some correspondence to go over with you."

Thank you, auntie. But Victor continued as if Marian hadn't spoken. "It will be wonderful. Fresh mountain air is Nature's own medicine."

"But your work . . ." Angelina said.

He ran a finger down the side of her face. "Everyone needs a night off. And I feel like celebrating. Marian is quite capable of working on her own."

He spoke as if she weren't sitting right across the table from him, and Marian watched, her pale, pinched face expressionless. Angelina felt helpless, trapped between them.

Then Marian offered Victor a tight smile, which he

didn't see. "Of course I can work alone. I . . . I appreciate your trust."

"Good." At last, he turned to Marian, but only for a moment. "Then I'll see you in the morning." He helped Angelina from her seat. "We'll have dessert in the meadow. Change into your riding clothes, my dear, and I'll meet you at the stables in half an hour."

Slowly she trudged up to her room, forcing herself to concentrate. If she hurried, she could get down to the stables before Victor and check them out.

Despite how rocky she felt, she managed to change in ten minutes. Another five and she reached the stables. A man was already there, saddling the horses, and she took a moment to introduce herself.

"Do you mind if I look around?"

"Help yourself."

She walked around, trying not to let the musky animal smell roil her stomach further. Most of the stalls were empty or contained bales of hay, and before snooping, she looked over her shoulder at the stableman. He was talking softly to the horses, paying no attention to her. She prodded the bales, shoved the heavy stacks back and forth, but ended up with nothing to show for it but more throbbing in her head and straw all over her. She sighed, dusted herself off, and continued exploring. Tack and grooming instruments hung from hooks on the walls but nothing out of the ordinary hung with them. She scuffed at the floor and scanned the wall for loose boards or secret compartments. Nothing. *Not much in the James Bond department, are you?*

She checked her watch. Five more minutes until Victor showed up. She strolled past an empty stall to the south corner of the stables and her gaze snagged on a small knothole embedded in the outer wall. She doubled back and carefully ran her fingers over it. Her breath sped up.

She'd felt a latch.

"Find something?" Victor's voice boomed in her ear. She jumped and her fingers pulled the knothole accidentally. With a screech, a desktop dropped into view revealing several compartments behind it.

Victor laughed and put his hands on her shoulders. "I didn't mean to scare you."

I'll bet. She'd almost chucked up the little food she'd managed to get down.

He came around to stand beside her and gazed at the compact desk. "Clever, isn't it?" He pressed a hidden switch and a light came on. The desktop was empty and so were the compartments. "My wife loved this place. This is where she did the stable books." His gaze lingered a moment on the desk, then he pushed it back into the wall. "Since Carol . . . since my wife passed away I'm afraid I've left the stables to deteriorate, but in the last few days I've felt rejuvenated. I'm going to revive them in her memory. In fact, you'll be the first to see my newest purchase. He arrives tomorrow. A stallion."

She tried to look enthusiastic. "How exciting."

"I've got a quiet little mare for you, though. Come, let's see if the horses are ready."

"I'll be right there. I want to take another look at this cute little desk."

She tensed, waiting for him to object, but he didn't, which led her to believe nothing sinister was hidden there. But just in case, she released the desk once more, and when Victor strolled over to the stableman she examined it thoroughly. Made with cunning craftsmanship, the whole thing mounted snugly and invisibly into the wall. She ran a hand down the fittings and over the smooth desktop, imagining the thousands of times her mother had done the same. Disappointment rippled through her. Honest as a preacher, the desk held no hiding places, no secrets, not even a small memento of her mother Angelina might have taken with her. Sighing, she closed it up just as the stableman came past leading two horses outside.

"Let's go, my dear." Victor put an arm around her shoulder and led her into the yard.

The stableman loaded a blanket and a hamper on the back of Victor's gelding and helped her mount the mare. Nervous and edgy, Angelina set off behind Victor, all her plans thwarted. Unless the plutonium was embedded inside a bale of hay, the stables were clear. That left the guest house and the staff quarters to search, a massive job for one person. Not to mention the locked room, which she couldn't even open without Finn's help.

Her head throbbed as she thought about it all. She looked over at Victor; somehow she had to move closer, break down his defenses, get him to confide in her. But the idea made her want to shrink back instead.

The horse seemed to sense her tension; she pulled at the bit and tried to shake off the reins. Above them, a suffocating blanket of sky hovered inky black and salted with stars. An enormous moon, white-hot as an interrogation lamp, glared down at Angelina accusingly, as though she'd already failed.

Victor led them the long way around the lake, a trail that would have been beautiful under normal circumstances, but right now made her feel frustrated and impotent. She had to get to Finn and he seemed farther off than ever.

They rode for nearly an hour, the horses familiar with the way and plodding on with little guidance. At last, Victor veered off to the east where a flat expanse sat atop a small rise shadowed by dark, looming trees. He reined in, then helped her down, his hands firm on her waist, his breath fast and excited.

The night smelled alive with possibility, earth and trees budding and ripe. Whether those possibilities boded good or evil, she couldn't guess. But an uneasy thread wound around her heart. She knew she should stay close, let Victor pet her, touch her, but she glided to the center of the plain, putting space between them. Facing west, she peered into the darkness where somewhere the three heads of Devil's Teeth butted into the sky. Finn was out there, waiting.

To her left, Victor spread out the blanket. He looked up at the night, fussed with the angle, and finally placed it a few feet from a small tree. He covered a corner with the wicker hamper, positioning it just so, as if the whole setup were a ritual of some kind.

A shudder passed through her. It *was* a ritual. He'd been here before, done this before.

Her mother's ghost floated up from her grave.

God, if Angelina wasn't already feeling sick, she'd feel sick now. To lie on a blanket with her mother's husband made her want to weep with revulsion.

But she said nothing—how could she when this was what she'd been sent here for?—and when Victor was satisfied with his arrangement, he came and put an arm around her shoulder.

"Sit down. I've made it comfortable for you." He

walked her to the blanket, saw her settled, and opened the hamper. Two champagne flutes nestled inside. He filled them with Eden's Gate water and handed her one. Ice-cold, it had been infused with the taste of berries, just like at the reception. The water slid down her throat like bitterroot.

"Look there." He nodded up to the sky, where the mass of stars seemed cold and far away. "Our souls are there, burning in a holocaust of white flame."

She gazed up at the glittering holes pricked into the endless black. "Do you think so? I . . . I've never been sure of an afterlife."

"Oh, I believe in the possibility of immortality."

Her pulse quickened. "By our deeds you mean? That what we achieve leaves a lasting legacy?" Arming a nuclear weapon could put him in the history books, that was for sure.

"That of course. But I'm talking about true immortality. The possibility of eternal life, eternal physical life." His voice drifted off, his gaze lost in the heavens. "Indefinite youth," he murmured. "Perfect health. Death vanquished."

She shivered and repressed the urge to move away. "I don't . . . I don't understand."

"Ah, but you should. You have done it, you see." He turned from the skies and looked at her with an intensity that made her want to disappear. "And I can only wonder if you were heaven sent."

Reel him in. She touched the back of his hand. "I'm very real, Victor."

"Yes, I know." He put an arm around her and drew her near. *Get close to him.* "And that is the beauty of it. My God," he whispered. "You look so much like her."

She looked down at her hands, chaste nails short and bare of polish, unable to face the obsession in his eyes. "You brought her here, didn't you?"

"Many times."

"I feel as though she's here, with us." A tiny shiver rolled over her as she thought of the portrait on the wall, the way the eyes followed her every move. The way her mother's perfume permeated every corner of Angelina's room.

He reached behind and undid the pins of her hair, the same way Finn had done in the hotel suite in Helena. Her stomach knotted at the comparison, but she did nothing to discourage Victor's fantasy.

This is your job. Sit still and do it.

"She always took her hair down at night."

Angelina shook out her hair, brushing it over her shoulders, and he stared at her, eyes dark and glowing in the moonlight. She tried to look away, but he took her face in his hands, his fervent gaze searching every inch of her.

"Are you here, *liubimaia*? Beloved, have you come back to me?"

Angelina's stomach twisted. Oh, God, he was going to kiss her. He would lay her down beneath the stars and do what Finn and Roper expected him to, what they expected her to do. A fresh wave of nausea shook her, but she raised a shaky hand and touched his face.

"I'm here, Victor," she whispered. "Tell me how I can please you."

Was it the sound of her different voice or the touch of her different fingers that snapped him out of his trance?

With a small moan of pain deep within, he released her. "I am sorry." He looked away, as though trying to regain his composure. "We should go back. You need your rest."

Relief at the reprieve nearly swamped her, and she had trouble getting to her feet. "I am . . . tired."

Rising, he gathered the glasses and extended a hand. She let him help her up, enduring his touch as she knew she had to. She looked forward to getting back. Every nerve stood on end; rest was exactly what she needed. It would give her time to get rid of her dizziness. And to get to Finn.

On the way back to the ranch, Victor hunched over the saddle, lost to the night and his memories, and she left him there, her own thoughts equally black.

In the last week she'd brought two men to the brink of seduction, and both had backed out. What did it mean?

That they don't trust you, party girl.

The explanation sank inside her like a stone. She wanted Finn's trust, wanted it badly, but to get it, she'd have to earn Victor's. And that meant . . .

An anxious ripple wobbled through her already wobbly stomach. She didn't want to think about what that meant. About Victor's bed.

A different stablehand waited to unsaddle the horses, and she tramped back to the ranch house at Victor's side. As usual, he escorted her to her room and standing in the doorway, stroked her face.

"I've left something for you. Put it on. I'll be back."

Now what? With a sinking heart, she slipped inside and saw the peignoir laid out on the bed. Sheer and soft, it was a far cry from the slinky red one she'd left in Memphis. This one was white, bridal white.

Her mouth went dry. Had Victor broken off the seduction in the meadow only to resume it here? Her hands went clammy; she wasn't ready. Not yet. A picture of Finn rose in her head.

Tell me not to do it, Sharkman.

But she knew he wouldn't. This was her job. Her talent, her only true skill. This was what they'd recruited her for.

A soft rap cut short time for debate. She opened the door and saw disappointment on Victor's face.

"I . . . I'm sorry, Victor. I can't. I'm not ready for . . ." Silently, she cursed herself for a coward, but he only smiled, as if gazing at a schoolgirl.

And then her breath hitched as comprehension dawned. My God. He approved. He expected her to resist him. Nice girls would.

"I just want to see you in it. I won't even come in. Just . . . let me look at you."

Relief swallowed up the eeriness of his request. She bowed her head, closed the door, and slipped out of her clothes with trembling fingers. The nightgown slid over her skin like sheer moonlight. She pulled the edges of the transparent robe together to hide the line of cleavage, placed her lifeline to Finn on the nightstand where she could see the circle of pearls, and braced herself with a prayer. She called softly to Victor, hoping he wouldn't notice the tremor in her voice.

He stood on the room's threshold as she steeled her nerve and walked toward him. The transparent material floated around her legs and thighs, and he inhaled a sharp, pained breath at the sight of her. Once again, tears misted in his eyes.

He caressed her head, sliding a hand along her neck below her hair. Breath erratic, he traced the line of her arm, her back, even her breasts and hips before moving back up to her face. She stood cold as marble while his hand skimmed over her body, heart drumming so loud she thought he might see it leap under her skin. But she choked back the icy revulsion and let him touch her.

Her mother's husband. Her mother's lover.

She wouldn't think about that. She would feel nothing. Be nothing. She could do this. She'd done it before. When Andy Blake had . . . hurt her, she'd gone away until he finished.

She would go away now. Become hollow, numb. No air, no breath, no being.

And then he spoke. "Thank you," he said in a hushed voice. He took her hand and kissed her palm the same way he'd kissed it the night of the party, deeply, intimately, in a way that made her skin crawl. "Good night, Angelushka. Sleep well."

The door closed behind him and she could breathe again. She stumbled to the bed, heart drumming, legs shaking. Mouth dry, she poured herself a glass of water from the bedside bottle and raised it to her lips with a shaky hand, hoping to forget the look on Victor's face when she'd walked toward him.

She checked her watch. She'd wait an hour; time for everyone to settle down for the night. She'd go the long way, skirting the stables in case Grisha was roaming. She'd . . . Her eyes drifted shut and blinked open. She lay down on the bed.

So tired. Need to rest. She closed her eyes.
Don't dream. Don't dream.

Angelina awoke with a start. *What was that?*

Moaning, she rubbed her eyes in the pitch-black room.

Her mother's spicy perfume wafted sharp and strong, piercing Angelina's aching head.

Another sound.

Someone was there. As her eyes adjusted to the dark, she saw a ghostly figure glide toward her.

Mother?

The figure moved toward the bed, an avenging angel coming to stop her, to protect Victor.

With a scream, Angelina bolted upright. Suddenly the light flashed on and she covered her eyes from the glare.

"It's all right, shh, everything is all right," the soft voice crooned. Angelina's heart slowed, and the spirit materialized into a flesh-and-blood woman in a chenille bathrobe.

Marian.

"You had a nightmare," she soothed, perching on the end of the bed. "I heard you cry out. Here." She poured Angelina a glass of water and she sipped at it.

"I . . . I don't remember dreaming." But she remembered how badly she didn't want to dream, to remember Victor. "Are you sure I cried out?"

"Yes, I heard you quite clearly. I thought something was wrong and when I came in you were tossing and turning."

Angelina frowned down at the glass. Dizziness made her head swirl. "I don't usually dream. I'm sorry I woke you."

"Don't be. I don't mind a bit." She brushed the hair away from Angelina's face the way she imagined her mother would have. For a brief, safe moment, she pretended that Marian was her mother, caring for her the way she'd always dreamed.

Smiling kindly, Marian said good night and left.

Angelina checked the time. Two A.M. She groaned. Finn must be beside himself. She took one last gulp of water, then stumbled out of bed to change. Her head felt like a giant boulder on her neck. Too heavy to lift. Too heavy to move. She braced herself against the nightstand and the glass clattered to the floor, spraying water everywhere. She stared at it.

Water.

The word boomed in her head like an echo between mountains.

She swayed, dizzy, and reached for the circle pin on the nightstand. If she could get it open . . .

Her hand closed around it and she felt herself falling. Her last thought was that she would never see Finn again. Then blackness opened its arms and she fell in.

CHAPTER
~14~

With only moonlight to guide him, Finn shimmied up the stone facing of Borian's ranch house and prayed he had correctly deciphered Angelina's crude map. Second floor, west, he was pretty sure that was the one she'd pointed out.

Pretty sure.

He reached for another handhold and hauled himself up in the darkness. Christ, he better be damn sure.

Fifteen feet up, he paused for a quick breath, sweat running under his shirt. Leaning against the cool stone, he still heard Roper's explicit order to stay away from the ranch.

Not on your life, pal.

Not after Angelina hadn't shown up for their nightly meeting. It could be nothing, but she hadn't looked good the night before. Something was wrong, and he could kick himself for not pressing her more about it. And if he didn't warn her about Copley no matter what else was wrong with her she'd be in serious trouble.

He swallowed the bead of worry that had been tightening his throat and checked his watch's luminous dial. Five minutes before the patrol swept this sector. He gauged the distance to the second-story corner window and pushed up another few inches. Reaching for a foothold, he suddenly slipped on air, loosening pebbles and mortar that fell away into nothingness.

Jesus Christ.

His heart slammed against his chest. Sucking in a breath, he dangled by his hands, swinging against the side of the house. Instantly, the universe collapsed into this one tiny quadrant: him and the wall. Every sensation sharpened. The cool air on his face, the scrape of fingers on stone, the echo of a loose pebble hitting the ground. He heard and felt it all, tight and close, precious as last seconds would be.

Squeezing his eyes shut, he channeled all his strength into the hands holding him upright, all his awareness into his feet. *Careful, now. Slow.*

Sweat dripped down his face. Arms strained under his weight. He gritted his teeth, determined not to fall. Angelina was somewhere inside that goddamn fucking house and he wasn't going anywhere until he made damn sure she was all right.

Grunting with effort, he held on by sheer will until his booted toe found a crevice between two stones. He lodged one foot in it and sagged against the building, suddenly secure again. With no time to relax and his heart thudding sickly in his chest, he clamped his jaw down hard and began to climb. No telling how much time he'd lost, but the faint light in the distance had to be an approaching vehicle. *Patrol.*

He might as well be a giant target under the plain light of the moon. He rolled one shoulder, feeling the weight of the Glock inside its holster. But the last thing he wanted was to draw attention to himself or Angelina by firing it.

Focus. He reached up and his fingers brushed the underside of the window casing. Another half inch, and they curled around the ledge. Over his left shoulder, the Jeep advanced relentlessly, its headlights sweeping the ground ahead, the spotlight in the back illuminating a wider, higher arc.

He pulled himself up so his eyes just barely cleared the bottom of the window. Inside, a bed. Whose? Impossible to tell from his position, but the window was cracked open.

The Jeep was almost directly below him, the spotlight sweeping the side of the ranch. No time to check another room. Bracing himself on one hand, he shoved the window open, and with a muttered prayer, slithered under and onto the floor.

The spotlight passed over the glass just where he'd been a second ago. As the light passed, it slid over a body crumpled on the floor.

He froze.

Crouched in the dark beneath the window, he stared, not sure he'd imagined it. Then his eyes adjusted to the dim light and he made out the lump on the floor.

He tore over to it, his belly twisting. White nightgown, light hair. *It isn't. Don't think it.*

With shaking hands, he checked the pulse in her neck. Relief flooded him. Gently, he turned her over on her back. No blood, no wounds that he could see in the stark, moonlit room. He yanked closed the curtains over the window, then risked turning on the bedside lamp.

Her golden hair sprawled over the floor, her beautiful

mouth lay half open, lush as a flower bud. Raking his fingers through his sweat-dampened hair, he glimpsed something wedged in her hand. Carefully, he pried the fingers open and saw the pearl monitor he'd pinned to her breast so many nights ago.

Something broke inside him. Had she been trying to contact him? Why the hell hadn't he noticed? He checked the back of the pin, but it was locked, the signal still intact. Panic circled low and pulsed in his veins. What had happened to her? He tossed the pin on the nightstand, then sat against the side of the bed and pulled her gently into his arms.

Softly, he brushed the hair from her face. "Angel," he whispered. He feathered a hand down her cheek and repeated her name again.

She groaned and he shook her. "Come on, Angel, wake up. Come back to me."

At last, her eyes fluttered open, glazed and cloudy. He watched the slow march of recognition as she tried to focus.

"Sharkman?" Her voice came out reed-thin, the word slightly slurred. Concern cramped his chest. She raised a hand to his face as if testing that he was real, and he covered the cold fingers with his own, pressing them against his cheek.

"It's me, Angel. Are you all right?"

She struggled to sit up, then collapsed back against him.

"Not . . . feeling well," she said, and ran her tongue over her lips.

"What happened? What are you doing on the floor?"

"Fell."

He let that pitiful explanation stand as her eyes closed again.

"Okay, Angel, let's see if you can get up." He tugged her to her feet, and when she swayed, he caught her to him. "Whoa, steady there."

He held her close, feeling her curved softness, the shape that had haunted him for days, and desire ripped through him.

Cut it out, Carver. Get your mind out of your pants.

As if she heard his thoughts, her eyes blinked open and her old defiance flickered through the green fog. "What . . . why are you here, Sharkman?" She smiled, a small, crooked tilting of her lips that squeezed his chest with concern. "Checking up . . . on me?"

Christ, she felt boneless against him. "What happened to you?"

"Couldn't get away. Sorry. Knew you'd be . . . mad."

He eased her onto the bed, stroking the hair away from her face. "I'm not mad." But barbed tendrils of worry pricked him. "What happened? What's wrong with you?"

She took a long time to focus. "Water," she croaked out at last.

A blue bottle stood on the nightstand next to the bed, the same kind of bottle Borian had brought with him to the Governor's Ball. Finn looked around for a glass, found one on the floor, and poured a finger's worth of water into it.

"Here." He held out the glass, but she pushed it away weakly.

"I thought you said you wanted—"

"No good."

"What's wrong with it?" He brought the glass to his

lips, but before he could tilt back, she'd lunged at him, knocking the glass out of his hand. "What the—"

The effort cost her and she ended up sprawled face-down on the bed. She groaned and the sound sent his fear spiking upward. He dropped down beside her and helped her turn over. Her green eyes closed, then opened. Something about their groggy appearance, about her slurred speech nagged at him. She looked and sounded almost . . . drugged.

His chest tightened and he glanced around, eyes lighting on the bottled water. Slipping something into it would be easy.

"Drugged," she whispered. "Water . . . drugged."

Her confirmation slammed into him with the force of a bullet. Only one explanation why she'd be drugged. Borian knew who she was and what she was doing here. *Christ and all the angels.* Without another thought, he scooped her out of the bed and into his arms.

"What . . . are you doing?"

"Getting you out of here." He started for the door.

"Wait. Put me . . . down." She squiggled faintly, trying to escape.

"Your cover's been blown, Angel. Why the hell they didn't just kill you . . ." He swallowed, thankful for whatever stupidity had left her alive.

"Can't go." She groaned against him. "Got things to tell."

He stopped just short of the door. "What things?"

"Think . . . found your stuff. Not stables. Locked room. Funny kind of . . . computer on the door."

The hodgepodge of words rocked him, all the more because he hadn't expected her to actually do much of anything, and every day she had. And now here she was, hopped up to within an inch of her life, spilling out intel that any ten-year vet would have been proud of. A wave of admiration raced through him and he tightened his hold on her.

"That's good, Angel," he said gruffly. "Good job."

The long speech had worn her out and her head had sunk against his chest. Now her eyes met his and through the cloudy gaze he saw a glimmer of something—pride or gratitude. Triumph maybe. Whatever, he didn't care. Once again, she'd earned his praise. "Thanks, Shark . . . man." Her eyes drifted closed. "Put me . . . down now."

But he didn't want to put her down. He liked the feel of her in his arms, supple and round through the thin white gown. He spied a ruffled armchair covered in a girly floral print, and he sank into it, still holding Angelina. The chair swung forward under his weight. A rocker. He settled her on his lap, her head resting on his shoulder, and rocked gently.

"Can you start from the beginning? Go slow. Tell me everything."

She snuggled up against him and he repressed a groan. Even sick with drugs she smelled wonderfully feminine, felt warm and soft. His fingers tingled with her nearness and he wanted to run his hands over her. But she was distraction enough, caressing her would only breed more. So he held her and listened, trying to fill in the blanks of her halting speech while he quietly rocked her in the moonlit room.

He took a moment to sift through her faltering report. She'd come up empty on the stables and hadn't searched the guest house or staff quarters—though they were a long shot. "Tell me about the lock on the door of that room. You said no one is allowed in but Borian?"

"Mmm." She nodded slightly. "Numbers. On a box."

"A keypad?"

"Mmm."

A metal door, closed with an electronic lock. A door that was out of the way so it wouldn't be spotted, that was off-limits to everyone. Out of all the leads, this had the most possibilities. "Could you draw me a picture?"

"Try."

"Good girl." Still holding her, he stood, then put her gently back on the rocker. He checked his pockets, but aside from a spare clip for his gun, he found only a couple of power bars—no pen and no paper. He'd run out of the damn mine without his notebook, another sign that he'd lost his perspective. But when Angelina hadn't shown up . . .

He stifled the memory of panic and refocused his efforts. Glancing around the room, he saw the tray that held the blue water bottle, grabbed the linen napkin off it, then riffled around the dresser for a pen. The best he could do was a tube of lipstick that had rolled behind a vase of flowers. He cleared the tray, upended it in her lap, and placed the napkin on top. Then he knelt in front of her and handed her the makeshift pencil.

She took the golden tube with wobbly fingers and peered closely at the label. "Rose Dawn. My favorite."

"Really?" He couldn't help teasing her. "I thought you were more of a Red Siren girl."

She threw him a small smile. "Former life. Now . . ." She leaned against the back of the chair and closed her eyes. She looked sleepy and drained, and his heart constricted.

"Now you're the Rose Dawn type," he prompted.

"Life is change." She made an effort to sit up, then twisted the lipstick open. "A Bic . . . would be cheaper."

"Yeah, but I'd have to go out for one."

She smiled wanly, and another surge of respect went through him. God, she was tough. And smart. And so achingly beautiful in the room's dim moonlight. Even wired and dozy, she looked good. He swallowed the sudden rush of feeling and stood, gesturing to the napkin.

"Do the best you can. I'll take the drawing and see if I can get a decoder for the lock."

She sketched out the keypad with shaky strokes, stopping frequently for brief respites. In the end, she'd done a good enough job for him to take it for analysis. They'd get an expert to look at it and figure some way in.

He looked over at Angelina. Eyes closed, she was breathing softly, the lipstick still in her fingers. He stared at the face he'd been seeing in his mind, and at her feminine form outlined by the flimsy gown. He remembered the feel of her body, the silky skin and lavish bow of waist and hips. He ran a shaky hand through his hair, pushing desire away.

Truth was, right now lust felt almost . . . sacrilegious. He laughed to himself, never believing he'd use that word in relation to Angelina. But she looked so young and vulnerable at the moment, almost asleep in the old-fashioned rocker. Moonlight glazed her face, softening the brittle veneer and leaving behind the girl she must have been once. A stab of anger pierced him at the thought of what had happened to her. If that small-town sheriff were here, Finn would strangle him with his bare hands, not to mention the bastard who'd hurt her in the first place.

Not that Finn was any better. Sending her here, putting

her in danger. This was *his* job, *his* mission, what *he'd* been trained for. She should be miles away, polishing her nails and driving every man in sight crazy.

Smiling slightly, he eased down beside her chair and gently extracted the lipstick from her grasp. Her eyes opened at his touch.

"Be better soon. Finish."

He looked up at her. Whatever they gave her wasn't deadly . . . yet. Maybe if she didn't ingest more, she'd be all right.

Maybe.

Did he want to take that bet? She was a civilian, his responsibility. She was doing him a favor, doing her country a favor. How far could he let her go? "Sorry, Angel. We have to get you out of here."

Her eyes, hazed and druggy, stayed on his. "Stay."

"Borian knows who you are."

Her head sifted slowly from side to side. "No. Wants me. Wants wife back."

He knelt in front of her and took her hand. He knew he should keep his distance, but he craved the touch of her skin, the solid reality that she was here where he could watch over her. "You can't stay. It's not safe."

"Can't find stuff . . . without me."

Fear gripped as the truth of this hit home all over again. Angelina was the only way they could get into the ranch, and therefore into the places where Borian could have stashed the plutonium. But Finn didn't want to admit it. "We'll find a way."

"What way?"

He didn't have a clue, but he didn't care.

And that scared him more than anything. He *should*

care. This was his job, why he was here. Why she was here. He couldn't let his personal feelings get in the way.

Her fingers squeezed his, the pressure feeble but there. "Need me."

A boulder settled on his chest. "Yeah." He sighed, reluctantly released her hand, and walked to the window. Another patrol was heading in their direction, and he ducked out of sight waiting for the light to pass. He cursed silently. All his protective instincts were on high alert, and that always meant trouble. But try as he might, he couldn't shake them off.

Reluctantly, he turned to her. "You'll stay until I come back with the decoder for the lock. A day at the most. If the plutonium is in that room, your job is over anyway."

She nodded. "'Kay."

"But you have to promise me something." In two strides he was back at the chair, kneeling in front of her. "No water unless someone else is drinking from the same bottle. If you're thirsty, use tap water." He searched her face to make sure his words were getting through. "Do you understand? I can't leave you here unless I know you understand."

"Understand. No water. Except . . . tap."

"Good." He brushed the hair away from her forehead, drinking in the sight of her. "Before I go, I'll wash out the glass and refill the bottle with tap water. You do the same every time you come back to the room."

She nodded again. "The same."

"And no food unless it's what everyone else is eating. I left a couple of power bars on the dresser. If you're not sure about the food, eat the bars. If you don't ingest any more, whatever they gave you should be out of your system soon. And, Angelina"—he took her face in his hands to force her concentration on him—"you can't let them know. If they figure out the drug isn't working, they'll find something else to use on you."

She blinked, trying to stay focused. "Pretend."

"That's right. Can you do that?"

"Been . . . doing it."

Another wave of respect ran through him, mingled with a burgeoning fear at the base of his spine that he didn't want to face right now. "Yeah, I guess you have." Then suddenly he remembered the other reason he'd broken into the house. "One more thing. Victor has an appointment with a Dennis Copley tomorrow. Do you know him?"

"Dennis?" He could see her trying to focus on the name.

"He was at your wake for Beaman."

She nodded slowly. "Horses."

"That's right."

"Friend of Beamer's. Went to . . . Kentucky Derby. Sat in . . . his box."

Christ.

"Okay, look. Stay in bed tomorrow. All day."

She gave him a small, crooked smile. "No . . . problem."

"Let's hope Copley won't stay the night. But if he does, stick to your room. You're sick. It's as good an excuse as any, and it's true."

"I like . . . bed."

Was that a joke? If she could joke, she couldn't be as bad off as she sounded.

He stood and let out a huge breath. "All right, then. Let's get you into it." He slid his arms under her and lifted her off the chair. She snuggled against him, sending waves of heat through him. God, just the smell of her made him crazy.

"You coming . . . too?" she murmured into his neck.

He smiled inwardly. God knew he wanted to. "Not this time, Angel."

He laid her in the bed.

"No sex on the job for . . . straight-arrow Carver?"

He tried not to let the smile show and ruin her impression of him. "You know it's against my code of honor."

He settled beside her, tucking the quilt around her, and studied her emerald eyes, now dull as moss. Another icy flash of fear rattled him. How the hell could he make himself go?

"You don't have to do this, Angel. Why don't you just walk away?"

Her luscious mouth tilted up in a small smile as she closed her eyes. "Because I'd . . . miss you, Sharkman."

With careful precision, Finn slipped through the trees toward the checkpoint, trying not to remember that Angelina was still inside the ranch, strung out and vulnerable. The thought made him want to charge forward but he forced himself to go slow, senses on alert for the slightest sound. No point getting caught now. Her life depended on it. He picked his way in the darkness. A few yards, and the Jeep and two men, automatics cradled in the crook of their arms, came into view.

Going back to the mine would've been easier, but getting transport from there was tricky and slow, and he needed to get his test sample out as soon as possible. He felt around his pocket for the aspirin bottle he'd found in Angelina's purse, the one he'd rinsed out and filled with a sample of the tampered water. He'd told himself she'd be all right, but he had to be sure. And he'd promised to be back within a day, so speed was essential. Mike and Jack were the fastest way out. They were due for a shift change in a few hours and he could hitch a ride back to town with them and deliver her drawing and the water sample.

He ducked behind a tree as a patrol Jeep passed by. The second Jeep stopped at the first and the driver called out.

"Fall back. We've had reports of a prowler and everyone's ordered up to the house for reconnaissance."

Finn stopped breathing. He swore he'd made it out with no one the wiser.

A big man with a clipboard jumped out of the first Jeep. "That's crazy. No one could get by us. And if there's a prowler, someone should guard the gate. Who gave the order?"

The man in the patrol Jeep thumbed over his shoulder toward the house. "Came from up there."

That seemed to stem the other guy's resistance. He grumbled, but turned the car around and wound toward the ranch house, the second Jeep following.

Now that was a lucky break. Maybe Borian wasn't as smart as everyone thought. Still as stone, Finn waited until both cars disappeared, then took a wary step toward the unguarded gate.

Behind him, the crunch of tires on gravel warned of a vehicle approaching from the ranch. Quickly he ducked behind a large rock. A black Suburban bumped over the path toward him. The all-but-invisible driver slowed as he neared the gate, then pulled into the trees until out of sight. The engine grumble cut off and a car door opened and closed. Heavy footsteps tramped in the underbrush.

Moments later metal scraped on metal like a latch lifting, and a slow, mechanical whoosh followed.

Whoever was in the car had opened the gate. Were they checking the outside perimeter? Looking for him?

He peered out from his hiding place into impenetrable darkness. The footsteps faded toward the highway, leaving him wondering who, if anyone, was left inside the car.

Trapped, he muttered a curse. How many more obstacles would he encounter tonight? He had to make sure Angelina was okay and the fastest way was to get that water sample to the lab at headquarters where it could be analyzed.

Eyes on the road, he strained to hear any sound that would tell him whether it was safe to venture out. Had he screwed up and revealed his position? Teeth on edge, he sat motionless, listening. Nothing but crickets and wind fluffing trees.

He'd tried checking in with Mike and Jack before he left the house, but couldn't get a signal on the sat phone. Now, he unhooked the phone, punched in the number, and waited for someone to pick up.

No one did. Wasn't the damn thing working?

His head snapped up as footsteps crackled in the brush again. He stowed the phone, listening, and like a movie going backward, the sounds he'd heard earlier repeated themselves in reverse order. The low, mechanical slide and metallic scrape of a latch, the click of a car door opening, the slam of it closing. Then the ignition turned over and the car backed up toward the ranch, setting off the way it had come, slowly, ponderously, wheels crushing gravel.

He stood rock-still. A cold sweat set in on his neck and

he shivered, waiting out the silence. Ninety seconds and nothing moved but the trees, topknots swaying. Sliding out from behind the shelter of his rock, he raced to the next, making his way toward the gate.

From the safety of the scrub line, he gauged how badly he'd be exposed once he stepped in front of it. But there was no help for it; an angel was counting on him.

A deep breath and he stepped out into the road, facing the gate in full view of anyone who happened by. His heart thudded in his chest, but he was concentrating so hard on estimating the height of the gate he barely noticed.

He leaped.

And landed halfway up. He scuttled the rest of the way as fast as he could, then dropped onto the road on the other side.

Dusting off his hands, he looked around quickly. The gate loomed unguarded behind him. If everyone was looking for him, they'd done a sad, sorry job of it.

He smiled to himself and scurried into the shadow of the roadside scrub. To his left he could make out the outline of the dilapidated shack across the road.

Ducking low, he slid through the rocky brush until he was opposite the hut, then jogged across the road and flattened himself against the side, easing slowly around to the front.

The old truck and rusty van were parked with their backs facing the shack. Finn took in the hay bales and pitchforks resting against the side of the pickup and wondered if Jack or Mike had dreamed up the props. Either way they were a nice touch.

He eased behind the pickup and over to the van,

rapped lightly at the back doors, calling low. "Hey—it's Carver. Let me in."

He waited for the sound of the lock turning, but nothing happened, and he rapped again. "Quit fooling around and open the door, Jack."

Nothing. He moved between the two vehicles and into the line of sight of the van's driver-side mirror, so they could see him. Since he wasn't where he was supposed to be he could only imagine what they were saying to each other. Nothing printable, that was for sure.

Returning to the van's back doors, he knocked louder. "Jack! Open the goddamn door."

He rattled the handle, but the door was locked. Muttering a curse, he slid along the driver's side of the vehicle.

His foot crunched on something and he shot a quick glance down. Visibility was nil, so he took out the penlight he always kept in his pocket and using his body to shield the glow, knelt and turned it on. The beam lit up a spray of broken glass at his feet.

He rose slowly, and the light rose with him, revealing the jagged remains of the driver's side window.

Jack's head lolled against the doorjamb, blood black against the light hair at his forehead.

CHAPTER
~15~

Finn sat grim-faced on the edge of a desk. The back room off the Helena airstrip was antiseptically clear of clutter, with only a couple of gunmetal-gray chairs and a steel filing cabinet to break the monotony of hospital-green cinder-block walls. Behind the desk, a broad window looked out over the airstrip, showing an empty runway and a bleak, overcast afternoon.

Roper stood with his back to the view, eyes sharp and focused on Finn. "Tell me again," he said for the umpteenth time, and again Finn repressed the acid rage of guilt blistering his heart and repeated what he'd seen forty-eight long hours ago.

"I saw the car, a black Suburban, pull into the trees. Someone got out. I heard footsteps, probably the gate lifting." Finn let the room's harsh bareness burn into his brain, whitewashing out the other sights branded there. Jack's lifeless eyes. The defensive wounds in the hands Mike had held up in a futile attempt to stop the bullet that killed him.

"Any sense of how big a person made the footsteps?"

Finn knew where his boss was going with this—
Grisha. Too bad Finn couldn't help out. "They were
footsteps. Scrabbling in the brush sounds. That's all." He
stood and shot a glance out the window. "Look, I can
guess as well as you can, but I didn't see whoever it was
and can't ID him."

Roper frowned. "Do you think Borian's men knew
you were there?"

Finn shoved away from the desk, fury making his neck
ache and grief taking up permanent residence in his chest.
"I don't know. Maybe. More likely Borian cleared the
area so no one could witness the car or ID the shooter inside."

He rolled his shoulders trying to loosen the tension,
and looked out the window again. No incoming planes
marred the horizon. He suppressed a growl and began to
pace the room, fear tightening the already tight ball of
panic in his gut.

Angelina was next. Every fiber of his being screamed
that she was in mortal danger, but the decoder was still en
route from Washington. A line of violent thunderstorms
had grounded the flight yesterday and today's arrival was
behind schedule. He scanned the glowering sky, reliving
the last few moments with her in the moonlit room. He
should have dragged her out of there by her hair.

As if reading his mind, Roper said mildly, "You
couldn't have known what Borian would do. Angelina
made the right decision to stay, and you did right to let
her."

"Tell that to her corpse."

Roper didn't respond, and Finn swallowed the nausea
that threatened to spew out his throat. He'd called the
ranch all day yesterday, and each time had been told that

Angelina couldn't come to the phone because she wasn't feeling well.

Not feeling well my ass.

But if Borian wanted her dead, he would have killed her not drugged her.

At least Finn could rest easy on that score. The water sample had turned up convallatoxin. The lab theorized that it was plant-derived, possibly from something as innocuous as lily of the valley, which was so toxic, even the water in which cut flowers were kept was dangerous. He remembered flowers in Angelina's room. Luckily, the sample contained only trace amounts, enough to sicken but not kill. If Angelina stopped ingesting it, she should be fine.

Unless the drug was only the first step. Maybe Borian needed more proof that the Feds were on to him. Maybe Jack and Mike were the proof, and now Borian would finish off Angelina.

Maybe, maybe. God, he was sick of the word.

They should have marched in there and hauled her out, case or no. Roper had gambled with her life and Finn had let him.

He peered up at the wide expanse of empty sky and ran a hand through his hair.

Christ.

Mike had two kids, and Jack . . . God, Jack.

Grief squeezed the back of Finn's throat. He'd protected Jack once only to fail him now. Immediately the pictures rose in his head. Jack's all-American grin, the crazy clothes. His endless gratitude. Finn nailed up the memories behind tight, closed shutters. If he let himself remember, he'd go crazy.

A black dot in the sky caught his attention. Instantly,

he fixed on it. The dot grew bigger, took the shape of an airplane, and dipped toward the runway.

His breathing sped up. "They're here."

Roper came to stand beside him at the window, his head barely reaching Finn's shoulders. Like Finn, he stood silent, watching the plane land. When the wheels touched down, he spoke, gaze glued to the runway. "The car is waiting. You're all set."

"Yeah." Finn adjusted the silk knot at his neck, straightened the sleeves of his suit coat. "I'm all set."

Payback time.

Angelina pushed the food around her dinner plate, avoiding the worried look on Marian's face as well as the concern she sensed in Victor. Her headache was finally gone and she felt stronger than she'd felt in days, but a hazy memory in the back of her mind told her not to let anyone know.

Instead, she forced herself to appear wan and lifeless, which was slowly driving her nuts. She'd spent most of yesterday sleeping off the effects of whatever she'd been given, and hugged her room most of today. She'd heard that Dennis Copley had delivered his stallion, but she'd managed to avoid all contact with him.

Last night she'd sneaked down to the guest house and searched it, but nothing had turned up and so far, she hadn't figured out how to maintain her sick act and also investigate the staff quarters during the day when they'd be empty.

Time was running out; a relentless metronome in her head beat out the seconds. Where was the plutonium? The smart money was on the locked room, but only Finn could open it, and he hadn't shown up yet. She'd expected him before now and couldn't help the small bud of worry nestled against her heart.

If he was coming and she hadn't dreamed his visit.

"It's good to see you're feeling better," Victor said, sliding a solicitous hand over her wrist.

She'd had to break her promise to Marian and let Victor know she was sick. As her aunt had predicted, Victor had turned into a nightmare of solicitude, hovering like an anxious parent, which made no sense as he knew damn well why she was sick.

She smiled at him, a thin affair that she hoped conveyed the effort she was making to hide her supposed unsteadiness.

"Eat a little more," he urged. "Get your strength back."

Then again, who could understand the ways of a twisted mind? She'd heard of people who induced sickness so they could nurse the patient back to health. Maybe Victor was one of them.

Obediently, she picked up a small forkful of mashed something or other. The vegetable had been served from the common bowl, so she guessed it was all right. Isn't that what Finn had said?

She thought back to two nights ago, trying to fix on a solid memory. Had that really been him standing there in the darkness? Had he picked her up and carried her, held her in his arms, rocked her?

Her hand shook at the possibility, and she put down her fork. Not that it mattered. Borian would only think the drugs were working better than she let on.

Gently, he pushed the water glass toward Angelina. "Some water will make you feel better." But the water had been poured before Angelina sat down.

"Thank you." She picked up the glass, and oops . . . let

it slip through her fingers. The crystal tumbled to the tabletop where the clear liquid soaked into the cloth. "Oh, I'm . . . I'm sorry."

Marian's smile was sympathetic. "Never mind." She called for a maid, who came with a towel to mop up the mess. "Fill Miss Montgomery's glass, please," she directed when the maid had finished. The maid did as instructed, filling Marian's glass from the same pitcher.

Safe to drink.

Angelina swallowed the water, wishing for a Coke with lots of rum in it. She looked at Victor and wondered what he'd say if she asked for one. "Degenerate drink. Weakens your essence."

Her essence. Part bad girl, part good girl yearning to be free. Would she ever figure it out?

Scuffling sounds in the hallway interrupted her thoughts.

"Take your goddamn hands off me—" A grunt, like someone had been punched in the gut, a muffled curse.

"Hold him!" Heavy footsteps, and three men burst into the dining room—Grisha, one of Victor's camouflaged goons, and between them, Finn, one arm wrenched behind his back.

Oh, my God. Her lungs backed up. She hadn't seen him in days, and for a moment all she could do was drink in the sight of him. Trapped and imprisoned, black hair disheveled, he looked wild-eyed and nothing like the cool, lethal operative she was all too familiar with. But at least he was back in uniform now, though his tie was askew and his shirt stretched across his chest.

Did they know who he was? Did they know about her?

Mouth dry, she watched Victor rise, his deep-set eyes sparking with anger. "What's going on here?"

Finn jerked away from the camouflaged man's hold, but he couldn't escape Grisha. "Tell Mr. Universe here to let go."

His face was taut, and she wanted to shout at them to release him. But instinct told her to sit still until she knew more, and she clawed her slacks underneath the table to keep from leaping up.

"He came to the gate asking for Miss Montgomery," the camouflaged man blurted out, wiping sweat from his forehead. "When he was told she was unavailable, he rammed his car through the checkpoint. We chased him up to the house."

Victor turned his piercing gaze on Finn. "Is this true, Ingram? You barreled into my home uninvited, upsetting my men and my guests?"

Finn flashed an appeal her way. "I tried calling for two days and no one would let me speak to you. They said you were sick." He seemed to be wilting under the pressure, but something she sensed below the surface made her think it was all an act and he was in complete control. He turned his attention to Victor. "The governor placed her in my keeping. She's my responsibility and I wanted to make sure she was all right." He squirmed again and Grisha wrenched his arm, making the muscles in Finn's jaw clamp down in pain.

"Victor, please," Angelina said quickly, unable to bear it any longer. "Stephen meant no harm. He was only thinking of me." She left her seat and crossed to the huddle of men at the doorway. "Grisha, let him go." She put a hand on the big man, ignoring the play of massive musculature that underscored his ability to inflict harm. He looked for directions over her shoulder and she assumed he'd got them, because he dropped his hold and stepped back.

Glowering at Victor, Finn rubbed his shoulder.

"I'm sorry, Stephen," Angelina said in a low voice. "Are you all right?" She looked deeply into those wicked baby blues and thought she saw a gleam of approval. She took a breath and scanned the group, playing along "I . . . I don't know what got into everyone. What an awful way to greet a guest." She spoke as if apologizing for Victor. "Have you eaten? Please, join us." She turned to Victor with a smile of entreaty, and was met with a moment of silence. Victor frowned. He wasn't pleased, but she knew he could hardly refuse without provoking questions he wouldn't like.

"Marian," Victor snapped, "set another place."

Marian rose immediately. "Of course." She disappeared into the kitchen.

"Thank you, Grisha," Victor said. "Have the men resume their posts." The two men wheeled around and left, but she knew Grisha went only as far as the hallway outside the dining-room entrance.

A few moments later Marian returned with a maid carrying plates, napkin, and a place setting of wood-handled silverware. They all watched in silence as the place was set, and then Finn sank into the seat, pulling up his chair roughly.

"You would have thought I was some kind of criminal." He straightened his clothes, jerking his coat sleeves back in place.

"I'm so sorry." Angelina watched him closely for signs that she'd gone too far or not far enough. "Victor is just trying to protect us."

"You hardly need protection from me," he grumbled.

"I don't believe we've met," Marian said in a soothing voice. She extended a hand to Finn. "I'm Victor's sister-in-law, Marian."

She saw the lightning-quick, almost-imperceptible narrowing of his eyes as he placed her.

"Forgive my manners," Angelina rushed in. "This is Stephen Ingram, an aide to the governor."

Finn took Marian's hand and nodded briefly. "Under other circumstances, I'm sure it would be a pleasure."

"I hope you'll forgive us, Mr. Ingram. As Angelina said, we're very isolated out here and Victor is careful. We're just doing our best to keep safe in an unsafe world."

At that moment, a maid scurried in with platters of food that she offered to Finn. He waved them away.

"Marian's right," Angelina said, an idea jumping into her head. She placed a hand on Victor's arm. "But surely you know that Stephen is harmless. He's my friend. In fact, why doesn't he stay a few days? There's plenty of room and I'd love to show him some of the ranch. I'm afraid I've been neglecting my work on land use, which is the reason I came all the way out here."

Victor frowned. "Are you sure you're up to that? You haven't been feeling well, remember."

"I feel much better. Really."

Victor exchanged a look with Marian. "I'm sure she's fine, Victor." Marian's voice was crisp. "These things last a few days and run their course. You're smothering her."

Unconvinced, Victor leaned toward Angelina. "You know how precious you are to me. If something were to happen to you . . ."

"I'll be fine." Angelina spoke low. "Please, Victor. It will make me feel useful."

A beat, while he scrutinized her, thinking it over. The silence seemed to stretch forever and during it her heart pounded loud enough to be heard all the way in Memphis.

Finally, he sighed and gave her a small pat on the arm. "All right. How can I refuse you anything?"

A weight lifted. Finn was here, and he would stay. She smiled, putting all the gratitude and appreciation she felt into it. "Thank you, Victor."

From that point on, dinner was a blur. She did her best not to stare at Finn, but her whole body felt newly awake. Eager to talk to him, she was thwarted by Marian and Victor, who never left them alone. At the stroke of ten, Victor shepherded her off to bed, while Marian showed Finn to his room. As always, Victor kissed her palm at the doorway, a tender gesture that never failed to disturb her.

"Rest, *milaia*," he said softly. "I'll be back to say good night."

Don't hurry. Don't even bother.

But she smiled as if his return would be a comfort she looked forward to. Slipping into the room, she spied an apple-green peignoir waiting on the bed. With a silent whimper of exhaustion, she closed her eyes, but when she opened them, the gown still lay pale and chaste, another memento of the woman Victor wanted her to be.

Reluctantly, she removed the clothes he'd sent that morning. As she undid the pins that held her chignon together, she saw herself in the mirror. For a moment, she stared at a stranger. Who was that quietly elegant woman in the ivory silk sweater and pearls?

She shook out her hair and the image cracked, reminding her of the other Angelina, the one who took control and fought back. But when she slipped into her mother's silky green peignoir, that other Angelina seemed far away. The light, floaty material slid over her body, making her feel weightless, like a ghost. Like she wasn't there at all.

She glided to the bed and her gaze lit on the blue bottle of water on the nightstand. A voice that sounded like Finn's reminded her to empty it in the bathroom sink and refill it with tap water. As the water gushed out of the bottle, a quiver of awareness rippled through her. Finn was here, close. Soon she would see him.

But not before she would see Victor. Shuddering, she refilled the bottle, dried it with a bath towel and replaced it on the table next to the bed. Victor would come, and soon he wouldn't be content with kissing her hand and caressing her face.

But when the door handle rattled, then opened, it was Finn who slipped in.

For a moment her world stopped. He looked so good, so real and solid in his white shirt. He'd taken off his suit coat, opened the shirt collar, and loosened the burgundy tie. His throat against the white cotton looked strong and tan. The sight of him released something warm and liquid inside her. Was he all right? Had Grisha hurt him?

She stopped breathing to gaze at him. His dark face was awash with hunger, blue eyes alight with it. His gaze raked her body and though she was wearing the most conservative nightgown he'd seen her in, she felt naked beneath his stare, as if he knew her heart was racing, her pulse quickening, her blood heating.

"Hello, Sharkman," she said softly. "Are you all right?"

He closed the door and leaned against it. "You don't think I'd let a caveman like Grisha do any serious damage." His eyes searched her face. "How about you, Angel? Feeling better?"

She tilted her head curiously. "So you *were* here the other night."

"Don't you remember?"

She shook her head. "My head is all fogged over. I thought . . . I thought you might have been a dream."

The barest hint of a smile touched his lips. "Some women think so."

She found her own mouth slanting up at his conceit. "Not me."

"No. Not you."

All at once, he moved toward her, and her feet responded of their own volition, steel drawn to a magnet.

"Any trouble with Copley?"

She shook her head. "I played invalid." But she didn't want to talk about Copley. "You held me that night, rocked me in the chair."

He admitted nothing. "I tried to get you to leave."

"But I wouldn't."

"Not until I came back with a way into your locked room."

"And did you?"

They met in the middle of the room, close enough to touch, to breathe the same air, to kiss.

"Yes." His gaze fixed on her face and her heart crashed against her chest. She was drowning and didn't care. He'd come for her because he'd been worried about her, and he'd let her stay because he had faith in the job she was doing. She felt giddy with happiness.

A soft rap on the door pulled her out of the surf. "It's Victor," she whispered.

Finn's face changed, hardened, cooled. "Coming here, to your bedroom?"

Another knock. "*Milaia*, it's me."

"Milay—"

"It's Russian. It means darling or dearest or something."

She looked around desperately. Where could she put Finn?

"Darling?"

"Just a minute, love," she called.

Finn's eyes were like two ice picks. "Love?"

She ran to the closet and swung open the door. "Get in."

"Nice work," he said in a low voice, and she pretended she hadn't heard the sardonic tone.

"For God's sake, Finn, he can't find you here."

"No," he said with a trace of resentment. "Of course not." He ducked into the closet and she pushed the door shut, but he stopped her from closing it all the way.

Victor's voice came through the door again. "Is everything all right?"

She tore into the bed, pulling the covers up demurely. "Come in."

Victor stepped in and scanned the room suspiciously. "I thought I heard voices."

"Voices?" She smiled faintly. "No, I . . . I had a bit of a headache and was in the bathroom with a wet cloth."

His face immediately took on an expression of deep concern, and he crossed to the bed. "I'm sorry you're not feeling well again."

"Oh, it's nothing, really." She put a hand to her head, rubbing the right temple, hoping she was convincing enough.

"Poor baby." He settled beside her, pulling away her hand and taking over the job himself. His gaze scoured her face, engulfing her, morphing her into the woman he wanted her to be. "Wait a moment," he whispered, then rose to turn off the light.

Returning to the bed, he leaned back against the headboard and opened his arms. "Come here." He drew her against him and darkness enveloped her.

Stomach heaving, she lay rigid, inhaling his suffocating aftershave and trying desperately to relax. But all she could think about was Finn a few feet away. Could he hear? See? Was he as sickened as she was? For a crazy minute, she hoped he would burst out and tell her she didn't have to lie next to Victor, touching him, letting him touch her.

But Finn didn't burst out of the closet. He didn't tell her to stop. He remained quiet and hidden because that was his job.

And this was hers.

"Do you remember how I used to hold you like this?" Victor murmured against her forehead. "It feels so good to hold you again."

Her heart squeezed, but she played along. "I know."

He kissed her temple, just below the hairline. "*Milaia*, you must get well. We have so much to do, and I need you beside me."

She swallowed her aversion and forced the words out in a soft whisper, hoping they would lead him to tell her what she wanted to know. "I want to help you, Victor. Tell me how I can help you."

"By getting well. I couldn't bear it . . ." His voice cracked, and he paused to clear it. "You must get well. I want you by my side always."

Yes, but for what? "I won't leave you. Ever again. I promise."

"Oh, God," he whispered. "*Dusha moia, radost'moia,* my heart my joy." His mouth trailed downward, over her cheek and onto her mouth. Her soul contracted at the touch of his lips, but she opened her mouth to him. She had no choice. This was her mission. This was what Finn wanted her to do. But she never dreamed he'd be there, listening, watching.

She endured Victor's kiss just long enough to make it real, but no longer, then gently pulled away. Tenderly, she ran a hand down his face.

"Tell me about your work. Tell me how wonderful it will be when we're working side by side."

He pressed her face against his chest, holding her tight. He was trembling. "Tomorrow, when you're feeling better. You must rest now."

Disappointment surged, but she quickly hid it. What more would she have to do to earn his complete trust?

A lot. The thought lodged in her throat like a lump she couldn't swallow, but sadly, she sensed she'd succeed. Victor was edging off the cliff that would bring him to her. A touch, a caress, the right whispered word might push him over. Tonight. It could happen tonight. Now.

But not with Finn listening.

Then Victor kissed her forehead lovingly, and the moment passed.

He rose, but before he left, he poured a glass of water, guiding her hand in the darkness. "Drink as much as you can. The water will strengthen you." He kissed her palm, rubbing her hand against his cheek, then left.

She stared down at the glass in her hand, feeling the weight of it in the darkness. Was the drug supposed to make her more compliant, more willing to submit to him? A wave of acid humor shook her.

She was all his. That's what she was here for. No chemical inducements necessary.

She put the glass of water on the nightstand, switched on the bedside lamp, and sank back against the pillows.

Deep in the recesses of the closet Finn stood rigid with tension. A thick, spicy fragrance filled his senses as the sound of two people on a bed filtered in. He heard their words, heard the sounds of lips smacking, and suddenly, the stink inside the closet was choking him. Pictures whirled in his head. Mouths together. Limbs entwined. Jesus Christ, Borian was going to . . .

Shut up and do your job. She's doing hers.

And getting the worse end of the deal.

A bitter wave of guilt washed over him. Unbidden, a picture of the first time he'd seen her rose in his mind. Body-hugging white dress with plenty of skin showing, drunk and gyrating for a pack of drooling men.

The closet closed in, so stultifying he almost couldn't breathe. But he suspected now what he hadn't considered then. That the dress had been a costume, as much a disguise as the clothes he'd made her wear for Borian. Underneath hid the fragile woman who'd been viciously hurt and would do anything to protect herself from that pain.

And he'd asked her to do the very thing that would hurt her again. To give up control to someone else and act the whore for him.

A constricting vine of nausea spread over his belly. His hand jerked, about to shove open the closet door, when the bed creaked. Someone stepped off. Water splashed in a glass. A murmur of good nights. The click of a door latch and then light flared beneath the rim of his hiding place.

Blood churning, he opened the door.

She lay against the pillows, eyes closed, and he remembered how she'd looked the other night when he'd carried her in his arms and put her in the rocking chair. Sweet and innocent in the moonlight.

Drugged and half-dead.

God, the things she'd endured because of him. And those that could still be on the horizon. An image of Jack's bloodstained head flashed in Finn's mind. Automatically, his hand balled into a fist and a muscle twitched in his jaw.

"Are you all right?" The question came out rougher than he'd intended, but the anger was at himself not her. Too bad she didn't know that.

She opened her eyes, darted a glance his way, then focused on the blanket at her lap, smoothing it out in nervous repetition. "Just dandy," she said with her familiar sarcastic edge. "How about you? You . . . look a little green around the edges."

She was fishing for comfort and absolution, and they were about the only thing he could give at the moment. He sat down beside her with a crooked smile, trying to make light of the situation. "I'm fine. Always wondered if I'd take to that Peeping Tom stuff."

"And . . . did you?"

He felt the tension vibrating her body, the held breath as she waited for the slap across her face. Instead, he covered her hand with his, gently ending the compulsive rubbing. "No," he said gruffly.

She turned her hand in his, gripping it. And suddenly

his arms slid around her and she folded into him, clinging like a limpet.

"Did he hurt you?" He held her close, his fingers threaded in her golden hair. "If he hurt you, I'll kill him, I swear it."

"No," she said in his ear, her voice sending ripples of heat through him. "He's barely touched me. Tonight was the first time . . . the first time he—"

Finn pulled away to look at her. "Then you haven't sl—"

Quickly she shook her head. "No."

A wave of relief clogged his throat, but she looked down at her hands. "But maybe that's why he hasn't told me where the plutonium is." An embarrassed blush stole up her neck and into her face. "You wanted me to get close. I guess . . ." She shrugged, then confronted him squarely, though he could tell it cost her. "I guess I haven't gotten close enough."

Silence descended, broken only by the moan of rising wind rattling the windowpane. Another storm was brewing, mirroring his turmoil. He wished he could scoop her up and carry her someplace where she'd be safe and protected. Where Borian would never touch her again.

"Maybe you won't have to," he said, trying not to let her see how desperately he clung to that hope. "My money's on the locked room. If we get in and find the plutonium, your job is over." From his pocket, he took a small black box, no bigger than a jeweler's ring box. "Here's the sequencer. We hook it into the keypad on the door and it will search for the locking combination."

He handed the box to her, his fingers accidentally brushing hers. She tensed at his touch, and something sharp buzzed through him.

Take her somewhere safe? Yeah and then bury himself inside her. Christ, he was no better than Borian.

"So when do we go in?" She handed the box back, and he noticed the slight tremor in her fingers.

"Tonight. We get in, we find what we're looking for, we get out."

He expected her to collapse in relief; getting out of there should have been her first priority. But instead, her green eyes looked troubled. "And then what? You get what you want and everyone lives happily ever after?" She threw the covers off, slipped out of bed, and walked toward the window, arms crossed defensively. "I've been there, Sharkman, and it doesn't work that way. You told me Victor's done favors for powerful people. With connections like that he could get away with anything."

"Not anything." *Jack. Christ.* But he said nothing about Jack. They had a big night ahead and he needed her sharp and focused. "This isn't small-town Texas, and I'm not some fat guy with a belly and a tin badge."

Her back was hunched and he stole up behind her, wanting to ease her tension, touch her, take comfort from her.

But he didn't dare. If he touched her now, he wasn't sure he could stop. And after what Borian had almost done . . .

He slid around until he faced her. She was frowning at the floor and he slipped a knuckle under her chin to tilt it up. "Borian will get what's coming to him. Trust me."

She searched his face, her expression part hope, part doubt. "I want to, Sharkman." She gave him a small brave smile. "More than you know. More than I should."

CHAPTER
~16~

The house was eerily still as Angelina led Finn down a stealthy path toward the north wing and the hidden corner where she'd found the locked room. The wind that had kicked up hours ago had ripened into a full-blown electrical storm, and she jumped at a boom of thunder.

"Easy," Finn said in a low, tight voice. "It's just thunder. If we're lucky the sound will cover our search."

To blend into the shadows, he wore a black hooded nylon windbreaker that had been packed into a tiny square that fit neatly in his pants pocket. Just before they left her room, he'd shaken it out and pulled it over his shirt and head, covering every speck of white. She had changed her clothes, pulling on her black jeans-and-sweater SWAT girl outfit. She'd even covered her hair with the scarf Finn had demanded. But she still felt exposed, the dead animals on the wall casting shadows in the dim glow of muted night lighting, shadows that seemed to follow her everywhere.

She and Finn had spent the last few hours going over the plan for the night in soft, low tones that wouldn't carry into the hall. Since she hadn't been able to map the north wing for him, she'd have to lead him to the locked room. He'd asked minute questions about the route, the habits of Victor, Marian, Grisha, and the rest of the staff, and made her describe the passage down to the room in endless repetition.

It had been torture. Every last minute of it.

Finn looked so damn good, so clean and strong. His crystal-blue eyes had fired her blood, his lean, dark body set off a rocket inside her. The bed was there, she was there.

But he hadn't touched her. He'd kept the dresser between them, the bed, the closet door. And when he couldn't find a piece of furniture to hide behind, he stayed on the other side of the room.

And coward that she was, she let him. For once, she didn't tease or tempt. She didn't ask herself why, she didn't want to know. Instead, she described her fruitless search of the guest house, the words as good a barrier as any he could come up with.

Until finally they'd drifted into a taut, awkward silence, he on the floor below the window, she across the room on the rocking chair. She tilted back and forth, her fingers clutching the arms. But white-knuckled as they were, they still burned to touch him. Even her fingernails felt hot.

Now she cut a glance his way. He was focused dead ahead and her heart skipped a beat. Something about the sight of him saving the world set her bad-girl heart racing. She'd always been a sucker for a nice guy, and try as Finn might, he couldn't completely hide the nice guy beneath the bastard.

She smiled to herself in the dark. She hadn't dreamt

him in her room the other night. He'd been there, tender and soft, the glow of admiration in his eyes. And not just for her body, but for her. For the person she was becoming, the person she could be.

Prove him right, party girl.

God, she wanted to. Desperately. And tonight . . . she had a feeling it would be tonight. They'd find the plutonium and prove Victor an accomplice to terror. And she wouldn't have to sleep with him to do it. Nervous excitement fluttered through her, the kind she imagined an actor felt just before the curtain goes up, minutes away from applause.

A flash of lightning buzzed neon as they came to the long, window-lined hallway that led to the north wing. Reflected glow from exterior lights just barely illuminated the way. Aside from being caught by someone inside the ranch, this was the most dangerous part of their journey. Through the glass, a patrol could catch them clearly in a searchlight sweep.

At the edge of the corridor, Finn pulled her back. Cautiously, he gestured her toward the wall opposite the glass, as far away from the windows as possible. He put a finger to his lips, then used it to point straight ahead, signaling that he would take the lead. She nodded and followed as he slipped into the passage. Heart pounding, her gaze fixed on his strong back, she slid soundlessly across the wide expanse of wall. The wind shrieked and somewhere a window rattled. To her right the night loomed through the long window, a dark, thick wraith ready to spring at her.

Suddenly, she was jerked off her feet, face shoved against the wall. *Finn.* Pressing her into the wood with the force of his body.

Her heart leaped into her throat. "What are you—?"

"Shh." His hand glided over her face to cover her lips. Out of the corner of her eye she saw a glow of light through the window. *Patrol.*

The light advanced, the shine increasing. Finn pressed in closer, blending them into the shadows, one hand over her mouth, the other imprisoning her between the wall and his body.

At last the searchlight faded, and he released her. Slowly, he turned her to face him. His big hands stroked her from forehead to chin. She closed her eyes, terrified that the softness of his touch meant something real. "Okay?" he whispered.

God, no, she wasn't okay. She would never be okay as long as he was around. "Fine," she whispered, and escaped into the darkness at the end of the glass hallway, darkness that would swallow up the flush that still heated her whole body. As if to underscore the havoc inside her, a clap of thunder split the air.

A few minutes later she slipped into the narrow passageway that led to the locked room. He was right behind her, so close she could feel the heat he generated. The path was even darker than it had been the first time she'd been there; they were deep in the bowels of the ranch, visibility zero, thunder a muffled thud. She dreaded going down the dark hallway with Finn's smell and body so overwhelmingly near. But just as she was about to turn and push him the hell away, he clicked on a tiny penlight and took the lead again.

When they got to the door, he shone the light on the lock, running his fingers over the keypad. He took out the black box and removed the sequencer inside. Kneeling, he peered up at the underside of the lock, then gestured her down beside him.

"Keep the light there." He handed her the light and aimed her hand. Her stomach fluttered at his touch, but she quickly suppressed the feeling to concentrate on the task at hand. Using a minuscule screwdriver he pulled from his pocket, he unscrewed the housing, then slid on the sequencer. He fiddled with the fit, muttered a low curse, then rocked back on his heels.

"Got it," he whispered, and pressed a switch she couldn't see. "Turn off the light."

In the sudden dark, a series of greenish numbers appeared. They seemed suspended in the air, but she knew they were embedded into the sequencer that was now attached to the lock. The numbers tumbled slow at first, then faster and finally too fast for her to follow as the device searched for the combination that would open the door. At last, one number fell into place and stopped rolling. Then another and another until a six-digit code hung ghostly in the dark. Finn switched on the penlight and punched in the code. A whirring sound, clicks, and when Finn pushed, the door swung open.

The room was dark as a tomb but ripe with a familiar scent.

"Jesus," Finn breathed. "It smells like that damn closet. What the hell *is* that?"

"My mother." The hair on her arms stood on end. The place smelled as if it had been bathed in her spicy fragrance.

"What do you mean?" Finn closed the door, then slid the narrow beam of light to his left and found a wall switch, which he flicked up.

"That's her"—Angelina blinked as light flooded the

room—"perfume." Then her eyes adjusted and she gasped, clutching a hand to her chest.

"Oh, my God," Finn said, slowly lowering the windbreaker hood to see it all.

She'd expected ugly linoleum and army-green file cabinets, metal desks and computers. Instead, the room was lovely in a spare, almost Asian way. Blond oak gleamed beneath her feet in a perfect square. In the center stood the room's only piece of furniture: a lacquered black bench, circular and unadorned. But on every wall, covering every vacant inch, were pictures of Carol Borian.

"He's crazy," Finn said quietly.

"Crazy with grief."

Angelina heard the despair in her voice; she could taste the disappointment. Without looking, she knew they'd never find the plutonium here.

She slid the scarf off her hair, letting the black silk pool around her neck, and stumbled to the low bench where she sank down before her rubbery legs gave out.

Numbly, she stared at the walls. In the middle of each a wide, central panel of fine, pale wood rose from floor to ceiling, a simple motif that set off the pictures on either side. Carol on horseback, around the lake, in a Jeep, in front of the porch. From poster size down to tiny snapshots, her mother smiled, laughed, threw her head back in joy, or pouted like a little girl. Every incarnation, every mood, every expression, alive on four walls.

Alive. Angelina's heart beat a rapid, painful tattoo. Her mother was alive. Here. Everywhere she looked. Laughing, teasing, having fun. *Happy.* God, she seemed so happy. And so real. Angelina could barely look yet couldn't tear her gaze away.

"We won't find anything here," she murmured.

But Finn was already running his fingers up one of the wood panels. "How do you know?"

"This is a church," she said. "A shrine. Don't you see?" Slowly she circled around, engrossed in the collective images. "It's the Carol Borian Memorial Chapel. He wouldn't do anything to put it at risk. Believe me, there's nothing here we want."

Finn paused in his exploration of the wood panel and came over to sit beside her. "I know this is a shock. It's not what we expected. You're probably right, but it doesn't hurt to look."

She shook her head. It did hurt. It hurt very much. "We've already stayed too long."

"The door's closed, there's no windows. That passageway is a good thirty feet from the main section of the house. We're safe for five more minutes." He pushed a stray piece of hair behind her ear. "You don't have to do anything. Just sit here while I look around."

But she couldn't bear that either. Action was better than sitting and brooding. "No, I'll help. Tell me what to do."

He pointed to two walls, one in front of her and one to her right. "Take those two. Look for seams that shouldn't be there, hidden latches, breaks in the plane of the wall."

Slowly, she rose and crossed to the right-hand wall. Fingers skimming over the surface, she felt around as he'd instructed. As she did so, her fingers brushed over her mother's face countless times and she wondered what it might have been like to do that for real. To touch her mother. To have her mother touch her.

Would she have claimed Angelina? Approved of her? Loved her?

The questions sent a pang of longing through Angelina. She'd never know. If she wanted someone to love her, she'd have to look elsewhere.

Elsewhere.

To her left, Finn's lean, dark shape seemed to loom larger. *Someday you're going to want me for real, Angel.*

Had someday come? Queasiness fluttered through her and she pushed the thought away. She glanced at him; he was gnawing the inside of his lip and staring hard at the wall to her left.

"Think you could ever love someone this much?" she asked.

"This isn't love, it's obsession. And it's what happens when you give too much of yourself away."

Even now, when she knew Finn had relented toward her, when he'd been on the verge of appreciating her for more than her measurements, even now, he kept his distance. "Is that how you view love?" she asked quietly. "The fastest route to losing yourself?"

He tore himself away from the display and shot her a pointed look. "Don't you?"

Touché, Sharkman.

She moved on to the next wall, running her hands up the side of the wood panel and expecting to find more of the same—nothing. But almost immediately, her fingers slid over a mechanism, tripping it.

With a silent lurch, the panel began to move.

"Finn!"

He took one look, saw what was happening, and raced across the room. Pushing her out of the way, he dragged her backward to the opposite wall, putting his own body between her and whatever was on the other side of the sliding door.

"My God, what is it?" Her heart was climbing up her throat.

"I don't know, but until we do, we stay back."

She stared at the ponderous glide of the panel, unable to accept that she'd been wrong about Victor. He couldn't have hidden the plutonium here. She could not believe it. She clutched at Finn's arms, fingers digging into the taut muscle. But the panel didn't hide a safe or a shelf with a container of nuclear material. Behind the door stood a . . . she didn't know what it was. Some kind of metal sculpture? Silver in color and tall as a man, it was capsule-sleek in shape with a three-dimensional design all over the surface. From here it looked like . . . like flowers. She blinked and peered closer at the top end of the sculpture, where a thickly paned window cut into the front.

"Stay here," Finn said.

No argument there, Sharkman. She watched him approach the thing.

"What is it?" He didn't answer and she began to get even more jittery. "What the hell is it?" She stepped forward.

"Don't!"

She stopped immediately.

"Don't come any closer." Something in his voice sent a chill skittering up her spine.

"Why? What's wrong? What's in there?"

He turned, his face ashen. "Your mother."

CHAPTER
⥼17⥽

Angelina's breath caught in her throat. Had she heard wrong? "My—"

In two strides, Finn covered the space between them. He pulled her into his arms, deftly turning her so her back was toward the window and the thing inside. "Remember the journal you found?" He spoke low and hushed into her ear. "It was about cryonics. That's the science of freezing human beings in the hope they can be revived sometime in the future when whatever killed them can be cured. This is some kind of cryonics tank. Your mother's been . . . Christ, Angel, she's . . . she's inside."

"In there? Her body is in there?"

"Look, Angelina—"

"Oh, my God. My God." She broke free and stumbled toward the container.

She could hardly breathe; her mind was on some kind of permanent lockdown. She put her hands on the tank, and cold steel bit into her fingers. Beneath them, frozen flowers extruded from the metal. Daisies. Perfectly shaped silver daisies. Her mother's favorite flower.

Eyes burning, Angelina stared at the body encased in liquid clear as gin. The window was double-paned, distorting the face behind it, but she didn't need a sharper view. She would have known that face anywhere.

Tears formed at the back of her throat.

It was her own face.

Her own, yet different. Pale and unearthly, like a Hollywood alien, yet so human, so very, very human.

Mother. My mother.

"That's what he meant," she whispered. "About immortality. About eternal life."

"That's what who meant?"

"Victor. Oh, God. He talked about vanquishing death. I thought he meant the plutonium, that he was going to perpetrate some great evil that would make him famous. But he was talking about this."

A great sadness weighed her down. She laid her face against the chilly glass window, as if somehow she could send her life force through it and receive Carol's in return.

I'm here, Mother. Can you feel me?

But it wasn't her mother who reached out. Not her mother who touched her head with a warm, comforting hand.

Finn.

"I have to search it," he said gently, stroking her head as though she were a child.

"God, no. He wouldn't hide it here. He wouldn't do anything to jeopardize what's most precious to him."

"I have to look anyway."

She closed her eyes and, nodding, stepped away. Carefully, he ran his hands up the sides of the tank, over the top, and around the back.

It was like desecrating her grave.

He examined the alcove, found pipes leading from the tank to a supply of liquid nitrogen. That's what her mother was swimming in. A sea of cool, clear liquid nitrogen.

She shuddered, tears burning behind her eyes.

At last he turned, empty-handed. "We should go."

She didn't want to go. She wanted to press herself against the tank, embrace the cold, dead steel, and somehow bring her mother back.

But she didn't. She stood quietly as he found the mechanism and the door slid closed over the steel cage imprisoning her mother's body.

And then Finn was there again, holding her, lending her his strength and his comfort.

"Are you all right?"

Not really. But she could be as brave as he was. "I'm fine." Yet on top of the shock and grief was the quick clutch of failure. Her failure. She squeezed her eyes shut as though somehow she could squeeze the truth away. "The plutonium isn't here, is it?"

"Doesn't look like it."

She let out a huge breath, feeling as though she'd let everyone down. "What now?"

He shook his head grimly. "We get you out of here. You can't pretend the drug is working indefinitely. Borian may decide to take other, more drastic steps."

Like strangling you in your sleep, party girl. She pushed that anxiety away, but it was soon replaced by another. She could still take Borian to bed. Sex for secrets.

A lump of cold settled in her stomach.

"He won't." She hugged herself, not wanting to face

that next, inevitable step. "He wants his wife, and right now, I'm the only way back to her."

"No." The word was deadly soft. She looked up to find his face set in hard, determined lines. "We'll find another way to get to Borian."

"There is no other way."

"You've done enough. You're my responsibility and I'm not losing anyone else."

Anyone else? "What do you mean? Who else have you lost?"

He glanced down as if debating with himself, then back at her, clearly weighing her ability to withstand whatever the hell he was about to say.

Alarm crawled along her spine. "What is it? You're scaring me."

He sighed. "Jack and Mike are dead."

"What?" All the blood in her body seized up.

"I found them in the shack the night I left you, two bullets to the head." He mimed shooting her in the temple. "Neat, quiet. Like sitting ducks."

"Oh, my God." Horrified, she backed away, tears clogging her throat all over again.

"Now you see why I can't let you stay. He'll be looking to you next."

Stunned into silence, she staggered against the wall and sank to the floor, a balloon slowly leaking air. She thought of Jack's warm brown eyes, Mike's easygoing grin. *Dead.* She could barely take in the idea.

Drawing her knees up, she laid her chin on top, trying to keep the iceberg in her chest from growing. Finn was right; the enormity of the risks had just multiplied a thousandfold. She should go. As far away as she could get from this house of death.

"Come on, let's get out of here before we overstay our welcome."

But she couldn't move; she felt so cold and heavy, a hulking block of ice. "You still need me, Sharkman."

"Not if you're dead I don't." He extended a hand to help her up. "Come on, let's go."

She ignored his hand and despite the chill creeping up her back, confronted him calmly. "Victor already has one dead wife; you think he's looking for another? He won't kill me."

"You don't know that." Without waiting for her help, he pulled her to her feet. He looked old and hollow, and she wanted to comfort him, but the only comfort he needed—to let him persuade her to leave the ranch—she couldn't give.

"Look at this room. It's a shrine to a dead woman. I'm that woman come to life. You said it yourself, he's obsessed with her, with me." She put a hand on his arm, felt his heat seep into her. She was so cold. "Don't you see? He wants me. I'm the dead ringer."

His eyes locked with hers, his face gray as stone. "Don't do this."

"We don't have a choice."

"I can get you out. Now, tonight."

"And then what?" She smiled at him, a pitifully sad twist of her lips. "You let him sell that stuff? Let some crazy make a bomb and use it?" He had no answer, his face angry and miserable. "What would Roper say? Would he want me to leave now?"

He recoiled the merest fraction but it was enough to tell her she'd hit a bull's-eye. "The hell with Roper," he snapped.

He'd left his penlight on top of the bench and she crossed over and picked it up.

"What are you doing?" He barked the question, fear rimming his voice.

I'm sorry. She started for the door, but he grabbed her wrist. "Where are you going?"

She twisted out of his grasp and continued into the dark passageway. She turned on the light and started running. He called after her, a low rasp of anger and anguish, but she didn't stop. She couldn't. Victor was waiting.

"Wait a minute! Wait a goddamn—" Finn cursed and dashed out the door, forced to stop and lock it, remove the sequencer and shove it back in its box in his pocket. By then she'd disappeared.

Christ.

If Borian caught her, if a patrol caught her . . .

Panic rising, he plunged into the darkness, desperate to find her before she did something stupid, something that made his gut clench and his throat squeeze shut. Stumbling blind, he wasted precious seconds and finally burst out into the main hallway.

He ran up the corridor, made a wrong turn, and forced himself not to shout. Where the hell was she? Lightning flashed through a window and thunder broke against the house, adding to his confusion. He closed his eyes and reached for calm, visualizing the route to her bedroom in his head. Left, then right, then right again. He retraced the path and found the stairs leading up to the second floor. She was almost to the top. He bounded up two steps at a time and caught her halfway down the hallway.

Breathless, he grabbed her by the arm. "What the hell do you think you're doing?" he whispered.

"Let me go."

He tightened his grip. "Not on your life."

"Let me go! Borian's room is right there. He'll hear us."

"Not if you stop fighting me." Immediately, she stopped struggling. "Good. Now listen—"

She broke away, dashing down the hall toward her room.

"What the—" He chased after and dived into her room in time to see her take some floaty thing out of the closet. A nightgown.

His chest tightened. "What are you doing?"

"What's it look like I'm doing?" She laid the gown on the bed and started to wrench off her black sweater.

He jerked her hand away. "Don't."

"Don't what? Don't find out what Borian's up to? Don't prove he's got the plutonium? Don't do what you asked me to do?"

He grabbed the nightgown from the bed and shoved it in her face. "Don't do *this*."

She plucked the gown out of his hand and cradled it against her as if stanching a wound. "Why not, Sharkman? Isn't that what I do best?" She raised her chin and faced him bravely, green eyes edged in a bitterness that he knew was aimed at herself as much as at him. "Isn't that why I'm here? To get him into bed so he spills all his secrets?"

Finn fought for patience, every nerve under rigid control. "You're here because I recruited you. You're under my orders, and what I say goes. And I say you're out of here." He grabbed her arm and tugged her toward the door.

"Get your damn hands off me!" She jerked away, then

rounded on, him. "I didn't come here to risk *my* neck, and *my* goddamn virtue, only to be sent away like a homesick kid at camp."

"It's not up to you!"

"The hell it's not! I'm the only hope you've got."

"I don't care."

Her eyes widened in surprise. "You don't—"

"I don't care!" He sank onto the bed and raked his fingers through his hair, his gut churning with the realization that he'd blurted out the truth. "I don't care how desperately the TCF needs you. I'm not going to be your pimp. I'm not going to sit here and let you whore for me. I'm not going to do it. We'll find another way."

Then the surprise was on him because her face kind of . . . crumpled. The luscious lips trembled, the chin she'd bravely stuck out lowered. He'd seen those gem-bright eyes fill with contempt, with anger and challenge, but this was the first time he'd seen them fill with tears.

He rose and stepped toward her, his heart doing a little crumpling of its own. "God, Angel, don't," he said softly, reaching out to wipe away the first splash of tears.

But footsteps sounded and his hand froze midway.

"Don't what?"

Finn whipped around. Borian stood in the doorway, tying the belt around a silk bathrobe. Frowning, he looked from Finn to Angelina and repeated his question. "Don't do what?"

Before Finn could come up with an answer, Marian hurried in. Also dressed in a robe over nightclothes, she peered around the room, wary concern on her face. "What's the matter? I heard voices."

"Nothing's the matter. Everything is fine," Finn soothed.

Borian's eyes narrowed suspiciously. "What are you doing in here, Ingram?"

"Nothing. I was just—" He stumbled, searching for an excuse, but his brain wouldn't work. What had Borian heard? And below that, like a dull pulse leading straight to his heart: were those tears of happiness or hurt?

"He was just . . . just checking up on me." Angelina tried to smile, but didn't quite succeed.

"At three in the morning, and in your bedroom?"

Borian turned on Finn with an angry glare. "This is outrageous. You barge into my home, wrangle an invitation to stay, and then upset my guests." His face softened as he turned toward Angelina, but his expression still held an air of mistrust. "Are you all right? What are you doing up this late? You should be in bed."

She looked down, put a hand to her brow. The gesture made it seem like she had a headache, but it also hid the telltale signs of tears. A shaft of respect tore through Finn; upset as she was, the woman didn't miss a beat. "Yes, I'm . . . I'm fine. I just couldn't sleep."

Not so fine, Angel. Slight tremors ran across her shoulders and she bit her lip as if to keep emotion at bay. Surreptitiously, he fisted his hands, itching to put his arms around her.

"Why are you dressed like that?" Marian's sharp voice pulled his attention from Angelina to the other woman. She was eyeing Angelina closely. Too closely. "Victor's right, you should be in bed."

Angelina looked down at herself, and his gaze followed. The black jeans and sweater she'd put on to steal through the house suddenly seemed completely out of place. As did his windbreaker. In fact, they were better suited for . . . He leaped at the excuse.

"That's what I told her when I ran into her in the hallway, but she was adamant about going down to the stables for a ride."

"A ride? On horseback?"

"I . . . I couldn't sleep." Angelina picked up the story in a shaky voice. *Nice work, Angel.* "I thought some fresh air would help."

"But the"—Borian's gaze skimmed the water bottle en route to the window, then quickly returned to Angelina—"the storm." He frowned, and Finn cursed silently. *Great thinking, Carver.* Of course, Borian would wonder about the damn water and why the drug wasn't working. But Angelina appeared frail enough at the moment; maybe Borian would assume she hadn't drunk enough to knock her out. God, he had to get her out of here. Sending her out into an electrical storm wasn't the smartest idea, but at least it would get her out of the house, which was all he cared about at the moment.

"You see? That's why we were arguing," Finn said. "I told her it was crazy to go out in this weather."

Angelina raised her chin with a stubborn glare, one he knew well. "It's just a headache. Riding will clear it up."

"But, my dear," Victor said, "it's the middle of the night."

"I know what time it is!" She looked from one to the other, settling at last on Finn. Tears still blazed in her eyes; she was on the verge of breaking down.

Go, he pleaded silently. *Take the excuse and run.*

But the bright eyes bored into him on high beams. "I'm a grown woman. I make my own decisions. I don't need permission to leave or stay." And she ran past Victor and Marian, and out the room.

"Angelina!" Victor turned to run after her.

"Victor, don't!" Marian tugged him back, and he yanked his arm away, but it gave Finn the seconds he needed.

A swift stride, and he stepped in front of the doorway, blocking the exit. "Let her go."

"Get out of the way," Borian growled, but Finn didn't budge. Borian's eyes narrowed to slits. "I thought you wanted to stop her."

"I did. But she clearly wants to go. And she's right. She's a grown-up. If she wants to go for a ride in a thunderstorm, why the hell shouldn't she? You saw how upset she was." Christ, that was thin, but anything was better than having her face Borian right now. He had to buy her time.

"Yes, and I blame you for it," Victor snapped. "What did you say to her? She never behaved so strangely before, and she certainly never cried."

"I didn't say anything. I told you, I tried to stop her."

"You have no business being here at all."

"If you hadn't barreled in, I might have persuaded her to go back to bed."

Marian put a soothing hand on Borian's arm. "The important thing is that she's safe. Do you ride, Mr. Ingram?"

"Why do you think I've got my windbreaker? If I couldn't talk her out of the ride, I wanted to go with her."

"Excellent idea. If the storm gets worse, she may need help finding her way."

Victor shrugged off his sister-in-law's touch. "Don't be ridiculous, Marian. If anyone goes, it will be me."

Marian's face tightened. "It could get dangerous out there. We can't risk losing you."

"Get out of the way, Ingram."

"She needs time alone."

"Victor, please—"

"I said, get out of the way."

By now Finn hoped Angelina would have had time to get out of the house; he stepped aside, bowing to Victor with a small flourish.

Borian shoved past him with a growl and rushed toward his room. Marian scurried after him, but the woman stopped at the threshold when he slammed the door in her face.

She looked back at Finn, mouth compressed in fury. Even from a distance, the heat of her hatred scorched him.

Poor Victor.

"Good night," Finn said calmly, and shoving his hands in his pockets, he sauntered away, leaving Victor to the wrath of his sister-in-law.

CHAPTER
⇜18⇝

Angelina raced down the porch steps, desperate to put distance between herself and everything inside that house.

Her mother's pale, fragile body encased in metal, Victor's suspicious eyes, Finn's abrupt about-face, and Jack . . . God, Jack and Mike . . . She couldn't think with so many images pinballing around her head.

She tore off, not caring where, unwanted tears pricking her eyes.

Dammit, party girl, you're tougher than this.

Not when it came to nice guys. She was a chump when it came to nice guys, and Finn had just been more than nice. In a million years she never would have thought he'd ask her not to sleep with Borian. She would have laid odds in Vegas and bet on it herself, a sure thing. She swiped the tears away with an impatient flick of her wrist. Why the hell couldn't he stay the bastard he was?

She ran toward the stables. The idea of a ride had been a straw Finn had plucked out of the air to appease Victor and Marian, but now it seemed the perfect way to escape the suffocating atmosphere in the house. And she needed escape, needed it like air to breathe.

If she'd been home, she would have put the top down on the Thunderbird, gunned the engine, and driven that machine to hell and beyond. But she wasn't home. She was stuck in the wilds of Montana. A horse would have to do.

Thunder rocked the heavens just as she put a hand on the stable door. She hesitated. Despite the lie to Victor, she couldn't take a horse out. Not in a storm at night.

Dammit. Dammit to hell.

She backed off, backed away, desperate for a safe place. A place that wasn't filled with men who wouldn't stay in the neat little boxes she wanted them to. Her feet picked up pace, she turned. And started running.

God, don't think. Just move. Run. Fly. Faster than ever before.

A cloudy moon lit the way, and night air brushed against her face, urging her to run faster and farther, as if somehow she could outrun herself.

But she couldn't outrun the pictures in her head.

Death. It was all around her now. Jack, Mike, Carol. Would Angelina be next?

Heart lurching, she bent into the wind. *Don't think about that. Don't think. Don't think.*

By some miracle she avoided Victor's patrols, and at last slowed to a fast walk. Heart thudding with exertion, she took in huge gulps of cool, bracing air, rich with the scent of pine. Thunder rumbled ominously but the chaos in the heavens seemed a pale reflection of the turmoil she was feeling. God, her brain was a muddle. Her mother. She'd been close enough to touch and yet still so unreachable. What was Angelina supposed to do with that?

Nothing. Take it on the chin, like everything else.

And Finn . . . The coldhearted cops she knew would never have sacrificed their assignment for her. Tears stung the back of her eyes. She thought she knew Finn Carver. A man who put duty first, a man married to his job. And now for some inexplicable reason, he wanted to throw that away and put her first.

"What do you think, Momma?" Angelina sniffed back the tears and looked up at the dark, snapping sky. "Should I let him do that?" Another clap of thunder. "Yeah, didn't think so."

Besides, someone had to save the world.

But what if saving the world meant losing Finn? Or worse, her life?

A chill settled in the middle of her chest. You pay your money and you take your chance.

Some chance.

She buried that thought. She couldn't worry about her personal safety. That was a risk she took when she signed on.

But she hadn't bargained on the other risks. On Finn.

Not that she ever had him to lose anyway. The familiar contempt hadn't appeared on his face lately, but what did that matter? He still thought her the worse for wear, didn't he?

Then why had he held her after he'd emerged from the closet earlier in the evening, and after she'd looked with horror and grief at her mother's body? Why had it felt as though she were precious cargo, treasured in his arms? At the memory, warmth rippled through her, liquid and dreamy. She remembered the tenderness in his face, the caring in his hands. She remembered . . .

Thunder cracked like a slap, bringing her back to her

senses. What was she doing? She'd lost herself to the giddy joy of a man once before, and been paid back with a vengeance. Like Finn, Andy Blake had been handsome and compelling. The town hero, a god who reached across the heavens for her. She wouldn't fall for that again.

She slowed to a stop. The air crackled with electricity; it smelled of earth and dust, of things older than time. In the presence of the ancient mountains, she faced the truth.

Finn was no Andy Blake. If he'd been your average asshole, he'd have taken what she'd freely offered over and over. But he hadn't.

Dumb, stupid cop.

Sweet, wonderful man.

She swallowed past the lump in her throat. Would Finn still want her after she'd been with Victor?

A gust of wind kicked up, blowing back her hair and sending earth and leaves at her face. She ducked her head against the debris and turned around. Finn may have given her the chance to run, but she couldn't take it. Not if she wanted to keep her self-respect.

Even if it meant losing his.

Heart heavy, she started back the way she'd come. A spear of white light severed the sky, exploding into an ear-splitting crash just over her shoulder. She leaped, turning and ducking instinctively. Her left foot slid sideways and for half a second she rocked, unbalanced, the outline of Devil's Teeth imprinted in white neon in the back of her eyes. Then the ground slid out from under her and the night went black.

The moment Finn was out of sight, he slipped down the passage and out of the house to the yard below. Marian may have been eager to have him go after Angelina, but Victor was another story. Finn didn't want a further confrontation with Borian, so he kept a low profile while he searched the area around the stables for Angelina. No luck there, so he headed for the garage where he hoped to find his car. He'd barely taken two steps when Victor and Marian burst onto the porch, both fully dressed and arguing. Quickly Finn ducked into the shadows below the porch.

"I had a groom check the stable," Marian said. "She didn't take the mare. None of the horses or cars are missing."

"She's on foot. That means she can't have gone very far."

"Let her go." A porch light showed her face distorted into a pleading scrunch. "Ingram is right. If she's crazy enough to go out on a night like this, what can you do?"

"Find her and bring her back." Victor pressed his lips in a grim line as a flash of lightning lit the sky.

A Jeep screeched to a halt, and one of Borian's goons jumped out.

"Any of the patrols spot her?" Borian asked.

"No, sir." The man hurried around to the passenger side and opened the door. Marian put a restraining hand on Victor's arm, but he paid no attention,

"Get Grisha," Victor said to her. "The men will search for her."

"They'll never find her in the dark," Marian said. "Why not wait until morning?"

Good idea. Give me time to find her.

But Victor wasn't buying it. "I don't want to hear your dire predictions, Marian. Do what I say."

Marian looked as if she'd been slapped, but she scurried away without protest. Finn swung around to do like-wise, but Victor caught sight of him.

"You're not welcome here, Ingram. Go."

"Not until I make sure that Angelina is okay."

"I'll see to that. Pack your briefcase and go before I have one of my men throw you out."

Fine by me, pal. Getting out was priority numero uno. But not without Angelina.

Finn retreated to the stairs as Victor shouted orders to his goons.

"Assemble the men. I want Miss Montgomery found immediately. Bring Mr. Ingram's car around. He's leaving."

Finn ran into the house, gathered his things and slipped out unnoticed in the tumult. Men were pouring in to receive instructions, then teeming out again into the night. His car arrived and he threw his briefcase into it, climbed in, and headed toward the gated exit. But instead of leaving, he drove into the trees. He retrieved a denim shirt, a pair of jeans and hiking boots from the trunk, grabbed a flashlight and his nine-millimeter from its hiding place under the spare tire. Then he covered the car's rear end with branches so it couldn't be seen from the road.

He changed in a flurry of quick, jerky moves, eyes pinned on the road. Once again the checkpoint had been cleared and the road was open. He dashed across, heading west. He hadn't gone far when the first drops of rain fell, quickly followed by a torrent.

Hair plastered to his head and water streaming over his eyes, he plunged on. The downpour would make finding Angelina harder, but that worked against Borian as well. Finn had no idea what had happened to her, but he sure as hell wanted to get to her before Borian.

If it was the last thing Finn did, he'd get her out of there alive and in one piece.

Drops fell on Angelina's face, increasing quickly to a cascade. She blinked her eyes open and moaned. For a few minutes she remained flat on the sodden earth, moving limbs in silent inventory. Nothing seemed to be broken. Slowly, she rolled onto her side and then sat up, bruised muscles making her groan. Lightning flashed and in the quick brightness she saw that she'd slid down a small ravine.

Terrific.

She tried her legs and found they would hold her. Through the now-raging downpour, she clawed her way back up the slope, clutching at scrub and brush for purchase. With a final grunt, she flung her arms onto what felt like a flat plain and pulled herself up and over, collapsing on her stomach and breathing hard.

Lying in the pelting rain, she remembered Finn's penlight and fished in her pocket to see if she still had it. *Lucky night.* She hauled herself to her feet and turned it on, but the narrow beam was almost useless against the thick curtain of rain. *Not so lucky after all.* She couldn't see a thing, had no idea where she was or what route would get her back to the ranch safely. Remembering the deep canyons Victor had shown her on the ranch tour, she stood still. Better to get drenched than take off in the wrong direction and walk off a real cliff.

She shivered, water soaking her hair and dripping down her back. But she welcomed it as a kind of retribution. *Come on, rain, wash my sins away.* She closed her eyes and held her face up to the blind, impenetrable sky, and the needles of rain hammered down on her.

For the sin of believing in possibility.

For the sin of hope.

For the sin of wanting to be better than I am.

Heal me. Cleanse me.

Thunder crashed on top of her. She snapped her head back down and forced herself to remain motionless. At last, the lightning came. In the seconds it lit the sky, she tried to pinpoint her location. The only familiar landmark was the three-headed shape of Devil's Teeth. Her own teeth chattering, she began walking toward it.

"Angelina!" Finn's shout vanished into the hammering beat of rain. Half a mile from the ranch, he stood in the flood, feeling like Noah abandoned by his ark. Jesus Christ, it was like her to disappear in the middle of a deluge. She'd been a royal pain from the start.

But what a pain. He wiped his face with his forearm and was immediately soaked again. She'd taunted and teased and challenged his very soul, and the worst of it was, he'd liked it. A lot.

You're in over your head, pal. Way over.

Maybe he was. But right now he didn't care. All that mattered was finding her safe before Borian did. So far, he hadn't run into any patrols. He hadn't run into anything, and that kept the icy tentacle of fear coiled in his chest.

"Angelina!" The storm swallowed his bellow, but shouting helped keep his imagination at bay.

Lightning cracked across the sky and thunder roared in his ears. The tentacle tightened. Was Angelina out in the open, exposed to the wind and the rain? As a boy, he'd once seen someone killed by lightning. It wasn't something he wanted to see again.

He sank into a mud hole up to his calves, and cursed.
He should have thought to steal a Jeep. At the rate he was
going he'd take all damn night to find her, which gave the
advantage to the more mobile Borian. And if he found her
first . . .

Finn didn't want to think about that. About what he
knew Angelina would do. He'd seen it in the stubborn set
of her jaw and the determined slant of her shoulders.

The thought of her with Borian curdled Finn's stomach. It would hurt her. It would be like Ruby, Texas, all
over again.

Would it?

An image of his wife rose in his mind. A dozen times
she'd pleaded for a second chance, had sworn things
would be different, blubbered all over him until sooty
streaks of mascara ran down her face and stained his
shirt, but in the end she always went back to the men and
the drugs.

Give it up. Angelina is not Suzy.

Damn right. And thank God for that.

He stumbled and almost landed flat on his face. A
glare of the flashlight showed a protruding rock. He continued on, but the near-accident brought home the danger,
and the fear. What the hell had happened to her?

Ropes of hair clung to Angelina's face and neck. Her
feet squished in the muddied earth and the downpour
thrashed in her ears, blocking out all other sounds.
Blinded by dark and rain, she crawled her fingers over
endless rock surfaces. The mine entrance was here,
dammit. Somewhere. She swallowed water, coughed, and
inhaled the wrong way. Half choking, water raging at her

face, she kept on, and suddenly her hand grazed scrub instead of rock, branches instead of boulders.

The entrance.

Heart drumming, she pushed her way through twigs and brush and finally stumbled past, sopping, bedraggled, and drowning in relief.

Shivering, she huddled in the cool, dry dark to catch her breath. Water dripped off her and plopped as it hit the rock floor. She retrieved the penlight from her pocket and switched it on. Free of the downpour, it gave off enough light to see the familiar inside of the mountain and the wooden supports left when the mine had been abandoned. Without Finn to distract her, she noticed what she hadn't before. That the place was falling down around her. Some of the supports looked sturdy enough, but others were bent and partially collapsed. She bit her lip, wondering how safe the mine was. Not too. A little nudge and it looked like it would all come tumbling down.

Let's pray the big bad wolf doesn't huff and puff tonight.

Shuddering with cold, she moved inward toward the campsite, where Finn's things were neatly stowed.

Thank you, Sharkman. Thank you, thank you.

Quickly she found the lantern and turned it on, creating huge shadows that played on the mine's jagged walls. Quaking uncontrollably, she rummaged through Finn's supplies until she located a couple of blankets, then shucked off her wet clothes and spread them over an outcropping in the wall, hoping they'd dry a bit. Using one blanket to towel off, she wrapped the other around her, figuring she'd stay until morning when she'd have enough light to find her way back to the ranch. She sank to the ground, pulled the sleeping bag on top of her, and leaned against a smooth spot on the mine wall waiting for the goose bumps to subside.

Slowly, she warmed up. The sleeping bag smelled like Finn and she tugged it tight around her, burying her face in his scent. God, she wished he were here. Wished they could have one night together before she had to return to the ranch. One night to see if she could fire his cool blue gaze and find out if the risk she'd be willing to take was worth the hurt it might produce. She closed her eyes, dreaming of him, and dozed off.

She woke with a start, her heart banging against her ribs. Someone was there. The crazy thought that her mother's ghost had followed her flew through Angelina's head. Irrationally, she sniffed the air for her perfume, but all she smelled was earth, rock and rain.

The sound came again. Footsteps. If Victor or his men found her here, they'd find the equipment and know what she was up to.

Heart flying, she doused the lantern, plunging the mine back into darkness, then scrunched against the wall to make herself as small as possible.

CHAPTER
~19~

"Angelina."

Ears tuned to the smallest sound, she picked up the familiar tone of the whisper. She gasped. "Finn?"

"Where are you?"

"Back here with your stuff."

She relit the lantern and stood. Then, like a miracle conjured from her dreams, he was there. Gilded by lantern light, bedraggled, drenched from head to toe, but looking better than she'd ever seen him. The ever-present suit was gone again, replaced by his cowboy clothes. Rain-slick jeans and a denim shirt molded to his body, outlining its hard, lean shape. Long legs, strong thighs, capable hands, muscled arms. She swallowed and hugged the blanket close, suddenly aware that she was naked underneath.

He stepped toward her, then stopped as if he'd seen her heart jump beneath her skin. Or was experiencing the same.

"Are you all right?" he said.

She nodded. "Haven't fallen in a ditch in a while though."

"No broken bones?"

"Nope."

He let out a breath. "Good."

An awkward silence stretched between them. He looked like he was going to say more, then didn't. Instead, he ran a hand through his hair and wrung out the water.

"You can use this." She toed the blanket she'd dried off with earlier, and he picked it up, using a corner to mop up his head. His hand slowed for a moment and she followed his gaze to the outcropping where her clothes lay. Her panties gleamed lacy white in the dim light. They weren't the sizzling scrap of cloth she would have chosen for herself, but he went still anyway. Then the moment ended and he continued toweling his hair as though he hadn't noticed.

But he had. And that notice radiated liquid heat to all her nerve endings.

When he was done with his hair, he shrugged out of his shirt, pulling it over his head without bothering to unbutton it. "I have dry clothes here somewhere." He bent over the backpack, shoulder muscles rippling.

The wisp of heat that had begun deep inside began swirling through her like thick smoke.

"Here." He turned, extending her a shirt to wear, but all she saw was the plane of his chest, the wide shoulders and slick of skin between them. She licked suddenly dry lips and raised her eyes to his face.

His blue gaze locked on hers. Slowly, his hand dropped away. The clean shirt tumbled to the mine floor.

He came toward her, his eyes eating her alive, and then she was in his arms, clinging to his tight embrace.

"Christ," he whispered into her hair, "I was afraid you'd fallen off a cliff."

"How did you know where to find me?"

"Because I know you. You're smart. I'd head here, I figured you'd do the same."

The praise elicited a warm flush that blossomed over the heat he'd already generated inside her.

He tightened his hold. "Mmm. Smart and so damn beautiful I can hardly breathe around you." He pulled away to search her face. Desire lit his eyes. Desire and knowledge. In the space of a breath she knew he wanted her. Knew, too, that he wouldn't back out. Not this time. But still, a doubt lingered deep in the blue centers. "No games, Angel."

No games. A quick stab of panic darted through her. Was she crazy? God, she was. A huge part of her wanted to give up control and plummet recklessly, not caring where she landed as long as it was in his arms. Her mind formed the words, but her tongue couldn't get them out. "I don't know. I . . . I'll try."

He ran a finger over her lips and watched her shiver in reaction. "For real," he whispered. "Say it."

She swallowed, her heart beating fast enough to fly. "For . . ." Oh, God. "For . . . for real."

He smiled as if to say, that wasn't so bad. Then slowly, agonizingly slow, he lowered his mouth to hers.

She shuddered with the contact, warmth prickling over her body as his lips heated hers. His tongue invaded, liquid and hot, and her knees buckled.

He scooped down and lifted her into his arms, still kissing her. She groaned. "Don't stop."

"Not for a minute."

He lowered her to the floor and laid her against the rock wall. Unfurling the crumpled sleeping bag, he pulled her onto the makeshift bed, sliding her on top of him so the blanket she wore wrapped around them both, her breasts one with his chest, skin to skin. He framed her face with his hands and kissed her again, warmly, deeply.

And then he looked at her, his gaze as warm and deep as his kiss had been. "You're in control, Angel. This is all up to you. Whatever you want, I want."

Tears stung her eyes, blurring his face, and he used his thumb to wipe them away. "No crying. Tough guys never cry and you're the toughest guy I know." He kissed her eyes at the corners, where they were wet. "And the softest."

She blinked back the tears and kissed his mouth, his jaw, and the line of his neck. "You're pretty soft yourself . . . for a cop."

He growled low in his throat and pressed her into the hard bulge at the top of his thighs.

She groaned. "Maybe not so soft." She whispered kisses down his chest. Her tongue made a slick journey toward the top of his jeans, which she unbuttoned and pulled off. He was hard and ready, and she grasped him between her hands, feeling him from base to tip. He arched at her touch, inhaling a sharp breath. But he didn't pull her down or force her onto her back. She felt the tension in his body as he restrained himself, waiting for her. True to his word, he let her set the pace, lead the dance.

She closed her eyes on a sigh. He'd always be true to his word. That was what she liked about him.

She rubbed her hands down one muscled thigh. His feet and toes were damp from the rain, but strong and powerful, like the rest of him. She came back up the other leg slowly, letting her hands wander over every part of him. But when her fingers skimmed the ridge near his right hip, they stopped and retraced their path along the edges of a long scar.

"What's this?"

"Nothing."

"Doesn't look like nothing." She kissed the puckered line and he trembled. "What happened?"

"Long story," he whispered, pulling her up and stopping the questions with a kiss. "Another time." He brought her hand to his mouth, and she forgot about everything but the way blue fire intensified in his eyes.

The blanket fell away and her breasts swung freely. He touched them with a sigh of pleasure. The nipples stiffened, peaking under his attention, and he raised his mouth to them. Slowly he ran his tongue in warm wet circles, and she arched back so that his liquid touch was the only contact between them. Desire swirled inside her, hotter and higher, like nothing she'd ever felt before. Fear jabbed—*don't lose control*—but it faded as he buried his head between her breasts and held her as if she were sweet and precious.

And when he raised his head and claimed her mouth, she gave it to him willingly, wildly, wanting to drink in his goodness and make it her own.

"I can't wait anymore," she said breathlessly.

"Then don't."

She slid over him and they fused into each other.

A gasp escaped her as she sheathed him completely, the feeling a wonder and surprise. They moved together gradually, the rhythm drugging and powerful. She groaned, her hips working. God, she never wanted to stop. He felt so good. *Finn.* God.

Sweat slicked his shoulders and his neck. His jaw was tight with holding himself back. But she couldn't stop the dance, she had to go on and on, riding faster, the blaze sizzling inside her. He held on to her breasts, squeezing and fondling and sending flames shooting into the deepest part of her.

"That's it," he whispered hoarsely. "Come on, Angel. Spread your wings for me."

And suddenly the inferno was too much; she couldn't stop herself. Party lights shattered inside her, bright and glittery and alive in the darkness.

Breathing hard, she collapsed against his chest. His arms went around her, holding her, stroking. He kissed her forehead at the hairline, and she lay quiet in the circle of his arms.

And then the voice in her head started. *You lost control, party girl.* The words hissed and rattled. *You lost control to a loose cannon. To the first man you couldn't manage. You can't even manage your own response to him.*

She tensed, heart racing, but for an entirely different reason now. Fear settled like a shard of ice at the base of her spine.

And then, as if he'd heard the voice himself, Finn spoke softly. "It's all right." He stroked her back, soothing, gentling. "You're okay. I won't hurt you. We can stop anytime."

His hands glided over her, slow and easy. They made no demands, just gave warm, sure comfort. And as they moved, the tension oozed out of her until she lay languid again. Safe in his arms.

Safe.

Something she'd never felt before with a man.

Safe and free.

A great weightlessness settled over her, boundless and buoyant, like floating on the ocean. No more manipulation. She didn't have to control Finn to protect herself. Because he would never ask more of her than she was willing to give.

That's what love is, party girl.

Not a power play, but a meeting of respect and caring between two equals.

Two equals like her and Finn.

She felt dizzy, light-headed with new knowledge. Carefully, she rolled to one side, still joined with him. "I don't want to stop," she whispered. "I want you to show me what the mighty TCF can do."

Slipping beneath him, she felt the pleasure of a man above, the broad width of his body, his shoulders and arms, so much more powerful than her own. Power leashed to protect and safeguard. To love and care for.

She smiled up at him and his blue eyes warmed. His tongue washed her lips, igniting a slow burn inside her, and she opened her mouth to him, tasting and exploring.

His hips moved in languorous rhythm, and she could feel him still hard inside her. She pressed him down over her, wanting him close and tight, wanting to make this beautiful and wonderful for him.

He started slow, supporting himself on his arms. His muscles bunched and strained, but he lingered, steady and exquisite. She quivered and he bent down to her, kissing her with sweetness, his tongue laving her with gentleness.

And then he pulled her into his arms and she felt the

length of him all down her body. His hips moved faster. He breathed into her ear and it felt like her own breath. She wanted to give him everything, wanted to lose herself to him, in him. She urged him on, his hips against hers a sea of desire; each stroke crashed against her shore reeling her in deeper and deeper.

"Angel, my God."

His ragged voice nearly sent her over the edge. She did have power over him, the power to please, to bring him mindless bliss. She wrapped her legs around him, brought him in tighter and deeper, all for him, to give him herself, anything he needed. But he held back as though waiting for permission, waiting for her. She felt it in the tense muscles of his arms, saw it on his sweat-slicked chest. She hugged him close, felt him shudder with need, and his desire for her set her on fire. She was a bomb about to go off, a scream about to shatter glass.

"Go," she said, the word a breathless pant. "Take me. Whatever you want."

"Come with me," he ground out.

Any last scraps of self-control vanished. She surrendered to the moment and to him. Utterly, completely, with everything that was in her. Without warning, she disintegrated around him, quaking with pleasure.

Finn bucked in her arms, his climax breath-stealing, shattering. Dead. He had to be dead. He closed his eyes and breathed her in. *That's right, pal, breathe. Just breathe.* Slowly, gradually, at last his heart settled into a jog instead of a race.

He kissed her on the neck, below the ear. "I always knew you'd be a handful, Angel. But Christ, I didn't think you'd suck my soul from me."

He looked down at her face, so beautiful in the lamp-light. Her lips curved in a saucy smile, but her eyes glowed with a different light. "The earth moved for me, too, Sharkman."

He laughed and pecked at her warm, full lips, then slid off to lie beside her.

"What am I going to do with you?" He opened his arms and she settled against him.

"Use me like the dog you are?"

He smiled up at the rock ceiling and gave her a short, tight squeeze. "Maybe. But not for about ten minutes."

"Mmm." She kissed his chest, setting his pulse off again. "I don't know if I can wait ten minutes."

He groaned, the blood thickening again in his groin.

She slipped one soft, fleshy thigh between his, rubbing against the hardening organ. "See? You have no faith in yourself, Sharkman."

"Come here," he growled, pulling her on top of him. He settled inside her, warm and wet and comfortable.

Above him her full breasts swayed softly as she rocked. The sight was excruciatingly exciting, but then, so was the sight of her hips, lusciously curved below his belly, and the place where they joined. Suddenly, need ratcheted up a thousandfold and he wanted to slam into her the way he'd wanted to moments ago. But like then, he bit down on the fierce desire and let her set the pace. It was sweet and languid, and in the end, just as blister-ing.

They slept for a while afterward, her head on his shoulder. He woke to find her leaning over him, her head braced on one hand, staring as though she were trying to memorize his face.

"Hey, sleepyhead." She ran a finger over his lips.

"Hey yourself."

She slipped down, nestling against him. Was she all right? Christ, he hoped so because he felt damn fine.

He pulled her close against him. "How you doing, tough guy?"

"Like I was starved and just had dinner."

He grinned up at the ceiling. He knew exactly how she felt. She skimmed a hand down his chest, past his navel and lower.

He groaned. "I need a time-out."

She laughed and her hand hung a right and skimmed the place where Morales's bullet had shattered his hip.

"Tell me about this then."

He captured her fingers, moving it away from the scar.

"It's a long story."

"So you said. But we're having a time-out."

She propped her head on her hand again and gazed down at him. For once the green eyes were soft and compassionate, and they sent a wave of uneasiness crashing against him.

He started to sit up. "We should get out of here." She pushed him back down. "It's still pouring out. I checked while you were sleeping. So suck it up; you're not getting out of this."

"I'll show you mine if you show me yours."

"You've already seen mine. You've got a file on me that's probably three inches thick."

"Don't flatter yourself. It's only two inches."

Her free hand found the scar again, fingers rubbing the raised edges. "Appendix?"

"Too low. Besides, that's the other side."

"Liposuction?"

He sighed. He really did not want to do this. "Bullet."

Her fingers stopped. Fear and concern flashed across her face. "Jack's bullet?"

He tensed and turned to her in surprise. "What do you know about that?"

"Jack told me you saved his life once."

Jack. He saw the face again, the easy grin, the teasing brown eyes. "That's not what happened," he said in a low voice. "Jack exaggerates." A hitch of grief while he remembered. "Exaggerated. He always . . . exaggerated."

"Bullshit."

He sat up. She sure knew how to ruin the mood. "Look, this is very old news. Sure you want to hear it?"

She nodded. "Oh, yeah."

An anxious pulse hammered at his head. He shoved a hand through his hair trying to figure out the quickest, least emotional way to explain. "Jack and I were working a case tracking down white supremacists who were funding their activities through the drug trade. We had a lead on the supplier, who turned out to be head of a ring handling distribution throughout the Midwest. The lead was through an informant. An ex-stripper and ex-addict who was the supplier's onetime girlfriend."

The words came out flat and detached, but he couldn't stop the memories from flooding his mind. Suzy's paper-thin body, wracked by crack and heroin, nursing bruises and broken bones, and so pitiful, his heart broke.

Come on, Suzy. Wake up. Walk it off. That's right, baby. You can do it. Hold on. You can do it.

"I helped her get cleaned up, and she gave us a lot of useful information."

Suzy's brown eyes wide and healthy again; a little weight looking good on her now. The new apartment he'd found for her, flowers he'd brought on the kitchen table.

Drinking her coffee, proud of her. Of himself. Of what he'd done for her.

The creep broke my arm. You bet I want to get the bastard.

"Using her information as a basis, we went undercover and worked the lead for over a year in a joint operation with the DEA. We were ready to make a move and close down shop. Jack and I went for a final meet and the whole thing exploded."

The smell of that vacant warehouse—concrete and metal and stale, empty air. The glazed smile back on Suzy's face. Nodding off. High again. Her arm around Morales, his around her shoulders, his hand creeping down to stroke her breast. In front of him. Daring him to do something about it.

We know who you are, Mr. Federal Agent. Thanks to your wife, we know everything about you.

Like a knife through his heart.

"Seems my informant had gone back to her old ways and sold us out for a lifetime supply of crack."

I'm tired of living your life, baby. Your stuck-up, boring life.

He'd pushed Jack out of the way and the shot smashed into Finn, an answer to a prayer.

"So you did save Jack's life."

"Saved it?" He snorted. "If it weren't for me, his life wouldn't have been threatened in the first place."

And now he was dead anyway. The thought hung between them.

"It wasn't your fault," she said softly.

He sighed. "Then why do I feel so shitty about it?"

"Because you take things to heart. Feel too much."

"I thought I was an unfeeling bastard."

"That, too." She smiled and kissed his shoulder. "So what happened to her? The informant."

Suzy. He didn't want to think about that loss, too. "She OD'd while I was still in the hospital."

She squeezed his hand. "I'm sorry."

"Yeah, me, too."

"Are you?" She looked at him curiously. "She betrayed you. She almost got you killed. Why should you care what happened to her?"

Now it came. Full confession. *Father, I have sinned. I have been stupid and blind and fooled by the oldest trick in the book. Love.*

But he didn't have to say it. Sudden understanding crossed Angelina's face. "Ohhh, I get it. Oh, my God. Shit. You fell in love with her."

Much worse than that, Angel. "I married her."

Was she laughing? She should be. It was a big fat joke all right. It cost him an official reprimand plus a suspension, and almost got him kicked out for good.

But no, only shock and sympathy showed on her beautiful face. "My God." She lay down, arms behind her head. "Well, that explains a lot."

"A lot of what?"

"A lot of what went on between you and me."

She was right, but he didn't want her to be. "One thing has nothing to do with the other."

"Doesn't it?"

He rolled over so he could see her. Sadness lurked in her eyes. Self-recrimination, too. "You're nothing like her," he said. "Do you hear me? You are not her. I was an asshole and it took me a damn long time to figure that out, but now I have."

Vestiges of the old defiance crept into her jade eyes. "What makes you so sure?"

He kissed her. She tasted like all his dreams. Wild and incoherent, in heightened Technicolor and damned exciting. "Because I know you. For one, you're harder on yourself than anyone has a right to be. A damn sight more than she ever was. For another, you never quit. She was a quitter from the word go. A lost cause, only I didn't see it."

"But now your sight is clear?"

"Crystal. I'm looking at you, Angel. At you." He kissed her again, taking her mouth deep into his.

They made love again and he took her, eyes open, watching, seeing, letting her see him. Their climax erupted in full view of each other, the explosion of pleasure exposed on her face as he was sure it was on his.

Only then did his eyes close. He drifted off, still holding her, still inside her, and when he woke later, he found her tangled in his arms.

Gently, he extracted himself and leaned against one hand to watch her sleep. Shadows mottled her creamy skin, but didn't mar the serenity there. His heart squeezed. He wished she could look peaceful like this all the time. But the storm would break soon, and when it did, they'd need a plan.

He stroked her face, moving the hair off her cheeks and neck. He couldn't abandon the case, but he couldn't use her to complete it either. Not anymore.

He knew what Roper would say. He couldn't let his personal feelings get in the way. He'd done that once and paid for it.

A smile tugged at the corners of his mouth. How the hell had she weaseled that sad story out of him? However she'd done it; it had worked. The weight he'd felt, the heaviness inside him whenever he thought of Suzy, had somehow lifted.

So how the hell was he supposed to stand there and let that slimeball Borian take Angelina to bed? He closed his eyes; the feel of her hot and wet and pulsing around him raced through his veins.

You do it by not thinking about that. You plant your damn feet and forget your damn feelings.

That was the only way they were going to find the plutonium and prevent a disaster. Angelina knew it. He looked down at the soft lips, gently curved now in peace and contentment, and knew if he ordered her to leave they would curl in defiance. She'd be right, too.

He stared into the darkness. What the hell was wrong with him? He was ready to sacrifice his case rather than hurt her. What's up with that? He thought he'd learned that lesson.

The answer shivered up from deep inside him.

You're in love, pal.

His breath caught, then started again. He smiled down at her, and the smile blossomed into a grin.

Jesus H. Fucking Christ.

He was in love.

And he wasn't about to let the object of his affection crucify herself for him or his mission.

He had to get her out of there. The thought bounced inside him like a ricochet. At least she trusted him now. They were together; she'd see he was right. He settled beside her, trying to still the edgy jitter in his chest. She'd come to him freely, with genuine emotion. If he could make her do that, getting her to leave would be a piece of cake.

CHAPTER
~20~

Angelina woke slowly, thinking for a moment she was back in her mother's room at the ranch. Then she opened her eyes to lantern light and remembered everything. Beside her Finn breathed softly and a searing jet of happiness soared through her. She stretched, smiling into the dim glow, slid off the sleeping bag, and checked her watch. Nearly seven-thirty. A brand-new day. Idly, she wondered what Borian had done all night. She waited for the fear to well up; she damn well should be afraid. But she couldn't summon the energy. Not when the night had been so . . . so . . . wonderful.

The shirt Finn had dropped hours ago still lay on the rock floor, and she slipped into it, letting the ends fall to her knees. Barefoot and wrapped in his clothes, she picked her way over the dirt floor and stepped through the scrub at the mouth of the mine to see what the morning looked like.

Sharp, cool air caressed her face, but the breeze had an edge of heat that promised warm weather. The mountain scents, full of pine and earth, smelled as fresh as she felt. Like a new beginning.

She hugged herself, embracing the knowledge of what she'd done last night. Capitulated to a man. Completely and totally. And instead of falling apart, she felt . . . whole. Young and clean. As if the girl she used to be had returned.

She rested against the side of the mine and looked out on the glistening morning, the granite mountains, and the silvery green scrub, and smiled. She couldn't stop smiling. It would be okay; everything would be okay. She closed her eyes and inhaled the day. Going back to Victor would be harder than ever, but at least now Finn would understand. He'd see they had no other options and she was just doing what she had to. What was right.

Footsteps sounded behind her, but she didn't turn. She didn't have to; she knew who it was. A burst of happiness exploded inside her. Finn came through the branches at the entrance and slipped his arms around her waist. "Good morning."

"Mmm." She snuggled against him. "It is a good morning."

The oversized shirt slipped off her shoulder and he kissed the skin there. "For a tough guy, you're awfully eager to bare your heart to the world."

She smiled as his lips nuzzled the beauty mark. "Adele—my adoptive mother—used to say an angel kissed me there. That's why she named me Angelina."

"And I thought it was because you were such a saint."

She laughed. "Yeah, well, I always wondered if she got it wrong. That maybe it was the mark of . . . of something else." The old, familiar doubts stirred inside her, but he turned her gently and his blue eyes kissed her with heat and affection.

"Believe in yourself, Angelina. I do."

Contentment bloomed over the qualms, smothering them. And when he drew her into his embrace, she came willingly. His hands found the edge of her shirt, sliding upward over her thighs to cup her naked bottom. "How long has it been since you've seen her?" His voice was a low, hoarse murmur.

"Who?" She could hardly think with him stroking her like that.

"Adele."

"I don't know. Years. When I needed her most, she threw me to the wolves."

He nipped at her ear, sending sparks through her. "People make mistakes. Maybe she deserves another chance."

But she didn't want to talk about Adele anymore. Turning in his embrace, she saw his jeans were half zipped, splayed like an open invitation. The hard ridge beneath the material beckoned, and she slipped her hands into the opening.

He kissed her neck. "You're changing the subject."

"Just going with the flow."

"We don't have time; we have to go."

"Do we?" She gave him an innocent look and withdrew her hand. Or tried to. His own clamped down on hers, keeping her fingers wrapped around him.

"We might have a few minutes." His eyes held a mischievous glint.

"I thought we might."

He pulled her back inside the mine and bracing his back against the mine wall, lifted her up, and she wrapped her legs around his waist, impaling herself on him. The sex was sweet and hot, and she tumbled again, losing herself totally and coming twice. Afterward, he held her against him and she shivered with pleasure and amazement.

Finally, he set her down with a mock scowl. "Christ, woman, we can't stay here all day." He zipped up the jeans and took her hand, entwining their fingers like high school kids. He kissed her knuckles, his eyes sparkling over their joined fists. "Borian's got guys in Jeeps looking all over for you. It's a miracle they didn't check here last night, but they're bound to remember this place eventually."

Hand in hand he led her back to the campsite, where she examined her clothes. They were still damp but she put them on anyway, wriggling into her panties and laughing when he groaned and turned away.

She slid into the black jeans and pulled the tank top over her head. "So, do I just, what—show up back at the ranch?"

He'd been lacing up his hiking boots and paused to look up. "We're not going to the ranch."

"What do you mean? Isn't Borian there?"

"Probably. But I've got to get you out of here. We'll have to go up the mountain. I'll call Roper on the satellite phone and he'll have a chopper waiting." Finn finished tying his boot and rose to face her.

A chill skittered up her spine. "But I thought—"

"You thought what?" He picked up his gun, checked the clip, and shoved the weapon in the waistband at the back of his jeans.

"Nothing has changed," she said quietly.

He grinned at her. "After last night, everything has changed."

A small ache formed at the pit of her stomach. "Not about Borian. The plutonium's still out there." She crossed to him and took his face in her hands. "I have to go back."

Beneath her fingers the lines hardened, his eyes freezing into blue ice. "I'm in charge here, remember? Going back is too dangerous; I'm not risking you. No arguments." He stalked off to pack the rest of his gear.

The ache grew deeper, and she put a hand to her stomach as if that could stop it. "If it wasn't me . . . if it were Jack or Mike or someone you weren't"—she paused, searching for a way to describe what had happened between them, but couldn't find those extraordinary words and had to settle for the mundane ones—"someone you weren't sleeping with, would you send them away?"

He hesitated for a fraction of an instant. "Absolutely," he said grimly.

But that tiny pause was all the answer she needed. She looked at him, sadness welling up. "I don't think so."

He was doing this for her; forfeiting his assignment to keep her safe. She saw it in the stubborn lines of his face, an expression that didn't quite hide his uneasiness and shame. He wasn't the kind of man to shirk his duty, but he would. For her.

Tears formed a lump in her throat, but she swallowed them. She couldn't let his feelings for her screw up his life again. Another woman he'd tried to rescue, ruining his career, his hope, his life. He'd never survive another wound like that.

After last night they were bound together, the two of them in a tight little bundle. And the only way to do what she had to was to cut him free.

So she shook her hair back, finger-combing the snarled

thickness, and choked off the tenderness he'd created in her. "You think because we fucked that you can order me around?" His eyes narrowed, but she plunged on. "I've fucked a lot of men. It's what I do, remember? You're just one in a long, long line." She watched the hurt creep into his face, and the dead look that quickly covered it. *Forgive me.*

"You came to *me*, Angel. That wasn't a game last night."

Her heart was breaking, the sharp, brittle pieces shattering inside her, but she threw him a pitying smile. "Wasn't it? I thought you were a better cop than that. Can't you spot a con when you hear it? I just told you what you wanted to hear."

He grabbed her arm. "Don't do this."

"Don't do what? Jesus." She shook him off. "Open your eyes, Agent Carver. One night of lust doesn't make us friends. It doesn't make us anything. But if you're a good little doggie, I might let you have another." She threw him a sultry look, tossed her hair, and laughing, walked out, hoping only that her legs would hold her long enough to get away.

Frozen, Finn stared at her retreating back, every word a knife in his chest. He was with Suzy again, coming home after two weeks in deep cover. Looking forward to sleeping in his own bed with his sweet new wife beside him. He remembered pushing open the front door and smelling the sweat and stale food, hearing her zoned-out laughter and a man's voice. His stomach had seized up then just as it seized up now.

Just one in a long line.

"No." He growled the word out loud, as though he needed the sound to confirm his refusal. *No.* Last night had been the most amazing of his life and nothing would convince him that Angelina had faked it. He knew her; she was reckless and didn't think enough of herself. She wanted to prove she wasn't as bad as she thought, as bad as he'd accused her of being.

She'd sacrifice herself to do that. Maybe she'd do anything to accomplish that. Even lie.

"Angelina!" He bolted after her, but only got a few yards before skidding to a stop.

Grisha rumbled toward him, one thick arm wrapped tight around Angelina's shoulders, protective yet menacing. Against him she looked small and vulnerable as a rag doll, and Finn went cold at the sight.

"Mr. Universe." He threw Grisha a tight smile. "Out for your daily constitutional?"

The bald-headed beastie gave him a hard, blank stare. "Miss Montgomery, she is found."

Angelina's eyes locked on Finn's. "I explained how I stumbled on the mine and sat the storm out here."

"That's right," Finn said pleasantly. He didn't like the way the big man was eyeing him, but the gun at Finn's back gave him a degree of confidence. *Stay cool, Arnold, and no one gets hurt.*

"Mr. Borian, he tell you to leave." Grisha's eyes drilled into Finn's, hostile and accusatory.

Finn shrugged. *We don't all do what Mr. Borian says.* "Well, the storm put the kibosh on that. In fact, I was about to take Miss Montgomery back to Helena with me."

Grisha's eyebrows rose, but he made no reply. Nor did he make a move to turn back the way he'd come.

Finn gestured toward the entrance. "First we have to . . . to go outside."

Grisha didn't budge.

"Marian told him to wait here," Angelina explained, emphasizing the name the tiniest bit.

Finn blinked. "You contacted Marian and not Victor?"

Again, Angelina answered for him, her voice calm, though he heard an edge of panic there. "She wanted to tell Victor herself that I was safe."

Interesting. Finn eyed the big man. Was Grisha's loyalty to Victor not as unwavering as it seemed? Or was it just that he had a crush on Victor's sister-in-law? Finn knew firsthand how a woman could get in the way of duty. Maybe Marian had gotten in the way of Grisha's.

A small wave of relief washed through him. This was good. Very good. He'd far rather deal with Marian than with Victor.

He smiled. "So, you and Marian are good friends?"

"She watches over Mr. Borian. And me."

"I'm sure she does," Angelina said, trying unsuccessfully to wriggle free. "But I'm safe now. You can let go."

Grisha ignored Angelina's struggles and focused on Finn. "Miss Marian say make sure she does not disappear again."

Angelina rolled her eyes, and Finn crossed his arms, trying to appear relaxed when in truth he was tense as razor wire. He had a weapon he couldn't use without blowing their cover, and an opponent that didn't seem inclined toward persuasion. "Well, surely Marian didn't mean for us to wait right here. We'd all be more comfortable outside." And as far away from the equipment as possible.

With a furtive glance, he scanned the campsite. His heart sank. The laptop, all the batteries, his holster, the monitor that tracked the signal from the pearl brooch . . . everything was in plain sight.

Before he could do anything about it, the sound of approaching footsteps reached them. Grisha continued to stare wordlessly at him, his bulging forearm tight around Angelina's shoulders. Seconds later, Marian appeared. She wore a light blue sweater over pressed khaki slacks and ushered in a wave of competency and civilization with her. Finally, someone they could talk to, reason with.

"Marian, please tell Grisha to let me go."

For a few minutes Marian stood silently, taking in the scene that greeted her. Then she smiled pleasantly. "Not yet, my dear. Not until you tell me who you are and what you're up to."

Angelina flicked a fast glance from Marian to Finn and back again. She smiled. "I'm not up to anything."

"I see you spent the night here with Mr. Ingram. How cozy."

Finn tried his best bluff. "I spent the night searching for Miss Montgomery and found her early this morning. We stumbled on this place and waited out the storm here."

"And did you 'stumble' on all this equipment, too?" She gazed around at the campsite and Finn held his breath, hoping she wouldn't understand what she was seeing under the lantern light. But the hope was short-lived. "There's enough here to outfit a small army." The word seemed to coalesce something in her mind. She turned to Finn with a cold, hard expression on her face. "Who are you? Do you work for Ivanov?"

She named the head of one of the Russian mob factions whose conflicts with Victor had compelled Borian to move stateside.

"See what he's carrying," Grisha said. "Russian made maybe."

"Do you have a weapon on you, Mr. Ingram?"

"Don't be ridiculous."

Marian jabbed a finger at Finn. "Turn around."

Finn smiled. "This is crazy." He gestured to the stash around them. "This is just a sleeping bag and some camping equipment I had in my trunk."

"Turn around."

And reveal his weapon? Not on your life.

"Grisha, show Mr. Ingram what you can do with those clever hands of yours."

Before Finn could move, Grisha's arms slid up from Angelina's shoulders to her throat. One hand nearly made a complete circle on her neck. The pressure brought Angelina up on her tiptoes. She turned white. Finn went stock-still.

"Let her go."

"Turn around, Mr. Ingram. Hands on top of your head."

Angelina closed her eyes and gave a small shake of her head. *Yeah, Angel, nice try.* But he couldn't risk it. Not with her neck stretched in Grisha's stranglehold. Reluctantly, he did as Marian bid and felt her slip the gun from his back. When he faced her again she was holding it up for Grisha to examine.

"Glock forty. Not Russian." Grisha turned his black eyes on Finn. "Government."

"Ah, federal agents. Just like those two in the shack." She aimed the gun at Finn.

The barrel caught a glint of lantern light, and he stared at the woman holding it, trying to disregard the muzzle pointing at his chest. Had she just admitted to killing Mike and Jack? A spurt of fury shot through him, but he shoved it back down. *Don't think about that. Focus. Get Angelina out of here.*

"What shack? I don't know what you're talking about. Look, I did what you asked. Now let her go."

But Marian ignored him. "I warned Victor, but he's been such a fool about . . ." Her gaze flicked to Angelina and back to Finn. "Who is she? Did she have plastic surgery? Is she some kind of warped experiment?"

He glanced at Angelina, his belly slanting in dread. She was breathing in quick, tiny gasps. Not a good time for evasion.

"She's your niece," he said flatly. "Now let her go."

A grim, deadly silence greeted that bit of news. As though Angelina were suddenly significant in a whole new way, Grisha loosened his hold, though his hand stayed in place around her throat. But as her feet met the ground, she began to breathe normally and her face took on some color.

The tension inside Finn relaxed a hairsbreadth.

Marian shook her head. "I knew you'd come up with something wild, but this is too much."

"It's true." Finn's voice was low and careful.

"Carol was barren."

"Not at fifteen, she wasn't."

Marian's eyes narrowed.

"The boarding school," Angelina said, looking directly at Marian. He could see her appealing to her aunt's heart, trying to make a real connection. "Remember telling me about that? We were having coffee and I asked you about Carol. You said she went to boarding school when she was fifteen. Well, it wasn't a boarding school, it was a home for unwed mothers."

Marian stared, face white and drawn. "I don't believe you."

"I was born there," Angelina said softly. "I can show you the papers."

Oh, Angel, I'm sorry. Finn knew how much this revelation meant to her. And how much was riding on Marian's response.

With a slow, painful chortle, she began to laugh. "What a joke," she muttered with a shake of her head. Her gaze shifted to Angelina's face. Carefully, she examined her from head to toe. "So you're the spawn of the devil."

Damn. Not the reaction they were hoping for.

The wire squeezing his gut tightened again and Finn stepped forward, but Marian raised the gun. He held up his hands. "Look, she can't hurt you. You have me. Let her go."

"No," Angelina said. "I won't let you do that."

He ignored her, as did Marian. The negotiation was between the two of them now. Good. He had to get her to focus on him. To see that he was her problem, not Angelina.

"Why should I let her go?" Marian said. "She'd only worm her way back into Victor's heart. I've gone to great lengths to protect him from himself. I don't intend to stop now."

"Please, Marian. Don't do this," Angelina said.

"Be quiet, Angel." Finn kept his voice low, his eyes on Marian.

But Angelina had never been very good at taking orders.

"You're my aunt. I came here to get to know you."

Marian turned the gun on her niece. Christ. So much for turning Marian's attention away from Angelina.

"No," Marian said through gritted teeth. "You came for Victor."

"That's not true. I swear it." Her eyes glittered with unshed tears.

"Don't say anything else, Angel." Finn's heart rate shot up.

"All my life I've wanted to find my mother—"

"Shut up."

"Angel, don't—"

"You're my family, the closest thing I'll ever—"

"Shut up!" Marian's face twisted in hatred. "Shut up! Shut her up, Grisha."

"No!" Finn jerked forward as Angelina started coughing and gasping for breath, but Marian turned the gun on him.

"Stay where you are."

"Like hell I will. He's choking her!" Again, he jolted toward her, but Marian fired the gun. The shot hit something behind him. Gravel and dirt fell in a heap of dust.

"Let him. Victor doesn't need her. All he needs is me, and soon he'll understand that." Marian's voice hardened. "Everything I've done has been for him. Starting with my pathetic sister."

Grisha's head snapped toward Marian, and his hold must have loosened again because Angelina stopped struggling and swallowed huge gasps of air.

"Mrs. Borian died of cancer," Finn said, eyeing Grisha's shaken expression.

"Yes, she did, poor thing." Marian gave a little shrug of dismissal. "So much pain. I'm sure she was glad to have her suffering cut short."

The implication caused another ripple of shocked silence. Silence Marian didn't seem to appreciate. "And now here's another weak woman blinding Victor to his destiny. I won't let him make the same mistake again."

She nodded toward Angelina. "She should have left when she got sick. The poison should have made her sick enough to go. But she's as stupid as my sister."

"*You* tampered with the water," Finn said.

"Who else? Victor needs a helpmate, someone who understands him. Someone strong and capable."

"Like you," Finn said softly.

She bowed, acknowledging the words as if they were a compliment. "Yes, like me. After all, where would Victor be without me? I caught your compatriots at their little spy game. I eliminated them. I would do anything for Victor."

He fisted his hands, desperate to control the rage about to spew out of him. This shitty excuse for a woman had murdered Jack and Mike. She'd nearly killed Angelina. And bragged as though she were proud of it.

Marian's eyes gleamed with a ruthless intelligence she'd hidden from everyone. She *was* proud. As the mask of dutiful submission fell away, the truth slammed into Finn with the force of a tidal wave.

They'd been watching the wrong person.

"*You* stole the plutonium," he said. "Not Borian."

"Of course. Victor appreciates cleverness. And I was clever enough to do what he'd never been able to—purchase one of the deadliest and most sought after items on the black market. In his name, of course. He appreciates money and power. And I'm going to give him both. Then he'll see how much I love him."

The theft was her gift to Victor, her sick, twisted love token. A chill stole over Finn.

"You're crazy if you think he'll ever love you back," Angelina said quietly. "He's still in love with your sister. And me."

Marian's eyes narrowed into menacing slits. "I killed

her once, I can do it again. Grisha, show Mr. Ingram what your hands around his throat feel like. I have something special for my dear niece."

But Grisha didn't move. "You kill Mrs. Borian." He repeated it as if he hadn't quite understood.

"And I'm going to kill her ghost. Get out of the way."

Grisha shook his head. "I have always do what you say. But always for taking care of Mr. Borian. But this . . ." He switched into a flood of what sounded like Russian. Marian answered him in kind, the sense obscure but the meaning obvious.

Grisha was balking.

Finn met Angelina's gaze. *Don't move. Don't do anything stupid.* Marian's attention was split between him and the big man. Finn inched forward.

"You've been Victor's true and loyal servant," Marian said, switching back to English, her patience clearly strained. "I've enjoyed our little . . . friendship. But if you want to continue in that capacity, I suggest you move away from that tramp."

Grisha dropped his hold and stepped toward Marian, shielding Angelina by blocking Marian's line of sight. "I don't listen. Not this time. Mr. Borian, he do not like it."

Finn caught Angelina's eye. *Now. Run.*

But before Angelina could escape, Marian sighed. "Very well." Without another word, she turned the gun on Grisha and shot him twice in the chest.

Angelina screamed as gunshots echoed inside the hollow mountain. Grisha fell, landing like a tree trunk at her feet, and two of the flimsier wooden supports wobbled. Dust rained down and suddenly everything moved at once.

"Run!" Finn dived for Marian, pushing her backward.

The gun went off, a shaky shot, not even aimed. But Finn was close, so close. A surprised expression crossed his face. He stepped, wobbled, then crumpled.

"Oh, my God, Finn, no!" Angelina raced to where he'd collapsed, and another shot zinged past her ear. Timber groaned behind her; one of the weakened wooden supports teetered and fell, bringing rock and earth with it.

She lunged on top of Finn to protect his body from the falling debris.

"I won't let this happen again," Marian said. She backed away from the cave-in toward the safety of the entrance. "Victor belongs to me. He'll always belong to me. And if he ever finds you, he'll think you came here to get out of the rain and the mine collapsed around you."

"You crazy witch!"

Angelina leaped up, but Marian fired, forcing her back. She tried to drag Finn's body into the clear, but another round blasted, making her duck. More rock and earth fell, and she covered her head, tasting dust and grit. When she looked up again, Marian was yards away, safe from the mountain's imminent collapse.

Through the powdery debris, Angelina saw her aunt pause. Their eyes met.

For a long, slow moment the dream Angelina had chased for years teetered inside her, and she made one last, desperate grab to save it. "You're my mother's sister, Marian. My flesh and blood." Her voice cracked.

With a hateful smile, Marian aimed at the main support pole. "Welcome to the family, kid."

She squeezed the trigger and emptied the gun into the wooden beam.

CHAPTER
~21~

Angelina threw herself on top of Finn as the timber cracked, swayed, and came down with an earsplitting boom that brought the mountain down on them. Plunged into blackness, she heard the sounds of destruction crashing and echoing all around. Metal severed, glass shattered. Something hit her shoulder and bounced off, another chunk hit the arm she wrapped around her head.

The shock was so great she didn't have time to be afraid until the thunder of the cave-in settled into vast silence. Only then did she realize her heart was pounding loud enough to be heard in the next state, her mouth dry, her skin icy tight.

Musty-smelling dust swirled into her throat, making her cough. Was this hell or was she really alive?

"Finn!" The body beneath hers shifted slightly. She heard a moan. "Finn, are you all right?" Another groan. Blind, she slid around until she found his face and could whisper in his ear. "Are you all right?"

"Ter-rific." His voice came out weak and hoarse. "What happened?"

She shuddered, remembering the vindictive pleasure on her aunt's face. "Marian shot you, then blew out the mine supports. The whole mountain came down on us."

"Then how come . . . we're still alive?"

She closed her eyes against his scratchy, whisker-stubbled cheek. They'd come so close to the alternative . . . "I don't know."

"Mmm." He tried to shift his position, and inhaled a sharp breath. "Shoulder hurts. Can't . . . move my leg."

A stab of panic hit her and she crawled frantic hands down his body to what felt like a wooden beam across his left knee.

"Something is pinning you down." She wished desperately for a light but had no idea where the lantern was or even if it was usable anymore.

"Finn—do you still have that little flashlight?"

"Pocket." She slid her hands over him again, searching for his pockets, accidentally brushing against his shoulder. He gasped in pain.

"God, I'm sorry."

"'S all right." He sounded drowsy. Was he slipping away? If only she could see!

"Finn! Stay with me."

"Can't . . . go anywhere, Angel."

She found the penlight in his right front pocket and by some miracle it wasn't damaged. Switching on the tiny beam, she panned it over the interior.

"Oh, my God."

Half of Grisha's body lay buried under rock and earth, only his legs visible. Rubble, dirt, and rock blocked the way out, but the worst of the wreckage had settled around, not on top of them. The main support beam had split down the middle. Half still stood, precariously holding up the roof just above them. The other half leaned heavily on Finn's leg. His shirt was a mess of sticky blood above his right shoulder.

"Bad?" he rasped.

"Better than it could be."

He grunted and fell into silence. She didn't know if he was asleep, passed out, or resting. But the longer they stayed here, the more dangerous it got. How much time before the rest of the support gave and all the mountain came down? Or the air ran out?

She bit her lip and eyed the beam across Finn's leg. It looked heavy, but she thought she could manage it.

No thinking about it; she'd have to manage.

"Let me see if I can get this off you." She tested the weight by running her hands over it and lifting slightly. He gasped in pain and she immediately stopped.

At least he was conscious. "God, Finn, I don't want to hurt you, but if I don't get this off we'll never get out of here."

He drew a harsh breath. "I know."

"I'm going to try and lift this off, but I'll need your help."

"I'm . . . all yours, Angel." His eyes were closed, his mouth pinched in pain. Her heart squeezed at the sight.

"We'll do it on three. I'll lift, but you've got to drag yourself free somehow."

"Give me a minute." He inhaled deeply as though steeling himself, balled and unballed his hands, then placed them palms down on the ground on either side of himself. "Okay."

She counted down, and on one, mustered every ounce of strength she possessed to lift the beam high enough for him to scuttle backward.

She managed to hold on until he was free, then dropped the heavy timber with an echoing boom. A shower of rock rained down and the other half of the support wobbled in reply. Heart thudding sickly, she whipped the light on it and stared hard, her breath stopped for what seemed a lifetime.

The timber held.

She sat down heavily, quaking too much to stand. A few feet away, Finn lay on his back, panting heavily.

"Christ. Should call you . . . Wonder Woman." And then his eyes rolled back in his head and he was out.

Running a trembling hand through her hair, she inched closer and gaped at his bloody shoulder. Before she could think too hard about it, she ripped his shirt away from the wound. At the sight of the blackened hole and the red blood surging around it, a wave of nausea hit. Swallowing hard, she forced herself to take a strip of his shirt and clean off as much of the dirt as possible. As she worked, blood from the back of his shoulder stained her hands, and when she looked she found a second hole there as well. Her stomach flopped. *Exit wound.* God, on what TV show had she heard that term, and who would've thought she'd ever use it? Steeling herself, she cleaned the second wound as well, and in a few minutes both had stopped bleeding. She made two pads out of the rest of his shirt and bound them with a sleeve.

For a moment she sat back on her heels and covered her mouth with trembling fingers so she wouldn't throw up.

Then she turned to his leg. His jeans were torn, but not enough to see what lay beneath them, for which she was monumentally glad. She did not want to know how much damage the heavy buttress had done.

Wobbly, she sank against a rock and closed her eyes. How perfect to sleep and not be responsible for anything ever again.

But though the body was willing, the mind was not.

So many lives hung in the balance. Those she'd never meet, who'd be maimed or killed if Marian sold the plutonium to someone willing and able to use it. And those she knew intimately, especially—Angelina glanced at Finn—this one particular life.

She hauled herself to her feet and trudged toward the entrance. A pile of rock and rubble blocked the way. Several smaller, easier-to-move pieces concealed heavier chunks she couldn't budge.

A wave of despair rolled over her. Without mechanized help, she'd never claw her way out.

If only she could contact Roper.

A spear of hope pierced her chest. The phone. If she found the phone she could get help.

She bounded over to where most of Finn's equipment had been. Setting the penlight on a wedge of debris, she scrabbled in the fallen rock, yanked and pulled at the rubble, breaking nails and scraping her fingers raw.

A bit of glass from what was left of the lantern sliced her finger, and she drew in a breath, cursing, then sucked at the cut. To maintain focus, she pictured Finn pacing outside in the dark, punching in phone numbers and . . .

Outside. Her heart sank. Even if she found the phone in one piece, she wouldn't get a signal from inside the mine.

Disappointment bit so sharp tears stung her eyes.

She leaned against the barricade and gritted her teeth in misery. In front of her, Finn lay battered and wounded. She was his only hope, and she'd just run out of options.

Come on, Angelina. Sharkman said you weren't a quitter. Prove him right.

She rubbed at her eyes with the heel of her filthy hands and took a deep breath. Then she swung the penlight around the dark space, desperate for a way out. Finn had set up camp several dozen yards from the entrance, but the mine itself went back farther. She shone the light into the dark interior. A pile of rubble lay there, but she made herself walk over and examine it. Amid the wreckage she found a small opening. She put the penlight in her teeth and squeezed through, scraping a knee and reopening the cut in her hand.

Blackness waited on the other side. She aimed the penlight into it and saw the mine continued endlessly. Starting down the passageway, she scanned the area with the light. Here and there, pieces of the mountain had fallen into the pathway, but for the most part, the way was clear. Channels led off the main one and she turned right down the first. It led to a warren of smaller arteries, all of which ended in rock. She retraced her steps and headed off to the left this time.

And there, halfway down, her heart stopped at the sight of a rickety ladder embedded in stone.

A ladder that went up.

She shone the light above her head, but the beam wasn't strong enough to penetrate to the top. She licked her lips and debated. The ladder looked a hundred years old; climbing up might destroy it. Which meant if she attempted the ascent, she should do it with Finn. But if she dragged Finn here and the ladder wasn't a way out, she would have expended what little strength he had for nothing.

She had no choice. She'd have to risk it; he couldn't stay where he was and this might be a way out.

She dashed back, wriggling through the small opening that led to where she'd left him. He lay still as death, and the sight sent a spurt of liquid fear through her veins. But under the steady beam of light, his chest moved up and down.

She swallowed hard, grateful for the small sign of life. She should let him rest. He deserved it.

But they had to get out of the mine, and she couldn't carry him out.

She shook him. "Finn, wake up. I may have found a way out, but I can't get us out alone. Finn!"

She nudged and shouted and tugged, even risking hurting him again if that would bring him to consciousness. At last, his eyes fluttered open and he looked at her groggily.

"My very own . . . angel." His eyes closed.

"Stay with me. Stay with me!" She jostled him again, and he groaned. "The entrance is blocked but I think I found a way out. Come on, wake up. I need you."

"Leave me here," he mumbled.

"Not on your life, Sharkman. Come on, up. Up!"

She put her arms beneath his shoulders and forced him into a sitting position. He was sweating by the time she succeeded.

"God, woman, you're . . . killing me."

"Don't confuse me with my family. Come on, one more push and you'll be on your feet."

Between her and the rock he used to prop himself up, she managed to get him upright, but the minute he put weight on his damaged leg, he gave a roar of pain and swayed heavily.

"Hold on! Don't fall. Don't—" She pushed him against the rock wall, forcing him to stay upright. He was breathing through his teeth, working through the pain.

"Christ," he panted.

"Look, your left leg's a mess. Try not to put any weight on it. Lean on me."

She gave him a minute to recover, then slung his arm around her shoulder. "Ready?"

He grunted a reply, which she took for an affirmative. Closing her eyes, she said a brief prayer for strength and took a step. He gasped, but didn't collapse. She took another step.

He was heavy as the mountain itself, and she staggered under his weight, but managed to hold on to him. They hobbled slowly, his body taut with the enormous effort of moving and holding back the pain, but she refused to stop until they reached the pile of rubble that blocked the way back. Then she propped him against the earth wall and wiped the sweat off his face and neck.

"Only a little bit farther. Can you make it?" She swiped at her own sticky forehead.

His mouth twisted up in the semblance of a grim smile. "Do I have . . . a choice?"

"No."

"Okay, then. Let's go before you . . . change your mind."

She pocketed the penlight to free both hands so she could maneuver them through the narrow opening. Crabbing sideways, she slid through first, half pulling, half dragging him behind. He cursed the whole way, each word laced in agony.

When they finally made it to the other side, she turned

the penlight back on and panned his face. He leaned against the pile of rubble, eyes closed, face gray.

"Please tell me you don't have . . . anything else as . . . entertaining as that lined up for me."

"No promises." She repositioned herself beneath his arm and they made the slow, excruciating journey down the passageway, off to the left fork, and up to the ladder.

"You're kidding," he said when she panned over it with the light.

"Afraid not."

She unwrapped his arm from around her shoulders so she could test the lower rungs. The minute she let go of him, he sank to the ground.

"Sorry," he murmured.

She looked down at him. He was pale and drawn; there was no way he'd ever make it up.

"You have to leave me, Angel."

She shook her head, not wanting to even hear that option. "I can't."

"Yes, you can. I'll be . . . fine."

"No. The mine could cave in again, the air could run out, you could—"

"Angel," he cut into her panicked rambling, and she took a breath, trying to control the fear spinning through her. "Come here. And stop . . . shining that thing in my face. You'll run down the . . . battery."

She sat beside him and switched off the penlight. In the darkness, his ragged breathing seemed louder and more labored.

"Give me your hand." His voice echoed in the darkness. She fumbled for a minute, but finally found his fingers. He squeezed hers, rubbing his thumb over the inside of her wrist. "I want you to . . . do this. I know you can.

Leave me here. Find a phone. Call Roper. Tell him what happened." He was running out of energy, his words slowing. "About Marian. Tell him . . . get men out here. Get Marian."

"I'll tell him to get *you* out of here."

He squeezed her hand again. "Marian first."

"But—"

"Promise."

"I—"

"Promise."

"All right, damn you. I promise."

He sighed and the hand gripping hers went slack.

"Finn?" She switched on the light, saw he'd fainted again. Another burst of fear sliced through her. Goddamn uptight, fricking hero. Why the hell couldn't he be a selfish bastard? Why the hell couldn't he think about himself first?

Because he wouldn't be Sharkman if he did, and you wouldn't love him.

Fear turned into a soggy lump at the back of her throat that erupted in a sob and splintered into tears.

All right, so she loved him. She'd done plenty of stupider things in her life.

Well, maybe not.

She swiped at her eyes, but the tears kept coming.

What the hell are you crying for? Crying's not going to get him out of here.

Standing around like a baby, waiting for, jeez, what the hell was she waiting for?

She sniffed back a shuddering breath and took a last glance at Finn. Sweat and dirt slicked his face, his makeshift bandage was seeping blood again; she didn't even want to think about what his leg looked like. But in spite of the mess, he looked good to her, and she didn't want to lose him.

"Don't you die on me," she said. He was out cold so he didn't reply, but his stillness seemed a silent reproach. "Okay, I'm going. I'm going."

She switched off the penlight and placed it in his still hands. Then she fumbled in the darkness for the ladder, put her foot on the first rung, and swung herself up. The rung held and she began climbing.

CHAPTER
~22~

The ladder led to an ancient trapdoor above her head. Without the light Angelina couldn't see if it was held by a lock, but a blind search only turned up a gummy lattice of cobwebs. She shoved on the damn door and it rained down debris and spiderwebs, but held fast. Swearing, she pounded until her knuckles bled and her shoulder and elbow were sore. Finally she budged it open, bit by creaking bit.

Relief washed over her as she poked her head out, taking in huge mouthfuls of the fresh morning air and blinking in the bright sunlight. The sunshine was a bitter reminder that the rest of the world went on fine without her or Finn, thank you very much, and would continue to do so, whether she got him out alive or not.

She slammed a mental door on the "or not." She wouldn't think about that. Or about the way she'd left Finn, his body broken and exhausted by pain.

Crawling out, she dusted herself off, wiped blood and bits of skin from her knuckles, and glanced around, orienting herself. Over her shoulder the three protuberances of Devil's Teeth loomed large and close; she was on the mountain.

A path overgrown with gray-green scrub and brush wound away from the trapdoor. One edge of the crude road butted up to the mountain, the other overlooked a nasty drop.

Don't look.

No, she wouldn't.

Ignoring the flutter in her stomach, she hugged the mountainside and scurried down. She stumbled a few times, going faster than she felt safe, but the thought of that unstable spur, split down the middle and holding up what was left of the mine, drove her on.

The path snaked down rocky and uneven, but she made steady progress for nearly ten minutes. Then she skidded to a stop.

A rockslide blocked her way.

She groaned. How about a break here?

You're alive. That's a pretty big one.

Right.

Okay, so she wouldn't whine. She'd find a way around this stupid rock pile.

But when she trudged the length of the slide, the path was blocked on all sides. She stared up at the mound. God. Where were her hiking shoes when she needed them?

Muttering a curse, she set her foot at the bottom and started up. Rocks tumbled beneath her steps, setting off mini avalanches. She slipped, held on, slipped again.

Dammit to hell.

Gritting her teeth, she continued up and at last made it to the top. For a moment she stood trembling, legs weak with relief.

And then she saw what was in front of her and smiled. About time things went her way.

A panoramic view of road and the country beyond spread out before her, good as any map. In the distance she could make out the blurred outlines of the Eden's Gate stables.

Sure of the way back to the ranch, she scrambled down the other side. The faster she got to a phone, the faster she could get Finn out of there.

A loose rock slid out from under her, setting off a fall of more rock. Suddenly the whole area was moving. She slipped, stumbled—oh, my God—and fell.

Fear thudding in her ears, she plunged downward, helpless to stop her heart-dropping slide.

An eon later, she landed on her feet with a screech of pain.

Oh, God.

She looked down. Her right ankle was twisted beneath her.

Great. Just great.

Gingerly, she put weight on it, but pain bit clear up her leg. She felt around the bone and sucked in a breath when her fingers pressed too hard.

She closed her eyes. Of all the goddamn stupid . . .

How the hell was she going to make it back now?

Compressing her mouth into a thin line, she took a step, then another and another. Pain streaked up her leg, but she pressed on, sweat prickling her neck and under-arms. Her limping gait slowed her progress to a crawl; twenty minutes later, she'd only gone a few dozen yards.

God. Why the hell Finn and the TCF would depend on her, she had no idea.

But depend on her they did, and she'd wasted precious minutes getting nowhere, time she couldn't afford with Finn trapped inside that wreck of a mine.

A sound drifted toward her. An engine. A car engine.

Shit.

Had Marian returned to check on her handiwork?

Panic sped through her. If Angelina could, she would've run back to the landslide to hide, but with her bum ankle she'd never make it.

Heart in her throat, she scanned her surroundings for another place to hide, but the car came into view before she found one.

She swallowed the scream that was about to burst out of her. It wasn't Marian, but a patrol Jeep. And the driver hadn't seen her yet.

Relief swamped her and on its heels came an idea, an idea so outrageous she wasn't sure it was sane. But she wasn't sure it wasn't brilliant either.

"Hey!" She shouted and waved her arms over her head to attract the attention of the man in the Jeep. "Over here!"

He saw her. Immediately the car veered in her direction. She bit her lip, her heart clattering in doubt. No turning back now.

"Miss Montgomery?" The driver jumped out and ran around to help her. He was a blunt-nosed youth dressed, like all Borian's men, in Eden's Gate camouflage.

"Yes. Oh, thank God. I don't think I could have made it back on my own." She extended her injured foot. "I did something awful to my ankle."

The young man made sympathetic noises and helped her limp into the Jeep. "Glad we found you," he said.

"That was a wicked storm last night. Mr. Borian and Miss Marian have been sick with worry."

I'll bet. "Well, I'm glad to be found. But please, hurry. My foot really hurts. I think I may have broken it."

"I'll get you back in ten minutes. I'll just call ahead and let them know so they can contact a doctor."

"No!" Angelina quickly placed her hand over the radio he'd picked up. "If you don't mind, I'd rather wait until we get there." She gave him her most dazzling smile. "I'm a little embarrassed and don't want to make a fuss. To be honest"—she lowered her voice to a throaty murmur and leaned in close—"I don't want to give Victor time to think about it. He can get so angry." She looked deep into the young driver's eyes and he turned a gratifying shade of pink.

He cleared his throat and replaced the radio. "I . . . I understand." He started the engine.

She braced her injured foot over her opposite knee, cradling it in her hand to protect it from the Jeep's jostling momentum. Heart hammering, she closed her eyes. What the hell had she just done?

Found the quickest way back.

Quick but not exactly safe.

Safe was not a priority. Not with Finn hurt and stranded in that godforsaken place.

Suddenly the events of the morning flooded over her. She and Finn had almost died. Finn still could.

Oh, God.

Tremors raced through her, tremors she hoped the driver wouldn't notice.

Marian had drugged her. Marian had killed Mike and Jack. Marian had stolen the plutonium. Not Victor. Marian. Her aunt. Angelina couldn't downshift that fast.

Out of nowhere, a spicy whiff of fragrance floated into the air. Angelina opened her eyes, struck by the familiar scent.

"Do you smell anything?" she asked the driver.

He gave her a puzzled look, then turned his gaze back to the road. "I don't think so." He sniffed the air. "Nothing but woods and rock."

She waved the idea away. "Of course. I don't know what I was thinking." But she did, she'd been thinking about what Marian had done.

She killed you, Mother, didn't she?

The whiff came again, as if Carol were nodding, urging her daughter on.

A chill rippled down Angelina's spine.

Marian had killed her sister. And that changed everything.

Angelina's heart sped up. Marian, not Victor. Marian.

The answer to the puzzle lit up inside her, neon and electric.

In a fury of impatience, she wished the driver would hurry, wished she could get there fast and finish this. Then her aunt would be someone else's problem and her mother would have the justice she deserved.

But the car bounced along at a steady, reliable hum.

After what seemed an eternity, the stables loomed in the distance. Her heart started to thud. Was Marian close by?

Angelina had figured out a way back to the ranch; now she'd have to sneak in without alarming her aunt. If she could get to Victor before Marian saw her, she might have a chance.

She put her hand on the driver's arm. "Could you do

me a favor? Find out where Victor is and if Marian's with him. I'd like to see him alone."

At her touch, the blush suffused the young man's face again, but he picked up the radio and called one of his buddies, who told him Victor had been out looking for Angelina but had been delivered back to the house fifteen minutes earlier.

"He went into his office to hear the patrols report on Miss Montgomery," the voice over the radio squawked.

She quickly put a hand to her lips to reinforce her request for secrecy. Her driver hesitated, then nodded.

"Ask him about Marian," she whispered.

"Any sign of Rover?" he asked into the radio.

Rover? Angelina gave a silent snort of amusement. Well, Marian did follow Victor around like a puppy dog, or so Angelina had thought before this morning. Now she wasn't sure who was holding the leash.

"Nope," screeched the radio. "But she asked for a detail to sweep out the trees and brush the wind brought down last night. Knowing her, she's probably supervising."

"Roger that. And out."

The driver replaced the radio. "Looks like Mr. Borian is in his office. Bailey's right; Miss Marian likes to oversee everything personally."

Angelina could definitely attest to that.

"The storm kicked up a lot of mud and dirt and brought down a bunch of scrub. If she's in charge of the cleanup, she's most likely there."

Angelina hoped so. But if not, it was too late anyway. They'd arrived. The driver hopped out and ran around to the passenger side to help her out of the Jeep.

"Let me take you in," he said, bending to swoop her up.

"That's all right," she said quickly, putting her hands up to forestall him. "I'll manage. Thank you."

"Are you sure? All right, then. And, miss, it was my pleasure." He got back in the Jeep and sped off.

Wincing in pain, Angelina hobbled up the stairs and into the house. She tried swallowing, but her mouth was so dry it was nearly impossible. She gulped a ragged breath and headed for Victor's office.

The animal heads lining the walls stared down at her just as they had the first time she'd entered his domain. Now, like then, they seemed an oppressive gauntlet she had to pass through.

Limping, she held on to the walls to help take the weight off her foot and kept her gaze focused dead ahead. The scent of spice wafted with her, as if carrying her toward the arena. Toward the sand and the sun and the waiting lion.

Every heartbeat sounded like a clap of thunder; her gait dragged in slow motion. She blocked out the throbbing ache in her foot so she wouldn't think about how helpless she truly was, how vulnerable.

If Marian was in the office and not on cleanup duty . . .

She couldn't finish the thought.

Rounding the corner to Victor's office, she leaned against the wall and listened as a collection of male voices inside discussed the search for her. She strained her ears, but heard nothing remotely feminine in the tones.

Pray you don't need your hearing checked.

She closed her eyes, grabbed a breath for courage, and took the last few hobbling steps into the room.

Victor sat behind his desk facing four men. All were intent on maps spread over the desk between them. As she stumbled into the room, Victor glanced up. A look of astonishment crossed his face and he leaped up.

"Angelina!" He ran around to where she stood and helped her into a chair. "Are you all right? We've just been talking about you. How did you—find her some water," he barked to one of the men and dismissed the rest.

"Where have you been? You worried us to death. What happened to your ankle? You!" He gestured to one of the departing men. "Find a maid and ask her to bring a pillow for Miss Montgomery's foot." He dragged one of the other chairs over to her and propped her injured foot on it.

The man dashed out of the room, and a few minutes later, two maids arrived. One carried a tray with a glass and a blue bottle of Eden's Gate water, and the other held a pillow that she fluffed and placed under Angelina's leg.

"Thank you," she murmured, and "No, I'm not thirsty," and "Please, don't fuss."

Victor wasn't appeased. "But what happened? Where were you? How did you find your way back?"

"I got lost in the storm and found an old mine to shelter in."

"An old mine?" Victor snapped his fingers. "Of course, I'd forgotten about that place. How clever of you!"

"Not so clever," she averred, looking down at her hands so he wouldn't see the lie on her face. "Grisha found me this morning and there was . . . oh, Victor, there was a cave-in. I'm afraid he's trapped inside." She clutched Victor's arm. "You must do something to get him out of there."

Victor's face paled. "But I saw him this morning. He was fine."

"Well, he's not fine now. Please, Victor, please hurry. He's badly injured. I don't know how much longer he'll last. Take as many men as you can spare, help him."

"Of course, of course." He picked up the phone and began barking orders. When he was done, he called for a maid to escort Angelina to her room. She quickly stopped him.

"I can manage. Don't worry about me. Just go, go!"

He kissed her bravely on the cheek and dashed out. The minute he was gone, she let out a huge breath and slumped in her seat. She'd gotten Victor out of the house. So far, so good.

She eased herself off the chair and limped to the desk. Picking up the phone, she glanced around, ears attuned to the slightest sound. Outside the office, men were shouting orders to one another; she hoped in the ruckus no one would remember where she was.

Fear made her fingers stiff and cold, but she punched in the contact number she'd memorized all those days ago. In two minutes, Roper was on the phone. In ten, she'd told him everything.

"I'll be there as soon as possible. Can you hold on?"

She chewed the inside of her lip. "Finn's in bad shape. And I just told Borian a whopper of a lie that will probably come back to bite me."

"All right, my dear. I'll get there as fast as I can. And good work."

She replaced the phone and leaned over the desk, drenched in sweat and chilled to the bone. Help was on the way, but would it arrive on time? She closed her eyes. She wanted to sleep for a week.

Her eyes snapped open. Oh, God. She'd forgotten the most important thing of all. Her hunch about the plutonium.

Stupid nit.

Now she'd have to risk another call to Roper. She reached for the phone again and froze as Victor burst back into the office.

Marian was with him.

Her eyes lit up in disbelief when she saw Angelina. "But you're . . . you were . . . I thought—"

Angelina took pity on her. "Surprised to see me, Marian?"

"You see?" Victor interrupted. "I told you she's perfectly fine. We'll have the doctor in to check her ankle, but I suspect it's only a bad sprain. Those cuts on her arms and hands look nasty, though. Marian, get some antibiotic ointment and help her clean up."

Victor started toward the door, but Marian grabbed his arm. "But Vic—"

"Really, I must go. There's been a terrible accident. Grisha is hurt." He pivoted toward the door, but Marian ran around to block his way.

"You can't leave her here. I told you, she's working for the government. She's a spy, a federal agent."

Victor tried to step past her, but Marian wouldn't let him, and finally he stood still, looking irritated. "Jealousy is unbecoming to a woman of your intelligence, Marian."

"It's the truth, I saw her and her partner, that so-called aide to the governor. They were together in the mine, surrounded by sophisticated equipment."

Victor flashed a wary glance at Angelina and then back at Marian. "Can you show me this equipment?"

Angelina dug her nails into her palm to keep from crying out. "What is she talking about? What equipment? You're wasting time, Victor. Grisha is hurt." She forced her voice to sound weary and harassed, even though chaos swirled in her head. Had she been wrong? In spite of his deep desire not to, would Victor take Marian's accusations seriously?

"Of course I can show you," Marian said.

"You can't show him what isn't there." Angelina met Marian's eyes. *The evidence is gone, remember? You destroyed the equipment in the cave-in.*

A stricken expression crossed Marian's face. "Well, actually I . . . I can't show you, not exactly, but—"

Victor exhaled an exasperated breath. "You're wasting my time, Marian."

He started to leave, but she put her hands on his chest, a gesture that was both intimate and supplicating. "You must believe me, Victor. You've always relied on my judgment, please, you know how much I care about you."

Victor removed her hands with a grimace of distaste. "Stop this. You're embarrassing yourself. And me." He stepped aside and clasped Angelina's hand. "I apologize. Marian is a bit unhinged about Grisha."

A long, slow cry wailed from deep within the other woman. Half-crazed, it sounded as unhinged as Victor accused her of being, and it stopped him in his tracks.

"Marian—"

"No!" she cried. "I won't let you ruin everything. Not again. Not after all I've done for you." With a spastic jerk, she reached into her pocket and came out with Finn's gun.

Victor stared at her with annoyance. "Put that away. You're being ridiculous."

Her face flushed bright red. "*I'm* ridiculous! I've worked and slaved for you. I've humiliated myself for you, done things no human should, but I did them because I love you. I love you, Victor."

"No, Marian. You're just upset." He pulled out a chair for her. "Here, sit—"

"I won't let her come between us again."

His brows scrunched together in puzzlement. "Again? What are you talking about?"

Angelina saw her opening and pounced. "She killed your wife, Victor."

"What?" He turned an astonished gaze on Angelina.

Stomach in a knot, she forced herself to look Victor in the eye and jump over the cliff. "Marian killed her sister. She admitted it to me. And now she wants to kill me."

"Shut up," Marian said.

But Angelina persisted. "She caused the mine cave-in. She shot Grisha because he tried to protect me, then left him for dead. She's crazy."

"Shut up!"

Victor eyed Marian with growing revulsion. "Is that true?"

The flush had gone, leaving Marian's face gray. Her disturbed gaze roamed around the room, as if searching for a way out. "Of course not. She'll say anything to save herself."

Out of nowhere, Angelina smelled Carol's presence, as though her mother were there, supporting her, lending her the right words. "Was Carol enjoying a slight remission in her cancer? A remission that seemed as though it might last? Did she have a few glorious days of happiness and then die unexpectedly in her sleep?"

Horrified recognition dawned on Victor's face. He stared at Marian in disbelief.

"It's not true." She shook her head and backed away, her voice desperate. "I swear. It's not—"

Victor lunged at her. "Did you do that? Did you kill my love? Did you?" She fired but must have missed, because he continued his dive forward and fastened his hands around her throat.

Marian's face turned red, then bluish.

Angelina tried to pull him off. "Victor! Let her go! Let the police—"

He elbowed her away and tightened his hold on Marian. "Did you kill her?" he roared. "Did you? Did you?"

Hoping to get help, Angelina hobbled painfully to the door. Behind her the sickening gurgle of Marian's struggle for breath vied with Victor's demented shouts.

A shot blasted in the room.

Angelina whirled in time to see Victor's hands slacken. Marian freed herself, coughing and gasping.

"Yes, I killed her!" she rasped. "I killed her, you stupid fool. She didn't believe in you. I believe in you. *I love you.*"

But Victor didn't seem to hear. He staggered backward, looking down at himself. Marian's eyes widened in horror, and Victor turned away from her.

And that's when Angelina saw the red flower blooming in the center of his chest.

Oh, my God.

"You shot me," he said. Then he fell.

"Oh, God, no!" Marian dropped the gun as if it were toxic. "I didn't mean it. I swear, Victor, I didn't mean it."

She bent down, caressing him, crooning to him. Tears streamed down her face. "I love you. I'll be your help-mate. You'll see. Everything will be fine. I promise. We'll conquer the world together." In a frantic gesture, she tried to stop the blood with her hands, but it was too late. A stream of red trickled from his lips. When she saw it, she moaned and covered her mouth with bloody hands.

Angelina stood stock-still, shocked to the marrow.

"Carol," he whispered, scanning the room for the familiar face.

His plea penetrated Angelina's disbelief; she couldn't refuse the dying man. Limping back, she sank down beside him. "I'm right here."

He fumbled for her hand and tried to squeeze it, but had no strength.

"Where's Marian?" he whispered.

Angelina turned his head so he could see the woman, sobbing on the other side of him. "Come . . . closer, Marian," he whispered. "Kiss me good-bye."

"Anything, my darling, anything. Oh, God, Victor, I love you." She leaned forward to brush his mouth, and his other hand came up holding the gun.

He blew the top of her head off.

CHAPTER
~23~

The gunshots sent a flood of people crowding into the room. Someone screamed. A uniformed arm shoved at Angelina to get a better view and a few moments later another shove pushed her in the opposite direction. One man looked at the mess of blood and gore and staggered back, white-faced. The young, blunt-nosed man who'd rescued her stumbled to a corner and threw up in a wastebasket.

All this Angelina experienced through a numb haze. Her mind registered sounds and sights from a great distance. Eventually, unknown hands lifted her from the floor and set her in a chair where she no longer had to see what was left of Marian and Victor.

Voice unsteady, she explained what had happened. Men swirled around, arguing what to do with her. Finally, Grisha's name penetrated the fog, and she glanced up to see a clump of men discussing whether or not to go to the mine. Then Finn and her assignment came back with a click, as though someone had turned a switch back on.

Roper was coming to arrest Marian and free Finn.

She looked around the room; no one was paying attention to her any longer. Quietly, she slipped from the chair, went to the desk, and called Roper again.

"Marian is dead," she said in a low, brusque voice, and briefly explained what had happened. "I'll give you the details when you get here. Make it fast."

In the meantime, she left the chaos in the office, crossed the central part of the house where the dining room and most of the public areas were. Slowly, painfully, she limped north.

Holding on to walls for support wherever possible, she slid down the glass-lined hallway, edged past the media room and the game room. Sweat dampened her shirt and pain rumbled with every step, but she didn't stop. Down the small, dark passageway to the steel door at the end.

She leaned her head against it, taking a momentary break. The cool metal felt good against the flush of pain. After a few seconds, she pushed herself away, gazed down at the keypad embedded in the front, and punched in the number Finn's decoder had uncovered the night before.

Had it only been last night?

The lock clicked open, she pushed the door inward, and once again was face-to-face with her mother's shrine.

At the sight of the photo-filled walls, an invisible hand squeezed her heart. The smiles, her mother's face frozen in happiness. So much pain to come, so much grief.

But Angelina didn't have time to dwell on the death of her dream.

Hobbling with care, she began the trek forward. With nothing to hold on to, the trip from door to wall was difficult. She bit her lip but managed to get there and trip the switch that opened the panel. Retreating gratefully to the circular bench, she watched the doors glide open on silent feet.

"Hello, Mother," she said quietly.

She imagined Victor here, sitting in the same place, gazing at his lost love, grieving, hoping for the miracle that would bring her back to him, and never once suspecting he harbored her killer.

The thick window in the tank blurred Carol's face, but Angelina knew she was there. She could smell her, the fragrance deep and rich, more pungent than ever.

She's dead, Mother. Marian is dead.

Was it her imagination, or did the sea inside the tank swirl momentarily? True or not, for a brief minute her mother's face came into sharper focus. She appeared calm. Serene.

As though she were saying thank you.

You're welcome.

Something happened then. Something strange and unsettling, but wonderful, too. A concept Angelina had given up on long ago came rushing back.

Maybe justice *was* possible in this world.

Maybe the good guys did get lucky every now and again.

She sat on the bench, surrounded by pictures of her mother and wanted to believe. Almost did. Somehow it didn't seem as unimaginable now.

Except for two tiny problems. Finn was still trapped in the mine, and the plutonium was nowhere to be found.

She scanned the space around her, gaze skimming hundreds of pictures lovingly placed, and at last came back to her mother's silver tomb. Now that she knew Marian was behind the theft, instinct told her the plutonium was in this room. Nothing would be more satisfying to Marian. Kill her rival *and* desecrate the grave.

But how? Where?

The key was there, if Angelina could only see it.

The tank was truly beautiful. She had to hand it to Victor, he'd spared no expense. The daisies stood out from the surface in three dimensions, so lifelike she could almost pluck them off.

Scattered over the surface, they formed a pattern of pretty daisy chains that wound around and around from top to . . .

One daisy way at the bottom had jumped the chain.

She cocked her head and stared at the misplaced flower at the lower edge, half hidden by the curve of the tank. It was slightly misaligned, easily missed by a quick glance. She would never have noticed if she hadn't been staring so closely.

Limping forward, she knelt and ran her fingers over the odd-man-out. It was metal like the others, yet on closer inspection, not quite the same. The petals were rounder, the center more prominent. And the whole thing stuck out from the tank at a greater depth.

Her heart began to thump. She shifted position to look closer, but her injured ankle got in the way and she lost her balance. Instinctively, she reached for the tank to steady herself, and her hand scraped against the flower. It moved.

She plopped onto the floor, staring at the thing.

It had moved.

Heart thudding faster now, she bit her lip and tugged at the petals. The entire flower came away in her hand.

My God.

Slightly larger than her hand, the flower had heft and weight, but she could still hold it easily in her palm. She turned it over, the metal cold and hard against her skin. A small rectangle, maybe an inch thick and attached to the back, gave the blossom its extra depth. Covering the rectangle was a thin piece of metal. She put the flower against the tank again and it stuck there.

A magnet. The thin strip was a magnet.

Quickly, she checked the others. They were all soldered on, solid and unmoving.

She turned the detached flower over in her hand, hunting for a way into the narrow box at the back. No latch, no entry.

She studied the daisy. The center bulged slightly. On impulse she pressed it, and the center popped open.

Her heart bolting into her throat, she jumped and nearly dropped the thing.

Jeez. Calm down.

But she couldn't. Not when she finally peeked inside and saw a small metal capsule.

For no apparent reason, she began to shake uncontrollably. Tears raced up her throat and in half a second she was bawling like a baby.

She'd done it. She'd found what they'd been looking for. Her job was over.

The corridor in Helena's St. Peter's Hospital was so well lit Angelina felt like a spotlight beamed down on her. *No place to run, no place to hide.*

She stared down at the Life Extension Foundation brochure Roper had just handed her and tried to concentrate on what he was saying. But all she could think about was Finn. He was there, somewhere in the hospital. Doctors were taking care of him, and he was going to be fine. Everyone said so. But a layer of uneasiness simmered inside her like a low-grade fever.

Roper's quiet, soothing voice melted into the white

noise of the hospital corridor with its bright light and anti-
septic smell, and she forced herself to focus on his words.

". . . company with experience in storing cryonics
tanks. I've made arrangements to have your mother's
body shipped there."

"Thank you."

"Is there anything else I can do for you?"

"You're sure Finn—Agent Carver—will be all right?"
She'd asked the question a dozen times and received a
dozen reassuring answers. Roper's was no different.

"The doctors tell me that none of his injuries are life-
threatening. He'll have a long healing period, especially
the leg, but he should be fine."

She nodded, needing to hear it again. He'd looked so
awful when they lifted him through that ancient trapdoor
and out of the mine. Strapped securely to a gurney, his leg
splinted and cushioned for the trip up, he'd been dirty,
blood-streaked, and unconscious. She'd stood on the
mountaintop, watching as they hauled his inert body into
the hovering medevac helicopter, and that was the last
she'd seen of him.

"How is your ankle?"

She glanced down at her foot, wrapped tightly in an
Ace bandage. "I'll live."

Roper patted her hand, covering the Band-Aids over
the cuts on her knuckles. "You've done more than I can
say. Marian had that flower custom-made so it could be
hidden in plain sight. You were clever to find it. Your
country is grateful, and so am I."

She shrugged self-consciously, embarrassed by the
official-sounding praise. "Well, if you're handing out
medals, I have a chest you can pin one on."

Roper coughed, which turned into a barking kind of

laugh, which in turn became an overdrawn attempt to clear his throat. "Yes, well, we all owe you a debt. Now, can I have someone take you to the hotel?"

Yes. Please. She was desperate to leave, but frantic to stay. "I'd appreciate a ride, but first . . . can I see Agent Carver?"

"I think he's sleeping."

"That's okay. I just want to . . . to see for myself that he's all right."

The little man shrugged, but escorted her to Finn's room. "I'll . . . uh . . . I'll wait outside," he said.

"Thank you." She took a breath and pushed open the door.

Finn lay on his back, eyes closed, body connected to a morphine drip through an IV in the back of his hand. His leg was wrapped and trapped, held still in some kind of Rube Goldberg medical contraption.

As she crept closer, she saw he'd been cleaned up, the blood and dirt replaced by sterile gauze and clean bandages. He didn't seem as scary as he had the last time she'd seen him, and the tightness inside her chest loosened a little.

She brushed the dark hair off his haggard face. Even in sleep, lines of exhaustion cut deep into his cheeks and around his mouth.

But his chest rose and fell in steady, reliable rhythm.

He looked broken but not destroyed. Worn out but not beat.

Alive.

And so damn good, tears welled up.

No use fighting it; she was a goddamn waterworks today. Once she would have died rather than cry over a man. But this man was worth it.

Besides, he was dead to the world and would never see.

She pulled the only chair up close to the unencumbered side of the bed.

"Hey, Sharkman," she whispered. "Looks like we're both going to live." His arm lay limply at his side and she ran her hand over his palm, straightening out the fingers.

Those fingers had made her body sing and she had paid him back with cruelty and lies. *Just one in a long line*. Would he believe it?

People always thought the worst of Her. What if Finn was no different? She didn't want to stick around to find out.

She swiped at her seeping eyes with the back of her hand. The important thing was that he was alive. He would heal. No matter what he thought of her, somewhere on the planet he'd be walking and talking.

The damn tears started again, clogging her throat and making her nose run.

Besides, she'd spent too much of her life using men as a shield between her and the world. It was time she stood on her own.

"Got something for you." Her voice was husky and thick. "Been carrying it around for hours." Reaching into her pocket, she pulled out the pearl brooch. "Something to remember me by." She pinned the circle to his pillow, and then, because she couldn't help herself, she leaned down and brushed her mouth over his.

"See you around, Sharkman."

Before she could change her mind, she turned and walked out the door.

CHAPTER
～24～

Finn didn't remember anything about the cave-in, but he read about it in the report Roper brought to the hospital. He would have preferred to hear what happened from Angelina herself, but since she never came to see him, that wasn't an option.

So he lay in bed while his leg and shoulder mended and read the cold, impersonal phrases that described how she'd dragged him to safety, sustained an injury but had been clever enough to use it to get to a place where she could call for help. Then she managed to keep herself alive while Marian and Victor killed each other, found the plutonium, and though she didn't dig him out herself, was the instrument that saved his life.

Every time he read it he was filled with pride; not many other men could boast that their woman was a superhero.

Of course, she wasn't his woman. Not yet anyway.

The gunshot wound healed faster than the leg did, but both required extensive convalescence. He bided his time, waited for his leg to bear weight again, and through

Roper, kept track of Angelina's whereabouts. She'd asked him not to reveal them to Finn, but Roper was never very good at keeping promises, so Finn knew that she'd moved out of Beaman's Memphis home. But where she went after that was anybody's guess.

She'd told Roper she was going to stay with a friend in Nashville, but when Finn called that number, it turned out to be a dry-cleaning shop where no one had heard of Angelina or her friend. On every document the TCF required her to fill out, she'd written a different contact number. Finn tried them all and they were all dead ends.

Nice going, Angel.

He spent most of his medical leave tracking her down. He had access to every database in the country; credit bureaus, the FBI's National Crime Information Center, state-by-state police and courthouse records. But she didn't show up on any of them, not even through a trace of credit card purchases.

As the weeks passed and no sign of her turned up, he gritted his teeth and refused to give up. He had to find her and talk to her in person. Tell her how much she meant to him.

And how much he meant to her.

Because no way was he falling for her bullshit.

Besides, he owed her a big-time apology for all the attitude he'd given her. Not to mention a world-sized thank you for saving his life.

A month after his release from the hospital, Roper banged on his apartment door.

"Thought you could use a beer," he said, lifting the six-pack he'd brought along.

Finn let the smaller man in. "Didn't know you drank beer. You must want something."

Roper smiled, not at all embarrassed to be found out. "I want you to come back to work."

Finn shrugged. "I've still got medical leave."

"The Finn Carver I know wouldn't let that stop him."

Finn grinned. "Someone once told me that all work and no play led to atrophy of too many important body parts."

"So?"

"So I'm getting a life. Isn't that what everyone's been telling me? I even went to the movies yesterday. Crutches and all."

"Did it take?"

"What?"

"Your experiment in ordinary living."

Finn thought about it. The movie had been silly and trivial, and despite himself, he'd enjoyed it. "I don't know yet."

Roper nodded, clearly unconvinced. "Well, I think you've just exchanged one obsession for another. And not that I want to encourage you down that road, but here." He took a piece of paper from his pocket.

"What's this?"

"An application for a bank loan from the Lone Star Bank in Ruby, Texas."

A bolt of pure energy shot through Finn. He glanced at the paper, then back at Roper.

His boss smiled. "Go ahead, check it out. She got the loan, by the way."

"You verified?"

"Twice."

Finn stared at the piece of paper disbelieving. He popped one of Roper's beers and leaned against the counter, drinking and rereading the same sentence over and over.

Ruby, Texas. "Why the hell did she go back there?"

"It's home, isn't it? She's got family there, unfinished business."

"Confront her past instead of running from it?"

"Stranger things have happened."

He fished in his pocket for the pearl monitor he'd found pinned to his hospital pillow. He'd kept it close to him ever since, taking it out a thousand times and wishing it was still pinned to her breast. Running his fingers over the smooth surface of the gems, he wondered what the hell she was up to.

Stranger things have happened.

Maybe catching the bad guys this time helped her see they don't always get away.

His hand closed around the brooch. Not much she could do about her own personal bad guy, though. Not after so many years. Not by herself.

He looked over at Roper. "Who do we know in Ruby?"

Roper shrugged. "No one. It's a small town. No TCF presence. Why?"

"I've got a bone to pick with the sheriff there."

Roper smiled. "How right can I be, Carver? If it's not one thing, it's another. Where's a piece of paper?" Finn tore off a sheet from a pad near the phone. "Here's the nearest FBI field office and the name of the Special Agent in charge." He pushed it across the counter to Finn. "So much for your medical leave."

Angelina adjusted the line of the halter top in the front window of Undercover Angel, the lingerie shop she'd opened with help from the Lone Star Bank. The nearest

Victoria's Secret was sixty miles away, and even the God-fearing women of Ruby wore bras and panties. Why not give them something to show when they took off their clothes at night?

Of course, she'd been perfectly aware that the shop was a long shot, especially in a small, uptight place like Ruby. But coming back and taking a chance had been like thumbing her nose at the whole town. After all she'd been through, all she'd accomplished, she no longer cared what anyone thought. *Take me or leave me, you'll never forget me.*

And big surprise, the shop had been a success.

She had Adele to thank for that. Her mother had burst into tears of joy when she saw Angelina at her front door. For the first time, Angelina accepted that Adele was truly glad to see her. And she found herself ready to forgive her mother for what happened all those years ago when she took the town's side against her daughter.

People made mistakes. They deserved a second chance.

This time, Adele got it right. Though the shop might have been denounced as sinful, she talked it up to all her church buddies and threw a lingerie shower for every bride and new mother in a fifty-mile radius. She not only eliminated the potential taint, she made the shop popular.

And now it was almost Labor Day. Women liked to buy when the seasons turned, and fall was just around the corner.

Angelina hummed as she changed the window display, switching out a hot pink camisole for burnt orange, and a turquoise bra and panty set for tiger-striped. A movement outside caught her attention and she looked up to see Sheriff Dodd being led in handcuffs from a Texas Ranger car toward the county courthouse.

It was early, but Ruby was an early-waking town and other people stopped to watch the spectacle, especially those in front of the Courthouse Café, who stood in little clumps of twos and threes. Angelina gaped along with everyone else, window display forgotten.

She hadn't seen much of the sheriff since her return; she'd stayed away from most of the trouble spots where she was likely to run into him. No bars, no back alleys—not that there were many in Ruby—no late-night parking-lot assignations. She'd lived quietly, and left lawbreaking and law enforcement to others. Once or twice she'd seen him on the street, an older, heftier version of the rooster she'd faced all those years ago, still recognizable enough to send a bolt of nausea ping-ponging around her stomach.

As for Andy Blake, she hadn't seen him at all. Adele told her he ran a car lot on the other side of the state, the kind of place that attracted used-up people and their used-up cars. He'd gone fat and bald and was working on his third marriage. Somehow that pleased them both.

Now she watched, dumbstruck, as a Texas Ranger escorted the sheriff around the car toward the courthouse steps. Well, what did that drama signify? She knew Max Dodd was an evil little twit, but she never thought he'd be caught at it.

The passenger side of the car opened and a man in a suit got out. He paused to say something to the Ranger, then turned in the vee of the door and gazed over the car roof across the wide expanse of road to the shops across the way. To her shop.

Her heart started thumping.

The man closed the door and strolled around the car to the curb and the street. Frozen, Angelina watched him cross, the same dark, lean strength she'd known and loved embedded in every stride. Whole again, safe, alive. Just as she knew he'd be.

But what was he doing here?

She stopped breathing. Her mind refused to work, refused to process the sight of him on the streets of Ruby, coming up to her window as if he'd lived there forever. Wordless, he looked at her through the glass. She couldn't move, her hands stuck to the stretchy tiger-striped material as though it were Velcro.

Then he tapped on the window and she jumped, released from the spell.

"I'm looking for Angelina Mercer," he said loudly, his voice distorted through the glass.

A rush of heat filled her face and she backed out of the window space, jumped down onto the floor, and unlocked the shop door, barring the way. She knew now she didn't need his approval; she could succeed on her own just fine. But she didn't want to face the possibility of his condemnation either.

"She's not here," she said, looking him straight in the eye.

A slight smile played around the corners of his mouth, and he leaned against the doorjamb, blue eyes taking leisurely inventory from top to bottom and back again. She straightened, hoping he wouldn't see through the changes. The shorter hair, the new color.

"That's too bad," he said at last, "I wanted to thank her for saving my life."

Another rush of embarrassed heat. Gratitude was definitely not what she wanted from him. "No thanks necessary," she mumbled and started to close the door, but somehow his foot got in the way and instead of getting turned out, he let himself in.

"And . . ." he said as he closed the door behind him, "I need her expertise."

She eyed him. How the hell had he managed to get inside? "I don't think she's doing much in your line of work these days."

He strolled around the shop, picked up a lacy camisole, and held it up to the light. "I was hoping to talk to her about something else. A gift. For a . . . special woman." He replaced the sheer garment and smiled pleasantly. "I know her measurements. Thirty-eight, twenty—" He stopped to give her another once-over. "Actually, she's about your size. But her hair"—he walked around her—"is longer, down to here"—he touched her shoulder and a buzz of unwanted electricity jolted her—"not here." He touched the nape of her neck where the soft curls stopped just below her ear, sending another electric quake through her. "And it's blond, not—" He was back in front of her now and he cocked his head curiously. "What is that color?"

"Natural," she snapped.

"Natural," he repeated. "Like in . . . God-given?"

"Exactly." She marched over to the door and swung it open. "We're closed."

He stuck his hands in his pockets and strolled toward her. "I like it. Kind of a reddish brown."

A treacherous tingle of pleasure threatened, which she quickly suppressed in a scowl. "We don't open until ten-thirty."

"Like honey with sunlight shining through it."

Now how was she supposed to ignore that? He closed in on her and she scooted away, if only so she could keep breathing. But that left the door unmanned, and he closed it again, resting against it with his arms and legs crossed.

"Here's the thing," he said softly. "I might not be here

after ten-thirty. And I really wanted to buy that gift. I have a major apology to make."

An apology? Seemed like she was the one who should apologize. Not that she would.

She raised her chin and challenged him with a look. "And you think a present will make it easier?"

"I don't think anything's going to make it easy. This woman . . . she holds a grudge."

"She does not."

He shrugged. "I know a grudge she held against a certain party for over eleven years. Now, I'm not saying this party didn't deserve it. In fact, he pretty much deserves everything he gets, and believe me, he's going to get the full treatment." For a moment his mouth hardened into a grim line, then softened again. "But me . . ."

She eyed him closely. "You're not as bad as him?"

"Let's just say I'm prepared to do my share of groveling."

"Starting with this . . . gift."

"Uh-huh." He pushed away from the door. "And anything else that's necessary."

"Anything?" Her eyes narrowed.

"Anything this side of the law."

Always the lawman. But wasn't that delicious uprightness part of the attraction? She smiled, then quickly looked away to hide it. She'd always be the party girl to him, and she couldn't live that way, no matter what he did to her breathing.

He sidled up beside her, close enough for her to feel his hip jutting into hers. Her stomach lurched and her heart did that jackhammer thing it always did around him. She dodged away, escaping behind the L-shaped cash-register counter against the wall.

"I think you better go."

"I will. I promise." But instead of heading for the door, he came right in after her. "In a minute."

Now she was trapped between him and the counter end. Her heartbeat ratcheted up another notch and wildly she looked for a way out, but there was none and he knew it. He smiled.

"First I want to return something that belongs to her." He fished in his pocket and came out with a circle of pearls. She let out a surprised gasp and felt tears at the back of her throat.

Before she could stop him, he was pinning it to her blouse, just above her heart. She was faint with his nearness, dumbstruck and dry-mouthed.

He didn't seem to care.

He stood back, cocked his head as he eyed the position of the pin on her chest. "The thing is, this woman I told you about? I'm nuts about her. Well, she drives me nuts, but I kind of like it." His gaze rose to her face, his expression heating and softening at the same time. "No, I love it. I love her." He stepped forward until he was so close she could feel his warm breath on her face. His hands cupped her cheeks and he tilted her head up so she was soaring into the depths of his blue, blue gaze. "I love *you*. I am sorrier than I can ever say about being the bastard I was. No excuses. I said a lot of things I regret. I misjudged you and hurt you, and I'll do whatever it takes to make it up to you."

He'd hurt her?

With great reluctance, she pulled away. "Starting with Sheriff Dodd."

He nodded. "Well, that wasn't hard. He's a scumbag of the first order. The Rangers were having trouble with an increase in drug distribution to high school kids in the county. Dodd got nowhere with the investigation, and it seems he never intended to; he was getting kickbacks from a consortium of dealers in the area. I would have liked to take him down for what he did to you, but . . . well, in the end I figured taking him down was all that mattered."

For her. He'd done that for her. "I don't know what to say."

"Just say you'll give me a chance."

A chance. "To what—prove how much you care?"

"Prove we're not all sleazeballs."

"We?"

"Cops. Men. Me. Mostly me."

"And how are you going to prove that?"

"I don't know yet. I figure it might take a while, though."

She barked a laugh. "Yeah, like a lifetime."

He stepped back as if shot, but the surprise was clearly feigned. "That's what I was thinking, too." He sobered, watching her intently. "A lifetime."

She stilled, seeing the gleam in his blue eyes. "What are you saying?"

He shrugged. "Nothing. Just that I might have to stick around past ten-thirty." He leaned against the counter and studied her. "If it's okay with you, that is. Ruby needs a new sheriff."

Her eyes widened. "And you're applying for the job?"

"I'm thinking about it. That is, if you'll think about this." He took something else from his pocket, this time placing it on the counter between them. When he removed his hand she saw the ring. The diamond ring.

Her mouth dried up. She cut a fast glance at him and then back at the ring. He couldn't be serious.

"What about . . ." She swallowed. "What about what I said in the mine?"

"What—that you were conning me? That it was all a joke and you didn't mean it?" He threw her a pitied glance. "You were right. A good cop knows a con when he hears one." He yanked her to him, close enough to smell the shaving cream on his skin. "And I'm a very good cop."

Her face heated, and he laughed, clearly enjoying her discomfort. "Bark for me, Angel. And if you're a good little doggie, I might be persuaded to give you some of what you had that night in the mine."

She pushed him away, untangling herself from the hard body and the sensations that flowed through her nonstop. "But, what about Arthur? What about the long—"

"—line of men?"

She nodded stiffly. "I don't give a shit, Angel. The past is past. I'm talking about the future."

"You don't care?"

"Why should I? Do you care that I was stupid enough to fall for a woman who didn't deserve me? That it almost got me killed? Seems my mistakes have been a whole lot deadlier than yours."

She eyed the ring. The diamond was square-shaped, simple and gleaming. Exactly the kind of ring she would have chosen herself. Not that she ever expected to choose a ring.

Not that she ever expected . . . anything.

"I never slept with any of them," she said softly, fingering the ring to avoid facing him.

Silence. "You never—"

"That was the deal. I hung around, looked pretty, made them feel alive, and gave them something to look forward to every day." She forced herself to face him. "But no sex."

"Not even Beaman?"

She shook her head.

"And they were . . . okay with that?"

She smiled, feeling wistful. "Very okay. You can't imagine what it's like to be pushed to the sidelines by life. To be old and counted out. I evened the score a little."

He shook his head and caressed her cheek with the back of his hand, sending a slow shiver through her. "You are one big surprise, Angel. But whether you did or didn't doesn't matter. I don't care." He pushed the hair behind her ears, a gesture as intimate as it was sensual. "So, what's it gonna be? You up for this?"

She met his gaze, saw the challenge there. *I dare you, Angel.* She raised her chin. She was never one to turn down a dare.

"No nagging about what I wear?"

He eyed her leisurely. "Honey, you can wear prison gray for all I care. As long as it's cut down to there and hiked up to here, I'll be happy."

She gave him one last chance to back out. "You ever stop to think what it will be like for a lawman to live with a bad girl?"

"Oh, I've thought about it." He shot her another sly, lazy smile. "And I think it'll be pretty damn good, Angel. As long as the lawman's me and the bad girl's you, I'd say it'll be pretty damn good."

ABOUT THE AUTHOR

A native New Yorker, Annie Solomon has been dreaming up stories since she was ten. After a twelve-year career in advertising, where she rose to Vice President and Head Writer at a mid-size agency, she abandoned the air conditioners, furnaces, and heat pumps of her professional life for her first love—romance. An avid knitter, she now lives in Nashville with her husband and daughter. To learn more, visit her Web site at www.anniesolomon.com.

More
Annie Solomon!

~

Please turn this page
for a preview
of
TELL ME NO LIES
an upcoming Warner Book
available in April 2004.

CHAPTER
~1~

The eyes of the dead held secrets. Detective Hank Bonner knew that just as he knew his job was to uncover them. He looked down at the body of Luka Kole.

What secrets did your eyes hold, old man?

Hank didn't want to find out. He had less than two weeks left as a cop, and he wanted to spend the time writing reports, cleaning up old cases and shutting down what had been a major part of his thirty-six years.

But two hours ago, Parnell, head of the Sokanan Police Department's Homicide division, had other ideas. "Dead body on Rossvelt." He'd handed Hank a scrawled address, the expression in his face daring Hank to object.

Hank knew what Parnell was doing. He could have given that DB to anyone. But he was using it to hook Hank in, playing out the line, trying to reel him back with one last case.

Hank had buried himself in a box of assorted memorabilia—a cracked coffee cup that had been a Christmas present years ago, books he never got around to reading, papers he still needed to sort through. "Let Klimet handle it."

"Klimet couldn't handle a cat stuck in a tree. Not yet anyway. I got your butt 'til the end of the month, Bonner. Get going."

So here Hank was, haunted by another pair of dead eyes.

He scanned the crime scene inside the Gas-Up on Rossvelt Avenue, the latest in a string of convenience store robberies that had plagued the Hudson Valley for the last month. Luka Kole, who evidently owned the place, lay behind the counter, a squat, gray-haired man with a hole in his barrel chest. The open cash drawer stood empty, the overturned candy bin lay on its side. Lindt truffles wrapped in shiny blue, green and red paper were strewn on the counter and the floor along with a display of Slim Jims, cigarette lighters, and Van Dekker County souvenir pens.

The mess was sure sign of a struggle. Whoever he was, Luka Kole hadn't gone down easy.

The only thing detracting from the obvious was the bank bag. Hidden beneath the cash drawer, it contained over a thousand dollars, fat and ready for deposit. Why would the robber leave it behind?

"Because he's a mope, not a rocket scientist," Joe Klimet scoffed, staring down at Luka Kole's sightless brown eyes as though he expected them to confirm his conclusion.

Hank studied the younger man. He wore a sharp black suit, silver gray shirt and patterned tie in yellow and gray. Slick and flashy with a grin to match. But Hank forgave him. Or tried to. He remembered what it was like to be cocky.

"So he leaves the money because he's stupid," Hank said.

Joe shrugged: Why not?

Hank bent to get a closer look at the body. He'd already scouted the scene, starting with a careful walk around the outside perimeter and gradually moving closer to the victim, who was always the last thing he examined.

"Seems to me a guy who's managed to get away with four of these jobs right under our noses is no dummy."

Klimet frowned. The homicide division's newest addition, he didn't like being challenged. "Something scared him off before he could check below the drawer."

Hank looked at him calmly. "What?"

"How the hell should I know? A customer, a car pulling in. Something."

"Maybe he wasn't after the money."

Klimet rolled his eyes. "You know, you're nuts, Bonner. The scene is clear—the cash drawer's empty. If the scumbag wasn't after money, what was he after?"

"Who knows? Revenge maybe. The other clerk said Kole argued with someone earlier in the day." Hank flipped through a small notebook. "Adulous McTeer, also known as Big Mac. Maybe this Big Mac wanted the last word."

"Then why take anything?"

"To make it look like a robbery."

"It was a robbery." Klimet crossed his arms, not hiding his irritation. "Just like all the others."

Hank was silent. "Looks like. But I want to talk to Mr. Big. We got someone rounding him up?"

"Already on it." Klimet ducked under the yellow

crime-scene tape to confer with the patrolman who'd been first on the scene.

Hank called to Greenlaw, one of an elite cadre of patrol officers trained as crime-scene technicians. "Still no brass?"

"No, sir," Greenlaw said.

No shell casings could mean a revolver. Or a smarter-than-average creep. "Keep looking."

Someone handed Hank the victim's wallet. Hands gloved, he examined it, hoping for something that would give him insight into Luka Kole. The clerk who'd found the body hadn't been very helpful; Kole had owned the store, but the clerk had worked there only a few weeks and didn't know much about his boss. The wallet didn't give away much either, except that Kole was no spend-thrift. The case was old and thin, the outline of credit cards imprinted on the worn leather in front. The guy must have been sitting on the thing for years.

Inside, Hank found the usual: credit cards, driver's license, plus fifty dollars in cash. Behind the bills he found a newspaper clipping, the headline half torn, but still readable: JOINT U.S. RUSSIA ECONOMIC VENTURE BRINGS JOBS TO VAN DEKKER COUNTY.

Quickly, Hank scanned the article. Normal press release stuff. Quotes from Mikhail "Miki" Petrov, the businessman who was bankrolling the Russian end of deal, and from A.J. Baker, the American consultant who'd set the whole thing up. Mr. Petrov was a big shot in Manhattan and Washington, and not easily accessible. A.J. Baker, on the other hand, apparently lived right here in the Hudson Valley.

Hank replaced the clipping and slipped the wallet into an evidence bag. So, like everyone else in town, Luka

Kole was looking forward to the deal with Renaissance Oil. But how many people carried around articles about it?

Hank ducked under the yellow tape. "Klimet." He handed the younger detective the bagged wallet. "Subpoena the phone records. Here and at the vic's apartment. Take Finelli with you to canvass the area. See if anyone heard anything, saw anything. I'll see you back at the station."

"Where are you going?"

But Hank had already walked off and pretended he hadn't heard.

Outside, he ignored the small crowd milling around in uneasy formation at the edge of the parking lot. He understood their fascination and their horror. When murder hit close to home the two things melded together. *It could have been me. Thank God it wasn't.*

He got in his car, backed out and called in to the station, waiting for the dispatcher to hunt down an address on Baker.

Then he turned down Highway Nine, Joe's question circling inside his head. What had the shooter been after?

Dead man's secrets.

Ten minutes later, he turned off the highway and slowed down to peer into the wooded roadside for addresses. The house was somewhere along this road.

At least Luka Kole was dead. And dead men were a lot more predictable than live ones. They didn't turn crazy, eyes wild and maniacal. They didn't come at you with guns or knives or . . . A chill shivered through Hank. Or screwdrivers. Instinctively he pressed a fist to his chest. Still there. Still beating.

As if he'd never felt that death blow, never experienced the certainty of his own mortality.

And then, somehow, lived.

"That's one strong breastbone," the emergency room doctor had said. "Deflected the blade. A little to the left or right and we'd be saying prayers over you. Count yourself lucky."

Oh, he did. Damn lucky.

But the problem with luck was, sooner or later it ran out.

A wave of sick certainty rippled over his skin. It welled up inside him as he found the address and turned the car into a long, gravel drive. Woods lined the road, thick, green and impenetrable. His heart started that upward chase, his hands gripped the steering wheel. This was crazy. No one was hiding back there. No one waited for him with murderous intent.

He swallowed, forced the runaway train inside his chest to slow down. He was here to do his job. Gather information. Find out what he could about Luka Kole.

Concentrate on the dead man, he'd be fine.

When the house came into view it was easier to remember the drill. He braked, paused to gape. The place was a sculpture of glass, stone and wood, but nearly overwhelmed by the natural forest overlooking the Hudson. Undergrowth tangled around it, thick as the briars surrounding Sleeping Beauty's castle in the book he read to his niece. A lair or a hideout, even a retreat. Hank sympathized. He understood the wish to submerge, to bury yourself. Did Mr. Baker? Or was he just too cheap to hire a crew to cut back the growth?

He pulled up to the house and noticed the tail end of a green van parked around the side. Out of the car, he walked around to investigate. EDIE'S FLOWERS, the van said. In front of it were two more vans. Caterers. A flurry of people swarmed in and out of the house.

Someone was throwing a party tonight. By the looks of it, a big one.

And then Hank remembered what day it was.

Alex Baker's reflection stared back at her from the large, gilt-framed mirror that hung above her dresser. She was all angles tonight, cheekbones like razor blades. Once, she might have cringed at the sharp edge in her eyes, but she was glad of it now. She felt well honed, a killing blade.

And if her stomach fluttered she ignored it. If that queasy awareness that she was alone, and always would be, haunted her thoughts, she pushed it away.

Hid it. Stuffed it deep down where it couldn't rise up and make her weak. Defenseless.

Instead, she concentrated on the way her silvery slip dress clung to her body, the way the barely-there straps blended with and exposed her skin. Her body was a tool, a smokescreen. It would compel and distract, and slowly, slowly open the door of the trap she was setting.

And it all began tonight.

She checked her watch. Nearly seven. She had a good hour or more before guests arrived; plenty of time to get ready. And yet, here she was, dressed and perfumed, hair perfect, makeup perfect. Only one small detail to add. She caressed the blue velvet case on her dresser. Inside was the necklace her father had given her more than a decade ago on her sixteenth birthday. She would wear it tonight, in honor of him.

She smiled at herself, a tight, deadly smile, and opened the case.

A knock sounded.

Her head swiveled in the direction of the sound. "Yes?"

The door opened to reveal Sonya, the shapeless brown dress over her short fat legs making her appear like a wrinkled mushroom. A worried mushroom, if her expression was any indication. Immediately, Alex crossed to the old woman and drew her into the room. She'd been fretful all day, not used to strangers in the house.

"Why aren't you in your room?" Alex spoke softly. "Let me bring you a plate of goodies. We're having blinis tonight. With caviar and sour cream. You love that. It's been a long time since you had real blinis."

Sonya shook her head. "Too much . . . noise," she said. "And now—" Her hands twisted together and a word burst out from her. A word in Russian. Police.

Alex stilled. "What are you talking about?"

Sonya emitted another torrent of Russian and instinctively Alex put a hand over the older woman's mouth, looking around as though the room held spies. "English, dear one. English. Slow down. Tell me."

The old woman bit her lip. Tears formed in her eyes. "Sorry, so very sorry." But the words came out in Russian. "He frightened me so."

"All right," Alex soothed. "Take a breath." She went into her bathroom and filled a cup with water. "Here. Drink this."

Sonya drank and handed back the cup with trembling hands.

"Now tell me, what is this about the police?"

"They are here."

"Where, at the house?" Alex smiled. "Of course they are. We have a security detail."

Sonya shook her head. "*Nyet*. Not . . . party. To talk. Questions. He said, questions."

A small alarm went off inside Alex, but she quickly silenced it. Sonya's English had never been very good; she often got things mixed up. "It's all right, darling. I'm sure it's nothing." She settled the woman into a large upholstered armchair. "Stay here and rest. I'll be right back. And don't worry."

Swiftly, Alex closed the door and made her way toward the front of the house. Preparations for the party were rapidly coming to a close. The house sparkled with lights and flowers. Silver trays and goblets, crystal bowls for candies and tidbits. As the sun set, fairy lights outside would turn the woods and garden into a magic kingdom seen through glass. A kingdom aglow with the rich, silky flush of oil. Russian oil.

She stopped just short of the entrance, where two workers from the florists were putting the finishing touches on the man-size centerpiece—a wire structure in the shape of an oil rig and entirely covered in thick golden mums.

"Quite an eye-catcher," said a deep male voice. The owner of the voice stepped from behind the structure and gave her a crooked smile. A big man with wide shoulders under a rumpled sports coat, he had fair hair and sun-kissed skin. A surfer stranded on land. A man out of place somehow. She met his eyes. Nothing out of place here. They were green. Sharp. Evaluating. Was this what had frightened Sonya?

His greeting replayed itself in her mind; had he been

referring to something other than the decorations? To her?

She stiffened, the ice she stored at the base of her spine rising like a protective shell. "May I help you?"

He flashed a badge. "Detective Bonner from Sokanan PD. I'm looking for A.J. Baker."

"I'm A.J. Baker."

His eyes widened and a mote of satisfaction clipped the iceberg building inside her. She liked surprising people.

"You're . . ." A jolt shook Hank. The shimmer of femininity in front of him looked no more capable of putting together an international business deal than he was. But perception wasn't always reality, as he knew only too well.

Quickly, he reassessed. Her ice-blond hair glistened and fell to her shoulders in a straight, silky waterfall, a perfect foil to the silvery dress, which swirled around her curves like mercury. Not beautiful in the classic sense, but in an outrageously exotic way, with high, angled cheekbones and eyes the color of sky before it rained. A pulse quickened inside him, and he saw the look of recognition come over her. The look that said, *I know what you're thinking, pal, and forget it.*

Yeah, he'd bet she did know. He'd bet A.J. Baker was used to men drooling over her. And he wasn't going to get in line. Ignoring his purely chemical reaction, he let out a breath to cover his initial surprise. "So what does the A.J. stand for?"

"Alexandra Jane. Alex."

He noted the drawn-out "a." Alex*aaa*ndra. Some kind of British thing. Or New England. Boston maybe.

"As you can see," she said, "we're preparing for a big

event tonight. Is this about the security detail? I hope there's no problem." She gave him an impersonal smile, and he saw hardness congeal behind those cloudy eyes. Not a street-wise toughness, but the cool confidence that only money and years of private schools could instill.

"Security detail? You mean for the big wing-ding half the department will be at? No, it's not about the security."

"Detective, I'm busy. How can I help you?"

Polite, but impatient. Eager to get rid of him. Because he was a cop, or something else? He glanced at the team of floral workers. On ladders and on the ground they hovered over the huge structure that probably cost more than his car. "Is there some place we can talk privately?"

"What is this about?"

Again, he glanced at the workers and she let out a small sigh of irritation. "This way."

She led him through the glass terrace doors and into a garden courtyard. The forest was even thicker here. Trees huddled over the house, enclosing it in a suffocating embrace as though hiding it from the rest of the world.

He nodded toward them. "I can recommend a gardener."

She looked in the direction he'd pointed, eyes narrowed in puzzlement. Then, as though she saw when he'd seen, "I like a lot of foliage."

Short, crisp, and by the aloofness her eyes, all the explanation he was going to get.

"I don't mean to be rude, but I'm expecting a lot of people. What can I do for you?"

The air smelled earthy and green and reminded him of the orchards of Apple House, the Bonner farm. But that memory brought up others, leading always to the two orphaned children who now wandered the grounds, and his own part in their fate. A bleakness descended, and he had to force himself to focus on the woman in front of him.

He leaned against the edge of the garden wall, a low brick structure that framed the patio. "I'm looking for information about a guy called Luka Kole. Ever heard of him?"

Her expression shifted, but quickly as the change came, her features composed themselves into disinterested lines. "Lu-Luka who?"

"Kole. Luka Kole. Know him?"

Did her shoulders tense? She frowned, looked down and then over at the woods beyond the garden as though trying to remember. "The name isn't familiar. Why? Who is he? Has he done something?"

Hank watched her closely. "Got himself killed today."

Her head snapped around. Shock charged her eyes. "Killed? You mean in an accident? Look, Detective, tonight is a very important—"

"Definitely not an accident. He was shot."

"I see." She sank into one of the wrought-iron garden chairs. Her silver dress shivered against the black metal, and the neckline drooped to reveal a dip of cleavage. "And what does that have to do with me?"

Hank tore his eyes away from her breasts. "I don't know." He cleared his throat. "Probably nothing. It was a long shot. We found an article about your Russian business deal in his wallet. Thought I'd see if there was any connection. We haven't been able to drum up much information about him. Who his friends were. His enemies."

She smiled, a dismissive, lady-of-the-manor curve of her lips, but something lurked behind it. What? "As I don't know him, I am hardly either." She rose, distant as a star. "I'm sorry I can't help you. And I am busy." She indicated the door back into the house and escorted him inside. "Will we see you tonight?"

He shook his head, dreading the evening ahead. "Got a previous engagement."

"Well, enjoy your evening."

Alex saw him out, closed the door behind her, then wilted against it, her legs suddenly gone.

Luka. My God.

One of the floral workers noticed her. "Are you all right, Miss Baker?" He started toward her and she drew a steadying breath. She could not draw attention to herself. Not now. Not when she was on the brink of everything she'd worked so hard for.

She straightened, brushing her dress as if nothing had happened. "It's all right. I'm fine. I haven't had much to eat today. Too much excitement."

The man nodded understanding, and Alex thanked him, then swept past, shoulders back, head high, though it cost her.

Get to the phone. She must get to the phone.

She was halfway to her room when she remembered Sonya. Oh, God, she couldn't face the old woman now. Not with this catastrophe. But she couldn't avoid all contact with her either. Sonya would only worry.

Retracing her steps, Alex forced her pace into a casual stroll and walked into the sunroom where a white-coated bartender was setting up a portable bar.

Take a breath. Smile.

She introduced herself. "Opening-night jitters," she confided. "I don't suppose you could spare a little vodka."

The bartender laughed. "We've got so much Stoli we

could swim in it. There's plenty to spare." He found a bottle and upturned a glass. "Ice?"

She shook her head. "Never."

He handed her the drink and she thanked him but didn't take a sip. *Luka, what happened?* Instead, she carried the glass out of the sunroom and into the kitchen, where the rich fragrance of stroganoff nearly turned her stomach. A platoon of cooks and servers made the place look like a staging area for a major battle. They stirred pots, checked ovens and plated canapés. Several were setting silver and glassware on huge trays to take to the buffet area. She filched a plate and spooned some of the thick beef and cream concoction on it, added blinis and Russian black caviar, herring salad and mushrooms in sour cream. Two finger-shaped *saikas* with jam for dessert, then up the small flight of stairs at the back of the house.

Please let this work.

Luka. Luka. The name echoed with every step.

Outside her bedroom door, she closed her eyes and breathed. In and out. Steady. Sure. She could do this. She'd been hiding her feelings for years.

THE EDITOR'S DIARY

Dear Reader,

Trick or treat? For both Angelina Mercer and Leah of Pecham, the two go hand in hand as deception leads them both to a love more electrifying than they could ever have imagined in our two Warner Forever titles this October.

Romantic Times raves **Annie Solomon's** work is "dark, riveting, and emotionally dense . . . one powerful read" so get ready because her newest Warner Forever title, **DEAD RINGER**, will knock your socks off. Angelina Mercer is Federal Agent Finn Carter's last hope. His hunt for a dangerous weapon has led him to her door with a proposition that could be her salvation or destruction. But it is surely her only chance to learn the truth about the birth mother she's been searching for her entire life. In return, she must infiltrate the inner sanctum of a tycoon's Montana ranch, walking the dangerous line between deception and discovery. With only each other to trust, Angelina and Finn must watch their every step because one false move could mean the end of their growing love . . . and certain death.

Leaving the thrilling world of espionage for medieval England, we find **Shari Anton's** Warner Forever debut **THE IDEAL HUSBAND**. *Rendezvous* says "she creates a spell that keeps her readers captured" and you'll be under her spell soon too. After all, what could be more romantic than a heroic husband risking his life to save his beloved from a shipwreck? But the gravely injured man Leah of Pecham tenderly cradles is not her husband but a gallant stranger who fearlessly came to her rescue. Honor-bound to care for Geoffrey's health yet certain he cannot survive, Leah decides to take him home to Pecham. There she will make everyone believe he is her lawfully wedded husband, washing away her dishonor and averting her father's wrath. And Leah will discover just how delicious—and how dangerous—a lie can be, for Geoffrey grows stronger and more seductive each day . . .

To find out more about Warner Forever, these October titles, and the authors, visit us at www.warnerforever.com.

With warmest wishes,

Karen Kosztolnyk

Karen Kosztolnyik, Senior Editor

P.S. Next month, Warner Forever offers you two titles that will make you think twice about being nice: Leanne Banks presents a hilarious romance about a bad girl whose life is turned upside down by a sexy neighbor and a special bundle that appears on her doorstep in WHEN SHE'S BAD; and Melanie Craft makes her writing debut with TRUST ME, an endearing story of a veterinarian who's a soft touch . . . until a client's brooding and gorgeous grandson accuses her of being a gold digger.